Arthur Arnold

Free land

Arthur Arnold

Free land

ISBN/EAN: 9783337278618

Printed in Europe, USA, Canada, Australia, Japan

Cover: Foto ©Andreas Hilbeck / pixelio.de

More available books at **www.hansebooks.com**

FREE LAND.

BY

ARTHUR ARNOLD.

. LONDON:

C. KEGAN PAUL & CO., 1, PATERNOSTER SQUARE.

1880.

INSCRIBED,

WITH GRATITUDE AND RESPECT,

TO THE

LIBERAL ELECTORS OF THE BOROUGH OF SALFORD.

CONTENTS.

FREE LAND.

CHAPTER I. .

IN the " New Domesday Books " prepared in 1874–75, at the instance of the fifteenth Earl of Derby, by the Government of which he was at that time a distinguished member, we find 525 persons returned as owners of one-fifth of the area of the United Kingdom. These are the nobles, and with few exceptions, they are peers of Parliament. They have each, on an average, three landed estates. The number in the several grades of nobility, the number, acreage, and annual value of their estates, are set out in the following table :—

	Separate Landed Estates.	Acres.	Estimated Rental.
Dukes 28	158	3,991,811	£2,357,655
Marquises 33	121	1,567,227	1,383,671
Earls 194	634	5,862,118	5,007,119
Viscounts 52	120	796,849	644,771
Barons............ 218	560	3,085,160	3,135,852
525	1593	15,303,165	£12,529,068

B

But this is an imperfect representation of the facts. From the list of nobility, peeresses are excluded; from the acreage, not only all forest lands and all woods (except saleable underwoods), but also the building estates within the metropolitan area, are omitted. Many lands held by trustees are not included, and as to the estimated rental, it is too low by at least a fourth, perhaps by a third, of the above sum. To some extent, this may be seen by observing that the estimated rental of the metropolis (now about £25,000,000) is not less than one-fourth of that of the United Kingdom, outside the metropolitan area, which, in the "New Domesday Books," is returned at £99,352,303. It may be added that the rental is in many places inaccurate with regard to Irish property, the return being based upon a valuation said to be 25 per cent. below the actual value, although it is unquestionably true that in Ireland some landlords have not raised their rents since the time of that valuation. In this return, no account is taken of the vast extent of common and waste lands, so large a part of which is claimed, and upon enclosure would certainly be allotted to these 525 nobles; nor is the area of any lands included which are not rateable for the relief of the poor. Their properties in roads and rivers, as well as in forests and in all timber-growing woods, in gas-works and water-works, in markets, bridges, docks, harbours, and canals,—are all excluded. I am sure I shall not greatly err if I assert that the property of the nobles amounts nearly to one-fourth of the extent and to one-eighth of the estimated rental of the United Kingdom.

No statement so remarkable can be made with regard

to the distribution of land in this country. There are other classes, but there is no class so small in number; the nobles are much fewer even than the elected representatives of the people. Yet there is no class which possesses an area of land within the United Kingdom comparable in extent or value to the estates belonging to the nobility.

Before we pass on to consider the possessions of other categories of landowners we may learn from the enumeration of the nobility how untrustworthy are the "New Domesday Books" in regard to the number of landowners. I am probably well within the truth in saying that the 525 nobles are in these books made into more than 1500 landowners. And this is how it is done. The Duke of Buccleuch, who has perhaps the largest income from landed property outside London, is also distinguished as possessing estates in a larger number of counties than any other subject of the Queen. His Grace is reckoned as 14 landowners in respect of the following properties:—

	Acres.	£.
County of Buckingham	894	2769
„ Huntingdon	1065	1312
„ Lancaster	370	418
„ Northampton	17,965	26,532
„ Surrey	8	708
„ Warwick	6881	12,568
„ Dumfries	253,514	97,530
„ Edinburgh	3545	28,409
„ Fife	60	15
„ Kirkcudbright	1000	100
„ Lanark	9091	1544
„ Peebles	248	273
„ Roxburgh	104,461	39,458
„ Selkirk	60,428	19,828
	459,530	231,494

I have set out the case of the Duke of Buccleuch as an example of the miscalculation of the number of landowners. He is returned as 14 landowners. There are 4 peers who are returned as 44 landowners, because these noblemen—the Dukes of Devonshire and Cleveland, the Earl Howe and Lord Overstone—each appear in the lists of 11 counties. Thus we have 5 persons returned in the "New Domesday Books" as 58 landowners; and if we include the Duke of Bedford, who has land in 10 counties, we may say 6 peers returned as 68 landowners. But errors of this sort do not affect merely the grand total of landowners, they vitiate all calculations based upon the plain record of these books in regard to the several classes of landowners. We may see this by a further reference to the case of the Duke of Buccleuch. In 4 counties, he stands for as many great landowners. He is returned in each as the owner of more than 10,000 acres. In 2 counties, he stands for as many owners of the second class. He is returned in each of these 2 counties as possessing more than 5000 and less than 10,000 acres. In 3 counties, he stands for as many owners of the third class, for in these he has property varying in extent from 1000 to 5000 acres. Again, in 1 county, he figures as a landowner of the fourth class, in respect of an estate exceeding 500 acres and less than 1000 acres. Yet once more, he is returned in 2 counties as two landowners of the fifth class, for in these he has property exceeding 100 and less than 500 acres. Finally, his Grace is counted as two in the number of the supposed yeomen landowners on account of his property of 8 acres in Surrey, which is evidently building land, and for his 60 acres in Fifeshire.

From this, which is undeniably a fair example, we may judge how fallacious are the general statements of the " New Domesday Books."

Below the peerage in rank, but superior in numbers, and hardly inferior in possessions and influence, are the lesser landed gentry, who, together with the nobility, are owners of about four-fifths of the soil of the country. It is not very easy, owing to the errors I have exposed, which are common throughout all ranks of the landed gentry, to form a trustworthy estimate of their number. But the " New Domesday Books " afford a necessary basis for calculation, and from those volumes I have compiled the following figures, which show the number of owners of 1,000 acres and upwards in the three divisions of the United Kingdom :—

	Owners of 1000 Acres and upwards.	Total Extent in Acres.
England and Wales	5408	18,695,528
Scotland	1758	17,584,828
Ireland	3745	15,802,739
	10,911	52,083,095

The total acreage of the United Kingdom (exclusive of the metropolis) as given in the " New Domesday Books," is 72,117,766, of which four-fifths would not much exceed the reported aggregate possessions of 10,911 owners. But we know from what has been now stated as to omissions which are acknowledged by the official compilers of these books, that the acreage is much more than this, and from what we have seen in the case of the peerage, we know that the number of owners is vastly overstated. If all the landed gentry, whom we have taken to be those possessing 1,000 acres and upwards, have been computed at the rate of 3 to 1, which we may say is the average multiplication of the peers into landowners, then we might conclude that four-fifths of the soil of the United Kingdom are in the possession of fewer than 4,000 persons. And it may be said that this would be a reasonable calculation. We should be amply justified in deducting nearly 1,000 for error in regard to the peerage alone. But it is certain that the same rate of error would not be found in the case of the lesser gentry, whose properties are not as a rule scattered in several counties. We can, however, form a confident opinion that the number of owners of four-fifths of the soil must be much fewer than 10,000, and that probably the true number approaches more nearly to 5,000.

Thus we arrive at the astonishing result that the representative owners of four-fifths of the soil of the United Kingdom could be placed within the compass of a single voice in one of the great public halls of the country. The landlords of more than 52,000,000 of acres might meet together in the Free Trade Hall of Manchester, and discuss the accuracy of these statements. Of this compact body of perhaps about 7,000 gentlemen, the House of Lords is strictly representative. With the exception of the Bench of Bishops, who may be said to represent the lands of the Church—an extensive property including 496,046 acres of some of the best and most highly rented land in England and Wales,*

---

* "Social Politics," by Arthur Arnold, p. 38.

—and of the Law Lords who, by their failures in regard
to reform have faithfully represented the legal system by
which this aggregation of property is unnaturally maintained—that House is composed of about 500 of the largest
landowners. The fundamental principle of the House of
Lords is the representation of the distribution of land
peculiar to Great Britain and Ireland. If that House
now and then annexes a successful lawyer, or statesman,
or soldier, he, as a rule, endeavours to justify the en-
nobling of his family by providing his less distinguished
heir with the proper territorial qualification.

Seeing, then, that -four-fifths of Great Britain and
Ireland are in the hands of some 7,000 persons, there remains but a comparatively small portion, the ownership
of which we have yet to consider. In the "New Domesday Book," the total area dealt with is 72,117,766 acres.
I have shown what is the ownership of 52,083,095 of
these acres. Over that immense area, the smallest estate
is not less than 1,000 acres. The remnant of the land,
belonging to the rest of the population, that is to 31,506,442
out of 31,513,442 of people, is therefore 20,034,671 acres.
Rejecting the parcels described as being less than one
acre, the area is reduced to 19,543,638 acres, which,
according to the "New Domesday Books," are distributed
as follow:—

	No. of Owners.	Estimated Acreage.
England and Wales	257,578	14,165,391
Scotland	17,346	1,332,542
Ireland	28,822	4,345,705
	303,746	19,843,638

The respective areas of ownership are as follow :—

Acres.			No. of Owners.	Estimated Acreage.
500	and less than	1000	8341	5,815,947
100	„	„ 500	42,673	9,339,255
50	„	„ 100	30,531	2,128,236
10	„	„ 50	83,855	2,023,225
1	„	„ 10	138,346	536,975
			303,746	19,843,638

These figures with regard to the owners of 1 acre
and less than 1000 acres are not, I regret to say, more
trustworthy than those relating to ownership of 1000
acres and upwards. To revert to the case of the Duke
of Buccleuch, we see on referring to the schedule of his
estates, that his Grace makes a five-fold appearance in
this supposed category of commonalty; and his case is
typical of that of the nobility generally. But there are
much larger errors than this. In the " explanatory
statement," or preface to the " New Domesday Books,"
we are warned that " where the owners appear to be
corporate bodies, or to hold their lands in virtue of a
public office, the names are printed in italic; but the
return must not be assumed to be complete in this
respect, as there is reason to believe that in many cases
the name of an individual is entered instead of the body
or office which he represents, and this remark applies
especially to glebe lands." It might be supposed from
this that the manifest error with reference to glebe
lands is of trifling extent. But in reality it amounts to
thousands. There are probably more than 10,000 parcels
of glebe land in the 15,000 parishes of England and

Wales. No one connected with the work of compiling
this return can have been so ignorant of the facts as
to suppose that in the county of Buckingham there are
no more than five parcels of glebe land; that there are
only three in the county of Hertford, and only seven in
the county of Lancaster. But this is exactly what the
italics in the lists of those three counties proclaim to be
the fact. Of course there is a very large error in the
statement, one which needed a much bolder allusion
than that given in the " explanatory statement." I have
taken the trouble to go carefully through the return of
"landowners" for those three counties, and I find that
in Bucks there are no fewer than 235 with the title of
" Reverend;" that in Hertford there are 159 "landowners " with the same prefix, and that in Lancaster the
number of "reverend landowners" is not less than 286.
It is certain that, with very few exceptions, these
"reverend landowners" are merely in official possession
of Church property, and their names ought therefore
to have been placed in italics. I selected those three
counties for no other reason than because the three chiefs
of the Government by which the return was issued
reside in those shires. The error is, however, as wide as
the kingdom.

But upon a fair showing of the tenure of public lands
by printing in italics, the names so distinguished should
not have been counted in the lists of persons returned
as landowners. The object of printing these names in
italics was to separate them from the landowners. Yet
the names printed in italics are included by thousands
in the above total of 303,746 "landowners." We have

seen that in three counties between 600 and 700 holders
of glebe lands are wrongly thrown into the total. We
may judge of the mass of errors by this discovery, and
by the following samples. In the list for the county
of Norfolk, " churchwardens," are enumerated as 136
landowners; in Essex, "churchwardens" are counted as
55 landowners. In the same county, the Gaslight and
Coke Company stands for 3 landowners. The North
Western Railway Company is returned as 28 landowners. "Trustees of Poor" figure as 40 landowners
in the single county of Bucks. "Colleges" swell the
total in the county of Cambridge by 22; and "Charity"
stands in the same county as 73 landowners. Errors of
such magnitude, affecting the total by tens of thousands,
might have been avoided by a more careful and intelligent compilation. But with every deduction made
in respect of public lands, the remainder is very far
indeed from presenting a true return of the ownership
of agricultural land.

Excluding the owners of less than an acre, the
number returned as owning more than 1 acre and less
than 1000 acres, form 95.5 per cent. of the total of
landowners in England and Wales; 90 per cent. in
Scotland, and 88 per cent. in Ireland. From this, a
foreigner might suppose that small holdings or peasant
properties were numerous in England.

Why is the percentage of the inferior of our two
classes of landed properties higher with regard to
England and Scotland? It is obviously because in
the manufacturing island the more opulent of the
population, especially in the neighbourhood of the large

towns, become owners, or lessees (a condition which, if the term be not less than 99 years, is counted as ownership in the return), of a few acres of land which are occupied in a pleasurable, rather than a productive manner. The number of owners of this sort throughout England and Scotland is legion. They are not agricultural owners; their land is bestowed in lawns, in gardens, in shrubberies, in paddocks, producing nothing but perhaps a portion of the fodder required for saddle and carriage horses, and every one of such owners appears in the totals last placed in tabular form.

No official calculation has been made concerning the number of owners of agricultural land in the United Kingdom. With no guide, except the certainty that the totals set out in the "New Domesday Books" are untrustworthy, I will not attempt to frame any precise estimate. We have seen what very large deductions must be made from these tabulated totals in order to approach a true statement. There are the holders of glebe imported by hundreds in each county to which our attention has been directed; there are the thousands of parcels of public lands to be deducted; there are other thousands of repetitions of the same owners in several counties; and then there are the vast number of suburban and other residential owners, whose property has no truly agricultural character. But the most careful study of the facts and figures leads me to believe that the number of agricultural landowners in the United Kingdom falls far short of 100,000.

I have now set forth a few incontestable facts in reply to the question, "Who has the land?" I shall proceed to offer other facts showing how the existing distribution of the soil of the country has been effected and how it is maintained; how the laws and customs which have led to this distribution operate to diminish the value of the landlord's interest in his possessions, and to restrict agricultural production and improvement. The argument of this book will be directed to securing the freedom of the soil; that is, its freedom from the operation of those laws and customs which, with injury to every class in the country, maintain an unnatural and injurious distribution of the land. No objection will be taken in these pages to the extent of the possessions of any man, or of any order or class in the United Kingdom. No one recognizes more thoroughly than the writer, the advantage of placing the heads of the families which own one-fifth of the country in a House of Lords. No one is more profoundly convinced that in the United Kingdom, as it is, there is no basis for a Second Chamber possessing anything comparable to the representative power and ability of the great landowners. The object of the author is to make the ownership of land accord with the free operation of economic laws. At present, there are three gentlemen in the United Kingdom, one in each of the three divisions, whose united possessions amount to nearly 2,000,000 acres of land. I have no objection to such a distribution of the soil if it should result from the action of laws which are most beneficial alike to the interests of proprietors and to those of the community. I shall show that the existing laws and customs have not that character; that they tend to reduce the value

of the landlord's property and to increase the dependence of the United Kingdom upon foreign supplies
of food. I shall make it plain that what is understood
by "free land" is at present most nearly expressed in
our land system by the well-known term "freehold;"
that our great need is to put the land of this country,
to the largest possible extent, in that condition of
"freehold," and to make the title to land and the transfer
of land, as far as may be, conspicuous and attractive
by simplicity, economy, and security. Further, it will
be necessary to give close attention to the peculiar
character of land as saleable property, having regard
to the fact that while land is one of the indispensable
necessaries of life, the security of property in land is
absolutely essential to the interests of production and
to the welfare of the people.

CHAPTER II.

WHO ARE THE LANDLORDS?

To whom does the land belong? That question touches the root of the matter of free land. We have seen, in the preceding chapter, that about 500 nobles are in possession of more than a fifth, and that, including the nobility, about 7000 persons are in possession as land-lords of four-fifths (more than 52,000,000 acres) of the United Kingdom. I say "in possession," because the landed gentry in this country are not "owners," in the strict and proper sense of the word, of the lands with which their names and titles are connected. Our word "landlords," which is as peculiar to the United Kingdom as our land-system is unique, fits their position more truly. It is a national evil of the gravest character, that the persons who are in possession of four-fifths of the soil are not, and can never be, responsible, interested owners of the fee-simple, or freehold, of their lands. Take the case of the leader of the peerage, the Duke of Norfolk, an exemplary nobleman and a good landlord. His Grace is not owner of Arundel Castle. There is no owner of the Norfolk estates. The Duke, like other dukes, has signed away his inheritance and

is but a life tenant. The superior title to the property
has passed to his baby son, the Earl of Arundel and
Surrey, who, when he reaches manhood, will in turn
be called upon to renounce the possibility of becoming
freeholder of the vast estates of the House of Norfolk.
I have no doubt whatever that the Earl of Derby, second
only in precedence among the earls of England, has
had far greater happiness in the affairs of the Foreign
Office than in the concerns of his family estates.   Why
should he not?   In Downing Street, he was the responsible Minister ; at Knowsley, his legal title is vastly
inferior to that which may belong to the infant son of
his brother, the Secretary of State for War.   Lord
Derby, after the manner of English landed gentry, has
by signature forfeited all possibility of being proprietor,
and the ownership of the estates now passing under his
name as owner, is devolved by deed of settlement upon
the eldest male child of his brother, who may, if he
refuse to re-settle the property when he arrives at manhood, be some day freeholder of the Knowsley estate—
a position which his distinguished uncle has, in accordance with the unwritten social code of England, been
permitted by most injurious custom to abandon for
ever for himself.   Lately, we have had the edifying
spectacle of a peer coming forward to denounce this
arrangement. On the 28th October, 1879, Lord Carington
gave a dinner to his Buckinghamshire tenants, and com-
municated to them his view as tenant for life, or nominal
owner, of the Carington estates, of the permissive law
and the general practice of entail and strict settlement.
Lord Carington said, " I ask you to consider the position

of the ordinary landowner of the present time—by that
I mean a man who derives the whole of his income from
land—tenant for life of an estate more or less incum-
bered with settlements and mortgages and other fixed
charges." Lord Carington then proceeded to state that
which gives especial interest to his remarks;. his "own
case." His lordship continued: "Following the advice
of my best friends during my father's lifetime, being
twenty-two years of age, I re-entailed the estate. I
inherited eleven years ago, property in Bucks, in Lincolnshire, and in Wales. I found property had been bought
in Bucks, and to pay for that property the Welsh estate
had to be sold, and the money re-invested in the land
purchased in Bucks. The farm-buildings were so bad
on the Welsh property that it was calculated that the
purchaser would have to expend one whole year's rental
on them to put them in decent repair. Mind, I do not
blame my father for this; but I do blame the strictness
of the entail, which prevented him putting the buildings
into such a condition as to enable the tenants to do
justice to themselves and the land by which they got
their living. The river Humber washed away five acres
of good land at Winteringham, and formed an island
in the bed of the river. As a tenant for life I could not
afford to repel the attacks of the river or to accept the
gifts of the ocean, for I could not charge the estate for
permanent improvements, nor could I sell a single acre
of the thirty-four square miles which I inherited. Under
these circumstances, what are the landlords to do? On
all sides we hear of reductions and returns to tenants·
These are duly chronicled in the newspapers with a

certain grim humour as 'liberality of a landlord.' It
keeps some tenants going and saves the landlord having
to cultivate, but ten per cent. reduction is no real use
and doesn't solve the question at all. . . . The time has
come that the great question of entail should be calmly
discussed. Many consider that the laws which allow a
landowner, by his deed or by his will, to prevent his
land being sold, seized, or lessened in size, either during
his own life, or for many years after his death, are
necessary for the very existence of the landed interest of
England. May these laws not be a positive danger to
the country, and one of the reasons for the present
agricultural distress ? In no way do I wish to introduce
a principle that a living man may not do what he likes
with his own—buy, sell, let, or farm as much as he
chooses, leave it all to his eldest son, divide it amongst
his children, or leave it entirely away. But though we
properly respect the rights of the living, ought we not
to curtail the power of the dead ? The largest landowner in England and Scotland has a total of 1,358,548
acres. I see no harm in that; there is no reason why
he should not own 2,000,000 acres; but what I do think
wrong is that a landowner should, either by his own
act or by the deed of his predecessors, be saddled with
an enormous tract of country of which it is impossible
for him to get rid of a square yard, however necessary,
however beneficial the sale of a small portion of it
would be to the country, the estate, to his tenants, or
to himself. I will try to show what the consequence is.
In the north of the county [Bucks] I have two strong
clay farms on my hands; one I cannot get a bid for,

c

nobody will cultivate it at any rent. I say to my agent,
'What am I to do?' He answers, 'The buildings must be
rebuilt, the worst land laid down in grass, the land
drained and cleansed, and in two years you may get a
tenant?' Very good, but all this ought to have been
done years ago and the tenant would have been saved,
and the land would never have got into so miserable a
condition. But the same millstone is round my neck
that hampered my father, that I must wear till my
death, my brothers as well, if they succeed me, and the
land is not free till after our deaths, or the twenty-first
birthday of an unborn heir. As tenant for life, I hoped
against hope, trusted to the good season of 1879 to put
things right; that season failed, the tenant is ruined,
and the land starved. It is a small matter, one farm in
hand, you will say; but look around us. I hear of a
proprietor with 4000 acres on his hands, a Berkshire
landowner with thirteen farms, and land thrown up
in all directions. People would improve their properties
if they could, but the majority cannot, as is shown by
the committee of the House of Lords, consisting of the
Duke of Richmond, Marquis of Salisbury, Earl of
Derby, and Lord Egerton of Tatton, who reported, in
1870, that of 20,000,000 acres in this country requiring
drainage, only 3,000,000 had been drained, and that,
taking into account also all other necessary improvements, only one-fifth of the land had been properly
dealt with. Is not this a serious state of things?
Farmers say, 'It is not so much the low prices we com-.
plain of, but the yield is so bad.' What else can you
expect? We shall be told that these views are dangerous

to the Constitution, to the Queen, to the House of
Lords, and to the welfare of England generally. But
is it possible to deny how much good has been done by
the gradual reforms that have been brought about in
the present reign? Is it not better that questions of
this importance should be properly and reasonably discussed on their merits than that strong opposition should
be offered to their very mention, that all the power of
intellect, position, and wealth should be brought against
the idea that such laws may be improved, until England
wakes up suddenly to find the measure of such reforms
brought forward by those who express themselves most
hostile to them, and a Land Bill hastily passed through
Parliament, with clauses that they may take away from
landowners the fee-simple of their land? We shall be
told that these restraints are necessary owing to the
temptations to young men coming early into their estates.
But, as a rule, peers do not inherit before middle age;
it is the exception, and many of the young ones recognize
the responsibilities of property. Are we, for the sake
of protecting a few, a very few, foolish men from the
consequences of their own folly, to hamper the whole
of the landed proprietors of England, and to make living
men, anxious to improve their estates and benefit their
tenants, feel the 'dead man's grip,' from which there is
no escape? I have reminded you of the disturbed state
of the country previous to the repeal of the Corn Laws.
In 1879 comes again a time of trial, and we have distress,
but not disaffection; disappointment, but not despair.
Is it too much to hope that the land laws will also be
calmly considered with a view to their improvement;

that landlord and landowners will become the owners
and lords of their land ; and that by free trade in land
the agricultural difficulty will be surmounted ?"

To that very practical, and, having regard to the
position of the speaker, it may be said, important, utterance, I will add the yet more recent declaration of the
Marquis of Ripon, who, on November 13th, in the
year just ended, said at Bristol: "The laws of every
country must favour either the distribution or the centralization of property, and I have no hesitation in
saying for my own part that the time has now fully
arrived when the law of England ought to favour, as
much as possible, a free and unfettered use of the land
by the actual present owner, and that it ought to promote the distribution and not the centralization of landed
property." Lawyers, who defend the existing system,
will probably say of these speeches, and especially of
Lord Carington's, that if a deed of settlement prevents
the sale of any part of the estate it is an exception to
the rule with such documents. That is the professional
way of evading the objection to such settlements, and
I shall show in a subsequent chapter, entitled "What
Parliament has done," how very little respect this
plea deserves to receive from those who are considering
the great question of the emancipation of the soil from
the bondage of such disabilities.

Now that we have seen, by an autobiographical
narration, what is the nature and consequence of entail,
we begin to have a more clear conception of the vast
difference between "landlords" and "landowners." But
it is necessary that we should bestow some further atten-

tion upon this bane of British agriculture, upon this method for depopulating the rural districts of our country—a system which, as we have seen, applies in all probability to not less than four-fifths of the United Kingdom. The family affairs of the landed gentry are all regulated on one pattern, the general outlines of which are easily understood. I have no intention to write a history of the laws and customs which regulate the devolution of land in this country. They are no more worthy of study than they were when Cromwell delivered the opinion that "The law of England is a tortuous and ungodly jumble." The laws relating to real property are not much better now than in the Lord Protector's time, two hundred years ago. But now there is a limit which did not then exist to the settlement of land. Any owner of land can by will determine the inheritance for the lifetime of any number of persons in existence, and for twenty-one years after the death of any one, or the survivor, of those persons. This limit, it cannot be denied, has been preserved in order that the land of England should not be free—in order that its freedom should be held in strict subordina-tion to the institution of a landed gentry. In this way land may be "settled" for a century, and it is fair to assume that the estates of the 7000 persons who are nominal owners of more than 52,000,000 acres are settled upon this plan. Let us endeavour to understand how this work of settlement is accomplished, avoiding, as far as possible, all legal jargon. We are now con-sidering entail and settlement with regard to the question —" Who are the landlords ? " Presently, in later pages,

we shall regard more specially the nature and operation
of this very important law and custom. We will first
take the case of a "new man," who has bought an estate,
perhaps has added to it all the outlying farms he could
purchase, and desires, as the phrase goes, to "found a
family." He has, we will suppose, a son, a minor. He
has brothers, to whom, if he or his son die childless, he
wishes the family foundation to belong. He instructs
the family solicitor to make his will, by which he con-
veys the landed property to certain friends who are
called trustees, for the benefit of his son; and should
his son's life fail, then to his brother; and should the
brother's life fail, to the children of his brother. If his
brother die without issue, then to his next brother; and,
that life failing, then to the unborn son of that brother,
and so on through all the members and heirs of the elder
generation, until not the poorest scrivener, paid by the
word, could suggest an addition to the precautions against
the estate falling out of the line of entail. These claims
are thus " tailed on " one after the other, the first "estate
tail" being obviously that of his son.

But, so far, the "new man" has only made a will
which he can revoke or destroy at pleasure. His land
is still "free;" if he is in debt, it can be sold; it is his
absolutely; he can deal with it as he pleases for his own
benefit, for the advantage of his tenants and his posterity.
He proceeds to deprive his land of this "free" character,
to make it, in aristocratic fashion, "no man's land;"
to prevent, to the utmost of his power, any one from
occupying his own position as a free landowner, perhaps
at the time when his son is about to be married. Then

the business of founding the family is consolidated and
secured. The "new man" now parts with his acres;
they are made over at once to trustees; he abdicates
the position of a freeholder, he accepts from their hands
that of a life tenant; he has bargained with his son
that he (the son) shall succeed him in the life tenancy,
and that they both together shall agree to place next
in the "tail" of possessors, the son who may be born of
the approaching marriage. The family is now founded,
the marriage is solemnized, and in due time, perhaps,
the "new man" caresses a grandson who, in noble
fashion, is born a landed gentleman. He, the baby, can
by no act of his grandfather, or of his father, be dispossessed of inheritance. He is the heir, and, if he survive them both the estate must be his. After him, in
the entail, come his expected brothers, his uncles, etc.;
so that if he live to manhood, and it is desired to continue the "family" in his line, that entail, which was
made by his grandfather and father, must be cut off, and
again his (the baby's) son must be placed next to himself
in the line of possesors. But much happens on the day,
or probably soon after the day, when he, whom we have
called "the baby," comes of age. With the consent of
his grandfather and father, or if both are dead, by his
own will he can exeute a disentailing deed, and lo!
the land is free again, and he is absolute possessor. The
law books call his tenure thus obtained "a base fee,"
but that does not matter. Yet this is not the practice
of the landed gentry. Even when the estate may be
free, the force of custom leads them to replace the legal
fetters. As a rule, the father is alive and is enjoying

the prospect of long life when his son and heir attains manhood, and it becomes necessary to guard the land, according to English custom, from lapsing into freedom. A new deed of settlement is prepared for the pen of the heir, and if he refuse to sign that deed, he may, after his father's death, possess himself of the freehold and deal as he pleases with the family property. Suppose, for instance, that Lord Hartington—I am mentioning by name none but the brightest ornaments of the nobility —had refused to re-settle the Devonshire estates, and to accept a life interest after that of his father—suppose he had declined to put his name to that parchment which carries on the entail to his son, if he should have one, and if not, then reverts to his brother, Lord Frederick Cavendish, and to his (Lord Frederick's) son,—he (Lord Hartington) would in that case, upon the death of the Duke of Devonshire, have been able to sell Chatsworth and Devonshire House at the auction mart. But, of course, Lord Hartington has followed long since, at the wish of his father, the fashion of English landed gentry; he has nothing more than a contingent life interest in the ducal estates—he can never be owner of Chatsworth. There are no owners over four-fifths of the soil of our country. Lord Hartington's position is just like that of the Marquis of Lorn; Chatsworth House can never belong to the one, nor Inverary Castle to the other.

It may be asked, Why do elder sons thus part with their inheritance? The answer is easily made; and seeing the inducements, it is certainly not surprising that an absolute refusal is, we may say, never encountered. The force of custom, especially when the observance of that custom is the distinguishing mark of a small and most powerful class, is very great. To withstand this influence alone, a very uncommon character would be needed. But even that is not the whole matter. The heir's reversion may not come for thirty years, perhaps more, should his father live to a great age. Meanwhile, he is, as a rule, dependent upon his father, and no parent has yet come out as an advocate for the avoidance of settlement in the case of all eldest sons. The reversion no man can take from him, but that, as any money-lender will remind him, is contingent upon his own existence. Assume that he is, as most men are, intelligent and of good behaviour, how much better does it seem for him to accept a suitable allowance from his father, and to re-settle the property upon the children which he himself may have. His expectancy of entering into possession is remote; the duty to his father, to his family, to the honoured customs of the distinguished class to which he belongs, is pressing, and so is his private and personal appreciation of the handsome income which will be his to spend how he pleases upon the completion of the legal business of that day. In fact, it seems to him, as it probably did to Lord Carington, when that nobleman was twenty-two years of age, that there is no choice, nor is there indeed practically. How could he otherwise obtain the pecuniary allowance he requires for those years—perhaps thirty or forty—which may elapse before the death of his father? Borrow? Yes, he may borrow upon his contingent reversion, but he will find that borrowing brings but little money to his pockets, and that it tends very rapidly to deprive him of all interest in his inheritance. It is obvious that a lender could only be secure by insuring the life of the son against that of the father, so that if the son died and never entered into possession of the family property, repayment might be obtained upon a policy of insurance. This is sometimes done, and Mr. Shaw-Lefevre, who is not only a useful member of Parliament but also a director of a life insurance company, has shown how onerous is the consequent charge.* Mr. Shaw-Lefevre says : " The charge depends mainly upon the age of the father, but as an illustration it may be stated that if the father be aged 45, and the property be worth £10,000 per annum, the value of the reversion of the son at the age of 21, calculated at five per cent., is not more than £15,000. A debt therefore of £5,000 will swallow up one-third of the future expectations of the son ; and how small such a sum as £5,000 must seem to the expectant heir to £10,000 per annum ! "

No surprise, then, need be felt concerning the ease with which more than 50,000,000 acres in the United Kingdom are continually re-settled,—continually, by that arrangement, preserving their ownerless character. In this statement, I have raised a general presumption that all estates of 1,000 acres and upwards are in strict settlement. That is not absolutely correct, but there is a sufficient margin for error in the very large area which is subject to settlement, composed of estates each less than 1,000 acres in extent. I do not think there is any exaggeration in the statement that four-fifths of the land of the United Kingdom are strictly settled, and at present destined to

* " Limitation of Settlements and Entails," by G. Shaw-Lefevre, M.P., 1877.

perpetual life-tenancy. In 1874, the heir presumptive of the very ancient barony of Dacre, stated that "seventy per cent. of the land in this country is held by men whose power over it is limited by modern settlement." *
But Mr. H. R. Brand wrote before the publication of the "New Domesday Books," and there can, I think, be no doubt that his is an understatement. It is probable that not less than eighty per cent. of the land of the United Kingdom is settled, and therefore without any real and responsible owner.

To whom belongs the comparatively small remainder? This question is not easy to answer. Thousands of the "owners" whose names are recorded in the "New Domesday Books," are only lessees of settled property. In the official directions for making the return, it was intimated "that lessees for terms exceeding 99 years, or with a right of perpetual renewal should be considered as owners." It is owing to the custom of entail, and to laws regulating the devolution of real property, that leases for 999 years have been common in the extensive building operations in the manufacturing districts of the North. In all such cases, few of which are of less extent than one acre, there is a fictitious return of ownership; and also with regard to leases for 99 years, there can be no doubt that the leaseholder often appears in place of the free-holder. The compilers of the return admit the " extreme probability " that " the names of the lessees have been entered in the return as owners, as neither the clerks nor the overseers would have had any reason to suppose that they were not the owners in fee."

* Mr. H. R. Brand, in *Fortnightly Review.*

When these and other considerations which tend to swell the vast area of settled property have been duly regarded, it is but a poor remnant of the soil that has responsible owners and is therefore marketable. We shall deal in due course with the fallacious conditions under which settled property is called saleable. As to the unsettled remnant, we shall see that the processes of transfer, and the ascertainment of title are so costly, so uncertain, and so vexatious, owing to the custom and law which encourage and permit settlement, as greatly to restrict transactions and to favour the acquisition of land by the wealthy. We shall see that the number of owners of agricultural land is dwindling, and must further dwindle, as a consequence of arrangements as unsuited to the circumstances of our time as the armour of a knight of the Middle Ages would be for a modern dinner-party.

CHAPTER III.

WHY is this area of land under settlement so immense and increasing? I have said that the custom and law which encourage and permit entail and settlement, favour the acquisition of land by the wealthy. Let us test this assertion by putting the matter into quite another form. Suppose that upon the purchase of a loaf of bread, the baker's right to the flour and to the shop, together with the history of his possession for forty years, had to be investigated at the cost of the customer, and that, as of land, there was only a limited quantity of bread. The price of bread would fall, and would remain low, because there would be fewer purchasers. All those who had but little money would take to rice, or some other farinaceous food, which could be obtained without the expense of this legal investigation. Especially would all the industrial and the more careful classes be driven away from' the bakers' shops by the uncertainty which must attend such an inquiry. No one would purchase a single loaf, for the uncertain charge for investigation and conveyance would be as heavy on that one loaf as upon a score of loaves. Bread would tend to become a luxury, which does not imply high price. Bread would be displayed with ostentation and pride in plenty upon the tables of the rich, and to possess bread in abundance would be an object of desire, not from fear of starvation, but because bread would be difficult of acquisition, owing to the expensive preliminaries. Somebody would propose that bakers' titles should be registered at a public office, so that anybody on payment, say of a penny, could see that all was correct, and would feel sure that the loaf might be eaten with safety. The reasonableness of such a proposal would be so evident, that some of the great leaders of society to whom the legal expenses were no object, would join, out of consideration for the national welfare, in the cry for registration of bakers' titles. But then it would be found that the rich kept long accounts with the baker in voluminous books, and that registration would involve the abolition of the bakers'-book system. Philanthropic leaders of society would admit the necessity of maintaining the system of books for dealings in bread, and would set themselves to work to frame ingenious schemes for uniting the book-system with the ready-money system in the registration of titles. Of course they would fail, and the family agents who had the custody of the baker's books would say, "We told you so; we told you that registration of bakers' titles was impossible." Although the habits of the people might, by the maintenance of this system, be turned as much as possible away from bread, yet it might come to be thought that a family which had not a baker's book could not be admitted to "county society."

The great organ of the wealthy classes in the press

would turn upon the reformers who suggested that by
this system transactions in bread were greatly restricted,
and would say, " Bread ! there is plenty to be had; there
are thousands of loaves advertised every day ; the sales
of bread for the year amount to so much sterling.   There
is a limited quantity of bread, and therefore it is found
unattainable by persons of small means." Then, perhaps,
some one who thought he knew a little more of the world,
and of the public welfare, than this upholder of the forty
years'-inquiry-into-the-baker's-title system, would mildly
state that the dealings in bread were ten times more
numerous in foreign countries, where the baker's title
was easily ascertained, and that though the price of
bread was naturally higher in those countries, yet that
everybody had enough, even if it was true that some
had a tendency to divide their loaf into morsels almost
too small for nourishment, a disposition which is always
tending to its own cure.   But if such a one calculated
that the qualifying character of the concluding words
would save his skin, he would be mistaken.   The party
of the bakers'-books at home would hint that he was
no better than he should be—that, in fact, he was a
Communist ; they would roundly assert that he was a
Red Republican, and plainly tell their neighbours that
the one object of his life was to adulterate the home-
baked loaf with foreign yeast, which would set all
England in a ferment.

This is a fanciful impossibility.   But with regard to
British land it is quite true that the small purchaser is
discouraged, and the purchaser of large areas is assisted,
and that for this reason land passes into the hands of

those with whom it is customary to "settle" it in order to insure the endowment of their heirs for the longest period the law will permit with immoveable, indestructible wealth. It is not the price of the land in the United Kingdom which makes its possession (I speak of agricultural land) practically the monopoly of families founded upon parchment settlements. I shall, as far as figures and facts can do so, easily and effectually dispel the erroneous opinion that land is dear in England, and that therefore, because of high price, it becomes the possession of those who have the largest command of money. It is not the pecuniary yield of land—which is only an indirect statement of price—which tends to make it the property of the leisure class. That is only another form of the same fallacy which in subsequent chapters I shall overthrow without difficulty. It is the onerous and uncertain demand in time and money which is made upon the small purchaser that drives him away from the sales of land. This, and the rarity of any opportunity of obtaining possession, as owner, of a small farm,—a rarity which will appear extraordinary when we contrast the sales of land in this country with sales in any other country of the world,— together with our manufacturing activity, have diverted the attention of the British people from the cultivation of the soil. Mr. James Beal, a well-known auctioneer, has stated that in his professional practice he has known cases in which the legal expenses of transfer amounted to not less than one-third of the purchase money. Suppose this to be the case with two lots of land, each worth, say £600. The two lots would cost the buyers

£1600. If sold together in one lot the cost would be £1400. A buyer therefore who was prepared to pay as much for the whole as would obtain each lot could afford to give £200 more; he could give £1400 for the land, and when it was conveyed to him, at a cost for legal expenses of £200, he would have made no greater outlay than the two purchasers of the separate lots. In the competition, he would always possess this advantage, and, although it may be admitted that the legal expenses in this supposed case are extreme, yet the advantage of the larger purchaser is always in a less or possibly greater degree certain and secure. But that is only the first of his many advantages. The proportion or percentage which legal expenses bear to the purchase money declines rapidly as the sum rises in amount. The purchaser of ten acres finds that the expense of conveyance makes a weighty addition to the cost of his land; the buyer of ten thousand acres finds that the price per acre is scarcely affected by the addition of the lawyer's bill. Yet it is not the actual cost and the increasing percentage of cost only which are against the small purchaser. That which more than these arouses his fear of dealings in land is the uncertainty—first, as to legal expenses. Fear magnifies without exception the object of dread, and the man who wishes to buy land as an investment for his labour as well as for his money, is sure, if he be resident in Great Britain or Ireland, to be preoccupied with fearful thoughts of law. He would give another fifty pounds gladly if he were sure the conveyance would not cost more than £5, but owing to the delay and to the uncertainty of ex-

D

pense, men of his class are not buyers, and the price of land is lower in consequence. I have known a terrified purchaser agree with a solicitor to convey certain land for a charge of two per cent. in a case with respect to which the solicitor told me himself, after the conveyance was completed, that if no agreement had been made he could not possibly (so simple did the title happen to be) have charged a sum higher than the amount of one per cent. To an industrial purchaser, the long delay, sometimes extending over twelve months, is a serious matter; the demand upon his time and thoughts, to say nothing of his capital, is a weighty hindrance. But delay does not in the same degree affect the man of leisure, and hence we perceive another advantage which the British system of conveyance by deed gives to him and his class. Yet even these considerations, which obviously draw the soil into the possession of the entailing classes, do not exhaust the long list of advantages which the landed gentry have secured for themselves by legislation tainted with imprudence. The industrial purchaser is the man likely to have need to sell again. In view of family arrangements, or at death, he may desire to turn his land into money for division among his children. In this case, his estate must pay a heavy fine from which that of the rich man is exempt. Upon the whole sum of his money probate duty will be charged, but upon the rich man's land the succession duty takes the mild form of a charge upon the life tenancy of the inheritor, who, moreover, is permitted to pay at his ease in a certain number of years. There is yet another matter which is of no slight influence and importance. One of the worst and most troublesome features of the British system of conveyance by unregistered and unrecorded deed, is the care it imposes upon the purchaser in regard to the custody of the documents by which alone his title can be maintained. The less educated a man is, very much the more difficult does such safe-keeping of written documents appear. It has been said with some truth that poor and uneducated men do not shave themselves because of the difficulty, which to them appears insuperable, of keeping a sharp razor. In rural districts it is well known that while the squire and the parson would think it unbecoming and extravagant to resort to the village barber, the labourer is the regular customer whose hardly earned penny affords a livelihood to that functionary. The custody of title deeds, which is an indispensable part of our troublesome system of landowning, is one of the peculiar drawbacks of the position of a proprietor in this country. But it is also one of the buttresses of that system which has been so long acceptable because it results in placing the land, at a low price compared with the soil of other countries, in the hands of the wealthy. We shall see, in glancing at other systems of land titles and transfer, how favourably the absence of responsibility in regard to the custody of deeds operates to promote the extension of proprietorship in land.

It is by reason of advantages of this sort that the business of landowning in this country is so injuriously restricted. We have seen, in the preceding chapter, by what means the soil is secured and settled when it is obtained by the landed gentry. It will be part of my

task to exhibit in succeeding chapters the operation of
these inequitable arrangements. It is said by some, who
ought to know better, that "in a free country like ours
the distribution of land depends on economic laws as
absolute as the law of gravity." * I shall maintain and
shall attempt to prove that with regard to the distribution of land this is not a free country, and that economic
laws have as yet no place in the agricultural land system
of the United Kingdom. And when, in this exposition,
there are manifested any symptoms of antagonism of class
with class, it should be remembered that such an attitude
is not of the nature of "free land." The antagonism
which does undoubtedly exist, and of which the exhibition cannot justly or dutifully be suppressed in these
pages, is due to the antecedent history of landownership
—to the fact that hitherto in the history of England the
laws relating to land have been made by landlords and
not by the nation. When these laws and customs, the
survival for the most part of the obsolete usages of feudal
times, have been revised and renovated and, as far as
need be, abolished by a parliament fairly representative
of the people, this antagonism, the consequence of self-
interested and essentially class legislation, will utterly
disappear and give place to the beneficial operation of
economic laws.

When we ask ourselves, "How does the land pass to
limited landowners?" we must not forget that law of
physics which is as true of landed estates as of celestial
bodies. The attractive force which is an attribute of
magnitude is a part of this question of free land, and if

* Mr. Froude on the Uses of a Landed Gentry.

we were to dwell upon such considerations as that thought suggests we might easily be carried into the realms of history. But the history of landed institutions and estates in this country is a field in which the modern labourer can only produce a crop of bitterness. I will not import the rancour of history needlessly into this inquiry. It is with facts and figures, not with rights and wrongs, that we have chiefly to deal. I have not a word to say against the landed gentry. It is true that they have resisted, and that, for the most part, they may be expected to resist reform. But they have inherited, they did not impose, the laws and customs of which we complain, and it is no new thing to find " the landed interest " (as the owners have been called, ignorantly implying that theirs was the sole interest) blind and deaf to counsels of improvement and reform. Though every step in the beneficial work must augment the value of their possessions; though no man who should seek to violate their rights of property to the extent of a single acre, or of a pound sterling, would obtain a hearing from the English people,—yet it is not to be expected that the majority of landowners will abandon their traditional policy of resistance. One reason why an unreasoning opposition may be looked for, is because the most intelligent of the landlords are the least concerned with the management of their property. If they were owners, it might be different; but as life-tenants, with fettered powers of improvement, they prefer the paths of pleasure or of statesmanship. As for the majority, they will oppose, partly because, as Mr. Disraeli has written of the British aristocracy in " Lothair," " they live in the open air and they never read;"—because, as Mr. Mill has written, "great landlords have rarely studied anything." * The same great writer upon economic laws refers in another place † to their "irrational hostility to improvement." The hostility may survive, but it must be ineffective. Their power of effective resistance is passing away with the extension of education and of the franchise.

If the British people do not now proceed to free the soil of their country from bondage in feudal forms of law the fault is their own. It is absurd to speak harshly of the 7000 life-tenants of these 52,000,000 acres, as though they were alone responsible. They are without question responsible for their own opposition to reform, and for the self-interested legislature of their time. I propose to consider in another chapter, the dealings of Parliament with the land. Here I will only assert that, being supreme in Parliament—a word which includes both Houses,—unquestionably supreme from 1688 to 1832, and in reality not less supreme from 1832 to the present day, the landlords have betrayed that weakness which I suppose is inherent in every class: they have not merely maintained laws and customs which favoured the aggregation of real property by the landed gentry, but whenever opportunity offered they have not abstained—as in Drainage Acts, in Contagious Diseases (Animals) Acts, and in regard to Local Taxation—from legislative policy which has had, to say the least, a very strong resemblance to class legislation. Yet this disposition cannot have surprised those who have taken even a cursory observation of the main stream of history. Land-tenure is the

* " Political Economy," vol. i. p. 283.　　　　† p. 418.

simplest of all its chapters; the proceeding is in outline uniform. In our country, those who possessed the land have at all times been unwilling to widen the borders of ownership. First the king, claiming all, and finding that he could not hold all against other kings, or against pretenders to his throne, called in great nobles that he might have the help of their swords at need; then the nobles, finding that they could not keep their neighbours out of their castles with their own weapons, admitted knights and esquires to landowning. Then the knights and esquires, so long as personal service was needed and until the reign of law was fully established, secured the strong arms of meaner men in the same way. Tenures of service matured through the influence of Parliament into freeholds. Then, when landlords no longer needed fighting men, the reactionary process commenced. There was at that time much subdivision of the land. But when intricate and costly processes of law were established then the re-attainment of the agricultural soil by the wealthy set in, has continued to the present, and is still in operation. The late professor of political economy at Oxford has recorded the fact that, in the last year of the reign of Queen Anne, nearly 4000 freeholders voted in a contested election for the county of Sussex. He adds, " It is not likely that, at present, 400 persons could be found in that county having estates of the same character as the voters had in the electoral contest of 1714."* The history of the world affords in our day no warning against class legislation so powerful as this ; we know that the uncontrolled action of any class tends to be selfish, and therefore

* " Transactions, Social Science Association," 1864.

injurious, and when our Parliament is, by the enfranchisement of the general population of the counties, and
by the equalization of the franchise in the three divisions
of the United Kingdom, for the first time representative of
all interests, we shall have in prospect a better guarantee
than has hitherto existed for equitable dealing with the
land of the country.

It is as true now as it was in the days of the Norman
Conquest, that naturally the strongest class in any State
is that of the landowners. And it is well that this
should be so. The danger menacing this country—a
danger from which nothing but Parliament can deliver
the State—is that, together with representative institutions of a practically democratic character, we are maintaining a mediæval land system. When millions rule,
the ownership of agricultural land may not safely be
confined to a few thousands. The reform of the land
laws is eminently a conservative measure. The present
system unwisely lingers here, because some people fear
that its dissolution involves the loss of continuity of
certain institutions. It would never have endured had
the monarchy and the House of Lords been less worthy
of admiration and honour; its fall will menace neither,
so long as they preserve their claims upon the regard
of the country. It is perfectly true that if the peers
were deprived of their estates, the real basis of their
authority would be gone. But there is nothing in the
programme of free land which of necessity involves the
distribution of their properties, and their titles of honour
have no connection with the subject. If their claim to
constitute the best Second Chamber that could be devised

must always be held to involve the placing in mortmain—that is what it amounts to—of 52,000,000 acres,
then I say, without hesitation, that the continuance
of the House of Lords is not worth the cost, which I
believe is at least equal to the charge for the naval and
military services. No one, however, who is wise will
defend the law of primogeniture and the custom of
entail and strict settlement upon that ground. The
nobility may count securely upon the good-will of the
great body of the people. Mr. Gladstone has lately
referred to this tenderness in the heart of the English
as an inborn love of inequality. That is, I think, a
profound mistake. I have not much belief concerning
inborn disposition, but certainly, if anything of the sort
exist, I should say that the rationalizing and independent temperament of the Teutonic and Anglo-Saxon
peoples rather disposed them to lean in the other
direction. That our people do not display this tendency,
that "a lord" has an undoubted advantage over other
men, is due to the characteristic which is as wide as
human nature—a preference for those who are in any
honourable way distinguished; to the tradition with
which that particular distinction is accompanied; and
last, but not least, to the personal excellence of many
of the nobility. It is probably true, as the *Spectator*
said *ápropos* of Mr. Gladstone's remark, that the
Duke of Norfolk, were he a Protestant, would be
the strongest Conservative candidate for Sheffield; but
that does not indicate an English love of inequality.
It betrays the existence of a sentiment, the absence
of which would be detestable. If other countries

had heirlooms as interesting and as respectable as the
Duke of Norfolk or the Earl of Derby, depend upon
it they would treat them tenderly. I do not believe
there is a cultivated Englishman in the world who
would not be sorry to hear that the dukedom of Norfolk,
or the marquisate of Salisbury, or the earldom of Derby,
had become extinct. But to call that feeling a peculiarly
English love of inequality, is surely a sad mistake. All
honourable inequality is attractive, and is therefore
desired. The first prize gained at school is an envied
mark of inequality. The prefix " Honourable," is always
acceptable, even to an ex-senator of the United States,
because it attracts the suffrages of men. Republican
peoples restrict or abolish titles of honour, either
because titles have become abhorred as connected with
oppression which has been defeated, or because they are
unwilling to expose themselves and their rulers to
temptations which they know it is not in all human
nature to resist. The reproach is constantly heard of
some one who expresses Radical opinions—" If he were
a man of family, he would talk in a different way."
The speaker never reflects that if the objectionable
opinions are but possibly well-founded, a more striking
condemnation of the institution of nobility could not
be uttered, for, in truth, it is implied in this reproach
that self-interest in regard to the maintenance of that
which is obnoxious to the public interest would prevent the free and dutiful expression of opinion. Those
who are the natural guardians of nobility, and of the
institution, as we may call it, of a landed gentry in this
country, must in this age be above all things careful

to keep its savour sweet before the enfranchised people, and they must be careful not to identify the uses of a landed gentry with those abuses of law and custom which have placed 52,000,000 acres of the United Kingdom in a condition of ownerless, sterilizing disability.

CHAPTER IV.

WHAT LIMITED LANDOWNERS DO WITH THE LAND.

WHAT do they do with the land? What can the landed gentry do with it? Own the land they cannot; alienate it, they cannot; improve the land, for the most part, they cannot, on account of their insufficiency of means. As a rule, they let it, some on lease, but most of it on yearly tenancy. As a rule, too, they think as much of sporting as of improvement. Of the nobles and squires, some are sportsmen first and landlords afterwards; some are practical agriculturists, energetic improvers and liberal to tenants; but what may be seen upon such estates as those of the Duke of Bedford, or of the Earl of Leicester, or of Mr. Walter, serves only to exhibit how almost universal is neglect of the duties and opportunities of landowners, in regard to the agriculture of the country. The neglect is inevitable on the part of the majority, and with all, is more or less consequent upon their position as mere tenants for life. I have named a great nobleman whose ancestral mansion is, to his knowledge and to my knowledge, in a very bad condition as to drainage. A much greater expenditure than that lately made by the State for the Prince of Wales at Marlborough House is requisite. If his lord-

ship were freeholder, I should think he would do what is
needed. But, however, to the public at large this matter
is of importance only in so far as it endangers the life of
a useful member of the community, and as the neglect
may poison some guest even more valuable than the
nominal owner of that great house. This is personal
matter. But land drainage, on the other hand, is of
public concern; if that is neglected the land will be less
fertile: and will any practical land agent venture to
affirm that of the landed gentry one-third have executed
those works of land drainage which are required upon
their estates? Many who could spare the money, do not
feel sufficient interest in land of which they are but life
tenants to undertake the work. The farmers are poor
and unenterprising, and do not wish to pay increased
rents. Others, who do take personal interest in their
property, prefer to expend their surplus in the purchase
of more land. But the majority are struggling to pay off
charges upon their estates, or to save money out of which
they may give portions to their younger children. Then
again, the condition of not a few is that in which improvement is regarded as a sheer impossibility. As a
published example of a condition by no means uncommon
(except in regard to the bankruptcy proceedings) among
the landed gentry, I take the following: " A property
of 16,000 acres, with a rental of as many pounds, was
settled upon the Earl of —— for life, with remainder
to his son, Lord ——, as tenant in tail. Upon the
coming of age of Lord —— the estate was re-settled.
In consideration of an annuity of £1500 per annum, the
son agreed to join in the settlement, and to assent to

charges which brought up the total encumbrance to £11,500 per annum, leaving a margin of £4500, out of which the son was to receive £1500 during the father's lifetime. The son gave up his reversion in tail, and took a life interest in succession to his father, with remainder in tail to his own issue. Within a year from the re-settlement, the son, having run into debt for a few thousands, was made bankrupt; the whole of his reversionary life interest was then assigned to the creditors, and the result is that during the lives of father and son, and perhaps for many years after, this great estate will be in the position of being in the ostensible possession of men absolutely without means, and without any motive or probably power to sell." Mr. Shaw-Lefevre, from whom I have taken this report, says of it, that "the consideration of such a case leads naturally to the more serious remaining evils which result from the present system of land settlements. The general effect of such settlements and entails is that the proprietors' rights and interests in the land are carved out into a series of limited estates for life and in remainder, each in succession, barren of power and of motive to meet the wants, the improvements, and the discoveries of the time." *

Of course we shall be told that Parliament has provided means for assisting limited owners in works of improvement. When, in a subsequent chapter, we look into the dealings of Parliament with the land, we shall see how far this assistance has been and can be made available. The most practical commentary upon

* "Limitation of Entails and Settlements," by G. Shaw-Lefevre, M.P. 1877.

the efficacy of any such assistance exists, however, in the immense extent of undrained land, in the want of cottages, in the rotten and insufficient farmsteads, in the waste of manure owing to improper buildings. In 1851, Mr. James Caird* found that "much of the land of England, a far greater proportion of it than is generally believed, is in the possession of tenants for life, so heavily burthened with settlement encumbrances that they have not the means of improving the land they are obliged to hold. It would be a waste of time to dilate on the public and private disadvantages thus occasioned, for they are acknowledged by all who have studied the subject and are seriously affected by it." Ten years later, Mr. Mechi, writing to the *Times*,† said—and his words remain true at the present day—"There are many millions of acres of exhausted grass-lands and poor stiff-clays, which now bind the tenant in poverty and discontent, that would be rendered profitable by an investment of from £20 to £36 per acre, in the following improvements :—

	£	s.	d.
Drainage	7	0	0
Subsoiling, or deepened cultivation	2	0	0
Removal of hedgerows, trees, and improvement of roads	2	0	0
Covered yards and good farm buildings	7	0	0
Suitable residence for tenant	5	0	0
Steam machinery	2	10	0
Burnt clay, chalk, or lime	5	0	0
Guano, bones, or other manure	3	0	0
Sewage irrigation where practicable	3	0	0

" So here is a total of landlords' and tenants' improvements which, conjointly, would certainly result in indi-

* " English Agriculture," by James Caird. † *Times*, July, 1861.

vidual and national profit. I am speaking practically on the matter, and I know that it would be a happy circumstance for the generality of clay-land farmers to have their present rents doubled, or even tripled, provided that the increased rental represented a fair interest on a sum expended on landlords' improvements."

The embarrassed landlord cannot do these things; the careless landlord will not; the rich landlord does not always do them, and the proof is, that they are not accomplished. Mr. Caird said that "the substantial and capacious farmeries of Belgium, Holland, the north of France and the Rhenish Provinces contrast most favourably with the farm buildings common in most English counties."* In every county, there is visible that indifference to improvement which is natural to limited ownership; but, as Mr. Caird has remarked, the "one great barrier to improvement which the present state of agriculture must force on the attention of the Legislature is the great extent to which landed property is encumbered. In every county where we found an estate more than usually neglected, the reason assigned was the inability of the proprietor to make improvements on account of his encumbrances." In 1878, this eminent authority upon British agriculture as it is, published another work,† in which he states that the holding of the land by tenants for life is "a condition which prevents the power of sale," and that the land so held, "is frequently burdened with payments to other

---

* "English Agriculture," by James Caird.

† "The Landed Interest and the Supply of Food," by James Caird, C.B., F.R.S.

members of the family, and in many cases with debt.
. . . There is no capital available for the improvements
which a landowner is called upon to make, in order to
keep his property abreast of the advance in agricultural
practice." This, Mr. Caird says, was the ground upon
which Parliament about thirty years ago " provided State
loans on favourable terms to the landowners, for the
drainage and reclamation of their estates." When free
trade in corn, was established, and it became impossible
for the landlords to obtain further gratifications of this
sort from Parliament, land-improvement companies were
formed, "the companies" says Mr. Caird, " necessarily
charging somewhat higher terms than those which the
credit of the State had enabled it to afford without
loss," and the result has been that " the total amount of
money charged on the land of the United Kingdom for
agricultural improvements under the system of periodical
redemption, in the last thirty years, amounts to about
fifteen millions sterling—twelve in Great Britain and
three in Ireland. About eight millions of it was advanced by the State, and seven millions by private
companies." Mr. Caird estimates that of this sum, so
trifling and insignificant when compared with the wants
of the agricultural soil of the United Kingdom, not more
than two-thirds, or £10,000,000, have been expended in
land drainage. With reference only to Ireland, I shall
presently show, upon the highest authority, that in the
smaller island there is at present great need for the land-
drainage of 6,000,000 acres, which, at the low estimate of
£5 per acre, would demand three times the sum expended
under the system of periodical redemption in Great

E

Britain in the last thirty years. Mr. Caird thinks it possible that in England and Scotland three times as much land-drainage has been carried out in that period by private capital without loans, and making the largest estimate of outlay, he finds that for Great Britain and Ireland "the capital wealth of the owners of landed property has been increased by three hundred and thirty-one millions sterling in twenty years, at a cost to them which probably has not exceeded sixty millions." And to what has this increase been due? To the augmenting wealth and numbers of the urban population, and to their demand for the more costly productions of agriculture. Says Mr. Caird, "The increase has arisen chiefly from the great advance in the consumption and value of meat and dairy produce, and is thus only in part the result of land improvement."

Some landlords grant leases, but we may judge that the majority do not from a statement made by an eminent land-agent to Mr. Mechi, in 1871, "that out of 1,500 farms which he has let, only one-fourth were on lease." The question of granting leases has no direct connection with that of free land. No one would propose to make the giving of a lease compulsory, and for my own part, I shall nowhere join in attacking landlords for withholding leases. My view of the rights of property is too absolute for that. A man has a right to do what he pleases with his own; it is for the law to restrain him from doing injury to others, or from withholding benefit from the community. Our interest in the subject of leases as part of an inquiry into the circumstances of the tenure and produce of agricultural land, is the degree to which the fettered condition of settled land, together with the customs which have brought the land into that condition, affect the granting and the terms of leases. But, however, in this chapter we endeavour to confine our attention to what is done by the landed gentry with their settled property. In granting leases or in accepting yearly tenants, the law is unduly careful of the interests of the landlord. By giving a preferential security to his claim for rent, he is led to be less cautious as to the character, the capabilities, and the capital of the incoming tenant. This leaning of the law to the landlords is directly opposed to public interest. The least responsible men are not seldom the highest bidders in the matter of rent, partly because, being ignorant, they are less able to judge the real value of land, and partly out of the carelessness which is often seen in men who have very little to lose. Speaking at Southport in 1864, the present Lord Derby said, " I think every good tenant who is expected to stay permanently on the farm he holds, is entitled to ask for a lease from the proprietor. It is a very simple alternative: if a man is not fit to settle on an estate with a lease, he is not fit to settle without one ; if he cannot be trusted with a lease, he cannot be trusted with the land. I say this—and in what I am saying, I am rather in my own mind addressing landlords than tenants,—I say, if a tenant is to be expected to lay out capital on his farm, it implies no distrust of the landlord—it is simply an ordinary and proper business precaution—that he should insist on having some lease. I believe that these two things—one, the making the giving of a lease a general rule, and the other, having leases drawn more simply than as a rule they are at present,—would go very far to settle that question of landownership of which we have heard something of late."

I am disposed to think that far too much is made by speakers and writers of the question of granting leases. As a rule, a good tenant can probably obtain a lease,—of a certain sort. Some landlords would rather suffer anything than make over peculiar privileges connected with their property for a period of years. But it is well-known to those who are practically acquainted with English agriculture, that tenants themselves do not always, or even in a majority of cases, desire leases. Some fear to take a lease because of that natural terror which the intricacies of the law relating to real property have implanted in every Englishman, especially in those of the middle class, with regard to parchment deeds; and others fear by taking a lease, and so giving a term to their occupancy, they may appear to suggest a time at which, upon the termination of the contract, the landlord may raise their rent, in part by an assessment of the value of their own unexhausted improvements. Where there is no lease, the landed gentry, especially those of "the good old sort," might never think of sending a valuer over the farm. But if there has been a lease, nothing is more likely than that at the end of the term, a new valuation will be made. Of course, all this tends to keep British agriculture in the old grooves, in all the unimproving ways of bygone times. Lord Derby invariably strives to impart to every subject a "business" character; but with the prevailing tenure of land in

England, complete success in that direction is impossible. In the ownership of land there is no "business," because ownership is merely nominal; and in the letting, 'the "business" character is diminished by the existence of the law of hypothec in Scotland and the law of distress in the other parts of the United Kingdom. Adam Smith said that "laws frequently continue in force long after the circumstances which first gave occasion to them, and which could alone render them reasonable, are no more;" and this is peculiarly true of the laws which give undue favour to the creditor for rent. That the feudal characteristics of landholding should now give place to business character is the object of this work, and the feudal relation injuriously survives in the laws of hypothec and distress.

I do not say that law should give no preference to certain pecuniary claims, but only that preference should be determined by public policy. If an indigent person die in the house of another, the common law gives him a "right" to Christian burial in the parish churchyard at the expense of the person under whose roof he has expired.* The law gives preference to expenses incurred in mortal sickness, and to funeral charges, with obvious advantage and propriety. That a similar preference should be accorded to the rent of a dwelling-house is also recommended by very strong considerations of humanity, and therefore of public policy. Many poor would be homeless and forced into pauperism were it not for the preferential security given to their landlord in the matter of his rent. But it is opposed to public

* Reg. v. Stuart, 12 A. and E., 773.

policy that the common law should give preference to the creditor in regard to premises devoted to trading, commercial, and professional enterprise; it is not advantageous to the public, that, if a bankrupt's estate is in process of liquidation, the landlord, who is a creditor for rent, can arrest the proceedings until his claim is discharged in full, and more unquestionably is it disadvantageous that extraordinary preference should exist with regard to agricultural rent. Some, even of the Tory members for Scotland, are converted to the abolition of the law of hypothec, but they are not ignorant that the English landlords will not throw down this buttress to their own law of distress. The law of hypothec—before its amendment in 1867—gave the landlord a preferential claim upon the crop, so absolute, that for any unpaid rent he might take any portion of it out of the hands of third parties wherever it went, unless sold in bulk in public market. By the Hypothec Amendment (Scotland) Act, 1867, this state of the law was modified. Crops cannot now be followed and brought back from a *bonâ fide* purchaser. The principle of hypothec, like that of distress, was in its origin not inequitable. The farmer was originally a servant, a serf, who, if he sold the crop before handing over his lord's share, was a wrong-doer. Distress is defined to be " the taking of a personal chattel out of the possession of the wrong-doer into the custody of the party injured, to procure a satisfaction for the wrong committed." * " Distress," says Lord Coke, " is a remedy of the feudal law. It was an incident inseparable from the fealty to the lord; so that," as Lord Coke laid

* " Stephen's Commentaries," iii., 342.

down, "a lord granting the rent to another, and retaining the fealty, the grantee of the rent could not distrain." These laws are injurious with regard to agriculture, because they prevent the introduction of that "business" relation in which Lord Derby evidently sees advantage. The rent of the landlord is protected and enhanced by these laws at the expense of the community. "It may be that a landlord does not always close with an actual adventurer, but merely uses his readiness to come forward as a leverage, either express or implied, to concuss a good tenant into submitting to more unfavourable terms than he would otherwise agree to. The knowledge that the landlord has it in his power to resort to this course, whether he do so or not, pervades the minds of all concerned. This is the true secret of the political subserviency of tenants, and of the arbitrary and oppressive conditions, such as those about the reservation and preservation of game, which are so much complained of, and for which, in so far as concerns game, the game laws are blamed. The game laws, with the exception perhaps of some trivial particulars, have really no more to do with such conditions than the currency laws have to do with them." *

Yearly tenancy prevails with no objection from many tenants, who prefer an "honourable understanding" (which is not "business") with their landlord, to one of those leases, the want of simplicity in which Lord Derby condemned. Yet everybody knows that what Adam Smith said of yearly tenancy is true—that "it is against all reason and probability to suppose that yearly tenants

* "The Policy of Hypothec," by Dr. Macleod Smith.

will improve the soil." It is not too much to say that
the agriculture of Great Britain is, to a great extent,
directed by consideration of what the landed gentry
understand to be sport. That is, as to a large area, the
explanation of the denial of leases; that is the cause of
vexatious covenants; and so long as the ownership of
agricultural land is by laws and customs restricted and
settled to the uses of a few thousand wealthy persons, this
sacrifice of national interests to sport must continue. It
would be well, as Mr. Mechi says, if on millions of acres
the rent were tripled in consideration of a further outlay
of capital by landlords ; it is against public policy that rent
should be so low as to encourage careless farming. There
are many great family estates on which rent is much below
what it would be if the occupation of land had a business
character. The consequent loss in production is a public
tribute paid to ancient feudalism and to modern sport.
The tenant likes a low rent; is glad to think that he and
his father have had the land on much the same terms ; it
is not difficult to get a living, and ambition tends to
wearing a red coat in company with fox-hounds. He
has no lease, but his landlord is a kind and honourable
gentleman, and so long as the rent is paid, and he neither
shoots foxes nor game, nor ostentatiously votes the wrong
way, and does not acquire a bad character in the neighbourhood, he is secure in his occupation. When he leaves
the farm he will be paid according to the custom of the
country, for the unexhausted improvements he has made.
This custom of course applies to farming of the old style,
and he is liable to the narrowest construction of it, or
even to the forfeiture of his invested and unexhausted

capital. Sporting has an enormous influence over British agriculture. A correspondent of the *Inverness Courier* of October 9, 1873, writing on the game question, under the signature of " a Ross-shire Factor," said that although there may not be a word of game in the bargain, "there is a lurking certainty on both sides, that if a hare or partridge be touched, out the tenant goes next term." As to England, Mr. Clare Sewell Read, who is a high authority upon such matters in Parliament, has said, " A landlord could now let his farm to a tenant upon the usual covenants, and eat him up with game without paying him the usual compensation. He could turn him out of his farm, and half ruin him with a six months' notice to quit, by confiscating every shilling of his improvements." Thick irregular hedgerows which are a hindrance to agriculture, are preserved because they harbour game. The rent of many estates is permanently low because sporting has to be combined with agriculture.

I do not seek to insinuate that a landlord is bound more than any other man to study the public welfare. I do not suggest that the abolition of what are called the game laws would do away with the preservation of game. No reasonable law could be framed which would prevent the tenant from giving facilities for the landlord's enjoyment of sport. The difficulty might safely be trusted to right itself, if a system of free land were established. But, with the present land system, it is a great and growing evil. I will take an instance I have met with, of disregard for public interests—the transformation of a sheep-walk, producing food and commodities valued at £381,000 a year, into deer-forest, producing food and commodities extremely valued at £37,620 per annum. The following figures are accepted as accurate in a work by Mr. D. G. F. Macdonald, entitled, "Cattle, Sheep, and Deer." The book was published in 1871; it is a practical work, intended for the use and pleasure of landlords, and is, with much adulation, inscribed to the Duke of Sutherland. The estimate is made, that in 1871, no fewer than 1,320,000 acres had been set apart for deer, at an average rental, as deer-forest, of 13d. per acre, which, as pasturage for sheep, would be worth only 10d. per acre. The account there-fore stands thus:—

SHEEP v. DEER.

1,320,000 acres @ 1s. 1d....	...	...	...	£71,500
„ „ @ 10d. ...	...	...	...	55,000
		Gain to proprietors ...	...	£16,500

This is followed by an account, the items of which do not appear to be in any way disputed, showing the interest of the community in the matter. It is presumed that the 1,320,000 acres of land would carry 156,000 Cheviot and blackfaced sheep, and that in its present condition of deer-forest, 8,800 stags and hinds are all the possible produce. The contrast is as follows:—

SHEEP.

156,000, 60 lbs. each @ 8d.	...	...	£312,000
300,000 fleeces (deducting lambs) @ 2s. ...			30,000
156,000 skins @ 5s.	...	...	39,000
			£381,000

DEER.

8,800 stags and hinds, 140 lbs. each @ 6s.				£30,800
8,800 skins @ 3s. 6d.	...	...	...	1,540
8,800 heads @ 12s.	...	...	...	5,280

£37,620

In this statement the annual gain to the landlords appears to be £16,500, and the loss to the community nearly £350,000. Whether these figures are accurate or not I give no opinion. I merely assert that although such use of British land is contrary to public policy, it cannot reasonably be prohibited. We shall find that this and other abuses have their source in the feudal laws and customs which prevent the most beneficial occupation of the soil. I will give another example from my own personal observation. A good many years ago, I was walking over the family property of Lord Dacre (the elder brother of the Speaker of the House of Commons), in Cambridgeshire, adjoining an estate which was then in possession of General Hall. Close by the border of Lord Dacre's property, which was for the most part laid out in very large barley-fields, there was a fenced enclosure of about eight acres on General Hall's land. The fence was strong and high, and in each of the four sides there were several trap-doors. Inside, the enclosure was rough and overgrown with gorse and brambles. The place was a famous cover for hares, and General Hall's keepers were in the habit of lifting the doors in order to allow the hares to roam in the neighbouring fields, and to eat the farmers' crops. Occasionally, illustrious and noble sportsmen enjoyed a battue at these trap-doors, and killed a waggon-load of hares. The district was admir-

ably and most carefully farmed, but to the farmers and
agriculturists of the neighbourhood the enclosure was a
nuisance and a serious detriment. Such a mode of game-
preserving is, of course, quite inconsistent with the
existence of anything like "business" character in the
ownership of the soil.   We shall seek to make landowning a "business," and agriculture a "business," by
taking care that the processes of undertaking the occupation or ownership of land are simple, expeditious, and
secure. "Is farming a business?" Mr. Mechi has asked
himself,* and his answer is, "Certainly not. There is no
free trade in it, but it is almost smothered in the swad-
dling clothes of old feudal customs and practices. Can I
wonder, then, that agriculture is poor, and comparatively
unremunerative?   I am constantly told by landlords,
that it is very difficult to obtain men of sufficient capital
to give full development to the powers of the soil."
Mr. Mechi gives some forcible reasons, and, among others,
brings forward the insecurity of a lease which may not
be transferred. He spent £20,000 on his business
premises in London, with the security of a lease; but
would he have done that, he asks, without power of sale
or transfer? It is, as he says, most true, that "to deprive
the widow or orphan of the beneficial interest in a lease
arising from a tenant's improvements, is a positive
cruelty and injustice, and few men of capital will expose
their families to such a risk."

Lastly, in considering what the landed gentry do
with the land, let us state the fact of greatest national
import, that, forced into their hands as land is by un-

* "How to Farm Profitably," by J. J. Mechi.

natural laws and customs, they obtain a poor rent, and that the annual produce of the soil does not much exceed £3 per acre.* But why have the people not clamoured for better agriculture ? Mr. Cobden thought it "astonishing that the people are so tacit in their submission to the perpetuation of the feudal system in this country as it affects property in land, so long after it has been shattered to pieces in every other country;" and he justly declared the cause of this tacit acquiescence to be, that "the great increase of our manufacturing system has given such an expansive field of employment to the population, that the want of land as a field for investment and employment for labour has been comparatively little felt. So long," he predicted, "as this prosperity of our manufactures continues, there will be no great outcry against the landed monopoly." I fancy the time has arrived, and the outcry will before long be heard, demanding that the land of the United Kingdom shall be free, and that the landed gentry shall be responsible owners, not merely life-tenants, of their property.

* Proceedings, London Central Farmers' Club, June, 1862.

CHAPTER V.

WHAT THE TENANT FARMERS DO WITH THE LAND.

IN every country of the world, agriculture is the most important, and, as a general rule, the least intelligently conducted, of all occupations. From the borders of Hungary and from the Grecian Archipelago to the confines of China there has been no general improvement in the implements of husbandry throughout all the ages of history. The plough with which the rich soil of Greece is idly scratched was of the same fashion in the time of Constantine, and the plough which the Persian peasant follows is identical with that which appears on the sculptures of Persepolis wrought in the time of Darius. Yet agriculture is, as I have said, of all industries the most important, for reasons which I prefer to give in the weighty words of Adam Smith.* "No equal capital puts into motion a greater quantity of productive labour than that of the farmer. Not only his labouring servants, but his labouring cattle, are productive labourers. In agriculture, too, Nature works along with man, and though her labour costs no expense, its produce has its value, as well as that of the most expensive workmen. No equal quantity of produc-

* " Wealth of Nations," book ii. c. v.

tive labour employed in manufactures can ever occasion so great a reproduction. In them, nature does nothing, man does all; and the reproduction must always be in proportion to the strength of the agents that occasion it. The capital employed in agriculture therefore not only puts into motion a greater quantity of productive labour than any equal capital employed in manufactures, but in proportion too to the quantity of productive labour which it employs, it adds a much greater value to the annual produce of the land and labour of the country, to the real wealth and revenue of its inhabitants. Of all the ways in which a capital can be employed, it is by far the most advantageous to the society."

The importance of agriculture could not be more clearly stated. Why then, it will be asked, is agriculture, as a rule, the least intelligently conducted of all occupations? The reply has only to be stated for its truth to be acknowledged. As civilization advances, the progress of manufactures greatly outstrips the progress of agriculture, because agriculture has less capacity for the division of labour than manufactures. Then, in the progress of manufacture, it is found that by the exercise of superior judgment, larger profits may be occasionally obtained than are possible in agriculture, in which the profits of capital depend upon the yield of the soil, and the highest intelligence of a progressive country is not therefore devoted to agriculture. In a new country, the investment of capital in land may be, and is generally, the surest way to the acquisition of great fortune; in a country of great manufacturing power, it cannot be so. An important cause of the inferior intelligence and enterprise of agriculture is the comparative isolation in which it is carried on. But this isolation of the agriculturist is implied in his inferior power with regard to the division of labour. Adam Smith says,* "The ploughman, the harrower, the sower of seed, and the reaper of corn, are often the same. The occasion for those different sorts of labour returning with the different seasons of the year, it is impossible that one man should be constantly employed in any one of them. This impossibility of making so complete and entire a separation of all the different branches of labour employed in agriculture, is perhaps the reason why the improvement of the productive powers of labour in this art does not always keep pace with their improvement in manufactures." The condition of agriculture is generally relative to the wealth of the country. The average capital employed in agriculture is higher in England than in France, and higher in France than in Poland, but the inferior intelligence of the agriculturist and the landowner as compared with the artisan and the manufacturer is universal. A man who should invest a considerable capital in cotton manufacture by hand looms would be regarded as a fool. All the factories of Lancashire are conducted upon one plan, one method, and practically with machinery of precisely similar operation. No employer would expect to make profits if he acted otherwise. Nor indeed could he by any other method obtain a suitable supply of labour, for the operatives are trained, each of them, to one department of mechanical work. But in farming it is quite otherwise. On one side of a hedge there is deep drainage and steam-plough-

* "Wealth of Nations," book i. c. i.

ing; the other side is soddened clay pressed into water-bearing "puddle" by horses, plough, and ploughman. I have heard farmers contend that the threshing-machine is not so good as the flail, because they had observed that their bullocks and pigs preferred the straw which issued from the flail; and it was not easy to convince them that the preference denoted their loss in grain which the irregular hand-work failed to extract from the ears of corn. With one farmer it is an article of faith that five bushels to the acre is the proper amount of seed, while another has proved that on land of precisely the same quality, a larger crop is obtained by sowing one bushel. Many a time I have seen farmers put aside inferior wheat and very inferior potatoes for seed. Yet, although they could not see the folly of such practice, they had sufficient understanding in regard to their cattle to know that a strict relation must exist between parentage and progeny. I have never known agriculturists who could not appreciate for themselves and their families, the comfort of warm houses and warm food in winter, and of shelter in wet weather, but I have seen scores of farms upon which it appeared that in the opinion of the presiding intelligence, animals would fatten most quickly upon cold food and cold drink, administered in cold yards and upon water-soaked manure. There is not a British farmer who does not like change of diet for himself, but there are tens of thousands who appear to suppose that their cattle have no similar disposition. The following is a sample of a conversation which, in its ignorant diversity of opinion, might be equalled by interrogating the farmers of almost any parish in the country

F

upon almost any subject. It is quoted from a report of one of Mr. Mechi's public meetings in Cumberland :—*

"*Mr. Mechi* (who was advocating thin sowing): I say to you farmers of Cumberland, make the experiment for yourselves and be convinced, for it is a very vital and important question for the British farmer and the British public. Let me ask you a question. How much do you think is the natural increase of ordinary crops throughout the kingdom, for every bushel you put in of oats, barley, or wheat ?

"*Mr. Bogue:* One hundred.

"*Mr. Mechi:* You say one hundred ?

"*Mr. Bogue:* The Bible says so.

"*Mr. Jefferson :* Seven.

"*A voice:* Eighty-eight to one.

"*Mr. Mechi:* Thank you. One gentleman says seven, and another eighty-eight to one. This is a nice illustration. Any more opinions ?

"*Mr. Bogue:* Thirty to one.

"*Mr. Lawson:* Ten."

And so on, with greater divergence than school-children would exhibit in reply to a conundrum. Certainly there are exceptions. As we proceed I shall have to allude to tenant farmers who have displayed great ability, energy, and enterprise. But the rule is otherwise, for the reasons which have been stated. For those reasons, both farmers and landowners are generally Conservative. But only those who misrepresent the words of Mr. Mill, ascribe to him the dictum that "all Conservatives are stupid." What Mr. Mill said was

* "How to Farm Profitably," by Mr. Alderman Mechi, p. 527.

this: "If you meet a stupid man he is sure to be a Conservative." I have met stupid landowners, but well knowing what was the manner of their life I was not surprised at their stupidity. "Where do your rushes come from," I once asked of a great candle-maker. "Chiefly from Cheshire." And when, some time afterwards, I met a party of Cheshire landlords, and told them of the want of drainage in their county, proved by the abundant growth of rushes, they assured me that the best cheese came from undrained farms, and that cows were very fond of grass which grows about rushes. "Are you convinced?" a good-natured Cheshire baronet asked. "Yes," I said, "I am convinced that there is no evil in this world which will not find defenders."

The tenant farmer would be less obstinate in his prejudice against improvement if he had the means to carry it out. But he has not, and though it is true that of all ways in which capital can be employed, it is by the farmer that its employment can be most advantageous to society, farming is the business in which the supply of capital is most inadequate. It was said by the late Earl of Leicester, a most intelligent landlord and a very skilful agriculturist, that when applied to for a farm, he used to ask the applicant: "How much money have you? and I will suit the acres to the money." If landlords were owners of their estates it is fair to suppose that they would be more generally anxious to obtain tenants possessed of sufficient capital to engage in the best cultivation of the soil. But they would probably not obtain more applications from such persons than at present, because the security for agricultural investment

is of such inferior character. Even in England, a farmer
is supposed to have ample capital who has £10 an acre,
and there is no other country of the world where the
capital employed in agriculture is so large as in Great
Britain. It is probable he would do better for himself—
it is certain that his occupation might be more beneficial
to the community, if he reduced his holding by one half
and had £20 an acre of farming capital. This is what
Lord Derby and Lord Leicester may be assumed to have
meant, when they said that the agricultural produce of
England might be doubled. The capital employed in
farming is spread too thinly, and part of the reason is
that the deeper a man sinks his capital in the soil the
less easily can he recover it. He is taught by habitual
insecurity of tenure to regard such outlay as a dangerous
investment. Tenant-risk and the absence of tenant-right
have contributed to drive capital away from agriculture.
I have before me several estimates of the capital employed in British agriculture, none of them exceeding
£6 per acre. But no estimate that I have met with
appears to have been made with so much circumspection
and inquiry as that formed by Mr. Mechi, and com-
municated with general approval by him to the London
Central Farmers' Club, in 1862. Mr. Mechi said he had
made "extensive enquiries;" that he had taken counsel
with "the most intelligent farmers," and that all agreed
with him "that something about £4 per acre is the full
average of the British farmers' capital." In endeavouring
to arrive at a correct conclusion, Mr. Mechi stated that he
had consulted "Spackman, McCulloch, Porter, the twenty
journals of the Royal Agricultural Society, Morton on

Soils; Morton's Encyclopædia of Agriculture; Stephen's
Book of the Farm; Noverre Bacon on the Agriculture of
Norfolk; Caird's British Agriculture; Low on Scottish
Farming, and many other works, besides making very
numerous personal inquiries and observations." His
estimate, we may observe, is in excess of that made by
M. Léonce de Lavergne, who in his "Rural Economy of
Great Britain and Ireland," estimated the capital of the
English farmer, about the time of the Crimean war, at
£3 7s. per acre. The same distinguished French statistician and economist estimated the produce per acre of
English agriculture at an equal amount, while Mr.
Mechi's estimate of English produce per acre is £3 12s.
In 1877, Mr. Mechi published another estimate, but
avowedly made with less care. He said, "the capital
now invested was not much more than £5 10s. or £6 per
acre, while for good and satisfactory farming it ought to
be double or treble that amount." It is a liberal dealing
with the matter to assume that in fifteen years the
farmer's capital has increased by £1 an acre. True it is
that those fifteen years have been marked by great national prosperity; but agricultural profits have not been
uniformly high, and farmers have contributed largely to
those foreign investments which seemed to them more
tempting than the improvement of settled estates of
which neither they, nor any one else, could become
proprietors. Whatever the capital may be in England,
it is always held to be less upon the entire average of
Scotland and Ireland. If we take it at £6 an acre, and
the cultivated area of the United Kingdom at 50,000,000
acres (which is more than the actual area), we have

£300,000,000 as the tenant farmers' capital. Upon many millions of these acres £20 to £30 an acre would not be an excessive capital for the occupying agriculturist. Mr. Mechi, upon poor land in Essex, finds £16 an acre the minimum allowance for the most successful farming; Mr. Walter Wren, in Surrey, allows £33 an acre * to himself as tenant's capital; in some places £50 an acre would be well bestowed. It is certain that the average of £6 might be enlarged to £12 with great advantage, both to the producer and the consumer of bread and meat.

Between the years 1862 and 1878 British people probably lost by foreign investments a sum nearly sufficient to have doubled the capital invested at home in agriculture. In that period, they lent £125,000,000 to Turkey and Egypt, to say nothing of their misadventures in other parts of Europe and in the New World. Why is no investment made in agriculture? With but £6 where at least £12 are required, agriculture is starving for want of capital. Every year the need grows greater. A wooden flail could be bought for a couple of shillings, and thirty years ago the thresher who used it was content with 9s. a week. That is, or should be, superseded by the steam-threshing machine which cannot be purchased for less than £300, and the hand that directs it will be worth not less than 25s. a week. A horse-plough costs about 30s. to 40s., but the time will come when it must give way to the steam-plough, which, with all appliances, will cost nearly £1,000; the scythe and the sickle, purchasable for a "trifle," will soon be found only in museums or in pictures of "Father Time" or of "The

* Letter to the *Daily News*, October, 1877.

Reaper." The promise of agriculture is good enough, but capital is not forthcoming.

Can there be a doubt as to the reason—in England, where the Metropolitan Board of Works can borrow millions at 3½ per cent. ? We have all been born and bred in the knowledge that the soil of England was no-man's land, that it afforded no security for tenants' capital, and that although a tenant might reap, if he lived, a recompense for his investment, yet that it has become habitual with the British people to shun investment under the usual conditions of agricultural tenancy. Every day, cases are occurring which confirm this habit to the injury of agriculture, and in every winter the farmer is reminded by occurrences upon his land that sport has precedence of production. The nobility are generally good landlords; their high sense of honour, and of public responsibility, keep them from acts of arbitrary oppression; and, probably, few are more honourably distinguished in this way than the Duke of Sutherland. We may judge, then, what felonious treatment tenants have in some places received, and what they may under less favourable circumstances expect to suffer when, in a book to which I have already made allusion, there may be found the following incident described as, " Noble Conduct of the Ducal House of Sutherland."* In the year 1849, when the late Duke of Sutherland " forced expatriation " upon a large population in the Highlands, it appears that a few poor people, evicted from their holdings, craved and obtained permission " to settle upon an unclaimed piece of moor

"* Cattle, Sheep and Deer," by D. G. F. Macdonald, LL.D.

at Knockferral, Strathpeffer." In 1871, Mr. Macdonald
"visited the little colony," and he says, "I was much
struck to notice what was in 1849 all but an unproductive waste, not worth 3s. an acre rent, now returning
annually 21s. per acre rent, and presenting a beautiful
picture of fertility, peace, and prosperity, with a thriving,
grateful, and attached tenantry." These "grateful and
attached" people, who were paying 21s. for that which had
been, when their labour commenced, worth 3s. per acre, were
living in much "fear" lest they should be turned adrift
in order that their holdings might be thrown into one.
Mr. Macdonald represented their case to the Duke, and
it should surprise no one to learn that his Grace promised
they should not be disturbed. Considering the harsh
conduct in which the settlement had its origin; considering that within twenty years they were paying seven
times the original estimated rental of the land, it is
certainly a "note" of our land system that this permission given to this "thriving, grateful, and attached
tenantry" to continue the improvement, at their own
cost, of their "beautiful picture of fertility, peace, and
prosperity," is described as "noble conduct."

Let us proceed to another case, that of the late Mr.
Hope, of Fenton Barns, which, often as it has been
narrated, has congealed in ten thousand hamlets the
current of agricultural capital. One such case, though the
money in question be but thousands, has the effect of
withholding millions from the soil. On December 30, 1874,
there appeared in the *Times* a letter from Mr. Hope, upon
the subject of "Tenant-Right." With regard to his occupation of the farm of Fenton Barns, he said, "For more

than twenty years I have bought manures and feeding cakes to the value of 2,000*l.* annually." He added, "I have known three adjoining farms on the same estate, where the leases expired the same year, and two were re-let to the old tenants, one a little above, the other a little below the old rents; but the third was let to a new tenant at an increased rent of fifty per cent., and this large increase was mainly due to the expenditure of the former occupier, and to his keeping up its condition to the last." I wrote to ask Mr. Hope if this third farm was not Fenton Barns, from which he had been turned out by his landlord. He replied that in the case of this third farm he was alluding to his own experience at Fenton Barns. Both he and his landlord are now dead. But if the latter were alive, I should say nothing against him for this transaction. It was immoral, but it was not illegal, and it is not my object to improve the morality of landlords, except so far as that would be effected by the teaching of better laws. This "landowner" had estates also in Lincolnshire, and before Mr. Hope committed the unforgiven sin of presuming to differ in a public contest from the political opinion of his landlord, he was, as for his great enterprise and ability he deserved to be, a favourite. While he was improving the landlord's property at his own expense, and, as it proved, to his own regret, he was a visitor in Lincolnshire, and, in company with his landlord, inspected some farms, .the like of which he had seen nowhere in England for high and careful, prosperous farming. That county is distinguished by the possession of an equitable custom of tenant-right having the force of law. In the same letter from which I have quoted, Mr. Hope said: "These [Lincolnshire] tenants had no leases, but farmed under agreements to quit at six months' notice, being paid, however, on removal, for draining, marling, or manuring by the use of feeding-stuffs or otherwise. Now, it is this Lincolnshire custom which I and Scotch farmers generally want to see added to leases for periods of nineteen or twenty-one years, being sure it would have the effect of adding one-third to the crops of the kingdom in a very few years."

In a speech which Lord Derby delivered, as President of the Lancashire Farmers' Club, in June, 1879, he said, "Farmers have great reason to complain." Not of the absence of Protection, for "it is mere waste of time to cry out for help of that sort." Nor was Lord Derby clear that the farmer has a legitimate grievance as to rates. He said he would not undertake to prove that the incidence of rates is, in all respects, perfectly just, but he was prepared confidently to contend that all increase of local charges falls ultimately upon the owner. If Lord Derby will reflect, I feel sure he will see that is a statement which must be withdrawn, because it is by no means in accordance with facts. Let him take the experience of the tenants upon his own estate. I have shown his lordship to be very favourable to granting leases, and it may be assumed that in his father's time the majority of the tenant farmers on the Knowsley estate were in possession of such contracts. The distress of the cotton famine led to a sudden and enormous increase of poor-rates, which, of course, were levied upon the occupiers. It would be impossible to prove that the burden of these increased poor-rates fell ultimately in any fair or just proportion upon the Earl of Derby. Later, we shall deal with this subject of rates, and contend that equity demands that the landlord should be bound to pay a moiety of rates in the same inalienable manner in which he is bound to pay the Property Tax.

Lord Derby does not think much of the grievance which some farmers make of the Malt Tax. Nor do I, nor, I fancy, do those English barley-growers who understand the consequences of that tax. Barley is, we may say, grown most largely in the east of this island, and from Sussex and Suffolk we have been accustomed, though not of late, to hear much declamation on the subject of the Malt Tax. I have made inquiry of many brewers, and th ey are unanimous in stating that it is the Malt Tax which secures the consumption of English barley. Two large brewers have told me very lately that if it were not for the Malt Tax, they would not use a single quarter of malt made from English-grown barley. They find a slight advantage in using malt made of English barley, because, while it has greater weight and proportionately higher beer-making qualities than foreign barley, the Malt Tax is the same upon all sorts of barley. They tell me that if the Malt Tax were abolished it would unquestionably be more advantageous to use foreign barley, and that, even if the Malt Tax were levied on quality, its operation would at once be found adverse to the interests of the English barley-grower. It is certainly true that of late years the agitation for the repeal of the tax has greatly declined, and this, I am informed, is the correct explanation of that fiscal phenomenon. Indeed it is by no means impossible that the time may come when the farmers of East Anglia will be found among the stanchest advocates for the retention of the Malt Tax. Lord Derby's reference to those English landlords, "who are owners only in name, whose estates really belong to their creditors, who are encumbered up to the eyes, and who are driven to press hard upon their tenants because they are hard pressed themselves," and his opinion that "the existence of that class of owner is a misfortune," are worthy of recollection. We shall not in this chapter deal with his suggestion of "some such summary remedy as was applied by the Encumbered Estates Court in Ireland."

As to the Game Laws, nothing can be more sensible and acceptable than the remarks of Lord Derby in the speech to which I am referring. He said, "Everybody agrees that over-preserving is a nuisance; that you can't have, and ought not to try to] have, a warren and a food factory on the same ground. But the remedy is not so simple. I assume that not many farmers wish to do away with Game Laws altogether. The effect of that would be, especially in these populous districts, to lay open your fields to perpetual trespass in search of game; and popular feeling would not allow of the passing of a trespass law sufficiently severe to put an end to the nuisance. The result would be a worse state of things than you have now. Speaking for myself, I should have no objection to such a change in the law as would give the game to the tenant, in the absence of any agreement to the contrary; but, as it would almost always be a subject of agreement, the change so made would be one rather of form than fact. Some people contend that the landlord should have no power of preserving the game, but that would not only be an arbitrary restriction, it would be an altogether useless one; for the tenant having the game might let it, and he would naturally let it back again to the owner. To prohibit that would involve the absurdity that every owner would be able to shoot on his neighbour's lands, but not on his own; to allow it, would leave things virtually as they are. It seems to me, therefore, rather a matter to be dealt with in detail, than to be made the subject of any sweeping legislation. A tenant has a right to protection from all damage by game, greater than what he bargained for when he took his farm; and if any method can be devised for securing him that protection more effectually than he has it now, I for one shall not object. I don't see that it is possible to deny that a farmer has a real grievance who takes a farm with very little game upon it, and finds the quantity doubled or trebled during his occupancy, though here, again, I must point out that the original cause of the mischief lies in the vagueness of the agreement, and that is a matter within his own power to remedy. So, farther, no remedy can be too prompt or efficient in the case of persons, whether owners or occupiers, who are injured by the game kept by their neighbours. In that case there is no dispute as to the wrong inflicted, and there ought to be as little as possible of delay or cost in redressing it." It only remains to be said upon this matter that the establishment of a free land system, and the dealing, such as will be proposed, with entail and settlement, with investigation of title, and with transfer of land, would, in course of time, entirely alter the position of the game question, because of the great diffusion of proprietorship in land which would result from those reforms. As his "last word" to tenant farmers, Lord Derby said in this memorable address, "Recollect that the relation of landlord and tenant in the long run will be regulated mainly by the need which each has of the other." An object of this book is to show that the need of the landlord has been grievously exaggerated in this country by their power in Parliament; that they have lifted this need of the landlord into a dogma, to their own injury and to the deep disadvantage of the country; and that what we have now rather to observe are the evils of the tenant's position in reference to agriculture, and to do what we can, without injury to the landlord's interest, to promote as far as possible the union of occupation and of ownership in the business of obtaining the production of food from the soil.

CHAPTER VI.

In this chapter, I propose to deal only with the question of tenant-right as it arises in Great Britain. The circumstances of Irish agriculture are so different that it will be advisable to make special reference to Ireland. It may be said that the matter of tenant-right has no direct connection with the legislation necessary to establish free land. But the recognition of tenant-right is part of any equitable system of land tenure, and the discussion of this claim may serve to illustrate with especial force the directions in which the peculiar objects of the landed gentry are opposed, in their dealings with the land, to the public interests. We have just seen that, in the opinion of a very eminent and practical agriculturist, the legalisation of tenant-right, together with the practice of granting leases, would increase the produce of the country by one-third. By those with whom that opinion is accepted, it would probably be regarded as a sufficient justification of the claim to have the right admitted and established by law. It is well worth while to investigate the demand for tenant-right, not merely because of this promised increase of food, but because the plea is of the same character as that which must be urged in support of the legislation necessary to liberate the land. We prove that certain laws and customs, which have placed 52,000,000 acres in the hands of about 7000 persons who are not owners, are injurious to the permanent interests of the country, and we have thereby established the strongest argument for reform. In like manner it has only to be admitted that the establishment by law of an equitable and inalienable claim on the part of tenant farmers is advantageous to public interests, and that those interests must greatly suffer by withholding the authority of law from the claim, or by giving landlords the option of evading that claim, to make the acceptance of such a law the duty of Parliament. I say " equitable claim," because it is made upon due consideration of the landlord's rights of property.

By no one have the arguments on the landlord side of the question been advanced so ably and fully as by the Duke of Argyll,* than whom, perhaps, no one is more capable of viewing the question in all its bearings. I am almost disposed to say that we need concern our-selves with no other arguments than those put forward by the Duke. We must repeat that while compulsory compensation for unexhausted improvements is a matter of first-rate importance under the present tenure of land, its value in promoting public interests with re-ference to production would naturally decrease very largely under a system of free land, because farmers

* " Essay on the Commercial Principles applicable to Contracts for the Hire of Land."

would then find it advantageous, and it would probably become customary, with the most prudent, to be owners of the soil upon which their labour was devoted. The examination of the Duke's arguments may therefore appear valuable in this inquiry, chiefly as an exposition of the tendency to defeat and disregard public interests which is characteristic of the system his Grace upholds and approves. His first admission is, " that the interests of society may require us to modify the existing rights of individuals "—a proposition which I am much too conservative to admit without the qualification that the rights referred to are rights not personal, but of property, and that in the latter case no modification should be made without clear proof of the resulting advantage to the community, and then not without full and abundant compensation. The question which the Duke starts with is, " Whether any such necessity has arisen ?" in the matter of tenant-right. We are all agreed in the proposition that, " Whenever the existing rights of individuals have to be considered—whether these are the rights of tenants founded upon custom, or the rights of owners founded on laws and usages still more ancient —all must be taken as they are ;" nor can there be a doubt that " the interests of the public, or of the State, are best served, on the whole, when men are allowed in all such matters [their own pecuniary and economic interests] to pursue freely their own natural instincts and desires." So far we go with the Duke entirely, but now we begin to part company. It is not a correct statement, " that the hire of land for the purposes of agriculture is a matter as purely economic or commercial as the hire of machinery for the manufacture of cotton fabrics ;" because, to the extent of four-fifths, the subjects of hire are by law and custom in the hands of men who are not interested as proprietors, and, except the very limited and restricted interest of a tenant for life, have no rights of property in them.   For the same reason, agriculture is not "a trade like any other trade." The Duke says that "what is called 'feudalism' is now a common subject of denunciation as a vicious element in the relationship between owners and occupiers of the soil." We know of no such "vicious element" as the principal element of "feudalism." We recognise the survival of "feudalism" in such broad and striking facts as that fifty-three persons of the Duke's order represent the ownership of 36½ per cent. of the land of Scotland. His Grace says: "The word has no definite meaning now except as a term of reproach for certain personal or hereditary influences which are disliked or disapproved by those who use it." Surely this is an extraordinary error; surely by "feudalism" we mean those laws and customs which have preserved a distribution of the land not very different from that of feudal times, which have placed more than 52,000,000 acres of the United Kingdom in the hands of some 7000 persons, who, instead of holding as tenants of the Crown, are, so far as the public interests are concerned, in the less beneficial position of tenants of posterity; in fetters with regard to agricultural improvements more severe than those of olden time.

The Duke assumes that his opponents take up ground which he chooses for them, and upon which it pleases his Grace to place them. He says that those who object to "feudalism, say that there is something in the nature of land which prevents it from being subject to the same economic laws as other commodities; and that as land is absolutely limited in quantity, it partakes of the nature of monopoly." The Duke then goes into very much argument, of which the object is to prove that the ownership of land is not a monopoly. But he is not apparently sure of his position, and proceeds to argue that "even if this classification of the ownership of land as a monopoly were correct, it is irrelevant to the question under discussion." The ownership of land, it has always seemed to me, is not a monopoly; but the reason why I think it cannot be called a monopoly is very different from that put forward by the Duke, and is precisely relevant to the question under discussion. Surely there can be no monopoly where there can be no such thing as absolute tenure. No ownership of land is conceivable which excludes the claim of public interest in regard to its occupation, and this public interest in regard to the occupation of the land is the proper basis of the demand for tenant-right. The public interest arises from the necessity for land to the existence and the maintenance of life, and from the limitation which exists as to its quantity. It is good political economy to say that all exchangeable commodities of which the quantity is visibly limited, are subject to monopoly. But although land is of that category, we shall see, in taking special observation of the nature of property in land, that the joint interest of the public has never been, and can never be, excluded.

The Duke says, " The more limited land is in quantity, the more important is it that the cultivation of it should be open to all the world." But that is not all. It would be well to add, "the more important is it that abundant capital should be employed in cultivation," and capital, we know, cannot be attracted without the pledge of security.

To the interest of the public at large, we have seen that agriculture is the most beneficial form of investment, and therefore it should be the most secure. The facts are, that less than two-thirds of the area which require drainage have received that improvement; that instead of having 16l. or 20l. an acre, farmers have, on an average, 6l. of capital per acre; that the produce of the soil does not average 5l. an acre, and that in the opinion of practical men, the concession of compulsory tenant-right would raise the produce to 7l. an acre. The public interest, then, in the discussion of this claim is not only, as the Duke puts it, how can the farmer be repaid for the expenditure of capital, but how can he be encouraged to make this outlay with due regard to the rights of the landlord. Of course, in a thoroughly healthy agricultural system, drainage and other works of permanent improvement would be done by the landowner; with our settled life-tenants this cannot always be the practice. The Duke puts "extreme cases," with the apparently useless object of setting them aside. He takes the case of an undrained field, worth 10s. an acre. "The man who has hired it, drains it at a cost of 8l., and thereupon the land becomes worth a rent of 60s., instead of only 10s." His Grace proceeds to assume that the demand is, either for the capitalised value of that improved rental at the expiration of the tenancy, or for so much of the expenditure as the tenant has not had time to recover out of the increased profits arising therefrom. But to us it seems neither to be this thing nor the other. The first would rob the landlord; the second would be unfair, perhaps to the landlord, and perhaps to the tenant. I have seen drainage rendered nearly worthless by partial sinking of the ground. This disaster occurs not seldom in the coal-mining districts. In that case (irrespective of the claim for compensation against the mine-owner), the outgoing tenant could not claim for effective drainage. But if that drainage, being a necessary work, had depreciated in value as an improvement by only twenty-five per cent. during his tenancy, the outgoing tenant is equitably entitled to receive 6*l.* per acre. The benefit of such an improvement to the landlord would be great, for the succeeding tenant would pay an additional rent sufficient to recoup the cost of the improvement in a few years.

We say that, ruled by just definitions of improvement and regulations under which such improvement should be made, the public interest demands that the claim should be unavoidable in law, and that this would be advantageous to landlord as well as tenant. The Duke says this proposition is partly founded upon the assumption "that, as a matter of fact, the capital of agricultural tenants is now exposed to special and exceptional risks, widely prevalent, severely felt, and which are not likely to be remedied by contracts or agreements." The Duke knows many facts which would invalidate this assumption, and so do I. Let us rather take ground not selected by the Duke, ground which no one can invalidate, and say that this proposition is made in view of the present beggarly condition of British agriculture in regard to capital and improvement. The Duke lays down " the fact, namely, of the sharpness of competition for the hire of farms," as, " perhaps, the strongest evidence to be found" that there is no widely prevalent fear as to insecurity of tenants' capital invested in permanent improvements. But it is no evidence whatever, because we have no information that these competitors contemplate the execution of permanent improvements. The capital they propose to embark is, no doubt, exceptionally secure; probably more safe than it would be in any other business.

We have now to deal with an argument which appears to be pitifully weak,—that farmers "are compensated for theoretical uncertainty of tenure, not only by a lower scale of rent, but also by habits, customs, and traditions of connection with the owner which are extremely powerful—so powerful as often to pass even undue limits on the management of ownership." I have already said that one of the evils of our "settled" land system is that rents remain so low, and I have quoted Mr. Mechi's statement, that rent might often be " tripled" with advantage to the tenant. It is quite true that in England, where leases are less common than in Scotland, " on many estates, the farms, except in the case of real vacancies, are never subject to any competition at all." It is also probably true that " in most parts of England it will be found that farmers, holding under the system of yearly tenancy, do generally enjoy longer periods of possession than the average of farmers holding under lease." It is an undoubted fact, as I have already stated, that English farmers are shy as to taking leases, because the period of commencement and of termination suggest to the life-tenant the idea of valuation, and valuation means adding to the rental at least that which Mr. Mill called the "unearned increment" of value. I entirely concur in the Duke's opinion, that "all over England; wherever the system of yearly tenancies prevails, farms are let below the full value to an extent of which the public has no conception." But the remarkable difference between us is, that the Duke pushes forward these considerations as tending to the public interest. Because a low rent would leave more money in a farmer's pocket, the Duke assumes "that this condition of things does afford a kind and a degree of security against loss from outlay upon improvements." I should say rather that it promoted sloth in agriculture, and deadened desire for improvement, was utterly injurious to the public interests, and is the destruction of the Duke's assertion that in the United Kingdom "contracts for the hire of land are matters purely economic." The risk is not "severely felt" because the expenditure is not made, nor is it reasonable to suppose that, under such conditions, it would or could be made in anything like a general manner. The argument which proposes to show that the facts of agriculture suggest the existence of abundant security for outlay upon improvements, breaks down at the first stages of inquiry in any county. The allied argument is, "that no legislation of the kind proposed

can possibly, in the long run, add anything to the security
which this branch of trade affords to those who embark
in it." To our surprise we find that the worst the Duke
has to say concerning compulsory legislation is that
" that form of security which is now so extensively
afforded in cheap rents would rapidly tend to disappear.
. . . The whole prospective value of the new privilege
would be discounted in the rent market. . . . It would
simply enter as a new element in the calculation of rent
among those who compete for the hire of farms." This
is as true, it seems to us, as it would most certainly be
beneficial. To whom would it be an evil that a compulsory law as to tenant-right " would compel owners
in self-defence to make the market price the standard of
letting value ? " Not, surely, to the landlord, whose income
would be raised by more than his payment ; not to the
industrious, intelligent, and enterprising farmer, who could
then deal surely and safely with the land, and, if need
be, could raise money upon the security of his claim ; and
most certainly not to the public, for the claim would be
void and of none effect, until, by the execution of improvement, their interest in the soil had obtained substantial advantage. It would probably reduce the power
of the landlord over his tenant ; and though the relationship is now so beautiful as the Duke describes, there will
arise, in the mind of many a man who has made much
outlay upon faith of yearly tenancy—possibly about
election time,—a thought that after all he is not quite his
own master, and disturbance would certainly tend to be
more rare when proceedings under a real Agricultural
Holdings Act would be of necessity involved. It might

add an additional complication to the affairs of life-
tenants. But then, life-tenancy is odious to public
interest. Is it not an amazing thing that landowners
who contend, in page after page, that the salvation of
British agriculture depends upon "freedom of contract,"
wish to retain that which is not freedom for their own
contracts with the tenant, by the laws of hypothec and
of distress. ? Occupiers will not, as we see, generally
execute improvements unless they have a compulsory
lien upon the soil by way of security; and adventurous
occupiers, who have not the means and cannot acquire
the means of farming land as the public interests
demand, will outbid more solid men, because of their
inferior responsibility, if the debt to the landlord has
a peculiar protection afforded to no other claim. Perhaps
the most triumphant sentence in the Duke's argument
might be described as the least sound. "Thus," his Grace
says, "the very plea which is used to show that security
for capital under freedom of contract cannot be obtained—
namely, the severity of competition—is the proof that
legislation is powerless to afford any other or any better
security than that which contract gives." Under "freedom of contract" the work of improvement is not done;
the belief is that with compulsory compensation it would
be otherwise: nor does the Duke deny this. And therein
lies the whole matter, so far as the public are concerned.
The rise in rent is merely an incident of beneficial
progress. Not the Duke of Argyll, who is ever ready
to fight in any arena upon his personal merits and
justly confident of achieving distinction, but rather the
average of landlords suggest, by their attitude on this and

kindred subjects, the talk of Boswell with Johnson:
"Upon my observing," says Boswell, in the "Tour in the
Hebrides," "that there must be something bad in a man's
mind who does not like to give leases to his tenants, but
wishes to keep them in perpetual wretched dependence
on his will, Dr. Johnson said, 'You are right; it is
a man's duty to extend comfort and security among as
many people as he can. He should not wish to have
his tenants mere *ephemeræ*—mere beings of an hour.'
Boswell: 'But, sir, if they have leases, is there not some
danger that they may grow insolent?' Johnson: 'Depend upon it, sir, a man may always keep his tenants in
dependence enough, though they have leases.'"

Lord Derby is a landlord as just and candid as the
Duke of Argyll, and Lord Derby's reasoning in connection with the Agricultural Holdings Act very much
resembles that of the Duke. Lord Derby says,* "As
to unexhausted improvements, no one wishes that the
landlord shall confiscate the result of the tenant's outlay,
and on the other hand, the landlord has a right to protect
himself against having to pay for so-called improvements
made by the tenant, which may be of no use to him and
may not add to the letting value of the farm." Lord
Derby indicates precisely the limitation of his view when
he adds, "These are the two rocks between which we
have to steer." But surely a broader and more beneficent
view of the subject would include the question, so much
more important, How shall we attract and induce that
considerable outlay for lack of which British agriculture
is so unproductive compared with the results that larger

* Speech at Liverpool, June 16, 1879.

capital would render possible ? Next we have to look
at Lord Derby's apology, admitting it to be the best that
has been, or perhaps that can be made, for the permissive
character of the Agricultural Holdings Act. His lordship
observed in the same speech, " I believe the last Act on
the subject—the Act passed by the present Parliament—
embodies as fair a solution of fhe points in dispute as we
are likely to arrive at, and I am told, and I apprehend,
that the results which it has produced are not to be
measured by the extent to which it has been formally
adopted, even when, as no doubt has very generally happened, landlords and tenants have preferred to contract
themselves out of it, and to make their own arrangements, they have mostly followed the lines in which the
Act is drawn ; and considering the great varieties of
custom in different parts of the country, I don't think it
is surprising that they should not have chosen to bind
themselves by a hard and fast rule." I should pity the
noble adversary who opposed Lord Derby in debate on
any other matter, with reasoning of this sort. There is
(1) an admission of high appreciation of the value of the
Act ; there is (2) an approving assertion that landlords
and tenants, though standing outside the Act, are nevertheless constrained to follow its lines ; and (3) there is an
apology for their escape from the Act on the ground of
the differences of custom which prevail. It cannot but
be observed how inharmonious the apology is with
the approving assertion. It is undoubtedly a good thing
that landlords and tenants should in their arrangements
follow the lines of the Act; their doing so must imply to
some extent an advantageous reduction of those differ-

ences of custom which surely no statesmen, and, least of all, such as Lord Derby and the Duke of Argyll, desire to retain. We have thus attempted to try the plea for unavoidable tenant-right by an exhibition of the objections of the most distinguished opponents of that claim.

CHAPTER VII.

ADAM SMITH, writing a hundred years ago, thought "the right of primogeniture, as of all institutions it is the fittest to support the pride of family distinctions, . . . likely to endure for many centuries," * and, he added : "Entails are the natural consequences of the law of primogeniture." The law directs (with the exception of the lands held according to the Old English custom of gavelkind), that the landed possessions of a person, dying intestate, shall be exclusively the property of the eldest son, or other eldest male heir. There is no law compelling this disposition, and if, in the next generation, the members of the House of Lords were, with the consent of their eldest sons to disentail their estates, there is nothing in the law to prevent distribution by will of the property of peers and of all other landed gentry among their children. But if, after that disentailment were effected, any eldest son came into absolute possession of the family estate, then, if he died without making a will, the right of male primogeniture would be asserted by the law and the estate would descend intact. It may be said that no estate is dealt

* " Wealth of Nations," book iii. c. ii.

with by an owner or a life-tenant in obedience to the law
of primogeniture, but that the landed gentry are accustomed to act in conformity with the law. The abolition
of the law would not therefore imply the abolition of the
custom of primogeniture. Those who seek to establish
free land, "not as a political, revolutionary, Radical, or
Chartist notion, but on politico-economic grounds,"* have
no hostility to persons or families. Is the law of primogeniture opposed to public interests, and are there any
compensating advantages to be taken into account ?
That is the whole matter. I maintain that the existence
of this law is opposed to public interests, and that the
alleged compensations are fictitious.

It is a feudal law. It was unknown to the Anglo-
Saxons before the Norman Conquest. Blackstone regards
it as a consequence of the Norman invasion, and it has
often been observed as evidence of its origin that William
the Conqueror's charter to London provides (as for a
point on which there might be apprehension), that the
children of an intestate shall inherit equally. In the
writings of the Duke of Argyll it is assumed, as we
have seen, that reformers speak with irrational dislike of
"feudalism," and that the "word has no definite meaning
now except as a term of reproach for certain personal
or hereditary influences which are disliked and disapproved by those who use it." That, as I have said, is
not an accurate statement. That which is "feudal" is
born of force, and that which is of what, in times wholly
feudal, was called "chivalry," is matter of honour rather
than of duty. It was to meet force with force that each

* Cobden, at Rochdale, November 23, 1864.

great family maintained its chief, whose authority was the local government of feudal times. The possessors of power thought that the welfare of the State depended upon the maintenance of their authority, or of an authority like theirs, and for universal duty they substituted a graduated law of honour, which demanded less from a churl than from a knight. The law of primogeniture—a law of that period—is in harmony with it, and in discord with our times. But the feudalism of that law has yet a powerful hold upon the country. Presently, when we look into the local government of the counties, we shall see that feudalism abounds. And it is an idea wholly feudal that we should maintain the law of primogeniture because it contributes to give us the institution of the House of Lords. The reign of law is not yet cleared even of rude and manifest traces of feudalism. The final appeal in law is, by patent fiction founded upon slender fact, to the barons and superior nobles of the realm, who are themselves, by privilege of strictly feudal character, exempt from the authority of the courts of law in regard to charges of serious criminality ; and the preference for sentiment of honour, rather than for sense of duty, survives in the declaration which, by feudal privilege, they are permitted to substitute for the common formalities with which the utterance of legal evidence is preceded.

The abolition of the law of primogeniture is demanded because it is opposed to the idea of natural justice which the State has set up, and which is perpetually reinforced as the basis of authority is widened by extension of the suffrage. That law decrees, in the case of intestate persons, the pauperisation of the younger sons and of all the female children. By the law they are left destitute, and by the law are left chargeable to the State. That is a disposition of property to which the reformed State is utterly opposed. Not only is the parent bound to provide during life equitably for his offspring, but he is, by modern law, obliged to see that they have such opportunities of education as may fit them to exercise human faculties with intelligence.

If the law of primogeniture had frequent effect, its immorality, its inconvenience, its evident disregard for the public interests as they are now understood, would long since have compelled its abolition. But its operation is rare, and, as a rule, is purely accidental. The landed gentry, for whose benefit it is maintained, take example from it, but avoid with scrupulous care its unnatural conclusion. Its authority is used by them to condone the practice of bringing up a family of children in equal luxury, with the understanding that the means by which that style of living is supported will belong to the eldest son. But the parents never allow their younger children to become the victims of this law, and by savings, which are not seldom arduous and difficult,—sometimes, by personal penury, which for obvious reasons is rarely pitied,—they repudiate, in the pittance they have scraped from the crumbs of primogeniture for their younger children, the direful authority of the Norman law. They know and feel that the law of primogeniture would work—as Mr. Walter, Member for Berkshire, once said—"flagrant injustice," and they avoid it; but when they are asked to abolish a law of flagrant injustice—

to remove a law, the bare operation of which is so re-
pugnant to their own conscience that, if they possessed no
property but such as was subject to its operation, they
would hold it a crime to leave their offspring in the
power of this law,—they hesitate, they demur, they say
that to abolish it would be to abolish heirship, and that
upon heirship the institutions of the United Kingdom
are founded. The public conscience and confidence are
stronger; the people, so far as my observation teaches me,
never make a vicious law to attain a much-desired end:
such laws always belong to some "interest," as that of
primogeniture does to the landed interest; and, moreover,
the enfranchised people know that institutions are now
dependent upon their will. It only needs a little more
awakening of the public conscience, a little firmer
grasping of the fact that bad law disgraces a nation,
and with the next impulse of conscientious policy this
law of primogeniture will disappear.

The general law of the country regards children
equally in reference to parental obligation, and upon the
death of the parent, if the law is to distribute his property and to make his will, the law, it is clear, should
operate upon the same principle. Injustice is opposed
to public interests, and this law of primogeniture causes
injustice. Let us take two of many cases which have
been quoted in Parliament. In the first, a tradesman
who saved money, had made a will in his wife's favour.
While he was in good health they agreed together that
his savings should be invested in a farm. He accordingly
attended a sale by auction, bid, became the purchaser,
and paid the deposit required by the auctioneer. He

died before the purchase was completed. His widow, the sole executrix of his will, to whom he intended to leave all the savings of their joint thrift and industry, was, of course, compelled to complete the purchase. Upon that being accomplished, the entire property was claimed, and was obtained by a nephew in accordance with the law which in England governs the inheritance of land. The widow was left destitute, and ultimately became chargeable to the parish for poor-law relief. The second case bears more strictly, though not more truly, upon the law of primogeniture. It is contained in a letter addressed to Mr. Locke King: "My father died suddenly in the year 1826, leaving a widow and ten children. His landed property cost between £14,000 and £15,000; his personal estate was sworn under £4000, which was all absorbed by his bond and other debts. His children were four sons and six daughters; the eldest son had long previously taken the name and fortune of his maternal grandfather, under his will, and was thereby handsomely provided for. By the intestacy of my father, my eldest brother succeeded to all the landed property. The personal estate being insufficient to pay the debts, which had been chiefly incurred to purchase some of the lands, the eldest son was thus enriched to the injury of his brothers and sisters. The nine brothers and sisters were, as regarded their father's property, left utterly penniless, and at the mercy of their eldest brother. My father left an inoperative will, whereby he evinced his intention to provide an annuity for his widow, otherwise provided for by her father, and to divide his property equally among all his children, giving the option to his eldest son to take the real estate at its fair value, otherwise to be sold, having bought it with a view of completing his eldest son's estate, under his grandfather's will. I need hardly state what heart-burnings and estrangements of feeling this untoward act of intestacy has occasioned." In fact, as has been said, "The law of primogeniture never works but to work an injustice."

The public injury which results from an unjust law far transcends the operation of its literal provisions, and the custom of "making eldest sons" is a pitiable burden upon those who are supposed to benefit by the practice. It must be a great drawback from the pleasure of life to have an eldest son, whom the father cannot disinherit, over whom he has no control, who is owner just as much as the father is owner, except in point of actual possession of the property, which can never belong to either. It must be a great humiliation for a gentleman who wishes to marry a second time, to have to ask his son's permission, in order to make some further settlement upon the family estate. The lives of not a few of those who are called "aristocracy" would win the sympathy of any prosperous tradesman, when he saw how, for the sake of that family idol, the eldest son, a thousand galling economies and probably some "meannesses" had to be endured, and must be, in many cases, of life-long endurance with some of the younger children of these noble families. A younger son, who has written a very lucid essay upon the law of primogeniture, says that, "Long before the heir to a great estate emerges from boyhood, he is made aware that his fortune does not depend on his father's will or on his own deserts. He soon learns to consider the estate as his, subject only to his father's life interest, and expects to receive an allowance, making him to live in idleness, so that a double burden is laid upon the land for the support of two establishments yielding no agricultural return. As the father grows older, and the son's expectation of succeeding becomes nearer and nearer, painful jealousies are very apt to spring up between them, till at last, not a lease can be granted or a fall of timber authorized, lest it may prejudice, or be represented as prejudicing, the reversion." This, of course, is not a result of the law of primogeniture, but of the law of entail adopted to the practice of primogeniture. In feudal times, the eldest son held the stronghold which was the protection of the family interests, and when men and women ceased to take refuge in castles and preferred the protection of law, then primogeniture was used as a force to obtain from the keepers of the public purse, a provision for the younger members of the family. For ages feudalism thus forced upon the country officers of all sorts, civil and military, and it is only in the memory of the present generation that this line of feudal operation has been rendered difficult by competitive examinations and by a scrutinizing publicity of all appointments. It is certainly not for the public interest that persons possessing such enormous influence as must pertain to the members of the House of Lords, who, as I have shown, are the reputed owners of one-fifth of the country, should, by the operation of law and custom be followed by perhaps a thousand young men, all landless and needy, whom they desire to dispose of to the country at the best advantage. It is to primogeniture that we have been indebted for so many unhappy histories of noble and honourable directors of public companies. We very rarely hear of an eldest son figuring as a decoy for the savings of the unwary. But there have been scores of cases in which noble names have been lowered to disgrace—cases in which the plea of the young men might, like that of a street beggar, be hung around their necks—" Primogeniture compels me to do this."

The abolition of the law of primogeniture is due because the law works injustice and because it avows a principle at variance with that view of parental duty which the State has undertaken to enforce. But I have no belief that the abolition of the law would be the cause of any remarkable change in the devolution of real property, and it is no part of the plan of "free land" to abolish the right of primogeniture, by which I understand the power of a testator to give his wealth exclusively to his eldest son. It is certain that in England the practice would long outlive the law; it is probable that the custom would not be in any great degree affected by abolition of the law of primogeniture. For most people it is enough that the Crown is the prototype, and the House of Lords the product of the system. But when the law, which clearly works injustice and disgraces the Statute Book, is abolished, why should not the practice of primogeniture remain in vogue? No valid objection can be offered on economic grounds to a preference in the matter of bequest to an eldest son. Even in the middle class it is not uncommon for parents to make larger expenditure

in putting the eldest son out in the world, in order that
if the father die he may assist the younger children. It
would not be surprising if primogeniture outlived all
the public privileges of peers.   Primogeniture is not
extinct even where the power of absolute disinheritance
of any child is forbidden to the parent.   It is true that in
most continental countries the parent's power of bequest
is much restricted.   But it is never defined as to the
whole property, and in some places, where partition is
decreed, the paternal house and a certain area of land
are first secured to the eldest son.   The nobility of the
United Kingdom are unwise and imprudent when. they
mingle in argument the practice of primogeniture, which
may easily be deprived in all cases, as it is in many, of
injustice, with a law the terms of which are so odious
that no man possessed of nothing but land dare avowedly
leave his children to its merciless and immoral operation.

CHAPTER VIII.

THE LAW AND CUSTOM OF ENTAIL AND SETTLEMENT.

HITHERTO we have not dealt with the obstructions to free land. Tenant-right has, strictly speaking, nothing but an indirect connection with the matter, and the same may be said of the law of primogeniture. The concession of tenant-right is advisable to promote the investment of capital in the soil, and the abolition of the law of primogeniture is due to the claims of natural equity and to the character of public justice. In the law and custom of entail and settlement, we touch the system of protection, by which landownership is, with so much injury, fenced against freedom. We have seen, in a preceding chapter, something of the process; we shall do well, perhaps, to refresh our memory by a reference to one of the works of highest authority upon the Law of Real Property. The method is thus explained by Mr. Joshua Williams : " In families where the estates are kept up from one generation to another, settlements are made every few years for this purpose; thus, in the event of a marriage, a life-estate merely is given to the husband; the wife has an allowance for pin-money during the marriage, and a rent-charge or annuity by way of jointure for her life in case she should survive her husband. Subject to this jointure and to the payment of such sums as may be agreed on for the portions of the daughters and younger sons of the marriage, the eldest son who may be born of the marriage is made by the settlement tenant-in-tail. In case of his decease without issue, it is provided that the second son, and then the third, should in like manner be tenant-in-tail; and so on to the others; and in default of sons the estate is usually given to the daughters, not successively, however, but as tenants-in-common-in-tail with cross remainders in tail. By this means, the estate is tied up until some tenant-in-tail attains the age of twenty-one years; when he is able with the consent of his father, who is tenant for life, to bar the entail with all the remainders. Dominion is thus again acquired over the property, which dominion is usually exercised in a re-settlement on the next generation, and thus the property is preserved in the family." It is probable that no exaggeration has been made in assuming that the ownership of more than 52,000,000 acres of the United Kingdom is controlled by settlements of this character.

We commonly hear complaints against this bondage of the land met by lawyers who are interested, or who fancy themselves interested, in maintaining the existing arrangements, with the statement that only a small portion of the country, such as the royal gifts of Blenheim and Strathfieldsaye are unsaleable. That is true to the extent that in many settlements, especially in modern settlements, a power of sale is reserved to trustees, but they omit to state that the power is always accompanied with directions to invest the proceeds in the purchase of

other lands to be settled in like manner, and, which is
infinitely more important, that no acre of this four-fifths
of the country can be sold upon default by the ostensible
owner and at the demand of his creditors. The nominal
owners of several of the finest properties in England are
now adjudicated bankrupts; their lands are racked and
impoverished, but those broad acres cannot be made free
without co-operation of the tenant for life with the next
tenant in tail, who in some cases is a minor and in others
is unborn and may never be called into existence. But
for every one of the landed gentry who is bankrupt there
are scores who are hopelessly embarrassed. The embarrassment of landowners is a matter of public importance,
because, and mainly because, their lands have by processes
of law become inextricably involved in their difficulties.
All consideration for public interest in the land is denied.
The cottages upon many estates are fever-nests, and are
few and far between; the homesteads are insufficient,
inconvenient, and in many cases they are in ruins; the
land is undrained, and there is no one with the interest
of a proprietor to look to the estate. The ostensible
owner, the lord or the squire of the district, who is
harassed for subscriptions and supposed to contemplate
with the benign interest of a seignioral lord the welfare of
all around, who is the great man in the church and in the
village, is in the dull reality of his own home merely a
poor annuitant, with eyes fixed, not upon the many fields
and farms which in the rate-book bear his name, but upon
the slender remnant of income which is all that charges
and settlements have left him for the daily and hourly
labour of providing for a family for whom ten times his

means would seem insufficient. He and his eldest son
have but one pleasure in the world, and as it appears to
cost nothing, they think themselves meritorious in that
they are content with the sporting which the estate and
the neighbourhood afford. Their tenants do not ask for
leases, and they have no wish to grant leases. They
believe they would do anything to increase the income
from the estate, but the rents are quite as high as the
average of land of equally good quality round about, and
and they cannot well ask for increase when they know
that every building on the property is falling to decay.
The younger children languish at home, well knowing
that upon the father's death they must find a new shelter
with very small fortunes. If the father were to spend
£100 of income upon the property in any one of the
many duties of a landlord, they would exclaim against
such an addition to the eldest son's inheritance. We are
supposing the case of an estate where the eldest son,
being of age, has accepted a life interest, cut off the line
of entail from his next brother and re-settled it in the
ordinary way, first upon the son which he may himself
have. In this miserable and mischief-making condition
of landownership, there is no remedy; the law and
custom of entail and settlement are doing their worst
for the family and for the country. Presently we shall
see what Parliament has done to mitigate the evils of
this condition of landownership. Here we are strictly
concerned with the operation of this law and custom.

Our first charge against the system shall be in respect
of production. There is no more cautious public man in
England than Lord Derby, and if the famous indictment

which he delivered in September, 1875, against British agriculture, is held to be an exaggeration, we must remember that his statement was shortly afterwards confirmed by that member of the nobility, to whom, of all others, the landed gentry would look with hereditary confidence for a trustworthy opinion. Lord Derby said, " High farming is not picturesque, and some sacrifices of profit may reasonably be made in the interest of that kind of taste, which we all desire to see more and more extended. But after setting apart all that can be required for that purpose on a liberal allowance, the fact still remains that we do not get, as yet, as much out of English earth, one-half of what we probably might with advantage, if all our present resources were brought to bear on the soil," and that statement of opinion was shortly afterwards confirmed by Lord Leicester. Now, when we remember—first, that the application of capital to the soil is the indispensable requisite for improvement; and second, the hindrance prevailing over four-fifths of the country established by entail and settlement, we shall be disposed to charge upon this system a weight of loss so grievous and appalling, that astonishment must be evoked in regard to its endurance. We are all more or less accustomed to boast our national immunity from the political troubles which afflict our neighbours, and of course the cost of wars and of misdirected revolution is not wholly to be estimated by any material standard. Yet, after all, that is the commonest form in which estimate finds expression, and in that direction it may be said that if to our land laws and customs this denial of increase in the produce of the soil is to be ascribed, then none of the nations of the continent have suffered from war or revolution losses at all comparable with those endured by the United Kingdom through the maintenance of these statutes and customs in blind idolatry to the institution of a landed gentry. If this be so, then as far as national prosperity is concerned, it would have been the most fortunate circumstance in our history had this island been successfully invaded by Napoleon, even though he had, together with the abolition of these laws and customs, demanded an indemnity twice as large as that which Prince Bismarck wrung from M. Thiers on behalf of conquered France. Is it loss of life we deplore? Then it may be said that had the agriculture of our country exhibited anything like the possible increase of production, unborn millions would have lived upon the food so created. So far as mere cost is concerned, even conquest would have been cheaper than the maintenance of entail and settlement. As an Englishman, I would of course rather bear the evils that we have, than that my country should sustain the indignity of conquest. But why need we bear these ills? When we come to compare the agriculture of this island with that of more populous and more purely agricultural islands in the United Kingdom, we shall see that, to the injury of this country, tens of thousands, if not millions, have been expatriated by the operation of those laws and customs which divorced them from the soil; and forced them, often unwillingly, often with long-ing in their hearts to remain in the land of their birth, with an affection for their mother country of which the wealthier and more cosmopolitan classes are quite ignorant, to quit this United Kingdom. And as they have become aware, in other countries where freedom reigns in the laws relating to land, how greatly such good and simple laws affect and mould the happiness and welfare of a population, is it wonderful that in their hearts there should have grown up a feeling of bitterness, and perhaps of hatred, against the exclusive and desolating land system of the old country ? And is it possible to doubt that in these matters we touch a great part of the hindrance to better cultivation ? It can be no exaggeration to say that one-third of the cultivated land of the country is still undrained; and if we had not direct evidence of the fact that this undrained land is entailed and settled, we should know it from the ascertained position of four-fifths of the soil. Whenever inquiry has been made of competent witnesses, their replies have been in this respect invariable. Mr. James Beal has quoted several opinions delivered to parliamentary committees.* Mr. Josiah Parkes, C.E. " had not the slightest doubt as to there being a quantity of land of entailed estates which requires drainage." Mr. Thompson of Reigate, who said he had " a good deal to do with entailed estates," was of opinion that " entailed estates generally required very great improvement." The well-known agriculturist, Mr. James Smith of Deanston, being asked if he had any observation to make, at once said, " The law of entail obstructs the substantial improvement of the land." It may perhaps be said that these opinions are not new, and that since they were delivered, entailed estates have been improved. We may

* " Free Trade in Land," by James Beal.

then call the present Lord Salisbury as a witness. He
drew up a report (to which large reference will be made
elsewhere) as recently as 1873, in which he stated that
what had been accomplished in the improvement of land,
"is only a small fraction of what remains to be done."
How this failure has been caused we shall presently see;
here we have the fact that the entailed land remains
unimproved.   Let us look at two cases, where the
blighting influence of entail and settlement upon embarrassed proprietors was removed.   In the first, Mr.
William Fowler, late M.P. for Cambridge, is the
narrator:—"A property in Sussex was purchased in
1810 for £50,000, or thereabouts, and placed in strict
settlement. So it remained until 1850, when it had
become so reduced in condition through neglect, that it
was sold to the present owner for £25,000.   He being
a man of capital and enterprise, has so improved it, that
recently he was offered £75,000 for the same estate."[*]
The second case was narrated by Mr. Bright, in the
House of Commons, on March 13, 1868.   He said, "The
other day I was driving in the county of Somerset, and
I was passing two villages, called, I think, Rodney Stoke
and Bleadon, and, seeing a great appearance of life and
activity, I asked the driver 'What was to do there?'   He
said, 'This is where the great sale took place.'   I said,
'What sale?'   'The sale of the Duke's property.'
'What duke?' I asked.   'Why, the Duke of Buckingham.   It was about fifteen years ago.   All the property
was sold hereabouts; the people bought the farms, and
you never saw such a stir as is going on in this neigh-

---

[*] " Aspect of the Land Question," by W. Fowler, M.P.

bourhood. All these new houses have been built since then,' and he pointed them out, and showed me that the new owners were cultivating very considerable tracts of land, which in former times had never been cultivated at all. The appearance of the villages, in short, was such as to astonish every person who passed through them, being so wholly different to that which you would see in any other part of the country. Now what had happened here? The great estate of an embarrassed duke had been divided and sold. He had not been robbed. The land had been paid for, the tenants were in possession, the old miserable hovels had been pulled down, new houses had been built, and new life had been given to the whole district." The public has been made familiar, through proceedings in the courts of law, with the embarrassment of the late Duke of Newcastle. In that case, the entail could not be cut off, because there was no one in a position to co-operate with the Duke for that object. There are a thousand cases not less urgent, but which have not been made public, in which entail and settlement bar the improvement of the land. And we should remember, in judging of this matter, to what a large extent the habits of the British people have been formed with regard to inalienable land. North, south, east or west, alike in all rural districts, it is often difficult to find a small piece of land for sale. In manufacturing towns, very few even of the largest factories are freehold. The dead hands of the late life-tenants withhold the soil from the living for the sake of the unborn. How deeply ingrained must the sense of submission to this system have become in British nature, when a man of such

rational mind and improving disposition as Mr. Caird
can write in the following manner of the practical
consequences of entail and settlement: "Cases may be
met with where the limited owner, who has inherited
a property from a succession of men in a similar position
of legal incapacity, finds himself in the midst of general
progress, constrained perhaps to keep half a dozen
parishes in a state almost of stagnation. The country
itself is most likely well-timbered and very picturesque,
with easy railway access to the metropolis or town, and
highly suitable for residential occupation. He could sell
it readily if he had the power, in small properties, for
that purpose, retaining still an important family estate.
It would not be difficult to point out cases in which this
might be done, with immense advantage to the landowners, the neighbourhood, and the public. Take, for
example, the case of a limited owner of 10,000 acres of
such land, yielding a gross rent of £10,000. If he were
enabled to sell 2000 acres, which might fetch a residential
price of £100 an acre, or £200,000, retaining his family
seat and 8000 acres ; his rental would then be £8000
plus the interest at four per cent. of £200,000 = £8000.
These sums together would make an income of £16,000,
or 60 per cent. more than he had before. He would thus
at once find himself in funds and in spirits to go on with
the improvement of the remainder of his estate, while the
neighbourhood would have the advantage of a circulation
of fresh capital and ideas, to brighten a scene formerly
rendered gloomy by dissatisfied indifference." Mr. Caird
concludes this example with the following remark :
" Landowners who are precluded by entail and settlement

from using this natural advantage of their position, are
deprived of an incalculable benefit to themselves and
their families," which surely is not only a striking con-
firmation of the truth of Cobden's remark, concerning
the "tacit" submission of the British people, but is
somewhat regardless of the superior public interests, in
reference to a legal bondage of the soil, sufficient, in this
single example, "to keep half a dozen parishes in a state
of stagnation."

I urge no duties upon landlords on philanthropic
grounds. I have not said that they ought to grant
leases, or that they ought to concede tenant-right. I
have not said that they ought to expend money upon
drainage; and in referring now to the disgraceful condition of many of the cottages of agricultural labourers,
I am certainly not about to charge that as a fault upon
the landlords. If it is for the public interest that the
tenant-farmer should be made secure; that the productive qualities of the soil should be improved, and that
the agricultural labourer should be more decently and
comfortably housed, these things are not to be requested
or begged from the landlords. The landlords might just
as well reply with a request that things should remain
as they are. We are contending for free land; not that
the owner of the land should "be expected" to do this
and that;—we would not rob ownership of any one of
its attributes. Let the man who likes to refuse a lease,
refuse it. If he be owner, we believe we can trust, in
the long run, to the promptings of self-interest. But we
have no owners on four-fifths of the soil, and the fact,
we believe, is a great part of the reason why we do not

I

obtain the vast increase of food which upon such high authority is declared to be possible. We shall see more of the character of this obstruction to free land in considering the recent dealings of a committee of the House of Commons with the matter.

The British peasantry is the most immoral in Europe. Any one may see this who compares the statements of the Assistant Commissioners who were appointed to inquire into the condition of Women and Children in 1869, with the books of travellers. I have myself seen something of the peasantry of every State in Europe, and I cannot, as I wish I could, assert the superiority of that of Great Britain. Just as I should trace the occasional cowardliness and meanness exhibited by Bulgarians to their exclusion from the military service of their country, and to a cruel subjection by the Turkish soldiery (an example of which was given in the account of a correspondent of the *Times*, who had seen a zaptieh force a bit into the mouth of a head-man of a Bulgarian village, and, in resentment for some faint show of independence, jump on his back and ride him through his village, then pull up at the inn door and stuff hay into his mouth, which, with tears of shame and suffering, the poor wretch was forced to chew and eat, while his comrades, in overwhelming strength, stood by without making any interference *), so do I regard the thriftlessness of the British peasant as due to his divorce from the soil in every capacity but that of a labourer; and his immorality, in part, to the condition of life to which he is perpetually, and without hope of independence,

* *Times*, February 7, 1877.

condemned by the British land system, and in part to the demoralization which is consequent upon the operation of the poor-law and his inevitable retirement to the public poor-house. Lord Leicester said, in 1871, that the farm buildings are "bad" in by far the greatest part of the country.* They remain bad; nor are the cottages much improved since Mr. Caird reported that "the inconvenient, ill-ranged hovels, the rickety wood-and-thatch barns and sheds, devoid of every known improvement for economizing labour, food, and manure, which are to be met with in every county in England, and from which anything else is exceptional in the southern counties, are a reproach to the landlords in the eyes of all skilful agriculturists who see them. One can hardly believe that such a state of matters is permitted in an old and wealthy country." The cottages of English peasantry were the subject of a special survey in 1869. Mr. Putman, one of the Assistant Commissioners, reported that there was "urgent reason for dealing with the evils now existing by some legislative enactment, which shall put an end to the state of apathy and indifference in many holders of encumbered estates, and open the doors for the spending of capital by those who are able, in place of those who are now unable to do so."† Mr. Culley, one of his colleagues, not a mere official, but also a practical agriculturist, described the evil in these words: "What, then, has led to the state of labourers' dwellings being such as to justify men in speaking of it as a national disgrace? And why are

* *Gardener's Chronicle*, October 21, 1871.
† Second Report, Appendix, p. 45.

so many landowners powerless to deal with it? If I were to answer these questions, judging from the history of the estates I have visited, I would answer at once, the encouragement given by law to the creation of limited interests in land, and the power of entailing burdened estates. What can the poor life-tenant, especially if his estate is burdened, do towards providing good cottages for his labourers? Nine times out of ten he strives to do his duty, and suffers fully as much as the ill-housed labourers on his estate." * Mr. Fraser (now Bishop of Manchester) reported to the same effect. He said, " Modesty must be an unknown virtue, decency an unimaginable thing, where, in one small chamber with the beds lying as thickly as they can be packed, father, mother, young men, lads, grown and growing-up girls, are herded promiscuously; where every operation of the toilet and of nature—dressings, undressings, births, deaths—is performed by each within the sight or hearing of all; where children of both sexes, to as high an age as twelve or fourteen, or more, occupy the same bed; where the whole atmosphere is sensual, and human nature is degraded into something below the level of the swine. It is a hideous picture; and the picture is drawn from life." † One more quotation out of a hundred which might be made with testimony of the same character. A country clergyman states, " that he never recollected an instance of his having married a woman who was not either pregnant at the time of her marriage, or had not one or more children before her marriage." ‡

* Second Report, Appendix, p. 95.   † First Report, Appendix, p. 34.
‡ " Free Trade in Land," by J. Beal, 1876.

But the clergy, pained and shocked as they must be at the condition of so many of the peasantry, have but one idea of remedy—that of preaching at the landlords, who, as we have seen, are often helpless, and upon whose philanthropy the country has no special right to count. Mr. Fraser's conclusion was, and I am rather surprised at it, of this sort. He thought, seeing this degradation and disgrace, "that the country has a right, in the interests of a class whose material and social condition is anything but one on which the mind can rest with satisfaction, to call upon those who own the soil to see to it that their estates are adequately provided with decent residences for those by whom they are tilled." Dr. Fraser, as Bishop of Manchester, is now, not by virtue of his office so much as by the virtues he has displayed in that office, a great power in the State; and I hope he will declare himself in favour of something stronger than this clerical mixture of Government inter- ference with compassionate good nature. The remedy prescribed in this extract is, in fact, simply impossible because there are no owners : but let that pass. What does it mean ? Does it mean that Government in- spectors are to see that every estate is well provided with cottages, as a passenger-ship with life-boats ? Then, is the country to find the money when life-tenants say they have not any, and cannot afford to borrow ? Where would the pauperism end ! Why should not " the country call " upon people to subscribe to soup-kitchens ? The landowners are not bound to be philanthropic more than others. Surely the duty which the results of in- vestigation impose is clear enough ; the evil is in the

system. And when, having got thus far, we find ourselves face to face with a system which, over four-fifths
of the country, gives us no "owners" to "call" upon
—for there is one in the tomb and there may be another
in the womb, and the man in possession is merely a
stop-gap between dead and unborn,—when we find this
state of things in the richest country the world has
ever seen, which pours out millions of wealth yearly
into illusory enterprises at the ends of the earth, while,
at home, agriculture—that most advantageous of all
industries and of all investments—is so neglected that
not less than £150,000,000 might be expended with
profit in drainage, then surely all doubt must be removed. We cannot be wrong in believing that part of
the evil consists in our having no landowners upon
whom we may call for the performance of philanthropic
duties, or to whom we may look for the beneficial operation of an intelligent sense of self-interest.

CHAPTER IX.

WE are still considering the character and consequences of entail and settlement, but now we propose to have regard especially to the operation of this law and customary practice upon the title and transfer of land. We have seen that entail and settlement are opposed to the improvement of agriculture, and to the most advantageous extension of villages and towns. We have seen that entail and settlement operate thus injuriously by depriving the tenant for life, or nominal owner, of the control which belongs to a freeholder, and of the motives and powers for improvement which the public interest demands should be inseparable from the ownership of land. We have seen that entail and settlement place ownership upon by far the larger part of the country in a condition of abeyance and stagnation. We have now to understand the obstacle which entail and settlement present to any adequate reform in the laws relating to the title and transfer of property in land, and to any suitable method for the record of title and the business of transfer, by an effective system of registration.

With this object in view, I propose to examine in some detail, first, the evidence lately given before the Select Committee of the House of Commons appointed, on the motion of Mr. Osborne Morgan, in 1878, " to inquire and report whether any and what steps ought to be taken to simplify the title to land, and to facilitate the transfer thereof, and to prevent frauds on purchasers and mortgagees of land," and, in a second chapter, to consider the report which that committee has lately presented to Parliament.

The volume of evidence containing the essence of the matured experience of eminent officials, conveyancers, and solicitors upon matters connected with their daily practice, and which, it is admitted by all parties, are ripe for legislation of some sort, was issued at the close of the first session of 1878. The examination of a master of the English law of real property, such as Mr. Joshua Williams, by a committee—including Mr. Osborne Morgan, whom I may call a conventional lawyer; Sir George Bowyer, the direction of whose tastes might dispose many to speak of him as an antiquarian, if not an antiquated, lawyer; and Mr. Lowe, whose questions have not seldom a destructive tendency—must have attraction. Indeed, after a careful perusal of the 200 pages of this Blue Book, I am disposed to say that no more interesting and useful work connected with the Land Laws of this country has lately been published than this Report of Evidence, to the contents of which I shall now endeavour to do indifferent justice, with the primary intention of exhibiting the influence of entail and settlement upon the main question of reform in the processes relating to establishing the proof of title, and the introduction of greater simplicity, economy, and security into the transfer of land.

Shortly before the committee was first appointed, the public mind had been greatly exercised concerning the Dimsdale frauds. Investors stood aghast between the disclosures of dishonest practices upon the Stock Exchange and the proceedings of a trial which showed in terrible reality the possible danger of the market for the sale and mortgage of real property. It has been said of one of the journals in San Francisco, that it never admits a report of an earthquake to its columns lest by doing so it should disturb real estate. Here real estate was and is seriously disturbed by the narrative of these frauds, and inquiry has been directed to many quarters, not merely by this committee, but by such personal inquest as Mr. Cross made during his recent visit to Scotland, especially as to whether liability to fraud, such as has been seen to exist, can be averted by adopting any system of registration.

It was not, therefore, extraordinary that the first witness called in by the select committee should have been Mr. Spencer Follett, the Registrar of the Land Titles Office, which Lord Westbury, it is assumed with good intentions, but with absurdly meagre results, set up by Act of Parliament in 1862. I have in other publications dealt with the results of Lord Westbury's Act. We will pass on to the operation of Lord Cairns's Act, which was committed to the official care of Mr. Follett, on January 1, 1876. The result of the Lord Chancellor's measure, which was to reform the transfer of land, is simply this, that up to February, 1878, after two full years of working, only twenty-eight registrations had been recorded. I calculated that, according to the rate of registration under Lord Westbury's Act, not fewer than 760 years would be required to place the land of England upon the register. But Lord Cairns succeeded in producing an Act of a much more dilatory character, and I hesitate to burden these pages with the number of figures requisite to exhibit the date at which the final object of his lordship's endeavour would, by the operation of his statute, be attained.

From July 1877 to February 1878 there were only four titles accepted in Mr. Follett's office, and it is estimated that with all the restrictions upon transfer that at present exist, the number of transactions completed in England every working day is not fewer than 1000. There have been no leasehold applications; and when the Chief Registrar was, in effect, asked, " Why stand ye here all the day idle ? " he replied, " I think that any voluntary system which interferes so very much with the ordinary custom of the country would not succeed; I think that is the chief reason." Mr. Follett is not, however, justified in that opinion by the facts of the case, because his office was somewhat less stagnant under Lord Westbury's Act. It was thought that the business done under the Act of 1862 was an irreducible minimum. But the further reduction since 1875 seems to show that the Act of Lord Cairns had some qualities or provisions peculiarly offensive to persons having titles to register. It required some ingenuity to frame an Act under which there would be a decline from the record of Lord Westbury's failure. But the Parliament of 1874 was equal to the task, and Lord Cairns's name is associated with a statute which, while it uses no compulsion to bring any one to the Registration Office, holds in perpetuity the very few that enter upon the register. It was not so under Lord Westbury's Act; estates could, up to 1876, be taken off the register. Now these twenty-eight titles which were all that Mr. Follett and an expensive staff had caught in two years, with a declining rate of registration, must remain for ever upon the register, the scanty monument— or shall we say the scarecrow ?—in the wide field of reform which has been Lord Cairns's barren possession for years of almost absolute power.

Failure is, therefore, clearly seen to be the feature of all that has been attempted in England in regard to the reform of land titles and transfer ; and the public mind is widely open to suggestions from every quarter. It is just to Mr. Follett to say that he is not content that his office should be dedicated to the memory of these eight-and-twenty titles; he would rather be doing more business. He suggested compulsion to Lord Selborne, and Lord Selborne, as everybody knows, attempted, when he was Lord Chancellor, to introduce compulsion. Mr. Follett recommended compulsory registration again to Lord Cairns, and the present Lord Chancellor "saw a difficulty in the way;" but Mr. Follett—perhaps because he has not to deal with the majority in the House of Lords, or with the great body of solicitors in the counties and boroughs of England—sees no difficulty whatever. Mr. Follett's idea is that of the compulsory registration of a possessory title. "A man, whenever he purchases

the fee or obtains the absolute fee, should enter it upon
the register. There would be no inquiry about it; he
would bring in a statement that he is entitled in fee just
as we enter a man now as the owner of a possessory title."
Mr. Follett's notion is that time would be on the side of
the man who was thus on the register; he does not think
persons would have their names entered on the register
out of fraud or mere fancy; or that if they did, harm
would come of it. He sees that in the registry of the
county of Middlesex about 150 deeds of title are dealt
with every day, and from this fact as a basis, with other
facts from the registry of York, he calculates "that the
deeds of title executed in England are something like
1000 a day." Mr. Follett, together with every practical
authority, is convinced, that "if the system required is
registration, there must be no power of removing property from the register."

Mr. Lowe, by very characteristic plainness of speech,
assisted the Registrar greatly in explaining why his
office has been so utter a failure. Said the ex-Chancellor
of the Exchequer, "Does not a great part of solicitors'
remuneration depend upon the length of the deeds which
they draw; and is it not rather unreasonable that we
should expect solicitors to give up profitable work for the
pleasure of coming to this Registry Office of yours?"
To which Mr. Follett meekly replied, "I think so."
"Then," proceeded Mr. Lowe, with a view, we may presume, to compulsory registration, "is it not like setting
up a clock and forgetting to wind it up, if solicitors have
every inducement not to avail themselves of it?" But
instead of further fouling his own nest by assent, Mr.

Follett diverged into an anecdote illustrating Mr. Lowe's fancy, and told the committee of an owner who, having registered his title, required a loan; "his solicitor found it extremely difficult to get a loan, because there was no title to investigate, and therefore no costs to be made out of the transaction." I am inclined to think that the most valuable portion of Mr. Follett's evidence is compressed in the statement—which, from his great experience of the way land is held in this country, and the general character of titles, is deserving of much respect— "that even with a forty years' retrospect a very large mass of property might be registered as absolute, and that the case of a bad title is extremely rare." If that be so with a forty years' limit, it may, for practical purposes, be said that the difficulty of bad titles would be altogether removed by adopting a limit of twenty years.

The evidence is unanimous and conclusive as to the fact that the main difficulty in obtaining a satisfactory registration of title is found in the practice of entail and strict settlement. The resulting complication of titles is very significantly indicated in Mr. Follett's reply to the following question by Mr. Marten: "Could you explain why the applications under the Act of 1862 pending January 1, 1870, were not completed in some cases until after July 11, 1877?" The Registrar answered: "In consequence of requisitions outstanding." Mr. Joshua Williams having said of Lord Cairns's Act, "What surprises me is this, that any person having a thorough practical acquaintance with the subject, should suppose for a moment that a scheme of that sort would succeed," proceeded to justify the English land system, and at the same time to show, in irrefutable language, that settlement was the real obstacle to reform and registration. Mr. Williams, like a true master of his art, appears to look upon the soil of England as a subject for the conveyancer's skill, and for that purpose to consider that it should be dealt with in large parcels as the property of opulent persons who can well afford to pay for the curiosities of English law. Said he, " In England, when a man buys land, it is very often at the end of a successful mercantile career; and he buys a large estate with the intention of making a family. He either settles it by his will or by deed, and then begin all the complications. *So long as settlement is allowed in the way that it is allowed, I confess that I do not see that we can have in England a satisfactory registration of title.* I think that it would be a good thing if it could be done, but in my idea it is entirely impracticable in the present state of circumstances in England." Subsequently Mr. Williams emphasized this opinion by saying, " You have your settlements, and the interests under the settlements are sometimes mortgaged again and again in different ways, and there is so much complication in dealing with land that *I do not think that the registration of titles will succeed unless you please to abolish settlement altogether.*" But Mr. Williams is far too faithful to the practice of his life to make drastic recommendations of that sort. On the contrary, as to abridging the retrospective length of titles, he confesses he is " rather doubtful of the expediency of the alteration that has already taken place from sixty to forty years," because " it certainly does open a door to fraud in cases of tenancies for life;" and as to making real property divisible in cases of intestacy after the manner of personal property, he will only say that his opinion is "rather that way."

No man in England is better acquainted with the usual form of settlements, of which it is often said that these instruments do not obstruct the sale and transfer of land, because, as a rule, they contain powers of sale conferred upon the trustees of the settlement. When Mr. Williams was asked if he had considered the possibility of inserting in all settlements a clause vesting in trustees a power of sale, or power of leasing, he replied that Lord Cranworth's Act is sufficient for the purpose; but he could not forbear from showing the cumbrous and obstructive nature of the operation in stating that the adoption of the provisions of that Act must involve " long clauses with regard to the sale of the property, ·the re-investment of the money in the purchase of other lands, to be settled to the same uses, and the interim investment of the proceeds of the sale in the Government funds or real securities, and the income to be paid to tenants for life; all these were rather long clauses to work out."

It was natural, perhaps, that Mr. Williams's enjoyment in detailing the processes of the English law of real property should appear to culminate when he was taken in hand by Mr. Gregory, a member of the Select Committee, and a well-known solicitor. Mr. Gregory began by speaking "with the greatest respect of the general body of conveyancers," to the high priest of that order, and seeming rather desirous himself of having the English system well supported, elicited the following

glorification of the conveyancer's recondite art, with
abundant apology for prolixity of the costly results:
"If," said Mr. Williams, warming with his theme, "you
have a thoroughly good settlement of land, with sufficient powers, you must have a very long instrument;
it is no use, if you settle property, settling it at all
unless you have the proper powers; that is the triumph
of the conveyancer; a thoroughly good settlement." Not
only is the more remote portion of a title the most expensive and difficult to investigate, but practically it is
there that the few "bad" titles are defective; but the
limitation of titles is, as Mr. Williams pointed out,
opposed by the standing difficulty with regard to estates
for life. Indeed, as a professional guardian of the system
of settlement of estates for life, he hardly approves of
the Real Property Limitation Act, which, coming into
operation at the commencement of 1879 abridged the
period of limitation. He doubts "whether it is not
going a little too far." His opinion is not an irrational
objection, if the country were resolved upon endurance
of the prevailing system of settlements. He objects
because "so long as you can settle property on a person
for life, and so long as persons are entitled after his life
interest, for so many years from his death, to prosecute
their claims, it may be an unsafe thing to take a forty
years' title. A man may be a tenant for life, for sixty
or seventy years, and during that time, if he were disposed to forge, he would have an opportunity of making
a title to the fee simple." In fact, it is quite possible to
read in Mr. Williams's replies either a cogent argument
for the abolition of settlement, or for extension of the

period of investigation to 100 years; because, as he says, "in some cases sixty years is not a sufficient title," and there are settlements now existing that were created in the last century, and in these cases "the abstract of title may go back for 100 years." Mr. Frere, a well-known solicitor, in his evidence also alluded to the dangers of the tenant for life system, and said he had known people to go on for years without the least idea that they were anything but owners in fee, and an old deed to turn up in their cellar which showed that they were only tenants in tail. Such is the "glorious uncertainty" of the English law of real property! Mr. Young, a leading solicitor, and ex-President of the Incorporated Law Society, to whose excellent address, delivered in his presidential capacity, I shall refer in another chapter, was of opinion that "the great difficulties which arise are upon settlements in this country. If you could have simply conveyances of estates, the titles would be very simple; and even by common conveyancing you might convey an estate of a large amount for a trifling cost, when you have mere conveyances on the title; but when you come to have settlements introduced on to the title, with charges and mortgages also, then come the difficulties." Referring to his experience, Mr. Young called attention to "the fact that landed proprietors like to enlarge or extend to the utmost their estates, and leave themselves no money," the consequence being that they have at their death no money to leave, and that they bequeath to their successor a title still more complicated, and cumbered with charges for their daughters and younger sons.

K

It remains for us to look at this great matter of settlement from the respective points of view of two members of the Select Committee, both baronets, one having apparently a thoroughly Liberal tendency; the other, as it seems, an ultra-Conservative bias in regard to the English law of real property. The latter—Sir George Bowyer—seeing in Mr. Young an irreverent regard for the present practice of entail and strict settlement, and having obtained from this distinguished solicitor an opinion that, with Mr. Frere, he was in favour of limiting the power of settlement to the attainment of the age of twenty-one by the first heir in tail male, asked, "Do you not think it is part of the political and social system of this country to preserve landed estates in families—and are you not aware that the House of Lords is principally based upon the possession of property, and the maintenance of property in families —and that the law of entail and settlement is intended for that purpose?" Mr. Young, having thus the whole weight of the British Constitution thrown upon his reply, said he could not consider that the law of entail and settlement was meant for that purpose, but he admitted it had that effect. "Then," demanded Sir George Bowyer, "are you prepared to get rid of that political law in order to simplify conveyancing?" It was quite impossible for any respectable family solicitor to say that to simplify the titles and transfer of land was a thing to be weighed for a moment against shaking the foundations of the House of Lords, and Mr. Young withdrew from the dilemma in the best way he could by saying that he advocated reform "generally in the interest of landowners, and at the same time to simplify conveyancing." The other baronet was Sir Harcourt Johnstone. Dealing with the same witness, and with his proposal that every entail should terminate on the first tenant in tail arriving at the age of twenty-one, Sir Harcourt asked: "It would be a more popular measure, would it not, to make everybody owner in fee of his property at the present moment, however much it was entailed and tied up?" To which Mr. Young replied, "I consider that it is very desirable to give perfect control over estates to the owners of them." Sir Harcourt pressed boldly forward with the suggestion whether it would be impossible for the Legislature to make provision for encumbrances, such as they might be, on any existing estate in tail, by directing that money shall be raised upon security of the estate, and put into the hands of the trustees for the benefit of those encumbrances, liberating the present owners and making them owners in fee ?

It is curious to note what was the form of objection which first presented itself to the mind of so able and public-spirited a solicitor as Mr. Young. He did not think it would be right for the Legislature to come in and say, "Here is an estate upon which there are charges of £30,000; we will compel the owner to sell part of the estate and pay off the £30,000, because the owner of the estate makes his own provisions as to charges when they arise; perhaps upon his own marrying; he marries a lady with a fortune, and he applies the fortune in releasing the charges on the estate, and he starts clear; but if the Legislature stepped in and

insisted upon sales of all the estates to pay off the
charges," Mr. Young did "not think it would be right."
Mr. Lowe was present at this examination, and I am
surprised he did not at this point repeat, for the instruction of Mr. Young, the argument he employed with
so much force in the *Fortnightly Review*, that "land
is a kind of property in which the public must from its
very nature have a kind of dormant joint interest with
the proprietor." Mr. Young, indeed, admitted that there
was a question "as regards the public at large having
an interest in land;" but, said he, "I am looking at
the estates themselves, and the owners of the estates
and in their interest." Probably he thought when he
uttered those words, that Sir Harcourt Johnstone's view
had no similar direction. But in that was he not much
mistaken, for is it not absurd to suppose that the proprietary interest in land would not be vastly enhanced
in value by the release of four-fifths of the soil of the
country from the bondage of settlement ?

We shall be able to look but briefly, and in general
outline only, at the suggestions thrown out by the more
distinguished witnesses. The solicitors were very frank
in the not unimportant matter of their professional
charges. Mr. Frere said, "The proper way to shorten
deeds is not to make them the gauge of the remuneration
of the persons who prepare them; there is no deed ever
prepared which might not be expressed in one-third of
the words with equal or more lucidity." "The draughts-
man is cutting his own throat," if he take pains and
trouble to abbreviate forms, because he is diminishing
his remuneration. It is indeed a monstrous system, as

absurd as paying doctors by the bottle of physic or for the pills they prescribe at so much per dozen. "We are paid," said Mr. Frere, "upon the most vicious principle; we are paid, first of all, by the length of our documents; we are paid by the quantity of time and discussion that can be thrown into the thing, and a man who understands his profession, and who can in half an hour put the thing so straight that there is no more trouble about it, gets paid nothing at all." The *ad valorem* scale of the Incorporated Law Society is one promulgated by solicitors; Mr. Frere says it is a great deal too high. He spoke of it with cynicism: "I cannot use it except with foreigners. I use it sometimes with mortgagors, when they are not particular so long as they get their money." There is an Act of Parliament (Lord Brougham's Act, 8 and 9 Vict., c. 124) for shortening deeds, but it is never made use of owing to the plan upon which solicitors are paid.

As to mortgages, Mr. Joshua Williams described that nefarious dealing permitted by law, known as "tacking." The method of "tacking," which would be abolished by any efficient system of registration, is this: I have a mortgage in land, and that land is mortgaged again to A B, subject to my mortgage; then, say, it is mortgaged a third time to C D. If I take the transfer of C D's mortgage, without prior notice of the mortgage of A B, I can tack his charge to my own, and I stand as first mortgagee for my own deed and C D's deed; and A B is excluded and postponed to a charge that was created after he lent his money. In the words of Mr. Gregory: "Though a man has done all that he can to protect

himself, he is squeezed out." The difficulty in our
present method of mortgaging is that the mortgagor,
having parted with the legal estate, has not the powers
of an owner, and though he remains ostensibly the proprietor, he cannot grant a lease. Mr. Williams thinks
that the mortgagor should have the power of granting
a lease, and that the lease should be good subject to
the mortgage. In Sir Robert Torrens's South Australian
system of registration, which he himself fully expounded
to the Select Committee, the old fiction of conveying
the legal estate is entirely abolished, and what is done
is this: If I want to borrow £10,000 upon my estate,
I hypothecate that estate by filling up a simple form
stating, "I hereby acknowledge to have received the
sum of £10,000 from C D, and further to insure the
punctual payment of interest and principal at the dates
arranged, I hereby mortgage to him all my estate and
interest in the land described in vol. — folio —, of the
register book." That is signed and attested; the certificate of title together with the memorandum is presented to the Registrar, who endorses the charge upon
the certificate, which is then handed back to the owner.
The mortgagor holds the title, and the charge being
inscribed in red upon the face of it, corresponding with
the entry in the Registrar's books, any one can see that
the land is charged to the extent of £10,000. Of course,
the proper way of making registration compulsory is
by giving legal recognition only to registered transactions, and this would obviously affect what are called
equitable mortgages—the deposit of deeds for an advance
of money. But Mr. Williams states his knowledge

"that bankers take deposit of deeds in Middlesex from their clients," a practice which in his opinion is unsafe. Mr. Bosanquet, one of the Solicitors to the Bankers' Protection Society, was asked as to the inconvenience to borrowers of having their mortgage transactions registered. He thought the feeling exaggerated, and contended that "if a person is entitled to know whether the person with whom he is dealing has mortgaged the furniture of his house [as he may know by the existing registration of bills of sale], he has a perfect right to know whether he has mortgaged his land, and whether he is the substantial man he purports to be."

Much difference of opinion was displayed as to the form of registration which should be adopted. But all the greater authorities seem to agree upon the point that registration should be permanent, that there should be no removal of property from the register. Mr. Joshua Williams has no doubt of the theoretical superiority of registration of title over registration of deeds. But he thinks the former impracticable, although he admits that "one of the great evils of our real property system is reliance on the title deeds," involving a burden of care and anxiety which has not to be sustained in any other country. He is favourable to the registration of deeds, especially in order to avoid "the insecurity arising from a man mortgaging property twice over." Mr. Frere is of opinion that without a simplification of the law, no system of registration of deeds could be devised so simple and inexpensive, and at the same time so effective, that it would be desirable to adopt it generally, and his first proposition is that which has been stated

—to sweep away all entails beyond the investment of the reversion of the fee simple in the tenant in tail on his attaining the age of twenty-one. It is interesting and important to note that this solicitor, of the very largest practice and experience, has expressed a deliberate opinion that English estates are just as much encumbered as Irish estates. Mr. Young thinks that any system of compulsory registration "would be practically unworkable, injurious to the landowners, and would only benefit the lawyers." He is prepared to say as much as this concerning the Middlesex and Yorkshire registries. He will not advise a client to go near the office which Lord Westbury set up, and which now administers Lord Cairns's Act. Mr. Young is not averse to registration; but he agrees with Mr. Frere that no effective system of registration is compatible with the complications of English titles. We could not desire a better reformer than one who, like Mr. Young, asks for simplification of the law from the Legislature, and condemns the practice by which, in this country, landlords " are so fond of entailing estates, and trying to provide for the future, that unless you can prevent them from making limitations, which are to be carried out at the expiration of 100 years, you will always have a difficulty." Mr. Holt, the Assistant Registrar, stated in detail the plan mentioned by Mr. Follett—a plan of charming simplicity, of which the benefits would be rather deferred than immediate. It is merely that everybody should register anything of which he chooses to declare he is possessed in fee simple, and Mr. Holt is not at all afraid of the registration of false or fancy titles. He was asked, "If a false title were registered, would it not after ten or twelve years create the semblance of a title?" To which he replied, "Once I heard the Master of the Rolls say that he did not sit there to legislate for fools. If people will buy a twelve years' title without investigating it, that is their own lookout." Mr. Holt's plan, nearly in his own words, is this—that after a certain date every person in the next transaction, dealing in any way with fee simple, should, in order to make that transaction valid, be bound to have it registered, without examination of title. He proposes that the person claiming to be entitled in fee simple should sign an application stating that he is in possession or receipt of the rents as owner in fee simple of the land described in a schedule to the application, which schedule should be written on parchment, and punctured in the corners, so that it may be removed for the purpose of actually forming the register; that the parcels shall in every case refer to numbers on the Ordnance map; that the registration should only begin in those counties where the Ordnance map on the 25-inch scale already exists; that the application, together with the schedule, be left in the registry office. There the applicant would be entered as owner of the fee simple, and set down as proprietor of the possessory title of the estate. Mr. Holt says that nothing must be voluntary, because "nothing which is voluntary succeeds in legal matters."

An interesting detail, illustrating the confusion which is caused by the present very defective index of the Middlesex Registry, was pointed out by Mr. Frere, who,

alluding to the Middlesex Office, says that there are
three names which, owing to the large number of separate
properties belonging to each, have especial terror for
clients in regard to the cost of search. Speaking of his
own practice, Mr. Frere said, "If one's property is in
the name of the Duke of Westminster, or Mr. Cubitt, or
Mr. Freake, I put it to my client—The expense will be
so much; will you have the examination or not?" It
seems that in Middlesex the registration is not kept up
very closely, but no witness said it was as bad as the
Dublin Registry, of which Mr. Wolstenholme, a conveyancing counsel of the Chancery Division, testified
that in 1877 "there was an arrear of four or five months
in making up the books; the memorials as they came
in were thrown into a box, and they had all to be
searched through." In Middlesex this is nothing but a
registration of names, which leads the searcher to in-
numerable memorials. Search in the Irish Registry
appears to occasion enormous expense. Mr. Frere re-
members one case in which he was concerned, where the
negative search alone cost £350, "before anything was
done with it, merely the references to the deeds registered." Mr. Wolstenholme added that in Ireland "the
searches are very expensive, and cause a great deal of
delay and trouble." In Scotland there is less cost, but
hardly less trouble. In Scotland all dealings with land
are registered, for the simple reason that "by statute all
land rights are preferable in order of the registration."
They are getting a better system of index in Scotland,
but, as Mr. Douglas suggested to the Select Committee,
"you cannot make *Bradshaw* simple." In Scotland there

are certain officials in the Central Registry who are paid by salary for their work as searchers under the Lord Clerk Registrar. But there are also private searchers who make search a profession, who have the confidence of the public, and whose charges are about the same as those of an official searcher. Mr. Douglas stated that a forty years' search costs from £12 to £16, but he added that in the great majority of cases such a search is not necessary, " because there has been a search already for part of the time, and you only want the last bit stuck on to it."

It is curious to note what discord of opinion prevailed on the subject of reform. Mr. Lowe, for example, put to Mr. Young " the opinion of the late Mr. Senior, that the best form of law of real property that could be made was to change all estates in fee into terms for 1000 years." On the other hand, Mr. Wolstenholme endeavoured to attain the same end, which is simplicity, in saying, " I would abolish everything except an estate in fee." Sir Robert Torrens showed that in regard to registration of title there is the certificate of title to deal with, and yet the title does not depend upon that certificate, as is the case with title deeds under the English system, because that certificate is representative only of the facts recorded in the Registrar's books. He showed too, and it is a very important matter, that " in the registration of titles, the title passes upon the entry in the register book." The difficulty in adopting the South Australian system, which its author, Sir R. Torrens, calls "transfer by registration of title," appears to lie not merely in the complication of English titles, but in dealing at first and compulsorily with the number of titles which would be brought for examination and acceptance. Colonel Leach, R.E., examined as an authority on maps, contended that the provision in Lord Cairns's Act by which registration under that Act is not conclusive as to boundaries, "is an extremely wise one." That appears to be an extraordinary opinion, because of what use is the irremovable registration of land if it does not fix the boundaries? The registered owner must continue to maintain that which Mr. Lowe happily termed the "mausoleum of parchment," from which registration, to be effective, should be a deliverance. Colonel Leach has made a careful estimate upon authentic data of the amount of business which compulsory registration would produce. He says that in Middlesex, where there is a densely crowded population, the number of deeds registered daily is one for every 22,300 of the population. In the North Riding of Yorkshire, which is not a densely populated district, the number is one in every 22,560, agreeing very nearly with the registration in Middlesex. Then in the West Riding, which is very thickly populated, the number is one in every 27,000. The agreement of these averages is very remarkable, and applying the result to the whole population, it gives about 1000 deeds as the daily demand for registration. Colonel Leach strongly supported Sir Robert Torrens in advocating the establishment of a central registry office in London rather than local registries. For the same reason that "practically the great bulk of letters come to London," so he argues that "power concentrated in London could deal with the work more easily, more cheaply, and more conveniently for all parties than if subdivided." What is that work to be? Sir Robert Torrens thinks that if we were to confine it to registration of titles of fee simple estates only, there would be no insupportable pressure, and that there would be no risk or anything to dread in bringing it at once into operation. There is no difference of opinion upon the point that effective registration of title is incompatible with the existing method of entail and settlement.

CHAPTER X.

ENTAIL AND SETTLEMENT ; TITLES AND TRANSFER—
(Continued).

IN dealing with the evidence in the last chapter, I showed a concurrence of opinion on the part of the most eminent witnesses, leaving no one in doubt as to their assurance that the custom of entail, and the practice of strict settlement, is a main cause of the difficulty which is found in simplifying the title to land. The Select Committee appear to have observed this in the evidence, but the point has no place in their Report, because they have not found in the scope of their instructions any reference to matters upon which the land system of these islands is founded. I think the committee had no desire to find themselves thus empowered ; that they are liable to censure for this restraint ; that they have been guilty of a too restricted ambition ; that they have made little of a considerable opportunity ; that those who were opposed to reform have been aided by others who, "willing to wound, and yet afraid to strike" at the abuses of the land system, have framed and adopted a Report which is not destined to bring about any great or valuable result in legislation.

In the preceding chapter, I have quoted the actual

words of their appointment, and that appointment clearly includes the reference to their consideration of all the impediments to simplicity of title, and of all the means by which transfer might be facilitated. But rather than deal, even by a paragraph, with the greatest of those impediments, the committee concluded their Report with the following apology : " Various suggestions will be found in the evidence for alterations, more or less radical, in the general law of real property, such as the total or partial abolition of entails, the alteration of the law of descent, and of the laws of perpetuity. Such proposals, however, involving as they do important matters of public policy, though incidentally bearing upon the question of land titles and transfer, seem to open out a wider field than that to which the inquiries of your committee are limited, and they have, therefore, not thought it within their province to report thereon."

It will, I fancy, be generally admitted that this is the verdict of an incompetent tribunal—incompetent in its collective, for I am not speaking of its individual, capacity—incompetent, perhaps, because of its numbers and of the mode of their selection. That apology contains, indeed, the vague expression of incontrovertible reasons why the committee should have taken a more courageous and public-spirited view of their task. But, on the other hand, the difficulty, perhaps insuperable, may be found in the composition of the committee. How, it may be said, is it possible for a committee of nineteen gentlemen, chosen, not to accomplish, or even to contribute to, a great project of reform, but simply and solely to give representation to all parties, and

sections of parties, in Parliament; how is it possible for
such a body to discharge adequately a great public
responsibility of this sort? There were, without question, members of that committee well-informed upon
the laws relating to land and the wants of the people
at large with regard to these laws, who would have
desired to deal fully and clearly, and with the most
liberal interpretation of the scope of their instructions,
with the great subject referred to their consideration.
But what were they among so many? Their only hope
of obtaining the necessary support of a majority in such
a motley association must be found in deferring largely
to the opinions of certain sections of the committee, with
whom they had no precise agreement, a need which is
well exhibited in the paragraph of Mr. Shaw-Lefevre's
rejected report corresponding with that which I have
quoted from the adopted Report of the chairman, Mr.
Osborne Morgan. There can be no doubt as to Mr.
Shaw-Lefevre's competence and willingness, then and at
all times, to enter upon propositions connected with the
titles and the transfer of land. But association with his
colleagues of the committee had so tempered his zeal
as a reformer with the considerations requisite to enable
him even to hope to obtain a majority in favour of his
report, that he himself was fain to let slip the weightier
matters of the law in the following paragraph: "Other
improvements of the law have been urged upon your
committee, especially with reference to the limitation of
entail and the Statute of Uses; as these changes, however,
involve other considerations which are hardly within the
scope of your committee, they consider they are hardly

justified in saying more than that changes in this direction would undoubtedly tend to simplify and cheapen the transfer and other dealings with land, and would remove some of the difficulties which have been urged to the system of registration of titles." Mr. Shaw-Lefevre, in this paragraph, candidly admits his desire for a bolder and more adequate report. But, upon reflection, he may acknowledge that the adoption of that paragraph would have involved stultification of the committee. They would have admitted that those larger matters, which the majority desired and intended to ignore, were actually within the terms of their appointment, while, in the same sentence, they would have twice declared them to be "hardly" within that boundary. In stating that an effective handling of the changes in the law, which the committee have in their adopted Report entirely and completely rejected, would tend to simplify and cheapen the processes to which their inquiry was directed, and to remove difficulties which they were specially engaged to investigate, their position would have been less consistent than it is rendered by the general acceptance of Mr. Osborne Morgan's Report.

It was necessary to say thus much before proceeding to deal with the exposition and recommendations of the Report, because the value and the reputation of that document are seriously affected by this limitation. Perhaps the most interesting expression in the Report is found in the unanimous agreement of the committee, with regard to Lord Cairns's Land Transfer Act of 1875, which is declared to be, "for all practical purposes, a dead letter." The Lord Chancellor, in the evidence

which he gave before the committee, said nothing to
shake their settled conviction of the failure of this, his
lordship's latest, attempt at reform. The Report deals,
or affects to deal, with the causes which have been
assigned for the reluctance of landowners and mortgagees
to avail themselves of the provisions of that Act. I have
good reason to believe that even of the forty-eight owners
who have registered land under the powers of Lord
Cairns's Act, not every one is aware that there is no
possibility of removing from the register a title which has
once been placed upon it, and therefore I am not disposed
to lay much stress on the absence of this power as a
cause of the unpopularity of the Act. In spite of his
lordship's admission that there could be no objection to
an amendment of the Act, by the provision of such a
power, on payment of a fee, sufficient to deter people
from acting upon mere caprice, it must be felt that a
power of removing a title from the register is a flagrant
contradiction to the arguments by which registration of
titles has been advocated. It may be natural that Lord
Cairns should have a feeling of sympathy for those forty-
eight titles, which are all that have been found in three
years and a half adhering to his scheme; but a healthier
manifestation of regard for their isolation would be
displayed by legislation which should lead—and I would
say, with Lord Selborne, should compel—others to join
them upon the registry of titles. Undoubtedly their
position is by its loneliness somewhat pitiful, but in
order that they may reap the full and rich reward of
their courage and promptitude, all that is necessary is
that registration should be in a fair way of becoming

general. Further, the committee find that the failure of the Act has been ascribed, "(a) to the disinclination of solicitors to recommend to their clients a course of dealing with their property which may tend eventually, if not immediately, to curtail their own profits; (b) to the general distrust of all projects of land registration inspired by the breakdown of Lord Westbury's Act; and (c) to the indisposition both of the public and the legal profession to familiarize themselves with a new system, and to run the risk of an experiment which involves so great a departure from established usage." That solicitors generally are averse to, or at all events are not trustworthy promoters of, all proposals to simplify titles and to facilitate transfer, must, I fear, be taken for granted. But much undoubtedly might be done, and therefore, looking to their power and influence, should be done, to mollify and conciliate their natural opposition. Solicitors can do pretty much as they please with the majority of their clients. But if Lord Cairns had laid before the public a real boon, and to all purchasers and possessors of land an undeniable advantage, in his Act, I will never believe that the solicitors could, with the utmost display of strength, have prevented all but forty-eight persons from availing themselves, during the space of three years and a half, of the provisions of his Act. There is not much in the remaining objections. One would like to have heard the former submitted to and argued against by Lord Westbury himself. But Lord Westbury never held largely of the public confidence as a legislator. The people have far more faith in Lord Cairns, who would manifest greater regard for his ultimate fame if he would show himself less ambitious of support from, and more earnest in educating, the Conservative party. Lord Cairns is named by some as the political successor of Lord Beaconsfield in the leadership of the Conservative party, and that expectancy is not ,favourable to any hopes of great measures of reform from the very distinguished lawyer who now occupies the woolsack. As to the public and the legal profession not liking to adopt a new system, that again cannot reasonably be held to apply to all but forty-eight persons of those who have had dealings in land since the beginning of the year 1876. The committee indeed dismiss these last two contentions with the very just remark, that they "seem to be scarcely reconcilable with the fact that, so far from the Act becoming more popular in proportion as it was better known, the applications under it have been steadily diminishing, until at last they have dwindled down to *nil.*"

Mr. Osborne Morgan succeeded in obtaining the concurrence of the committee in his own estimate of the causes of failure, which is admirable so far as it goes, but it does not go to the root of the matter. It is true, though few lawyers have put the matter so tersely, that the English people are deterred from any effective registration of titles by the "almost superstitious reverence for title deeds" which prevails in this country; by the more or less ignorant impatience concerning official scrutiny and surveillance which obtains as generally, as well as by a reasonable fear that their titles when examined on application may not prove to be without a flaw. The committee could not but be aware—though they chose, as I have already pointed out, to make no recommendation on the subject—that the difficulty of having a clear and simple record of title is opposed, as their Report admits, by the notorious fact "that not only large but small properties, both in England and Ireland, either already are, or at any time may be, settled on successive holders, either by way of trust or without any trusts at all," and it cannot be forgotten that in exact proportion as the registered owner is left free and unfettered to deal with the land, the owners of unregistered interests are exposed to the risk of having their property dealt with behind their backs, and are left to protect themselves, as best they can, by a system of cautions and inhibitions. These considerations omit that which, in regard to registration, is of greatest importance. One of the titles registered under Lord Cairns's Act has been that of a considerable area of building land intended for sale in small lots; and there being a great number of lots, the shrewd Member of Parliament, who is the owner of the property, estimates, and no doubt rightly, that before many of the lots are disposed of, the reputation of the title for simplicity and cheapness in the case of purchasers upon this building estate will become renowned to his own advantage. The ultimate benefit of registration, of course, consists very largely in this value which the purchasing public attach to land the title to which has been registered. And this benefit can only accrue widely when registration has become generally, if not universally, adopted. Unless a rapid increase in the number of titles on the register can be insured, any system of registration must prove a failure. Voluntary adoption of registration is not to be expected from any large body of proprietors until their abstention from the register is likely to appear an exception to the general practice, and so to prove injurious in dealing with their property. They must therefore either be tempted by advantageous terms, or compelled in certain circumstances of sale, or other transfer, to come in to the register, of which it is as true as of anything else, that nothing succeeds like success. It is essential to the satisfactory establishment of a system of registration of titles that means should be taken to insure the placing of a concourse of titles upon the register, and for this reason the machinery of a Landed Estates Court has been made available, as the Lord Chancellor proposed to make it subservient in England. The advantages of registration must not only be apparent; they must be in high repute, before those who register can reap the full benefits of the system.

The Select Committee, which had no spirit for dealing with the weightier questions in dispute, nevertheless recorded their deliberate opinion "that to legislate for the registration of titles without, as a preliminary step, simplifying the titles to be registered, is to begin at the wrong end." In saying this, they uttered their own condemnation, because while they in one place acknowledge the superiority of registration of titles over any other form of registration, they have taken no pains whatever to propound reforms for the simplification of titles. And there is so much that might be done in that direction. Take, for instance, the suggestion of the committee, that registration is neglected because of fear on the part of reputed owners of property that application for an absolute title may result in the detection of a flaw in their title. That fear would be, we may . say, practically removed if the limit of investigation were brought down from forty to twenty years. Such an abridgment would be a reasonable and valuable reform, and it would be acceptable if it were not for the difficulty and complication due to the English system of settlements and life-estates. In Australia the term is only twelve years; and here, till lately, it was not less than sixty years. Why can it not be reduced to twenty years? The committee did bestow a feeble consideration upon this point, and of course immediately bowed before the fetish of entail and strict settlement. The result of their fearful thoughts on this matter, which is one of the greatest inportance, is embodied in the penultimate paragraph of their Report, in which they say:—

" Your committee have considered whether the period of commencement of a title which a purchaser under an open contract might require, at present fixed at forty years might not, in view of the recent Statute of Limitations, be still further shortened. But, as the term in question depends not only upon the time during which claims against land may be kept alive, but upon the estimated duration of human life, during which such claims may remain in abeyance, they believe that such an abridgment cannot be made as long as the rights of reversioners and other persons having future interests, are, for the purposes of the statute, held only to arise when they fall into possession. Whether the latter rule might not advantageously be altered, they consider to be a matter for grave consideration."

In their criticism of the causes of failure of Lord
Cairns's Act, I should have said that the committe might
with reason at least equal to their average, have included the absence, to which I have already alluded,
of any provision in the Lord Chancellor's Act for the
assurance of boundaries. Under the Act of 1875, an
owner of land may acquire an indefeasible title to certain
lands; but if there is no definition of the lands over
which that title extends, the value of the registration
may not be very evident. The essence of such registration is indefeasibility, and the value of indefeasibility
is in the security of the boundaries of property. An
object of registration is to do away with the necessity
for the preservation of title deeds, a necessity which has
led to that which Mr. Osborne Morgan has described as
"superstitious reverence." This reverence may be exaggerated, but it is undoubtedly the consequence of the
immense importance of the title deeds under our system
of conveyancing. But Lord Cairns's Act does not enable
a proprietor to be less anxious and careful concerning
his parchments. He may have the certificate of the
Land Registry Office as warrant for his title; but in
order to maintain his boundaries he must continue to
be charged with the custody of title deeds. There is no
real relief for him from the evils of the system of conveyance by deed. Mr. Shaw-Lefevre has stated with
reference to this matter in his draft report, that "the
importance of determining the question of boundaries
is over-rated;" and he adds, "the exclusion was deliberately adopted in 1875, with the object of lessening
the expense of putting properties upon the register in

the first instance." There can, however, be no advantage in cheapening processes at the cost of depriving them of efficiency. There was, and still remains, in the mind of Parliament, an almost superstitious terror of the cost of maps, and the advice tendered upon this matter has not always been of the most practical and well-informed sort. There need be no considerable expense in the provision of boundary maps, nothing at all commensurate with the benefit and security conferred by the indefeasibility of the deposited boundary.

All through the first four pages of their Report the committee are engaged in arguing against a mode of procedure, that of registration of titles, for which they have no mind, and against which the majority exhibited throughout the inquiry a fixed objection. In one place, they assume that such changes as the prohibition of the power of tying up land in settlement, or giving to the possessory proprietor the right of dealing with it as his own, "would be so opposed to the general feeling of the country, that for the present, at least, it would be idle to consider them seriously." This is the mode in which the committee arrive at what they are pleased to call their "conclusions." But surely that is not a proper conclusion for a Select Committee. They are not embodied for the purpose of studying the general feeling of the country. The presumption is rather that what they call the general feeling of the country is made up of the self-interest of individuals, and that this self-interest may be led anywhere in the direction of generally advantageous alterations in the laws relating to the security and transfer of property. The position in

which the committee was placed may be thus described:
They find that the most eminent living, and late, lawyers
have shown themselves desirous of establishing a system
of registration of titles; they find that nothing has
occurred to impair the arguments by which the superiority of that system was vindicated at the time when
those attempts were made. They find that those attempts
have proved abortive. Then they make mention of
changes in certain directions, the result of which they
admit would be that "the registration of titles would
be as easy as the title itself would be simple." The
ordinary mind would naturally suppose that, as their
efforts were specially to be directed to the subject of
registration, the committee would deem the investigation, and probably the recommendation, of these changes
their first and nearest duty. It would never occur to
any one who knew nothing of the method and composition of a Select Committee, to suppose that they would
shirk the consideration of these changes on the ground
that they were opposed to the general feeling of the
country, that they would say that on that ground it
would be idle to consider them seriously. Least of all
would it be supposed that words of this sort would be
dignified with the name of a "conclusion," and made
use of as a sufficient preliminary to the virtual laying
aside of the system of registration of titles.

The utility of giving instructions to such a committee is not discernible, because it seems so very
apparent that the majority of the committee—to whom
only I must be understood to refer when mentioning
the committee in relation to their Report—had a pre-

conception of what the people do want in regard to the laws relative to the titles and transfer of land. Their Report betrays a misunderstanding of their proper function. The Lord Chancellors who have laboured to establish registration of titles may be as good judges of what the people want as any members of this committee. . But the committee were not appointed to consider what the people want; they were appointed to consider and report what is the best that can be given to the people in the way of legislation tending to secure and to simplify the titles and transfer of land.

Let us take another example of their reasoning. They are informed in evidence "that no system of registration of titles can be devised which will be voluntarily adopted; and, on the other hand, they are told by the Lord Chancellor that he has not yet seen any way in which the registration of titles could be made compulsory," and then, "without expressing any final opinion" upon the Lord Chancellor's observation, the committee "think it sufficient to observe that it would be very difficult to force upon every purchaser or mort-gagee in this country a mode of dealing with his property which not one purchaser or mortgagee in twenty thousand at present adopts of his own accord." But although the committee have shown that they are informed of particular objections to the system of registration of titles established by the Act of 1875, and although they cannot be ignorant of the unequal advantages of a voluntary registration which they are informed next to nobody will adopt, and a compulsory registration to which at least Lord Selborne saw his

way, they report of their own proceeding as their arrival
"at a conclusion." The Lord Chancellor, timid for
obvious reasons in the direction of compulsion, was deliberate in the proposal of a landed estates court on the
Irish model, to be presided over by a judge of the first
importance. It would, of course, be .unbecoming the
dignity of the first judge in the land, and of the Speaker
of the House of Peers, that he should offer a suggestion
for legislation to a committee of the House of Commons,
and the Lord Chancellor accordingly put his proposal
in the past tense, and pointed out that if in the original
instance the measure for the registration of titles had
been preceded by the establishment of such a court, it
would have commanded a greater degree of confidence
in the public mind. But this did not at all square with
the preconceived idea of the committee as to what the
people want. They quickly arrived at one of their
"conclusions" with respect to it, and their Report upon
this matter of high importance in regard to the deliverance of the soil of England from the comparative
sterility to which, because of the poverty of insolvent
landlords, so much of it is doomed, is that "your committee are afraid that the time for carrying out such a
proposal has gone by, and that now it is too late to
resuscitate it."

Before proceeding to the affirmative recommendations
of their Report, the committee take their stand and
justify their "conclusions" upon an axiom borrowed
from the Royal Commissioners of 1868, which "they
believe to be perfectly sound." It is that "for an institution to flourish in a free country, it must offer to

the people the thing that they want." This committee
seem to have a notion that there is inspiration in that
most unmeaning phrase. I suppose that in its original
employment it was used by men who had no doubt
whatever that the land system of England flourished in
a free country. But would any one have the hardihood
to say that what the people want is to be found in that
system ? What the people want, in regard to matters
in which, from inherent complexity, the people cannot
and do not attempt to devise improvement, is the legislation which is the most clearly directed to certain ends,
such, for instance, as this committee were told off to
accomplish when they were directed to have regard to
the steps which "ought to be taken to simplify the title
to land and to facilitate the transfer thereof." This high
charge and grave duty the committee resolved of their
intrinsic mediocrity to abandon altogether ; and having
assigned for this remarkable neglect the reasons or
"conclusions" of which I have made mention, they preferred to write their own commission, which is to be
found in their Report in these words :—"Is the present
system of English and Irish conveyancing in any, and
what respects, capable of substantial improvement ?"
That is the question, and the only question to which
this Report. is an answer, and to that question, owing
to the limitations too readily accepted by the committee,
it is obviously a very lame and imperfect answer. Still
it must be admitted that by far the more interesting
and—if the word may be applied to any part of the
document, I would say valuable—portion of the Report
is that which follows upon the ignominious miscon-

struction of the task which the committee received and accepted from Parliament. From this point the tone of the Report acquires a greater resemblance to vigour, because the committee then enter upon the ground of the preconception which had occupied their minds from the time of their first meeting. Here they brush aside, with quite natural contempt, the idea of radical reform. They have, indeed, no toleration for reformers. They tell such that, "as they have already pointed out, simplicity of transfer presupposes simplicity of title, and simplicity of title in a country like England or Ireland is more or less unattainable." But if we stoop to the view of the committee that their function was properly confined to considering how the registration of assurances might be improved and extended, we shall find at least something to applaud in the latter portion of this Report. It is hard, even in the moment of severest disappointment, to withhold sympathy from men who seem not unconscious of the inadequacy of their course: With aspect of apology, they indicate, and the remark has a certain merit, "that if every assurance relating to land were registered, a basis would be laid which would make the registration of possessory titles a comparatively simple matter. In fact, each purchase deed would serve as a starting point in the title, at which the purchaser, if he wished it, might pass from one register to the other."

When difficulties appear to thwart their own conception of details, the committee have a very short and simple way of dealing with them. In their own happy method they "conclude" with a simple denial of the existence of any difficulties. Take, for example, their decision "that local registries might be advantageously established in convenient centres." They incline even to such minute subdivision as that of the County Court registries, and they say, "the objection that such a proposal would involve more than one search where properties situated in different localities are comprised in the same instrument, does not seem to be entitled to much weight, as such cases, it is believed, are, in England at least, comparatively rare." If this means that properties are, with very rare exceptions, conterminous with the·areas of County Court registries, it is certainly the most hazardous opinion that was ever printed for Parliament at the expense of the country. Surely no one possessing the least claim to practical knowledge need hesitate in opposing even a solitary opinion to that of the committee in this matter. The adoption of such small areas of registration must produce severe inconvenience. The committee have generally ignored the question of cost; but there can be little doubt that the expense of a system of registration would be proportionately increased in the ratio of the number of offices of registration. It is, moreover, open to those who are in favour of larger areas of registration, to argue that with such minute division of the country, the buyer and seller would not seldom be residents in different registration districts, and that in such case it would be easier for both to transact their business by post with a more central office. The committee lay much stress upon the superior advantages of small areas in regard to the difficulty of search, but in this matter also the cost

would be greatly increased by their method, and they omit to say whether the certificate of search, which is to be accepted as evidence of the state of title up to its date, is to be indefeasible, and if the sufferer from any error in such a certificate will be entitled to compensation. In the Australian system, as the committee were made aware, a compensation fund is provided by hypothecation of a trifling portion of the registration fees. The point is not unworthy the attention of the committee, because, were the certificate not indefeasible, both solicitors and searchers might be disposed to promote unnecessary frequency of search. The final· recommendations of the committee are preceded by a paragraph, which by a special vote was introduced *ab extrâ* into the Report, and which has, it must be confessed, a somewhat irrelevant and unnatural character. It ostentatiously records the obvious fact that the committee do not recommend the repeal of the Lord Chancellor's Act of 1875, and neither, though they have emphatically declared it to be "a dead letter," do they recommend its amendment in any direction. They only think that "the two systems of registration might be consolidated, or at all events that the registration of deeds and that of titles in England might be carried on upon the same premises or, at all events, under the same superintendence." This lumbering paragraph may have been intended humorously. Perhaps it was introduced on the motion of Mr. Lowe, who may have meant nothing but a grim joke. Seeing that the committee had already in their Report declared the Act "a dead letter," and that the applications under it "have dwindled down to *nil,*" it is nothing but funny to record an opinion that the business of the Act might without difficulty be consolidated with other business, under one roof or one superintendence.

Of the positive recommendations of the committee, some of them are excellent. But so far as they are novel, so far as they differ from recommendations—such as the conversion of a mortgage from a conveyance upon conditions to a simple charge, defeasible in the event of repayment of principal and interest; and the immediate completion of the cadastral survey for England and Wales : both of which have been put forward by nearly every writer on the subject of reform—their recommendations are in strict harmony with the "conclusions" of the Report. The first is "the abolition of the present scale of conveyancing charges, and the substitution for it in all cases, where it is possible, of a graduated *ad valorem* scale of payment." Well, all that need be said on this point is that it is a little wonderful to find a committee including lawyers and solicitors in large practice believing that the public would gain much by the establishment of such a scale. The project, moreover, is not new. An *ad valorem* scale is now permitted; solicitors frequently offer it to their clients; and clients, knowing little or nothing of the matter, and craving only some sort of fixity, often accept it. I have before mentioned a case of this sort, in which a solicitor told me he had prepared a conveyance upon an agreement for an *ad valorem* fee of two per cent., and he said he was glad his client had accepted the scale, for such was the simplicity of the title that his

M

charges could not have much exceeded one per cent. Then we have the scale of charges promulgated by the Incorporated Law Society, a body which we may be quite sure would exercise very great influence in framing the suggested new scale of charges. The committee heard in evidence, from an eminent solicitor, what was the character of the fixed scale of payment. Mr. Frere, whose evidence on this point is referred to in the preceding chapter, said the charges were so high that he could only use them in the case of foreigners, or of those who were so pressed to obtain money on mortgage that they were somewhat unusually indifferent as to what they paid for the advance. The committee recommend in the second place the compulsory use of short statutory forms. But just as in regard to their first recommendation they use the words "where it is possible," so in this matter they do the same, varying the formula, and prescribing the reform "as far as practicable." While the complexity of English titles is continued, that practicability will not be found to extend very far. There are fashions in the work of lawyers as in that of milliners, and while four-fifths of the soil of England are bound in settlement, defying the adoption of short statutory forms, the length of deeds will for some reason or other be found to be undiminished.

The same circumstances will tend to vitiate, though they might not wholly obscure, the benefits to be obtained by the recommendation with regard to mortgages, the character of which I have already indicated. The further recommendation, which is intended to insure the presentation of a real representative as owner of land, "having the same control over, and power to make, a title to freeholds which a personal representative now possesses in regard to chattels real," implies mere homage to a policy which the committee have shrunk from endorsing. Nothing is more to be desired for the national welfare than that every rood of land should have a representative and responsible owner, free to sell if that be desirable, and forced to sell if he is obliged to make a declaration of insolvency. But the recommendation, even if carried to its extremest limits, would give only a sham resemblance to that wholesome state of things. There would be names, but the persons so represented would be no more the free and responsible owners than the members of the House of Lords are landowners. The peers of England are not landowners; they are land-holders only; and not less fictitious would be the ownership of four-fifths of the land of Great Britain and Ireland as it would appear in the names of those appointed representatives under this or any other recommendation of the committee. The fifth recommendation refers to the cadastral survey, and the sixth to the repeal of the Statute of Uses. The seventh deals with the establishment in local centres of district registers of assurances respecting land. This has been already discussed. The recommendation introduces the Ordnance map for the purposes of index, the need for which has been illustrated by an exhibition of the horrors of search in the business of the Middlesex Registry, owing to the very defective system of index which obtains in that establishment; but it says nothing about making the map serve for the identification of boundaries in connection with Lord Cairns's Act. The eighth recommendation, making registration virtually compulsory, is one which is indispensable to the success of every system of registration, whether of titles or of assurances,—"that (except in cases of actual fraud on the part of the party registering) every instrument shall rank in priority according to the date of its registration." The ninth proposes the appointment, in connection with each registry, "of an official searcher, or staff of searchers," whose certificate is "to form part of the title, and to be evidence in the case of subsequent dealing with the property as to the previous title disclosed by the register." Upon this, I have already asked who is to be liable, and is compensation to be provided for errors in the search ? The tenth and last recommendation, containing the only reference to the registration of titles, proposes nothing by way of amendment of the Act, which has been pronounced to have no operation and to be "dead," but simply—and from what is said by the committee, we may presume, idly—recommends the "localization of the registration of titles," with the formula "as far as practicable," and "concurrently with the establishment of district registries for the registration of assurances."

Although this report is substantially the work of the chairman, Mr. Osborne Morgan, it would be unfair to charge upon him an equivalent responsibility for its shortcomings and defects. The chairman of a Select Committee is bound by an unwritten contract with Parliament to do his utmost to evolve the most definite expression of a majority of the committee which he can succeed in obtaining, and probably nothing better than the Report which is now before Parliament could be expected from a majority of the nineteen gentlemen, of whom Mr. Osborne Morgan was one and the president. Besides two members of the Government, there were not fewer than four thoroughly Tory lawyers on the committee—men who revere the principle and practice of entail and settlement, with all that is involved, as forming the basis of the most important political institutions of the country. But whatever be the cause, the result is matter for regret. Mr. Morgan was the instigator of the inquiry, and he, together with the majority, has failed to make the best use of the opportunity which was conceded. The revision of the laws relating to land will now surely and speedily be undertaken. There will be a great development of public opinion upon this most vital of social questions; and when the people of this country have considered, so far as it is possible for the population to consider, what it is they want, we may safely predict that their requirements will not be found within the paragraphs of this Report.

CHAPTER XI.

EVER since the existence of classes in the population
of this country, that of the landlords has been practically
dominant. Up to the formation of Mr. Gladstone's Administration in 1868, their rule in the British Legislature had been unquestioned; it was not endangered
by the admission in 1832 to the electoral body, of a
section of the community including so many of their
dependents. The most stupendous and striking illustration of class legislation has been the work of the
landlords in Parliament. Their error has been that
which is common to all classes—the error of wilful
blindness to the interests of the country, when the
proper direction of their eyes would be averted from that
which they regarded as their personal interest. Not
long ago, I was painfully affected by the evidence of a
most honourable and competent authority, as to the
survival of this class legislation. Lord Hartington, the
next life-tenant of the Devonshire estates, assumed
the existence of a conspiracy in the majority of both
Houses of Parliament, to maintain the law of hypothec
(the English regarding it as a buttress for the feudal

law of distress in their own country) as quite a natural policy of legislation. He thought, indeed, that it was "scarcely honest"* that Scotch county members should give a popular vote without intending to endanger the law, and without reference to their own convictions. But he had no doubt whatever as to the fact that, so long as the landed interest maintained a majority in Parliament, the obnoxious law was quite safe ; and that landlords, who liked to please the farmers with vain votes and speeches at variance with their secret wishes, could do so "with perfect safety, without the smallest effect." This opinion, gravely uttered by one of the most distinguished of the nobility, was received with "applause!" As I read this, I tried to think it was not true. Corporations, we know, have no souls, but there is no Englishman who is not proud of Parliament, and this charge is one which no individual could sustain without dishonour. Unhappily it is true and trite—so trite, indeed, that Lord Hartington, the last man to befoul the class of which he is an ornament, spoke of it, perhaps thoughtlessly and quite as a matter of course. This class, so noble in some of its traditions, so justly proud of its history, so patriotic towards the fatherland for which its members have, in all times, laboured in the cabinet and fought in the field and on the seas, has not in legislation proved superior to the influence of self-interest. The process has been invariable, but it has not always been a conscious process. Probably no class is wholly conscious of its own selfishness. If the masons who were lately on strike were to make laws

* Lord Hartington at Glasgow, Nov. 7, 1877.

for labour in England, they would probably find an honest inspiration in the importance of their craft, in the dignity of labour, and in a strong national sentiment. But we should expect the outcome to be more favourable to the masons than to the community. It has been just so with the landlords, but with this difference: they have moulded customs and made laws with all the authority of the greatest power in the country. This is no indictment of the landed gentry. In the history of property they have played their part after the manner of men. They have seen the soil of the kingdom passing away from freehold into strict settlement, and they have said in their hearts, "It is good for us to be here," sincerely deluding themselves, for the most part, with the comforting belief that the aggrandisement of families was the welfare of the State. The traditions of an age of force they have transmuted in an age of law, so that our county government remains a sort of government according to acreage. We shall make special inquiry into local government, as affecting agriculture; in this chapter we are engaged with the legislative efforts made by Parliament to increase the production of the soil.

I have often referred to the House of Peers as the House of Landlords. The ownership, by their families, of one-fifth of the soil is the real basis of the power of the House of Lords. In this sense, the Peers are representatives, each of his county or district, and each embodies a local reputation and interest of high importance. More than a third of the House of Commons is of the same composition, and the influence of the landed gentry commands a large number of younger sons and relatives who are members of Parliament, or who hold other places of authority. The business of this important class is the letting of land for purposes of agriculture and, to some extent, for manufacture, for trade and dwellings. Their interest in the land is limited and often languid because they are only life-tenants, and but few have any practical acquaintance with agriculture. " Landlords are, perhaps, the only great body of men whose interest is diametrically opposed to the interest of the nation." * I am not one of those who think that this statement is applicable to the present circumstances of this country. It is, however, unquestionable that rents must be lowered if we could import meat from the New World at 6d. a pound, and wheat from the Mississippi and the Punjab at less than 30s. a quarter. If a country is stationary, then it is obvious that agricultural improvement would tend to reduce rent. If, with no increasing demand for food, land could by drainage be made to produce five quarters of wheat instead of two and a half quarters of wheat per acre, then there would be a surplus produce, inferior soil would cease to be cultivated for wheat, and all rent must decline. But with a rapidly increasing demand for food, such as exists in this country, with augmenting capital and population, agricultural improvement will surely tend to increase rent.

The landlords in Parliament have long perceived the deficiencies of agriculture. Such men as the late Duke of Bedford and the late Earl of Leicester, could not fail to notice the difference between their own well-managed

---

* " Buckle's Fragments," p. 350.

estates and the general aspect of the country. Those who had less acquaintance with the subject, had the opportunity, upon the appointment of committees, of hearing the evidence of experts. That the members of the House of Lords took a practical view of the inquiry will be seen from the following extracts. I have before alluded to the evidence of Mr. Josiah Parkes, C.E. :—

"*Mr. Parkes.*—I conceive that if rents have a tendency to fall, the drainage of an estate which is waterlogged may keep them up to what they now are, and even increase them.

"*Question* 150.—Consequently, if any rents at any time are lower than the existing value of the land, the drainage would have the operation of enabling the tenant to pay a higher rent?

"*Answer.*—Clearly so, or to maintain his ability to pay the same rent for his farm."

Mr. John Thompson, of Horley, near Reigate, was another witness for the information of the Lords. He was asked :—

"*Q.* 183.—Was the produce more than trebled [of a farm which the witness had described as having been drained, but only with bushes laid in trenches and covered in] ?

"*A.*—Yes; and of that farm I can produce the account. Since then, it has grown on an average from seven to eight sacks, taking bad years and good years; and turnips, swedes, and mangel-wurzel, and all such things, have been grown in great perfection, which could not be done before, from the great tenacity and wetness of the soil.

"*Q.* 222.—Then you are of opinion that the draining of land generally increases its value ?

"*A.*—Very much."

A great mass of evidence was taken prior and subsequent to that quoted, all of which tended to show that drainage was generally needed ; that farm buildings were badly planned, and in bad condition ; that there was an insufficiency of cottages and so on. It is always clear that the public interest demands the improvement of agriculture, and Parliament being, therefore, thoroughly concerned in the matter, loans have been from time to time applied for and voted for application to these objects. We shall do well to bestow some attention to the history of these and other loans, because it affords evidence that the landlords in Parliament had no difference of opinion from ourselves in regard to the fact that entail and settlement prevent the application of capital to the soil. The testimony of witnesses could leave no doubt upon that point. Lord Beaumont, a peer and agriculturist, had taken a seat at the witness table, and was asked :—

" *Q.* 986.—Is your lordship aware of many entailed estates in the part of Yorkshire where you reside, that would be much benefited by efficient draining ?

" *A.*—A great many ; my own especially."

Nothing could be more complete. Conviction was forced upon the minds of the least intelligent. They could learn by analogy with manufacture. If the peers who were life-tenants of land in manufacturing districts had not by the help of their own order in the Legislature obtained leasing powers so extensive as to be indistinguishable from freehold, the manufacturing prosperity of

England might never have been attained. They saw that whenever they wished to attract capital to the soil, they must make their own inferior position as life-tenants approach that of freeholders. And, accordingly, this has been the basis of all their legislation. The life-tenant is to act as a freeholder for certain purposes and with certain objects. But he is not to have the incentives nor the advantages of the freeholder in regard to the free disposal of his property, and, therefore, this legislation has had but a very limited operation. The propositions and the limitations were of a very simple character:—The land is thirsting for improvement, which is hindered because it is held in life-tenure by persons who have not always the will, and rarely the means, to carry out the necessary works. Therefore we will relax this bondage so far as to let them charge the estate with the costs of improvement. It is hard to suppose that persons who reasoned thus, and who acted upon this reasoning, could be insensible to the lesson they had learned—that free land was the proper legislative conclusion. Let them look at their policy in plain terms. They saw that the application of capital to land was in proportion to its freedom; for their own advantage they obtained leasing powers for 999 years, thus abandoning the ligatures of entail and settlement where great profit was to be obtained. It was the national interest more supremely than their own which demanded the freedom of agricultural soil, and in regard to that, they permitted just so much departure from the legal bondage of the land as would meet a case such as Lord Beaumont's, and would enable such a prudent man to charge the life-tenure of his successor. But after a small preliminary experience of Drainage Acts, they were emboldened to plead that agriculture had peculiar claims upon the public purse. They would not let the land be free to meet the swelling capital of the country, because they and their position were, they supposed, the products of its bondage. In most States, it is manufacture which receives public doles. But here manufacture has had freedom, and the land has not had freedom, and the Legislature of landlords, which withheld freedom from the soil, thought proper to administer to agriculture doles of public money.

No class in the country can pretend to superiority in honour and character—I would even say to an equality—with these gentlemen. Yet, by way of warning against any class legislation—see what they did! Holding the land in fetters of entail and settlement; displaying their knowledge of the consequences, by assimilating their position as life-tenants to that of freeholders, for purposes of urban improvement, though in that respect insufficiently to accomplish a general advance; made aware by the preamble of the Acts which devoted public money to agricultural improvement, how deeply the public interest was concerned in such work, it never occurred to them that their obvious duty was to liberate the soil before the application of public money could be touched upon with honour or propriety. The plea for the use of public money in works of agriculture is only one of degree; it only arises from the fact that capital so employed is in degree more beneficial to the people than capital engaged in manufacture. But that is all. With free land the Drainage Acts might have been impolitic;

with the land settled to the uses of a few thousand families, and so withdrawn from the free application of capital, they were—I fear I must say—scandalous. They were made by a Parliament composed, as to the great majority, of the chiefs of those families; they were made consciously for the benefit of those families, attracted by the promises of increased rent. Seeing that entails were created, the landowners were performing an obvious duty in passing Acts to permit the life-tenant to charge the estate; there could be no better way of dealing with the disabilities of their own position; so far, these Acts were not only proper, but laudable. But seeing how deeply wronged are the public interests in regard to production by the continuance of those disabilities, which they felt it necessary to attenuate in order to make way even for partial improvement, an equitable Legislature could not have conveyed public money to those uses, while nothing was done to bring capital and land into free and unrestricted co-operation. In the 9 and 10 Vict. c. 101, the landlords of England first permitted themselves this departure from public duty. It would have been as easy to drive six omnibusses abreast through Temple Bar—when Temple Bar was standing— as to pass the preamble of that Act through the reformed House of Commons. It contained the following words : " Whereas it is desirable that works of drainage should be encouraged, in order to promote the increased productiveness of the land, and the healthiness of the districts where it is required, and to supply the demand for agricultural labour, especially at that season of the year when other sources are expended," etc. With these words, £2,000,000 sterling were granted in mitigation of the disabilities of landlords, whose tenure was and remains the great obstacle to the improvement of the soil. How was it spent? We have noticed Lord Beaumont's remark as to the great need for drainage upon entailed estates in Yorkshire. The Yorkshire landlords took up a large sum, and not long afterwards Mr. James Caird, now a Tithe and Enclosure Commissioner, then a Special Commissioner of the *Times*, made a survey of the agriculture of Yorkshire, and this is what he wrote: "The Government Loan is repayable in twenty-two annual instalments of $6\frac{1}{2}$ per cent., which repays both principal and interest. A few landlords charge their tenants 5 per cent. of this annual sum, and themselves pay $1\frac{1}{2}$ per cent. Most frequently the tenant is bound to pay the whole, and in addition, to cart the tiles free of charge; and we are sorry to say that more than one instance exists in Yorkshire where the landlord charges his tenant $7\frac{1}{2}$ per cent., thus putting into his pocket 1 per cent., besides securing a permanently higher value for his land by an outlay to which he does not contribute a single farthing. This grasping conduct, so utterly at variance with the intention of the Legislature, is quite unworthy the character and position of a respectable landlord." * Of course it was not by the greatest landlords that a loan was needed. Nobles like the Duke of Portland did not want any of the public money. Of his Grace, Mr. Caird said at the same time, "He drains to any extent at 5 per cent.," † and in doing so, Mr. Caird calls him "a wise landlord." But if

* "English Agriculture," by James Caird.　　　† Ibid.

drainage was "wise" at 5 per cent., and no one can
doubt the prudence of such outlay, then what are we to
say of the borrowing landlords, who, as Mr. Caird says,
"most frequently" laid upon their tenants, not only the
entire charge of 6½ per cent., but also the cost of carting
the tiles?   What we must confess is simply this—that
public money was given to them upon false pretences ;
that the public interest in the improvement of the land
was made secondary to their own advantage.   In
Scotland, we are told by a good authority "that the
custom was to charge the tenant a yearly percentage
of about 1 or 1½ per cent. in excess of the Government
rate." *   This is not very different from the rate which
still prevails, for although it remains true that "a wise
landlord" may "drain to any extent at 5 per cent.," with
advantage to himself and to his estate, the Duke of
Argyll tells us, in the essay before referred to, that " it
is quite common, under the system of Improvement
Loans, for tenants to be willing to pay interest at the
rate of £6 14s. per cent. on drainage outlay made by
the owner."

Let us turn now from this rather unpleasant subject,
which however could not be avoided, to a more general
consideration of the dealings of Parliament with the
land, and to the results.   Mr. Shaw-Lefevre has stated
with precision what Parliament has done to mitigate
the evil of family entails and settlements, both to the
limited owners and to the public.   He says their "efforts
have taken two directions :—

"1. Power has been given to the Court of Chancery,

¹ " The Land Question," by John Macdonell.

on application of the tenant for life, to sanction leases
for agricultural, mining, or building purposes, extending
beyond the possible lifetime of the tenant for life.
Power is also given to the Court of Chancery to authorize
the sale of settled property, subject to this,—that the
purchase-money shall be devoted to paying off any
existing charges, or to the purchase of other lands, to be
settled in the same manner.

" 2. Power is given to the Enclosure Commissioners
to charge settled property with money expended in
improvements, such as drainage, and the building of
farms and cottages, the principal and interest of which
is to be repaid by annual instalments, varying according
to the permanence of the improvement; and various
companies have been formed for facilitating such charges
and carrying out such improvements."*

The former of these powers relates to urban land ; the
latter, to agricultural land.   The exercise of the former
has added enormously, that of the latter considerably,
to the income of landlords.   By the former, the land has
been made free, in cases of 999 years leases, in all but
securing the reversion of the increased value to the
descendant of the landlord.   By the latter, there has
been no approach to free land ; the position of the life-
tenant has been advanced in regard to improvement loans,
and that is all.   Manufacture bribed the landlords into
the concession of land, practically free from settlement,
for its use ; agriculture could not do that, and it remains
in bondage until the people vindicate that which Mr.

* " Limitation of Entails and Settlements," by G. Shaw-Lefevre, M.P.

N

Lowe has termed their "dormant joint interest " * in the soil, by giving to it the condition of free land. I have said that by the latter power the income of landlords has been considerably increased. In proportion as they approach free land, so does their income augment. Were free land established their wealth would unquestionably be very much enlarged. But we must admit that to a great extent this would accrue to posterity, and remote posterity has but few friends. In order to be just, we must never forget that the landed gentry now in both Houses of Parliament, did not make their position, nor that of their eldest sons. They were born heirs of entail ; they accepted life-tenancy for an income in their youth, and because it was the established custom of their class; many of them have eldest sons tailed on by the same process. The pleasures and solid advantages of ownership can never come to them, and men are most apt to think that they are themselves a pattern for posterity. The power of judging for the country in this matter has hitherto most injuriously been placed in the hands of these very men who, whatever may be their personal excellence, are least of all the persons whose judgment should be final upon matters in which they are peculiarly unfitted by tradition, by custom, by law and by interest to adjudicate for the welfare of the community.

Their attempts to make agricultural land free for purposes of improvement, while they held it fettered by entail and settlement, have resulted, as we should expect, in failure. In this matter none of them will

* *Fortnightly Review*, January, 1877.

dispute the authority of Lord Salisbury, who, with all
the tenderness which his lordship reserves exclusively
for concerns of feudalistic character, drew up the Report
of that Committee of the House of Lords which inquired
into the improvement of the soil, as resulting from the
exercise of the above-mentioned powers, in 1873. We
learn from Lord Salisbury's report that—

"The general result of the evidence is to show that,
although considerable use has been made of Improvement
Acts, and extensive improvements have been effected
under them, the progress has not been so rapid as was
desirable, and that what has been accomplished is only
a small fraction of what still remains to be done. Mr.
Bailey Denton states, as the result of his calculations,
that out of 20,000,000 acres of land requiring drainage
in England and Wales, only 3,000,000 have, as yet,
been drained. Mr. Caird, the Enclosure Commissioner,
speaking not only of drainage, but of all kinds of
improvements, estimates that we have only accomplished
one-fifth of what requires to be done. The case for
Parliamentary consideration lies in this, that the improvement of land, in its effect upon the price of food
and upon the dwellings of the poor, is a matter of public
interest; but that, as an investment, it is not sufficiently
lucrative to offer much attraction to capital, and that,
therefore, even slight difficulties have a powerful influence in arresting it."

"The interest at which the land companies lend is
4½ per cent. The sinking fund, to repay the loan in
twenty-five years, together with the interest, bring up
the average payment upon the effective outlay to a

little more than 7 per cent. It appears that, sometimes, though not in all cases, the tenants will pay to the land-owner, in the form of rent, the full 7 per cent. which he pays to the company. In that case, the landowner is, for twenty-five years, neither a gainer nor a loser upon the transaction. At the end of that time, if the drains are effective, he gains the whole 7 per cent.; but this consideration is by no means a certainty.

" On the balance-sheet of cottages it is unnecessary to dwell. All witnesses agree that, apart from any land that may be attached to cottages, no pecuniary profit is to be obtained from building them.

" The average rent which they bear, after maintenance, appears not to exceed 2½ per cent. The replacement of bad cottages by good is an even less remunerative operation.

" A complaint against the existing system is directed to the function of the Inclosure Commissioners. A needless minuteness, and a rigour which refuses to bend to local requirements, are imputed to it. It is manifest, indeed, from the evidence of the Commissioners and their inspectors, that the latter claim a control so complete over the execution of works, as to leave little discretion to the landowner or his agent. In the selection of sites, in the arrangement of plans, in the choice of materials, in the drawing up of specifications, it is no unusual thing for the inspector to take a view opposed to that of the landowner and his agent ; and whenever this contingency arises the landowner must give way. Mr. Parkin, an experienced solicitor, says :—

" I find, from my experience, that landowners do not

like the interference of surveyors and inspectors sent from public bodies. Control of any kind, however wise the controlling power may be, especially when it comes from a public office, is distasteful to men in the management of private affairs; and where the profit of an operation is small, the necessity of submitting to such control may be sufficient to deter men from undertaking it."

"The case for Parliamentary consideration" is plain enough to any but those who, like Lord Salisbury, accept primogeniture, entail, and strict settlement as of divine institution. It is clear enough that application of capital to entailed and settled land is accompanied with so much friction that it is not accomplished. "The price of food" and "the dwellings of the poor" are indeed matters of public interest, but they are made subordinate to the maintenance of entail and strict settlement. The "difficulties" to which Lord Salisbury's report refers arise out of that condition. If the land were made free by such legislation as we shall advocate, the borrowing of money for works of improvement, with security upon the land, would be half an hour's work. But with no owners over four-fifths of the country, and with all ownership depending upon the accuracy of a long history written in legal jargon, which none but experts can understand, and which each owner or limited owner must keep in writing, safe from fire and fraud, at his own risk, or in the costly care of a solicitor, it is no easy matter to get at security. As it is, the poor life-tenant, who sets the machinery in motion, and then finds himself tossed about from directors to commissioners, from commissioners to inspectors, and from inspectors back to his family solicitor—he is to be pitied, as, with costs of all kinds to pay, he finds no adequate satisfaction in the resolution to make his tenant pay a fair rate of interest as increased rent. The Lords of this committee must have shut their eyes very tight against seeing that the evidence they had received was a condemnation of the practice of entail and settlement, as opposed to the improvement of the land, and therefore to the public interest. On this point, I can regard no opinion as of more value, or even perhaps as of equal value, with that of the chief of that branch of the legal profession which is generally assumed to be deeply interested in maintaining the intricacies of the British system of nominal ownership. I quote the words of the late President of the Incorporated Law Society, as of great weight. The gentleman, who held that office in 1876, said, " It admits of question whether it is for the benefit of the country generally, or even of the owners of landed estates as a class, that entails should prevail so extensively as they do in England. This prevalence assumes that the majority of a generally educated class are improvident and incapable of doing justice to the estate and their families, and, for the sake of the spendthrifts and their families, hampers the much more numerous class, as I venture to estimate them, of the reasonably prudent proprietors and their families. Nor does the entail protect the spendthrift himself. He can and does still squander his life-interest; and the estate itself, under such circumstances, is likely to be neglected. This may last for thirty years or more, and what damage may accrue during that period, to those coming after him, for whose benefit the entail has been created!"* To the family solicitor, the family estate is something like the ark of the covenant, something sacred to a family whose interests obscure all wider considerations. How bad, then, must entail and settlement be when this respectable gentleman, who perhaps is one of those conveyancing practitioners who have made a fortune by the greatest abuse of law known to the civilized world—how bad must it be when such a one will add, " A parent has no power, under an ordinary entail, of depriving of the estate a lunatic or proved spendthrift son in favour of a younger son, or of a child of the eldest, nor can one will provide for every contingency. . . . In ordinary families, I think many of the entails created are more for the benefit of the lawyers than of their clients. Some will call this rank heresy, but it is the result of forty years' experience in a branch of the law with which I have had the most intimate acquaintance."† What Parliament has done in regard to improvement of the land is to leave undone that which Parliament ought to have done. In touching the matter of Taxation I may be obliged to refer to the history of the land tax, but I will not needlessly rake up wrongs of the forgotten past. The landlords, as an hereditary body, have much reason to desire that the history should remain closed. " It is not wise " said Mr. Gladstone, " to provoke the examination of the history of our Statute Book with a view to ascertain and enumerate the instances in which the narrow and oblique purposes of

* Address, at Oxford, by Mr. L T. Young, October 4, 1876.
† Ibid.

class have been pursued by Parliaments in the choice of which the upper orders had it all their own way." *

The latest act of the Legislature in connection with agriculture has been the appointment of a Royal Commission which will probably in a year or two produce an interesting report. There are two gentlemen upon that Commission, Lord Spencer and Mr. Goschen, to whose remarks I look forward with much interest. They are men highly qualified to represent the interests of landlords and of the country in such an inquiry. But it is matter for serious complaint that the question of reform in the laws relating to land should be now referred to a Royal Commission. In one of the many reports upon the subject mentioned in this volume—that, drawn by Lord Salisbury, from which I have made a long quotation in this chapter—we read: "The case for Parliamentary consideration lies in this, that the improvement of land in its effect upon the price of food and upon the dwellings of the poor, is a matter of public interest." It seems to me that this sentence contains a condemnation of the policy of the Government in postponing reform by handing over this great interest to yet another Commission. "The case for Parliamentary consideration" has long since been established, and that which is urgently needed is the introduction, by a powerful Government, of suitable measures of reform.

* "Last Words on County Franchise" *Nineteenth Century*, January, 1878.

CHAPTER XII.

ON PROPERTY IN LAND.

To be in a fit state of mind to comprehend the matter
of property in land, "the first thing the student has
to do is to get rid of the idea of absolute ownership.
Such an idea is quite unknown to the English law. No
man is, in law, the absolute owner of lands. He can
only hold an estate in them."* That is a strict interpretation of property in land from the legal point of
view, and is written by the most accomplished authority
upon the English law of real property. No claim to
absolute ownership of land upon the basis of law can be
maintained. We say that a man has an estate in fee
simple in those lands with which he is himself free to
deal unreservedly, and in order to establish free land,
we must put all owners of land, as far as possible, into
that position. The tenure of many lands in England
is copyhold; an estate which should be abolished, not in
the tardy fashion in which that obsolete tenure is now
wearing out, but by a much more swift and speedy
process. The estate by which the greater part of England is held is, as we have seen, estate tail, and the

* Williams, on the Law of Real Property.

power of settling land in estates tail must be denied,
if free land is to be accomplished. Free land implies
freehold estate, which in legal phraseology is known
as an estate in fee simple.

But there is higher authority than that of law which
is opposed to the conception of absolute property in land.
The thing is impossible. No nation would admit that
they exist upon sufferance, that they hold their liberty
to exist upon the soil of their country at the pleasure
of a minority. Yet that would be implied by acceptance
of the doctrine of absolute property in land. Mr. Froude
has written very appropriately upon this point. His
opinion is that "private ownership in land is permitted
because Government cannot be omnipresent, and personal
interest is found, on the whole, an adequate security that
land so held shall be administered to the general advantage. But seeing that men are born into the world
without their own wills, and, being in the world, they
must live upon the earth's surface, or they cannot live
at all; no individual or set of individuals can hold over
land that personal and irresponsible right which is
allowed them in things of less universal necessity."
Taking thought of the whole matter, it is not possible
for any person to differ seriously from that statement.
Does any one suppose that if, for example, the fifty-three
peers who are nominal owners of two-fifths of Scotland,
designed simultaneously and with one accord to depopu-
late their territory, the State would or could, with any
pretence of justice, allow such a proceeding ? By the
intervention of Parliament, the State would at once
declare that these landowners had exceeded their rights

of property in the soil. But there has been depopulation effected over a large tract of a single property, and
although displeasure was intimated by members of the
community, there was no intervention by the State.
Why is this ? The reason is obvious. The interest of
the community in the security of property is immeasur-
ably greater than the interest of the community in the
tenants of a small district. Moreover, the interest of the
community, which is primarily concerned in the most
productive occupation of the land, may in certain cases
be promoted by the removal of population from a particular place. In regard to the important matter of
water-supply—there is none so good as that collected
in the natural reservoirs (or lakes) of mountain districts.
From their elevation, and consequently abundant rainfall,
as well as from the purity of such water, lakes should
always be regarded as the best sources of water supply.
And inasmuch, as lakes are generally surrounded by
scenery of great beauty or grandeur, which in densely
populated countries will surely attract residents upon
the slopes, producing impurity in the water, and de-
stroying by numerous erections the charm of nature, I
can conceive nothing more desirable from union of the
sanitary and æsthetic points of view, than that, to the
widest extent to which it is found possible to utilize the
lake waters for the supply of town populations, there
should be upon the water-shed of such lakes a clearance
of the population, and a prohibition of agriculture, which
would involve the use of manure in tillage.

In the case of injustice committed by a landowner
against an individual, the State, representing the com-

munity, cannot look on unmoved. It has provided in several directions, laws regulating compensation in such cases; it has hitherto withheld justice from the farmer in such a case because the representative body is at present controlled by landowners, and its policy is directed for their supposed advantage. When individuals are deprived of any pre-existing right, they should obtain compensation; when the deprivation is hurtful to the State, to the community, then it is met with prohibition. All landed property must be held subject to the claim of the State, whether that is specified or not. There is no Session of Parliament in which this supreme claim is not asserted for purposes of local improvement, or for the execution of necessary public works. The State confiscates, by Act of Parliament, any land, with or without houses, required for waterworks, or railway, or canal, or some other public object. The act is complete in itself; it is an exercise of supreme ownership which none can dispute. The compensation is not needed to give legality to such an act; it is legal by virtue of the authority inherent in Parliament. The compensation obtained may not be such as the owner approves, but for that reason Parliament will not permit him to retain his land. The land belongs to the State, and that prime right of property may be exercised anywhere and to any extent. Equity and the interests of the community demand that fair compensation shall be given. But that compensation is given, not as the price of a bargain made with the State, in order that the confiscation of the land might be permitted, but it is awarded by way of satisfaction for the antecedent issue of an irresistible decree. The compensation is, moreover, a part of that policy by which communities endeavour to obtain the most productive employment of the soil. The security of property, of all kinds, including land, is very firmly based upon the self-interest of the members of every community, and just as it is our interest as consumers to give stability to the farmer's tenure, so far as to insure him against the danger of loss by sudden removal, involving the forfeiture of his expenditure, so it is our interest as consumers, and our interest as owners of property, to strengthen the title and the hold of the landowner, and to make it subject, not to vexatious demands, such as will prevent the investment of capital for the due and proper improvement of the soil, but only to such requirements as render obvious and permanent advantage to the neighbourhood, or to the welfare of the people at large.

The land belongs to the nation, to the State, to the people. It is not possible to sever the interests of a beggar crouching at the gates of a park from that land. Infinitesimal they may be, but their existence cannot be denied. The land from which he is to-day thrust out with perfect justice, may in a short time be taken without the owner's consent to make a cemetery in which that beggar's body may be laid, or to build an asylum, a hospital, or a workhouse for him and others like him to inhabit. We thrust that beggar from out our gates or doors, and we have the support of authority in doing so, not because we have absolute property in the land from off which we bid him remove himself, but by virtue of that limited property which the State permits and encourages

for the advantage of the community.   It is not long since
Mr. Lowe wrote those very true and telling words which
I have quoted before, words which put the case plainly
and with proper simplicity.   "Land," said Mr. Lowe, " is
a kind of property in which the public must, from its
very nature, have a kind of dormant joint interest with
the proprietor." *   The existence of that " dormant joint
tenant " will never trouble the mind or vex the peace of
the landlord who is doing the best he can for himself in
the production of rental, or of food, with his land.   We
all concur in private ownership and maintain its rights,
because we believe that such property in land yields the
strongest inducements to increase the produce of the
earth and the happiness and well-being of its population.
But those who are in the position of landowners—a responsible position, as a share of something which every one
needs, and of which the supply is limited, must ever be—
should always remember what is the nature of the bond
which holds the State to sanction and support property
in land.   The "joint interest" of the public is existent,
though dormant; it would certainly become rampant
were the obligation upon which property is held to be
very extensively disregarded.   And the public must be
the judge of its own interests.   There was a landowner
who, for a half-insane freak allowed his estate to lie
untilled, to grow weeds and brambles, to become in fact
useless.   His freak was undisturbed; the public suffered
loss and wrong, but there was no interference, because
the interest of the public in the security of property, is
far greater than the interest of the public in the manage-

* *Fortnightly Review*, January, 1877.

ment of one estate. Interference in such a case would indeed have made those few neglected acres productive, but it would have seriously alarmed the owners of every other acre in the kingdom, and therefore the public is in such a case inactive, because the balance of evil largely preponderates upon the side of interference. But it is not difficult to imagine cases in which interference would not only be justifiable in regard to the interests of society, but also in which neglect to interfere would be fatal. For instance, a foolish or evil-minded man who desired to make experiment or to bring evil upon the country by breeding the Colorado beetle in his fields would find himself restrained by law and his property invaded by officers of the State. In fact, the saying of the late Mr. Thomas Drummond, that property has duties as well as rights, contains the assertion in another form of the "dormant joint interest" of the public.

Property in land differs essentially from various kinds of personal property. Take, for instance, property in three per cent. consols. There the State promises to pay a perpetual annuity of three per cent., and nothing but the inability of the State to redeem that promise can deprive the fund-holder of his property. But it is not so with regard to land. The State, it is true, supervises and permits the transmission of land, as it does of personalty from testator to inheritor, but in the case of land not only is there no promise that it shall remain his, but it is held upon the clear and distinct understanding that the State may and will take it, with the assent of Parliament, whenever the inalienable joint interest of the public demands its confiscation. Not merely is it true that, as

Mr. Mill said, "the greatest stickler for the rights of property will hardly deny that if land, the gift of nature to us all, is allowed to be the private property of some of us, it is in order that it may be cultivated;" but that right of private property in land is, and from the character of the property must ever be, subject to interference for every cause which can be sustained on behalf of that "joint interest" of the public. With regard to a promise to pay £3 a year for ever, the man from whom that promise is confiscated has an equitable claim, not merely to the present value of that promise, but to all future conditions of value which by any reasonable statement he can attach to it. Even an extreme and fanciful valuation of his right must be given, if it is sought to redeem that promise with equity. He may allege that in 50 or 100 years the promise will have a peculiar value, and his speculative view must be examined and, if sound, must be conceded. But it is far different with property in land. If the State need a meadow in which to build a dockyard or a fortress, or if the State lend its authority to a local government or to a private undertaking, the owner must resign his land, and his claim for anything beyond its present value will not be admitted. Were he to contend that in 50 or 100 years the land might become part of the site of a great town, he would meet with no attention. He would be rudely taught to know his place and his true position—that of a landholder whose right is subject to the superior right of the public. Mr. Gladstone's reference to the matter is one of the most recent, and his opinion is in complete harmony with that of the best writers upon political economy. Mr. Gladstone, in his speech at West Calder on Nov. 27th, 1879, said : " In my opinion, if it is known to be for the welfare of the community at large, the Legislature is perfectly entitled to buy out the landed proprietors. It is not entitled morally to confiscate the property of the landed proprietor more than the property of any other man ; but it is perfectly entitled to buy out the landed proprietor if it may please for the purpose of dividing property into small lots. I do not wish to recommend it, because I will show you the doubts in my mind about the proposition. But to the principle no objection can be taken. Those persons who possess large portions of the space of the earth are not altogether in the same position as possessors of mere personalty, for personalty does not impose the same limitations on the action and industry and the well-being of the community in the same ratio as does the possession of land, and therefore I hold that compulsory appropriation, if for an adequate public object, is a thing in itself admissible and even sound in principle."

I am a determined adherent to the principle of private property in land, but I wish to display its limits. I have no wavering inclination towards any of those vague and unsound proposals for " resumption," or " nationalization " of the land. I am firmly and profoundly convinced that in a community so various in its industry, and I may add, in its leisure, as ours, private property in land is salutary, beneficial, and necessary. The policy which is commended in this volume has for a primary object the firmer foundation of private property in land. In England, at the present day, with our system of conveyance by deed, the right

o

of property in land is understood to mean merely this,—
that in the opinion of the owner's lawyer, his title to
the estate is the best that can be found. That opinion
may be, and sometimes is, a dishonest opinion; it may
be a mistaken opinion. To make the title and right of
the owner absolute against all other claims, except that
of the State, is part, and no small or unimportant part, of
the policy of free land.

It is manifestly within the competence of the State
to obtain possession of all the soil of the kingdom—to be
itself the one sole landowner and landlord of the country.
This is what is meant by the "nationalization" of the
land. But the State would surely make a very bad
bargain if it were to confiscate all real property, and
give to the owners a fair and proper compensation for
their interests. That is the first objection to a policy of
"nationalization." Mr. Fawcett wrote in 1872[*]a powerful
argument against this policy, but the figures he adopted
contain exaggerations of estimate, which he did not
point out. For example, it is stated that the net annual
rental of the land and house property is £150,000,000;
and in order to get at the capital sum required for
purchase, this is multiplied by 30, and to the advocates of
"nationalization" is presented the difficulty of raising
£4,500,000,000. Of course the buildings are not worth
30 years' purchase. Even 20 years' purchase would be
too high a valuation for a very large proportion of the
buildings. Having got to the £4,500,000,000, it was
very easy to show—especially with the help of Sir John
Lubbock's assurance that the raising of such a sum

[*] " The Nationalization of the Land," *Fortnightly Review*, December, 1872.

would require an advance of 1 per cent. in the rate of
interest—that, in fact, a loss of £50,000,000 per annum
would result. The bargain might not be so bad as that,
or it might be much worse, for the difficulty would come
in maintaining and in raising the rentals. That the
management would be commercially competent and
politically honest seems impossible. How could a
Government determine competition ? By the highest
bidder ? That would not settle the difficulty which
might take the form of demand for subdivision.
Could a Government decree the practical exclusion of
a merchant from the money market or the wool
market by denying him offices within the narrow
circle to which these trades are confined, in the city
of London ? Competition takes so many forms, and
no Government could be so intelligent in its ownership as are private individuals. The main object for
which private property in land is sanctioned by the
State, with the concurrence of all rational people, is the
belief that such ownership is most successful in promoting production. Production is at present very much
neglected, but that is because private ownership is
baulked by settlement, and by the "ungodly jumble" of
our legal processes. Production would undoubtedly be
much greater if private property in land were more
firmly and fully established. I cannot think it possible
that a Government could promote production with anything like the power which may be obtained from
private ownership. With reference to this proposal,
Mr. Mill said : "I have so poor an opinion of State
management, or municipal management either, that I

am afraid many years would elapse before the revenue realized for the State would be sufficient to pay the indemnity which would be justly claimed by the dispossessed proprietors. It requires, I fear, a greater degree of public virtue and public intelligence than has yet been attained to administer all the land of a country like this upon the public account." * I do not go so far as Mr. Mill in this matter. I am inclined to say it is absurd to suppose that an official administration of real property could in a country like this be successful.

One of the chief points of contention on the part of the advocates of this plan, has been that the poor are driven into unwholesome dwellings by the competition for land arising out of private ownership. They argue that the State might protect the people against competition, and that through "nationalization" it would come to pass that every man would dwell in his own separate house. Together with this, there is expressed a conviction that land ought to be cheaper for the sake of the poor. I cannot comprehend arguments of this sort. If the land were the property of the State, by what other intelligible method than competition could private lesseeship be determined? There is no other method which would not still more quickly produce confusion, tumult, and revolution. Again, is it true that the poor are overcrowded in unwholesome houses, because the land is not cheap? There is no basis for such an assumption. It would have an aspect of truth if these overcrowded houses were always upon the cheapest

* "Papers on Land Tenure."

land; but that is not the case. The landscapes of
rural England are, to me, sadly remarkable for the
absence of cottages. The houses of the poor in England
—especially in southern districts—are disgraceful. But
it is not because of competition for the land. It is not
because land is dear; I should rather say it is because
land is cheap. Look abroad in countries where agricultural land of equal quality is much dearer than in
England, and this horrible, this bestial overcrowding
is not seen! What does the highest authority—that of
M. de Laveleye, say of Belgium?—"The farm labourer
is generally well housed. For himself and his family
he always has a house, with at least two, more frequently four rooms, generally kept in good condition,
and having an acre or half an acre belonging to it,
where the man grows vegetables, potatoes, and rye;
and there is besides, a goat, which gives milk to the
household :—

" No. of families for every 100 houses in the Rural Districts of—

	1846.		1856.
Flanders, West	103	...	101
Flanders, East...	104	...	102
The Entire Kingdom ...	104	...	104

" Thus the number of houses in Flanders has increased
as compared with the rural population, who have by
this means found better accommodation." That is the
ideal of the nationalizers, but it is not the result of
"nationalization;" it is the natural consequence of free
land.

The just limitation of the rights of property in land
has been disregarded in the construction of railways

in this country, because the owners of property have held exclusive control of the Legislature. There has been an excess of cost in the construction of railways in the United Kingdom, compared with railways of the Continent, amounting to not less than 100,000,000*l.*, of which the landlords received by far the larger part as payment over and above the extreme value of their lands, the balance being absorbed by unnecessary payments to lawyers and for other professional services which the opposition and vexatious processes of the landlords demanded. However ignorant and short-sighted, this opposition would have been legitimate had it been confined to their private capacity. It was because the landlords sat as judges with a perpetual majority in Parliament that the British railways have been so heavily weighted with excessive expenditure. It was natural enough that peers and squires should believe that fox covers and game preserves would be injured by railways; it was to be expected that a brand-new baronet should say to Robert Stephenson, " Why, Mr. Stephenson, if this sort of thing be permitted to go on, you will in a few years *destroy the noblesse !* " * and perhaps it was natural enough that the Lords and Commons determined to make a good thing out of the innovation. In narrating the history of the Bill for the construction of the London and Birmingham Railway, Dr. Smiles tells us that " the promoters found to their dismay many of the lords who were avowed opponents of the measure as landowners, sitting as judges to decide its fate. The Bill was thrown out. Thirty-two thousand pounds had been expended

* Smiles's Life of Robert Stephenson.

in preliminary and parliamentary expenses up to this stage. But the promoters determined not to look back, and made arrangements for prosecuting the Bill in the next Session. Strange to say, the Bill then passed both Houses almost without opposition. The mode by which these noble lords and influential landed proprietors had been 'conciliated' was the simple fact that the estimate for land was nearly trebled, and that the owners were paid about 750,000*l.* for what had been originally [and we may be sure very excessively] estimated at 250,000." *

At last these unjust judges in their own cause learnt something of the value of railways to their estates. " Landlords found they could get higher rents for farms near a railway. They became clamorous for ' sidings.' Owners who had fought the promoters before Parliament, and compelled them to pass their domains at a distance, at a vastly increased expense in tunnels and deviations, now petitioned for branches and nearer station accommodation." † The Marquis of Bristol, speaking in favour of a line, said with magnanimous effusion, " If necessary, they may make a tunnel beneath my drawing-room;" and Dr. Arnold of Rugby, as he stood watching a train from a bridge over the Birmingham railway, exclaimed, "I rejoice to see it, and to . think that feudality is gone for ever; it is so great a blessing to think that any one evil is really extinct." Had Dr. Arnold survived to the year 1880, he would have seen that " feudality " is still rampant in Great Britain and Ireland.

* Smiles's Life of Robert Stephenson.   † Ibid.

· CHAPTER XIII.

TITLE AND TRANSFER, PROJECTED REFORMS.

I HAVE dealt incidentally, in preceding chapters, with the title and transfer of land in this country. In England, the title to land is proved by the production of deeds, the existence of which may be known only to those who have custody of the parchments; and in the small areas in which registration of deeds is carried out, there is nothing on the record to indicate precisely the nature or circumstances of the contract. No land system in the world affords such facility for the commission of fraud, while none gives such slender security as to title. There is no more eminent practitioner than Mr. Frshfield, and that well-known solicitor has testified against the English system in these words : "Title by deed can never be demonstrated as ascertained fact, but can only be presented as an inference more or less probable, deducible from the documentary and other evidence accessible at the time." It cannot be denied that such a demonstration of the insecurity of title to land, is likely to sustain and to strengthen the existing distribution of the soil. There has been no Lord Chancellor in this generation equal in power and ability to Lord Cairns

who has said so much and achieved so little in regard
to reform of the laws relating to land. In 1859, Lord
Cairns said in the House of Commons, of which he
was then a member, that " upwards of 200 years ago
Sir Matthew Hale, writing of a property he had purchased, said he would willingly give one year's purchase
more for it, could he be sure thereby to have a good
title. That was a moderate bid for a simplification
title." Sir Hugh Cairns continued : " Coming down
to more modern times, I find, in 1846, a Committee
of the other House of Parliament reported : ' They are
convinced that the marketable value of real property
is seriously diminished by the tedious and expensive
process attending its transfer.' . . . Then in 1856, a
Royal Commission having been appointed to take the
whole matter into consideration, I find witness after
witness addressing himself to the injury sustained by
landed property, and to the actual loss consequent upon
the difficulties incident to transfer." Such having been
the views of peers and members of Parliament for more
than 200 years, I think it may be stated, with a considerable degree of indisputability, that if the title to
land were a registered fact, demonstrable with the same
simplicity and certainty which obtain in the case of
ownership of Railway Debentures, the middle classes
would be much more desirous of obtaining possession of
land.

From the evidence of eminent solicitors given before
the Select Committee on Land Titles and Transfer, we
have gathered that the English system is one which
encourages this intricacy and uncertainty of title. The

members of a great and highly responsible profession depend largely for the amount of their fees upon the retrospect and examination of title. To such an extent does this view of their remuneration prevail, that a solicitor having a client's money to advance upon mortgage, or to invest in the purchase of land, will often display a distinct personal preference for dealing with a title which is the least clear, and which will invite the largest number of interrogatories, and will require the most research. A friend of mine has purchased a building estate of which the conveyance cost him about £200. This has been plotted out into small divisions, and the cost of the conveyance to purchasers of each building lot is very small indeed, because the conditions of the tenure will be based upon the examination made with reference to the whole property at my friend's cost. A purchaser of a plot upon this estate is not unlikely to speak well of the English system of conveyancing, when he gets his little deed and his little bill of costs. But let him beware, when he wishes to mortgage that land, lest the mortgagee's solicitor should insist upon investigation of the £200 title. The distinguishing feature of the English system, is that a purchaser or a mortgagor cannot be sure that he will not have to pay for an investigation of title during the past forty years. The description of the system by Lord Chancellor Cairns cannot be too often quoted. The following sketch of some legal phases of the English land system was uttered by Sir Hugh Cairns, in February, 1859, in the same great speech to which I have already referred :—

"You buy an estate at an auction, or you enter into

a contract for the purchase of the estate. You are very anxious to get possession of the property you have bought, and the vendor is very anxious to get his money. But do you get possession of the property ? On the contrary, you cannot get the estate, nor can the vendor get his money, until after a lapse—sometimes no inconsiderable portion of a man's lifetime—spent in the preparation of abstracts, in the comparison of deeds, in searches for encumbrances, in objections made to the title, in answers to those objections, in disputes which arise upon the answers, in endeavours to cure the defects —not only months but years frequently pass in a history of that kind ; and I should say that it is an uncommon thing in this country for a purchase of any magnitude to be completed—completed by possession and payment of the price—in a period under, at all events, twelve months. I pay the expense—the considerable expense which is incurred—in addition to the price which I have paid for an estate, and I obtain a conveyance. About a year afterwards I desire to raise money upon mortgage of this estate. I find some one willing to lend me money, provided I have a good title to the land. The man says, ' It is very true you have bought this estate, and that, you investigated the title, but I cannot be bound by your investigation of the title, nor can I be satisfied by it. My solicitor must examine the title, and my counsel must advise upon it.' And then as between me, the owner of the estate, and the lender of the money, there is a repetition of the same process which took place upon my purchase of the estate, and, consequently, the same expense is incurred as when I bought it ; and for the whole of that I, the owner of the estate, and the borrower of the money, must pay. Well, that is not all. Months or years after all this is completed, from circumstances, I find I must sell my estate altogether. I find a person willing to become a purchaser. The intending purchaser says, 'No doubt you thought this was a good title when you bought this estate, and no doubt this lender of money thought he had a very good security when he lent his money ; but you are now asking me to pay my money : I must be satisfied that the title is a good one, my solicitor must look into it, and my counsel must advise upon it.' Then, again, commence abstracts, examinations, objections, difficulties, correspondence, and delay. I am the owner of the estate, and I must pay substantially for the whole of that, because, although the expense is paid in the first instance by the purchaser, of course, in the same proportion as that expense is borne by him, in the same proportion will he abate the price which he will give for the estate."

The evils of the English system are peculiarly evident in the case of mortgage. In this country the legal estate of the borrower upon real property is conveyed to the lender of the money, subject to a right of redemption ; and the mysterious and costly evidence of title, contained and exhibited only in the deeds, passes into the possession of the lender or of his solicitor. As possession is "nine points of the law," and as there is no other record of title than that which is contained in those parchments, it is evident that the proprietor of the land must be placed at extraordinary disadvantage if he require a second advance upon his estate. He will have to bid high in

order to find a second lender. As a general rule, it is
never prudent to advance money on second or subsequent
mortgage in this country, without taking full consideration of the risks and obtaining, by indirect means, security
against them.   If there is default in payment of interest,
the second or subsequent lender is not like the first, in
a position to deal as owner with the property.   It is even
difficult and expensive for him to obtain access to the
documents upon which the ownership is based.   But that
is not all.   In a preceding chapter I have explained the
monstrous plan of "tacking," to which the second or
subsequent lender is liable, and by which his money is
endangered.   The result of all this is, that trustees are
generally prevented from making advances of funds upon
second mortgage, and that such security is, for the most
part, accepted only by persons of incompetent judgment
—too often widows and spinsters who are craftily and
cruelly advised by self-interested persons—or by those
who, knowing the risks, make the borrower pay heavily
for an advance.   In England, if a man possesses an
estate worth, say £100,000, upon which there is a mortgage of only £10,000, and he wishes to obtain from
another quarter a further advance of £10,000, though
he has £90,000 of security to offer, he may find great
difficulty in obtaining the money, and will certainly
have to pay a higher rate of interest because of the
English system of title.   One of the most beneficial results
of such reforms as I shall advocate, would be to give to
a second mortgage in this case a security quite as good
as that of the first.

   We have seen that the chief difficulty in reforming

the transfer of land in this country arises from complexity of title owing to limitation of ownership. If we turn for a moment to regard the land system of the United States, we shall see that while there is but little restraint in dealing with land, yet that the customs of the country do not, at all events at present, tend to prolixity of legal documents or to complication in regard to title. In 1869, the British Government obtained and published an elaborate report upon the tenure of land in the United States. We were informed that "the system of land occupation in the United States of America may be generally described as by small proprietors;" that "the proprietary class throughout the country is on the increase;" that "the theory and practice of the country is for every man to own land as soon as possible;" that "the American people are very averse to being tenants;" that "land is so cheap in the sparsely peopled portions of the country that every provident man may own land in fee;" that "the possession of land of itself does not bestow on a man, as it does in Europe, a title to consideration;" that "absolute titles to land are easily and quickly acquired;" and that while in the United States the landowner "has entire freedom to devise his property at will, in the event of his dying intestate his real estate is equally divided among his children, without distinction as to sex, subject, however, to a right of dower to his widow should there be one." We further learned that tenancy of agricultural land was not only rare, but was also much restricted; that, for example, in the State of California, "no lease of agricultural land can be for a longer term than ten years;"

that, by the Constitution of the State of New York, adopted in 1846, it is declared that "no lease or grant of agricultural land for a longer period than twelve years, in which shall be reserved any rent or service of any kind, shall be valid;" that Michigan in 1850 adopted the same term; that in many States, in regard to rent, "the law confers no privileges upon the landlord above other creditors;" that in the United States "the sale and transfer of land are conducted with about the same ease as would be the sale of a watch," and that "very large quantities of land are seldom held undivided by one family for more than one or two generations"—a fact of which an illustration was given "in the case of the Livingston family, whose noble domain in the State of New York, embracing upwards of 160,000 acres, and which was granted to them under patent of the Crown, by the colonial governor, was divided in 1790 by the third and last landlord of the manor, he being imbued by the progress of advancing ideas and the changing character of American institutions." *

The phrase with which "her Majesty's representative" concluded the above quotation is not well composed, but it may be taken to indicate that which I believe to be truth: that the institutions of the United States and the feeling of the American people are opposed to the establishment of a landed gentry. We may not say that never in the future history of the United States will there be a landed gentry possessing a great part of the agricultural land, and, together with it, large power

* Part I. Reports from H. M. Representatives respecting the Tenure of Land in the several Countries of Europe (*sic*), 1869.

and influence, but we may certainly affirm that such an
institution cannot be indigenous as in England. We
can fancy a time, and that not very remote, in which
the Homestead Law of 1862 may be placed among the
curiosities of American legislation, when there will be
no "unappropriated territory of the United States" on
which new settlers can be placed, when the current rate
of interest on capital will have declined to an equality
with that which is general in England, when all the
present conditions of landowning will be changed, when
the ambition of many of the wealthiest citizens of the
United States will tend towards the acquirement of
land. But economic considerations, we may be quite
sure, will never in the United States be put out of sight
as they have been in England in deference to the landed
gentry, because of the radical difference in the foundation of the two communities. The English nation was
founded at a time when the idea upon which the origin
of society is based—the rule of the Family—governed
the world; that idea has survived in England. The
American community has been formed upon quite a
different model. Among all the great contributories to
the formation of the English people, the elementary
group was the Family. The Family, House, and Tribe
of the Romans may be taken as the type. Sir Henry
Maine's researches in "Ancient Law" may well be referred to upon this point. He says: "The aggregation
of Families forms the Gens or House. The aggregation
of Houses makes the Tribe. The aggregation of Tribes
constitutes the Commonwealth. . . . The history of
political ideas begins in fact with the assumption that

kinship in blood is the sole possible ground of community in political functions; nor is there any of those subversions of feeling which we term emphatically revolutions so startling and so complete, as the change which is accomplished when some other principle—such as that, for instance, of *local contiguity*—establishes itself for the first time as the basis of common political action."

English society was founded and is still vastly influenced, if not altogether ruled, by the ancient idea; the United States differ essentially in that they were founded and are altogether governed upon the modern idea of a community. To make this more clear, we cannot do better than follow a little further the lucid argument of Sir Henry Maine. "The idea that a number of persons should exercise political rights in common simply because they happened to live within the same topographical limits was utterly strange and monstrous to primitive antiquity." "They recruited themselves by factitious extensions of consanguinity." They became aristocracies when "a fresh population from any cause collected around them which could put in no claim to community of origin." Perhaps one of the closest survivals of the *Patria Potestas* of the Romans which endures in our time is the Royal Family of England, with of course the signal difference of feminine headship. With the Romans, the maxim "*Mulier est finis familiæ*" prevailed, as it prevails in this day among the British and Irish landed gentry. The history of civilization is distinguished by the gradual dissolution of family dependency and the growth in its place of individual obligation. As Sir Henry Maine puts it, "The Individual

P

is steadily substituted for the Family as the unit of which civil laws take account." Admitting that society in the United States was based and is formed upon the Individual as the unit, I contend that there is a substantial difference yet discernible in English society, and that this distinction is largely due to the survival of the ancient idea, represented, with so much needless cost to the people, by the landed gentry.

In the United States, the force of public opinion, the power and intelligent self-interest of the people, together with their settled habits and customs, and the provision of adequate and admirable surveys of the country, combine to maintain simplicity and brevity in the documents and processes pertaining to the transfer of land. Land is conveyed by deed in the United States. But in order to be valid, every deed must be recorded. There is a registrar appointed by the County Court for each county in the Union, whose duty it is to register deeds of title to lands in their several counties respectively. The record becomes notice of the title to all parties. The fees for registry of deeds are very small. They are regulated by the number of the folios, and so much per folio of 100 words is charged. An ordinary deed is written for two dollars, and the cost of the registry is about one dollar. Each conveyance bears a United States revenue stamp of fifty cents for each 500 dollars. When valuable lands are conveyed, legal opinions on title obtained, and careful abstracts made out, the cost may amount to more than 100 dollars. But on an average in the State of New York conveyances cost from £1 to £2, and the registration of them from 10s. to 20s.

I cannot within the necessary limits of this volume, give, to an extent which is perhaps desirable, examples of instruments connected with registration of deeds, or with registration of titles. But I cannot refrain from quoting in this place a blank form of deed of conveyance, such as is common in the United States :—

Know all men by these presents, that　　　, of　　　, in the State of　　　, for, and in consideration of the sum of dollars, to　　　paid before the delivery hereof, and the receipt whereof is hereby acknowledged, do hereby grant and sell unto　　　the following parcel of land, situate in the City of　　　, and known as lot numbered　　　, in block numbered　　　, according to the plan thereof, as recorded in the Registry of Deeds for the City of　　　, in book　　　, page　　　, be the contents of the said lot more or less : To have and to hold the said parcel of land, to　　　the said and to　　　heirs and assigns for ever.

And the said　　　, for　　　and　　　heirs, hereby covenant with the said　　　, heirs and assigns, that　　　will warrant and defend the said premises against the lawful claim or claims of any person whomsoever; excepting however from this warranty, any claim which may exist against said premises arising out of unpaid taxes, and assessments laid on said premises since the　　　day　　　18　　, the date of the contract of sale of said premises to　　　.

In witness, etc.

From the United States we obtain that which is probably the most favourable example the world presents of registration of deeds. At this point we may call attention to an assumption, which is commonly made by Englishmen, in regard to the transfer of land in new countries. They are too ready to assume that, even apart from the complications introduced by entail and settlement, the ownership of land is a more difficult business to deal with in this country, simply because it is an old country in all that concerns the distribution of land. It may well be doubted if there is not error in such an assumption. In

the Australian Colonies, it is found, with regard to 40
years' titles to the most valuable estates, that, owing to
frequent changes of ownership and to unskilful conveyancing, the complications are at least as great as any
which lawyers have to encounter in this country; and,
again, as regards boundaries, the ancient landmarks and
hedgerows of England afford facilities unknown in newly
settled countries. In England, the great estates have been
held for ages by the same families; in America, and in
Australia, ownership is rather, as a rule, brief and uncertain.

In examining the proceedings of the Select Committee
which sat lately to inquire into the Titles and Transfer
of Land in the United Kingdom, we gathered that the
highest authorities have displayed a preference for a
system of registration of titles. Lord Cairns, to refer
again to his speech of 1859, said : " A register of titles
has nothing on earth in common with a register of deeds.
The objections to a register of deeds in this country are
so manifest, that hardly any persons in the present day
would venture to propose it. Those objections are of this
kind : To be worth anything, a register of deeds must be
compulsory, and you must have it for the whole country.
When you have got it, it will not simplify title in the
least. It only puts on a formal record all that multitude
of deeds and conveyances, of the extent and complexity
of which we have already so much reason to complain.
You have to investigate and search just as before. In
addition to that, you have to pay for searching in the
register, and also to pay, in some shape or other, the
expense of placing the deeds upon it." These requirements have been found so onerous in the United States,

that a personal covenant by the vendor, that he will
warrant and defend the said premises against the lawful claims of any person whomsoever (see form of conveyance, p. 211), is generally accepted in substitution.
That the land system of the United States will tend to
complexity there is certainly some danger. But with
such a registration of titles as that which Sir Robert
Torrens established in Australia, land transfer can never
become difficult, if the people may be depended upon,
as they certainly may, to prevent the establishment of
customs and practices which would introduce troublesome complexity of title. In the South Australian registration, there is indefeasibility of title, together with
simplicity of transfer. The essential point in a system
of registration of titles is that the title should pass, not
upon the execution of a deed, but upon the entry of the
record of the title in the register. The process may be
said to be based upon the practice in copyhold tenure,
which it much resembles—the register book of titles
standing in place of the court-roll, and there is great
analogy in such a simple system, to that which takes
place in the sale and transfer of shipping.

"Perhaps," said the present Lord Chancellor, in the
address above referred to, " the most extraordinary facility
of transfer obtains in the case of ships. In five minutes,
and at an expense of less than five shillings, you may
make a contract for, and actually transfer such a ship as
the *Himalaya* or the *Great Eastern.* The mode in which
the transfer of a ship is effected is by a document of
simple form and by the entry upon a register that the
transfer has taken place." Aided by the courtesy of the

officers of the Custom House, I have made some inquiry as
to the transactions in shipping in the port of London for
the year 1877. The title to land would in rational circumstances be less complicated than that of a ship, which
is always divisible, for purposes of ownership, into 64ths.
An estate in land is, it may be said, also divisible. But
in regard to land, there is the obvious advantage, that by
survey, the separate share of each owner may be detached
from the original estate ; whereas, in a ship, it is essential
that the shares should remain undivided. There is no
way of indicating upon a plan a separate share of any
vessel. I found that the register books made use of for
shipping formed an admirable example of what could be
done in regard to land, and there is encouragement also
in the smallness of the staff required to manage the
transactions—which, however, as compared with land,
are very few—in shipping. I found that the total
number of ships registered in the port of London was
only 2,853, of which 961 were steam vessels, and the
number probably remains about the same ; that in twelve
months the number of vessels in respect of which application was made for registry, was 201, and that the ap-
approximate number of transactions recorded upon the
London registry was as follows :—

Transfer by bill of sale	1,440
Transmissions by death, and probates registered ...	55
Mortgages dealt with (whether recording the mortgage or the discharge)	401
Certificates of sale dealt with	48
Other transactions (bankruptcy, marriage, etc.) ...	45
Struck off the Registry (192 ships=107,858 tonnage)	192
	2,181

Sir Robert Torrens stated lately, in evidence before

the Land Titles and Transfer Committee, that the idea
of his highly successful Australian Act occurred to him
from having been Collector of Customs, and having
had much to do with the transfer of shipping. He
said, "Land is brought under the Act upon the application of the owner in fee-simple, or as we commonly say,
freehold. He is obliged to produce his deeds with an
abstract, which is examined by a solicitor appointed by
Government for the purpose, and if it is found that a
primâ facie title is made out, and it is proved by
application and inquiry that the applicant is actually
in possession, then advertisement is made that so-and-so
claims to be recognized as owner in fee of such-and-such
lands, and a time is appointed within which persons
desiring to oppose his receiving an indefeasible title
shall put in their objections; after that advertisement
and no claim arising, then an indefeasible title is given
to the applicant, and it is issued in this form : All the
deeds are set aside, and a certificate is drawn out stating
upon the face of it all that the land is then liable for,
such as jointures, mortgages, leases, and everything of
that description; and all the certificates of title are in
duplicate, just as the old ships' registry used to be."
One certificate is given to the owner in fee-simple, the
other has its place in the register. If the owner should
lose the certificate, he can, upon proof of identity, get
another. If he should wish to transfer the land, he may
attend with the purchaser before the registrar, or if
he is at a distance from the office, he may attend before
a notary or a justice of the peace, provided with the
introduction of a householder or a solicitor, so as to guard

against mistaken identity. Then and there the owner
fills in the memorial in the printed form, which is on
the back of the certificate, and which is simply to this
effect :—" I   , in consideration of the sum of £   ,
transfer to   all my estate and interest in the lands
described in vol.   , folio   , of the register book."
Suppose the owner wishes to transfer part only of his
estate. A memorandum of transfer is made out, including a brief description of the property, and referring
to its number as to volume and folio ; a map has to be
deposited, showing the portion cut off for sale, and these
papers, together with the owner's original certificate, are
brought, in the manner above described, before a public
officer. The plan and memorandum of purchase, together
with the certificate of title, are then given to the purchaser or to his solicitor, upon payment of the money,
and are conveyed, by hand or by registered post, to the
Land Registration Office. There the original certificate
of title is endorsed with the facts of the purchase, before
it is returned to the owner, and a new certificate is made
out for the purchaser of the portion of the estate, with
no embarrassing retrospect of title, and not carrying on
the face of it anything that does not affect the land
he has purchased.

Sir Robert Torrens displayed the advantage of this
method by referring to a building estate at Bromley, in
Kent, in which he was interested, and which was valued at
about £1000 an acre. It was purchased by a speculator
who wanted to cut it up into sites for villas. The examination of the title occupied about eighteen months, and cost
£300 ; the person who subdivided the property amongst

the holders of the several plots of land, gave to each of them "a printed form of conveyance, which cost a mere nothing; 10s. or something of that sort." Now, under the English system, how do those purchasers stand? The vendor's solicitor approved of their title, and they have accepted the cheap conveyance with perhaps a thought that, after all, the English laws relating to property in land are not so bad as some reforming people make them appear. But suppose that after expending £2000 or £3000 in building a villa, they should want to mortgage, or to deal in any way with their interest in the property, the solicitor of the mortgagee, or of the purchaser, will, they may depend upon it, require to make a full examination of the £300 title; and their true position is this, that having each bought a plot of an acre, which cost, say, £1000, the investigation of their title may, at any time, cost £300. That terrible drawback to obtaining possession of land in this country is at once swept away by such a system of registration of titles as that we are now considering. It is probable, in regard to the improvement of land, the enlargement of towns in connection with works of public utility and sanitary improvement, that the benefits secured by registration of titles in connection with mortgaging, exceed and outweigh all those accruing with reference to other dealings with property in land. The old and troublesome fiction, already described, of conveying the legal estate, is altogether abolished, and, in the words of Sir Robert Torrens, what is done is this: "If I want to borrow £10,000 upon my estate, I hypothecate that estate by filling up a simple form, stating—'I hereby acknowledge to

have received the sum of £10,000 from   , and
further, to insure the punctual payment of interest
and principal at the dates arranged, I hereby mortgage to him all my estate and interest in the land
described in vol.   , folio   , of the register book.'
That is signed and attested in the manner before described. Then my certificate of title is taken, together
with this little memorandum that I have signed, and
presented to the registrar, and he endorses upon my
certificate of title : ' The land is charged with £10,000
in favour of   , interest payable   ,
principal payable   ;' that is then handed
back to me; the mortgagee does not hold my title;
I hold it, and the certificate of charge being noted in
red on the face of that document [and also upon the
duplicate in the register book] nobody can look at
it without seeing that I have already mortgaged the
land for £10,000." The lender of the money, on his part,
retains the memorandum of mortgage, upon which the
registration officer makes the following endorsement :—
"The particulars of the within mortgage were entered
in the register book, and on the certificate of title
of   on the [date]." The owner, who
retains the certificate of title, may want to raise a
second, third, or fourth, or tenth mortgage, and there
is no obstruction to his doing so beyond the record upon
the certificate. The mortgagee can transfer the mortgage
by simple endorsement upon the certificate of mortgage,
the transaction being acknowledged in presence of a
registration officer or any other authorized public functionary. The first or any succeeding mortgage is discharged by filling up another printed memorandum on

the back of the certificate of mortgage, which simply states: "I hereby acknowledge to have received the sum of £   , in full satisfaction of my claim for principal and interests for the within mortgage." This is brought to the registrar's office, where it is duly authenticated, and the registrar makes a memorandum cancelling the record of the mortgage. The record is struck out from the certificate held by the owner, who, if he shall desire it, may have a new certificate, free from all trace of the charge. In a transfer of mortgage there is no necessity for the production of the certificate of title. One of the points of greatest advantage in the system is that land is thus rendered a basis of credit as available as Stock. Upon default in the terms of the borrower's contract, the second or any subsequent mortgagee can sell the property, subject to the claims of preceding mortgagees.

In order to give assurance to the system of granting unquestionable, indefeasible titles, it is the practice where this method of registration of titles is in operation, to establish an insurance fund, by levying a halfpenny in the pound upon bringing land under the Act. This is to provide compensation in case there is some valid claim which has been lost sight of, and in order to avoid disturbance of the registered owner and possessor of the land. But it is found in practice that this provision is almost unneeded. In twenty years, and in 50,000 transactions, there have been no more than six applications to this fund, which now amounts to a very large sum of money, and Sir Robert Torrens believes that £1000 would cover the total amount which has been paid by way of compensation.

CHAPTER XIV.

HOW TO MAKE FREE LAND.

IN the year 1871, at the request of Mr. T. B. Potter, M.P., the Chairman of the Cobden Club Committee, I prepared a short treatise,* in which I suggested that legislation should be directed to the following points :—

1. The devolution of réal property in cases of intestacy in the same manner which the law directs in regard to personal property.

2. The abolition of copyhold and customary tenures.

3. The establishment of a Landed Estates Court, for the disposal of encumbered settled property.

4. A completion of the Ordnance Survey of the United Kingdom upon a sufficient scale.

5. A system of registration of title, which shall be compulsory upon the sale of property, the fees upon registration—sufficient at least to defray all official expenses—being a percentage on the purchase-money; the same percentage for all sums. A certificate of title would be given free of all costs in respect of any freehold lands, of which the reputed owner could prove undisturbed

* " Free Trade in Land," by Arthur Arnold. Cassell, Petter, and Galpin, 1871.

possession for thirty years. Any title could be registered in the Land Registry Office upon evidence of title for thirty years; the fees being the same as in case of sale, when registration would be compulsory.

6. That, preserving intact the power of owners of land to bequeath it undivided or in shares, no gift, or bequest or settlement of life estate in land, nor any trust establishing such an estate, should hereafter. be lawful; the exceptions being in the case of trusts for the widow or the infant children (until they attain majority) of the testator, or for the benefit of a posthumous child.

To the first of these points Mr. Potter has, in the interval, himself directed personal efforts in Parliament. In a preceding chapter, I have dealt specially with the law of primogeniture, the abolition of which is demanded in the Bill Mr. Potter has urged upon the attention of Parliament.

With reference to the second point, and in explanation of its significance, I cannot do better than quote from a statement lately made by Mr. James Caird, who is one of the Commissioners for the Enfranchisement of Copyholds, in a report to the Council of the Royal Agricultural Society. Mr. Caird writes :* "In 1841, the Legislature passed an Act for commuting manorial rights, and facilitating the enfranchisement of copyhold property. This was amended and extended by subsequent Acts of the Legislature. Since 1841, upwards of 12,000 enfranchisements have been completed under the Copyhold Acts, and they are now proceeding through the instrumentality of the Copyhold Commission at an

* " The Landed Interest, and the Supply of Food," 1878.

average rate of 600 a year. Besides these, a very large number have been effected throughout the different parts of the country, without the intervention of the office, owing to the stimulus to voluntary enfranchisement given by the Copyhold Acts. But though the number seems large, it represents probably but a moderate proportion of the whole, as wherever there is a manor, there are many copyhold properties; and much yet remains to be accomplished before this injurious and obstructive kind of tenure shall altogether cease to exist. The Copyhold Commission was formed with the intention gradually to abolish copyhold tenure, beginning by offering facilities.for voluntary enfranchisement, after which it should proceed to its object of extinction on the compulsory principle. Accordingly, after ten years' trial of facilities under the voluntary system, compulsory powers were given to either lord or tenant to demand enfranchisement, with further facilities again in 1858, which led to a rapid increase in the number of enfranchisements. Under the present Acts, either lord or tenant (except where the copyhold is held without a right of renewal) may now apply to the Copyhold Commissioners to compel enfranchisement, upon terms to be fixed by two valuers, one appointed by each, or by their umpire. And in small cases, not exceeding £20 of annual value, the amount may be assessed by a single valuer, nominated by the justices of the locality."

" The complete extinction of copyhold is still far from accomplishment. And a great bar will be presented to the profitable use of copyhold property so long as any

considerable extent of the land of this country, embracing
a vast number of the smaller estates and houses, remains
subject to manorial fines, whether certain or arbitrary;
to joint right in timber under which the tenant cannot
cut without leave of the lord, nor the lord enter the land
to cut without leave of the tenant; and to vexatious
demands for heriots, and a species of control worse than
double ownership. These are evils naturally most felt in
the populous parts of the country. The Copyhold Commission has now been in operation for thirty-five years,
so that full time has been given to prepare and provide
for the final extinction of this kind of tenure as originally
contemplated by Parliament. The simplest mode of
doing so would be by enacting that within some definite
number of years, say thirty, all copyholds then existing,
should become freehold. Till the termination of that
period, the right of either party to compel enfranchisement should continue, and the obvious interest of the
lords to make the most of their opportunity would quickly
bring about this transformation."

That is a very important statement made upon the
best authority. I concur in every word of it, except in
the suggestion of thirty years. I think ten years would
be quite sufficient, and with the substitution of " ten "
for " thirty," I would adopt Mr. Caird's remarks as satis-
fying the second of the above-mentioned provisions for
the attainment of free land.

The suggestion of a Landed Estates Court for the
sale of encumbered settled property naturally leads to
a reference to that which was done in Ireland. I have
known a Conservative lawyer who is a member of Parlia-

ment argue that Lord Cairns proposed, in the Bills which he introduced in the House of Commons, as Solicitor-General in 1859, to establish in England a Court similar in power and in operation to the original Encumbered Estates Court of Ireland. I need hardly say that is a delusion. Lord Cairns (then Sir Hugh Cairns) delivered, as we have seen, an admirable condemnation of the English system of title and transfer. But when he came to deal with the question of an Estates Court, this is what he said: "What has been done in Ireland by the Encumbered Estates Court? I beg the House to observe what were the particular objects for which the Encumbered Estates Court was in the first instance established in Ireland. These objects were two, and they were perfectly distinct; and it is important that we should keep this distinction prominently before us. The first object was to obtain the means of enforcing the compulsory sale of an encumbered estate ; the second to give to the purchaser a parliamentary title. Again, I say, these objects were perfectly distinct—the one might have been obtained without the other. To which of these objects was it that the objections originally taken to the institution of the Encumbered Estates Court were directed? Unquestionably to the first—to the compulsory sale of the estate. To force a sale at a period of depression, it was said, was unfair to the owner of the estate, because if he were allowed to keep it until a more favourable period, he might sell at a price so advantageous as to enable him to pay off the encumbrances and have a surplus remaining. But no objection was made to the parliamentary title being given to the purchaser. Why? Because it increased the value of the property, and was therefore beneficial to the owner. The Bill passed; the value of estates sold under it rose; and it finally became matter for consideration in this House, and in committees of this House, whether a system which applied so well to encumbered estates, would not apply equally well to unencumbered estates; and it was decided, and I think most wisely, that it was impossible not to extend the system to them."

Lord Cairns proceeded, in a very subtle argument, to exclude compulsory sale and to exhibit the attractions of a parliamentary title. He said that if unencumbered estates had not been included in the operation of the Court, fictitious encumbrances would have been created in order to obtain a judicial investigation of title. He dwelt solely upon the question of title, and never once glanced at the vast interest of the people in the compulsory sale of encumbered settled estates. Gradually, with masterly skill, he reduced the operations of the Irish Court to the secondary object, although he was bound to admit that in the compulsory sale of landed estates worth £20,000,000, involving no fewer than 7000 conveyances, the Encumbered Estates Court had proved its efficacy as an instrument for the liberation of the soil, by making but two unimportant mistakes, in one of which—a bogland whereon there was "no physical boundary"—an angle having been laid out "somewhat more obtuse" than it should have been, caused a mistake to the extent of thirteen acres of land having only a nominal value. The most beneficial object of that Court was to pass the land of Ireland, for the benefit and advantage of all, from

Q

enfeebled because embarrassed hands, to the possession of
those who were in a better position to undertake its cultivation. Had the circumstances of Ireland resembled those
of England, the advantage of the operation of that Court
would have been even more apparent. A landowner, whose
estate is overwhelmed with encumbrances, and who is
therefore an incapable proprietor, has no ground whatever
for complaint if his creditors are enabled to force a compulsory sale at a time of depression. It is then that the
public interest becomes most urgent and imperative, and
that his inability to further the public interest in connection with the soil becomes most evident. The estates
of the English landed gentry are as much encumbered as
those of the Irish gentry, and in this island also the compulsory sale of encumbered settled estates is as urgently
demanded for the welfare of the community. Anywhere,
a limited owner, with the concurrence of the heir in tail,
would be able to bring about a voluntary sale in the
Encumbered Estates Court, or a sale could be forced by
the accepted petition of unsatisfied creditors. When,
upon the attainment of free land, there were no longer
any settled estates to be dealt with—a position which will
be considered in following pages of this chapter,—then
the functions of the Court with regard to encumbered
settled property would come to an inevitable end. But
after demonstrating the evils of the English system of
conveyance, with which no one is better acquainted than
Lord Cairns,—after showing that these evils are so largely
traceable to the practice of entail and settlement,—the
lame and impotent conclusion at which he arrived in his
proposals of 1859, with reference to a Landed Estates

Court for this island, was expressed in the following words: "There is no valid reason why we should hesitate to apply to this country, one part, and one part only, of the system which was introduced by the Encumbered Estates Court. The part which I think we could with safety apply to England, is the part by which the Court is authorized to grant an indefeasible title. The part which I would be sorry to see introduced here—because there is no occasion for it—is that which enables the Court to impose a compulsory sale of encumbered estates."

It may be from a lamentable want of energy, the sad result of ill-health; it may be from a too intimate knowledge of the dead weight of opposition which the standing conservatism of the House of Lords would present to adequate proposals of reform; but whatever the cause, the fact is certain, that Lord Cairns will, unless his career is in this respect suddenly amended, be remembered in the history of England as a great lawyer, who, in the possession of talents unrivalled by his compeers, and of unexampled influence in the House of Lords, has culpably and conspicuously failed in the achievement of reforms relating to land. At the time when the present Lord Chancellor asserted that there was no occasion for the compulsory sale of encumbered settled estates, the solicitors of England knew, as Mr. Frere has lately affirmed in evidence which has already been referred to, that " English estates are just as much encumbered " as Irish estates, and it is not possible to doubt that a mind so economic, so practical, and so sagacious as that of Lord Cairns, fully comprehended and comprehends the advantage to the community which must result from land

passing through the hands of such a Court—passing from
a condition of mortmain,—for that is what settlement in
these cases amounts to,—into the condition of free land.

The Encumbered Estates Court, which I proposed in
1871, and the establishment of which I advocate again,
might, as in Ireland, be empowered to deal with long
leasehold interests as well as with entailed estates.   In
Ireland, I believe, "a term of 50 years absolute, unex-
pired, or a greater estate," was subject to the operation
of the Court.   The entailed and settled properties, which
came—upon the petition of creditors, or upon the voluntary submission of those entitled to the fee-simple—
within the jurisdiction of the Court, were by its fiat
made free land, the entail and settlement being protected
by the Court so far as the claims of those entitled in
reversion could be made good to the proceeds of the
sale.   If anything remained of the value of the life
interest of the tenant for life, he was, of course, entitled
to receive it, and the heir in tail was, as to his right,
protected by an investment made with the authority of
the Court, if there was anything to invest after the
discharge of all liabilities upon the interest of the life
tenant, and of the encumbrances settled upon the reversion of the estate.   I venture to assert that there is
occasion for an Estates Court in England to enforce a
compulsory sale of encumbered estates ; and to hope the
establishment of such a Court will form part of a great
measure of reform with reference to the land system
of this country.

With regard to the Ordnance Survey, and the provision and utility of maps, there is general concurrence of

opinion. Nobody denies that the Survey ought to be completed, or that maps are valuable aids in dealing with the title and transfer of land. To a system of registration, such as is here advocated, maps are simply indispensable. It is discreditable to our Governments that more rapid progress has not been made with what is called the Ordnance Survey. In July, 1878, Colonel Leach stated that Ordnance maps are published of only fourteen counties in England, and that the survey is a-head of the publication of the maps. The survey is always laid down on the 25-inch to the mile scale in the first instance. That is the basis of all scales, and from that basis enlargement might, of .course, be made to any desirable dimensions, which would differ in urban and rural districts. Colonel Leach, who is an Assistant Tithe Commissioner, and has had great official experience in the use of maps in connection with dealings with landed property, stated in evidence before the Select Committee on Land Titles and Transfer, that the revision from time to time of the Ordnance Survey, for purposes of registration, would not be difficult, and said, from actual experience, " in four or five counties " (Ans. 3621), that " the alterations were practically much smaller in extent than might have been supposed, and were such as would not affect the question of registration." But registration of titles need not be deferred until the completion of the Ordnance Survey, although there can be no question that the Survey should be pushed forward with all reasonable rapidity. I have myself somewhat carefully examined a good many parish or tithe maps (which have been made throughout the country, at a cost, estimated by Lord Cairns, in 1859, at £2,500,000), and in testing their accuracy, have found them generally quite as serviceable as the Ordnance map. On this point, Colonel Leach said (Ans. 3542), " Under Lord Westbury's Act, we had upwards of 400 cases of first registries; we had not in all cases an Ordnance map, but we had no difficulty in any case in getting maps sufficient for the identification of the property." (Ans. 3545), " It is a fallacy to suppose that there is the slightest difficulty with maps; and I may go further, and say that there is very little expense." Conveyancers under the existing system are in the habit of setting forth in detail all the enclosures and buildings included within the limits of the estate—a proceeding which affords opportunity for largely increasing the length of the deed, and consequently enlarging the bill of costs; but it must be borne in mind that, for the purpose of conveyancing by registration of title, the external boundary of the property is alone required to be delineated on the map or described in the certificate of title.

As to the large and difficult matter of registration, it would be imprudent for a layman to appear dogmatic ; yet it is clear that the subject must not be left entirely to the decision of lawyers. There must be a public opinion in favour of a generally defined system of registration, but the arrangement of details need not be dealt with in a work of this sort, the furthest object of which is simply to inform and direct that public opinion. In the evidence which is quoted and referred to in preceding chapters, it is made clear upon legal authority of the highest character, that registration of titles has present and permanent advantages which can never be obtained from any system of registration of deeds, and that an effective system of registration of titles is incompatible with, and, indeed, impossible, so long as, the complexity of titles introduced by the practice of entail and settlement is continued. I shall propose that the power of entailing and settling life estates in land be withdrawn as inconsistent with that freedom of the soil which it is my object to attain. I shall suggest that there should be no interference with existing settlements, but that, after the passing of a Land Act, no entail should be valid, nor any settlement of land, with the exceptions which are mentioned in the commencement of this chapter. I shall propose also that the limit for investigation of title be reduced to twenty years. It will perhaps be contended by Mr. Joshua Williams and others, with regard to this limitation, that it would prejudice the interests of certain persons entitled to reversions under existing settlements. It might be possible to retain in those cases the 40, or longer, years' limitation until the expiry of the existing settlement. These changes would obviate many of the objections which have been made, and would greatly clear the way for the establishment of registration of titles. After giving such attention as I could to the matter, I incline very strongly to believe that the Torrens system of registration of title, which has been so successful in Australia, might be established with far larger success in this country. I would suggest that at first nothing but freehold, or fee-simple, should be registered; that registration should be compulsory upon sale or transfer;

and that voluntary applications for the registration of such title be received with particular favour and with especial advantage to the applicants.

Let us endeavour to understand in some slight degree how the main body of the land of this country would be affected by the enactment of such proposals. And first with regard to entailed estates, which, as we have seen, comprise probably four-fifths of the soil. Where an entailing deed of settlement has been executed it would hold good. Let us revert to the supposed case of the Earl of Derby, because there is great advantage in taking a personal case, and because that is a name which it is pleasant to recall, as it suggests no feelings but those of admiration and respect. We have presumed that, Lord Derby having no male issue, the Knowsley estate is settled upon Colonel Stanley for life, with remainder to his son, who is at present in legal infancy. Not until that son arrives at manhood, could the position of the Knowsley estate be affected, nor could it be placed upon the register. But when Colonel Stanley's son arrives at manhood,—supposing an Act prohibiting the practice of entail and settlement to have been passed and to have come into operation,—the young man would not then be able to do as his uncle has done, and to re-settle the estate in his own line. He would then become heir of the fee or freehold, and by no inducements could he be made to forfeit that position. On the day that he reached the age of twenty-one, he could, in concert with his father and his uncle, constitute a freehold title to that estate, and the title would at once be fit for registration. It would be open to his uncle and his father to agree with

him that, in consideration of a certain yearly allowance
for himself, he would place certain charges upon his
inheritance; and then, if he survived them, he would be
absolute master of the property subject to the redemption
of those pecuniary charges. He could sell any part of
the estate, and if he became embarrassed—which in the
case of the Stanleys is a most improbable contingency—
and unable to meet the cost of encumbrances, the property
could be sold in the Landed Estates Court. In regard
to the succeeding generation there would be yet a further
change. If Colonel Stanley's son, having, as we suppose,
inherited the Knowsley estate, himself desired to effect
a settlement upon his own marriage, he would no longer
be at liberty to settle the lands of Knowsley upon his
unborn children, but he could charge the property for
their benefit or for that of his wife. If he had a family
of sons and daughters, he could bequeath the property
to any one or to none of those children, or in partition
among them; and if he desired to make provision for
them by charge upon the property, it would stand in the
old form if the estate had not been registered, but in the
new form of a mortgage upon the property if the estate
had been placed upon the register of titles. Then again
at his (Colonel Stanley's son's) death another compulsory
change might occur. If the estate had not previously
been placed upon the register, that process would then
become obligatory, because of the transfer which must
then take place; and thereafter it would escape the functions of the Landed Estates Court, because all trace of
settlement having worn out, the owner of the Knowsley
estate would stand, in regard to pecuniary liabilities,

exactly in the position of any ordinary purchaser of freehold property. All this might happen, without the least reduction of the area of the family estate in the possession of the Earl of Derby of that day, but it could not happen without giving a greatly increased value to those magnificent possessions.

In that case we have followed a long interval which might elapse between the enactment of the proposed reforms, and the transformation of an entailed and settled estate into free land. We might take the very different case of a landlord whose eldest son will be of age a month after the time mentioned in the Act, at which the practice of entail and settlement would be invalid. Then the father and son could together make a freehold title, place the property upon the register, and that being done, all charges must appear upon the register in the order in which they are agreed to, and the estate would more quickly pass into the condition of free land.

I do not think that the amount of business which would thus be thrown upon the hands of the registration examiners and officers, would present any insuperable difficulty. It is estimated that 1000 dealings with property take place every day in the kingdom, and that of those not more than one-fourth are freehold transfers, which at first would alone be placed upon the register. It is a trifling number, and with a system of free land a large increase might undoubtedly be looked for. But that increase would be gradual, and the number actually to be dealt with in the first instance is not likely to inspire terror. Let the adverse critics of these proposals remember that in suggesting the delays which would occur from pressure of business, they must not draw example from the existing system. The reduction of the limit of investigation to a period of 20 years would make a very considerable difference, and, I may almost say, there is no title which would not pass easily through such an abbreviated trial. Except on transfer, I see no reason why the examination of a freehold claim should be compulsory. There might be no objection to the registration of a possessory claim, but it might be desirable that, at the expiration of 20 years, compulsory steps should be taken to make the title indefeasible. It is of the essence of effective registration that titles should be indisputable and irremovable. It is always said, in objecting to registration, that there are a number of defective titles, the exposure of which could not be compelled with equity. In that speech to which I have so often referred, the Lord Chancellor said, " I believe in point of fact there are very few titles in the country which are not good." But his lordship was then speaking with reference to a sixty-years' limit of investigation. I have made inquiry as widely as I could among solicitors, and am prepared to assert that there are practically no titles which would not sustain a twenty-years' investigation; and that, for the sake of possible exceptions, the enormous benefits of compulsion must not be lost. I do not undertake to give a decisive opinion as to whether district registries or a central office would be the better arrangement. I have dealt incidentally with this point in commenting, in a previous chapter, upon the report of the Select Committee upon Land Titles and Transfer. Some however, are inclined to think that, at all events at first registration would be more smoothly worked by district offices, perhaps together with a central office, so that persons seeking registration might have local or central registration, or, possibly, might have both.

District registration would certainly be more costly, but there is no doubt it would be more popular, and if ever these reforms are enacted, popularity and the conciliation of important interests must be regarded. District registration would provide appointments for many qualified solicitors, and that might be no small advantage. I shall not affect to overlook the opposition which must be expected from solicitors, who regard themselves as having vested interests in the present method of the conveyance of land. I should look upon any suggestion which would give satisfaction to that highly important and most influential body of professional men, as a matter which ought to meet with earnest and, if possible, with the most favourable consideration. To those who are growing old in the practice of their profession, I would say that the system to which they have been educated and accustomed will, in any case, last their time. To others, I would say, that the new system would diminish the very heavy responsibilities, the unfair liabilities, with which they are now weighted; while it would bring undreamed-of activity to the business of land transfer, and to the investment of money in connection with land, in this country. If they compare the stagnation of landownership in England with the transactions I have recorded in a subsequent chapter as taking place in that other island of the United Kingdom called Jersey, they may well think it rash to suppose that the general income of the profession would, by these reforms, be diminished.

I can hardly place bounds to my sense of the importance of conciliating the good-will of the great body of solicitors to the necessary proposals for liberating the soil of the country. I find that Sir Robert Torrens has not been unmindful of this view of the subject, and that, in a paper which he read at the meeting of the Association for the promotion of Social Science, held at Cheltenham in 1878, he said, "Whenever we come to consider the possibility of adopting registration of titles in England, this obstacle of professional hostility stares us in the face. How can it be got over? One of our Australian judges, arguing that the conveyancers had a freehold interest in the old system, arising out of the money, time, and labour expended in mastering the highly artistic and very intricate science of conveyancing, proposed to be superseded by my Act, suggested that ten to fourteen years' purchase on the average of each man's income from that source might be a reasonable compensation, and their opposition might be bought off at that price. I agree with him ; for, after all, the conveyancer's costs are but a small item in the loss sustained by the nation, through holding on to this peculiar system. The delays, the uncertainties, and the disabilities are far heavier items." I have expressed the importance of this part of the subject, but I do not wish it to be understood that I impute to the members of a very distinguished profession, a sordid interest in their opposition. For my own part, I do not admit that solicitors can be interested in opposition to reforms which would clearly prove advantageous to those amongst whom they live. I believe that the enactment of such reforms with regard to the conveyance of real property, would lead to a re-arrangement of the branches of the legal profession, which would prove advantageous to the status of solicitors. I am confident that the result of free land would be to increase eight or tenfold the transactions in real estate. Nor do I fail to give to a highly educated body of gentlemen, including two of my nearest relatives, credit for a public spirit and patriotism which are superior to other considerations. But while I refrain from offering an opinion, which could be of no value, as to their right to make any such claim as that suggested in the above quotation from Sir Robert Torrens' paper, I do not fail to observe that the enactment of such reforms as I am suggesting would, in the judgment of most competent witnesses, add three or four years' purchase to the value of the landlords' interest in the soil, and that the landlords would still be great gainers by these reforms if they paid taxation upon transfers, sufficiently abundant to cover every possible contingency in regard to the execution of these proposals.

It has been stated in evidence before the Select Committee on Land Titles and Transfer, that "there are between 900 and 1000 deeds dealing with land executed in England every day, which makes 300,000 in one year" (Quest. 3157); and upon the very competent authority of Sir Robert Torrens, it is stated with reference to an objection against making the system of registration compulsory, upon transfer or sale, on the ground that "any staff appointed to conduct it would be overwhelmed by the mass of business," "that by limiting the application of the measure, for a time, to dealing with fee simple estates, and with lesser estates in lands, the fee simple of which has been previously registered, the block may be avoided and the pressure reduced by at least three-fourths." The probable pressure of applications for registration does not, indeed, appear to present difficulty. An examining staff of any requisite number could be appointed and set in action without inconvenience. Some do not think that a central office should be, at all events at first, established. Obviously there is no precise and present analogy between transactions in the Funds and those in land, because in the former there is no prolonged examination of title, and there is no map. But once the land is on the register, there is then considerable analogy, and it is both surprising and encouraging to notice with how few clerks, and with what perfect accuracy, the registration of title to portions of the National Debt is conducted at the Bank of England. There can be no doubt that these transfers, amounting upon an average to more than 150,000 per annum, are far more numerous than the transactions in fee-simple estate. These transfers involve 300,000 alterations of account, because, for every transfer made, the amount must be taken from one account and added to another. But Mr. Thomson Hankey states that all this work is performed by 200 persons, dealing easily with 1700 books, and at a cost not exceeding £200,000 per annum.*

The system of transfer of land by entry upon the

* "Banking" by Thomson Hankey.

register, and of tenure by certificate of title, to which, by the mere exhibition of the duplicate, or by memorandum of its number in volume and folio, official reference can at once be made, disposes of the troublesome and costly business of search, which is so great a defect in the registries at present in operation. There is no such thing as search in Sir Robert Torrens' system, except it might happen in the case of a man drowned at sea, or of one who committed suicide, or who became insolvent. Persons interested might then require to search in order to see of what he died possessed. And again, there is no difficulty whatever as to deeds which are not upon the register. With regard to property of which the fee simple has been registered, deeds which are not upon the register are simply non-existent. Of course, in bringing the register into operation, time would have to be allowed for the registration of deeds affecting lands of which the fee simple was by compulsion placed upon the registry, and for recording them in the order of their execution. For examination of title, qualified legal assistance would be requisite; but for the ordinary routine business of working such a registration of titles when it was once established, it is quite a mistake to suppose that lawyers would be required. No man in the world can speak with such authority on this point as Sir Robert Torrens, and he said in the evidence referred to (Ans. 3238), " It is simply bookkeeping. The man you want for the kind of work is a man used to cataloguing; the man who has catalogued the library at the British Museum would be the man. I maintain that legal study, though it generally improves the mind, does not give any special qualification

for the work of registration; if I had the work to do
now, I would go to the British Museum and see if I could
find who is cataloguing the library, and get him."

It must not be argued that registration would not be
popular because it has never yet been popular. With free
land inevitably in prospect, the large landowners would
have inducements to register which they never had under
the Acts of Lord Westbury and Lord Cairns. The expense of putting land upon the register must in the first
instance be considerable, and perhaps this expense would
aid rather than retard the enactment of reform. Those
who have vested interests in the business of conveyancing may rely that there would be no diminution of work
for some years to come. But all who are interested in
the land would be abundantly repaid by the greatly
increased saleable value such property would immediately
acquire, when the title to a large area of the soil had
passed upon the register, and the middle-classes had
become accustomed to the operation of the new system.
It would be well, as I have said, to offer special attractions to voluntary registration; and it may be remarked,
that it is not a sound or judicious plan to charge by percentage for investigation of title. Even a low scale might
in that way involve a charge of £10,000, or more, upon
the possessions of a great landowner, and it is most
desirable to induce the great landowners to come by
voluntary application upon the register, in anticipation
of the time when, upon transfer, the registration of their
freehold estates would be compulsory. The charge for
investigation should bear close relation to the amount
of labour involved. Where compulsion is employed, the

R

registration fees might with advantage be a percentage, but such a mode of charge should be carefully avoided. where it is desirable to induce landowners to apply for registration.

I shall not now dwell at any length upon the proposal for the abolition of entail and settlement, because the arguments in favour of that policy form the greater part of this volume. It is justified by due regard for the interests of the commonwealth; it is justified by respect for the interests of the landlords; it is justified both by considerations of morality and of expediency. Without this abolition there can be no effectual reform; there cannot be free land. I am at a loss to find words that will better express the object which, in advancing any one and all of these suggestions, I have in view, than those employed by Mr. Bright * in his very interesting contribution to Mr. Joseph Kay's work, in which I will take the liberty of substituting the plural for the singular pronoun and verb: "We seek to give that freedom to the soil which our laws have given to the produce, and which they give to personal property of every kind; we would leave to their free action the natural powers which tend to the accumulation of landed property on the one hand, as well as those which tend to its dispersion on the other; we would so change our laws as to give to every present generation an absolute control over the soil, free from the paralyzing influences which afflict it now, from the ignorance, the folly, the obstinacy, or the pride of generations which have passed away." We must, to this end, obtain the abolition of power of entailing land and of

* Preface to " Free Trade in Land."

settling it for life estates in the manner which is now so widely practised in this country. We shall injure no man by denying to him the power of fettering the land, and of fastening it—it may be for 100 years—upon those who may neither be desirous of such possession nor qualified for such inheritance. The claim thus to settle land is a claim which works positive injury to the saleable value of the landlord's interest, and it is a claim to a more absolute property in land than can rightfully be sanctioned by the State with due regard to Mr. Lowe's excellent definition of " the dormant joint interest " of the people at large. The latest contribution of importance upon this point has been the speech of Mr. Gladstone at Dalkeith. As to " the law of entail and settlement," he is reported to have said, " I am in favour of the abolition of that law. I disapprove it on economical grounds, and I disapprove it on social and moral grounds. I disapprove the relations which it creates between the father and eldest son. I disapprove the manner in which it makes provision for the interest of the children to be born. Was there ever, gentlemen, in the history of legislation a stranger expedient ? Let us take the ordinary case. The ordinary case is this : The son is going to marry. When he marries (because under that law, supposing he does not marry, and his father dies, he becomes absolute owner)—when he marries his father gives him an income for life, and he, the son, in consideration of the income, re-settles his estate on his issue to be thereafter born. Now, what is the meaning of the process ? It is that the actual owner of the estate induces the son to make provision for his own children by giving him an income for his life. Provision for the children is not made by the free will of the father, but by the free will of the grandfather, in order to secure the further tying up of the estate. It appears to me that there is one law written more distinctly than any other on the constitution of human society by the finger of the Almighty, and that is that the parent is responsible for a sufficient provision on behalf of the child. But the law of England is wiser than the Almighty; it improves on Divine Providence; it will not trust the father to make provision for the child; it calls in the aid of the grandfather, and commits to him the functions of the parent, introducing a false, and in my opinion an unnatural relation into the constitution of that primary element of society, the sacred constitution of the family. Not only to liberate agriculture, gentlemen, but upon other grounds, and I will say upon what I think still higher grounds, I am for doing away with this law of settlement and entail." It may be observed that there is no interference proposed with the power of bequest, except in the direction that the power of bequest would be enlarged and made free, for it is a power which at present does not belong to the landlords of this country. Their lands are settled; they cannot leave their estates to whom they will. They would by these changes be made free, as the land would be made free. We are not concerned in this chapter with any conjecture as to the results of the policy which is proposed. But it is clear that by none of these suggestions would the large estates be divided, except by the will of the freeholder, or as a consequence of the estate passing out of his hands, either by compulsory sale in the Encumbered Estates Court, or by voluntary transfer.

The abolition of the power of entail and settlement would enhance the value of all private interests, while it would do justice to the public interest, in the soil. The owner of land would be at liberty to impose charges upon the land at his pleasure, and settlements of personal property would continue to be made as at present. Personal property is to a certain extent a necessity of life, but it is obviously unlimited in quantity, and it is evident that the community is greatly benefited by the sanction given to settlement of personalty. And there is in this respect no analogy between the two forms of property. The absolute ownership of land is, as we have seen, inconceivable, and the practice of settlement implies an unjustifiable disregard for the "dormant joint interest" of the public. It is sufficiently condemned by the unanimous opinion of the most distinguished conveyancers that it renders the adoption of any effective form of registration of title impossible; it is sufficiently condemned in the fact, profusely illustrated in these pages, that it is opposed to the improvement and to the better cultivation of the land. The only plea for retention of these practices is that put forward by Sir George Bowyer, to which I have already alluded, that "it is part of the political and social system of this country to preserve landed estates in families." It may be truly said of the reforms which are here proposed, that they would not defeat that end.

In order, then, to establish free land, a great Act of the Legislature, such as only a Government supported by a majority of the nation could carry through Parliament, should be directed to secure the following provisions:—

1. Immediate abolition of the law of primogeniture, by directing the distribution of real property in cases of intestacy in the same manner as the law directs in regard to personal property.

2. Abolition, compulsory upon sale or transfer, and in any case, within a period of ten years, of copyhold and customary tenures.

3. Establishment of a Landed Estates Court for compulsory disposal of encumbered settled property.

4. Completion of the Ordnance Survey, with the utmost reasonable speed, for the United Kingdom, upon requisite scales and with arrangements for periodical revision of maps.

5. Abolition of entail and settlement of land, with exception in the case of trusts for the widow, or infant children (until they attain majority), of the testator.

6. Establishment of a system of registration of freehold and indefeasible titles, compulsory upon the sale or transfer of property, together with voluntary register of possessory titles, and a reduction of the period for investigation of title to twenty years. All lesser interests in the property registered to be recorded.

CHAPTER XV.

THE foundation of rural Government in England remains, as it has ever been, the possession of land. The Lord Lieutenant, the highest officer in the county, is always, as a matter of course, a great landowner. A Lord Lieutenant who had not a park in the county is simply unimaginable. If a man choose to invest £20,000 in a landed estate, and is a person of fair character, he has no difficulty—especially if he be a Churchman and is not vehemently opposed to the political policy of the Lord Lieutenant—in obtaining for his name a place upon the Commission of the Peace. Then he is a member of Quarter Sessions, is specially clothed in his own district with the majesty of the law, he is an *ex-officio* member of the Board of Guardians and of other local bodies. Formerly, the necessary qualification for a magistrate was the possession of landed property valued at £100 a year, or the right to one in reversion of not less than £300 a year; but lately, assessment for two years to the inhabited house duty at £100 has been accepted as sufficient. This concession was made in order that the rural bench might now and then obtain recruits from the urban and suburban residents generally possessing special qualifications. From first to last our rural government is based upon property; even the guardian must be qualified, and in the election of a guardian the rich man may throw in his six votes, while the poor man is a mute and unrepresented subject, in a system which is not merely concerned with expenditure but with extensive powers affecting personal rights.

Mr. Goschen, in presenting the Rating and House Tax Bill to Parliament in April, 1871, said that "we have a chaos as regards authorities, a chaos as regards rates, and a worse chaos than all as regards areas." I am convinced that examination will produce agreement in opinion that this chaos results from an attempt to unite the legitimate principle of representation with the dubious principle of government by acreage. There are about 820 petty sessional divisions in England and Wales, but these do not correspond with any other areas. The parish is the most ancient division of the rural districts, but government by clergy, and government by acreage, commingled with government by representation of the people, have despoiled the word of any distinct signification. The civil parish is sometimes a very ancient and sometimes a very modern limit; for purposes of local government, it simply means an area "for which a separate poor-rate is or can be made, or for which a separate overseer is or can be appointed." * The same may be said of the ecclesiastical parish, which is sometimes a thing of yesterday, made through the operation of the Church Building Acts, and sometimes

* "Local Government," by W. Rathbone, M.P., and S. Whitbread, M.P., 1877.

a survival of all the centuries of English history. But no good reason could now be given for the areas of parishes, of which some are very small and some are very large, some very populous and some very thinly populated. In the chaos and confusion of rural government there is one statement which may be made with the certainty of hard fact, and it is this—that the boundaries of parishes never cut the boundaries of unions "which are merely aggregations of parishes, and there are only eighty-five parishes which extend into more counties than one; but parishes are frequently cut by the boundaries of boroughs and of local board districts." *

In this chapter, I propose to deal with our local government only so far as it is based upon or is affected by the tenure of land. We have seen that the possession of land is the governing principle of selection in regard to the county magistracy. Orthodoxy is also an element of selection. An interesting episode in regard to the government of counties, illustrating very forcibly this part of the subject, occurred in 1873–76, in connection with the contest by the present writer for the representation in Parliament of the Borough of Huntingdon. The mayor, who, as returning officer, took no part in the election, was a Nonconformist of station and high character, a near neighbour of the Lord-Lieutenant; and I was informed that the Lord-Lieutenant, with conspicuous disregard, had not placed the name of a single Nonconformist on the Commission of the Peace;

* "Local Government," by W. Rathbone, M.P., and S. Whitbread, M.P., 1877, p. 4.

in fact, that there was not a Nonconformist in that position in the county of Huntingdon. The claims of the mayor, and of one other gentleman in the county, whose acquaintance I made during the election, but who gave me no assistance, appeared so palpable, and the advantage of their appointment to the districts in which they resided so considerable, that I felt it my duty to address a letter to the Prime Minister, impugning the conduct of the Lord-Lieutenant. In his reply, Mr. Gladstone expressed concurrence with my complaint; and, in consequence of the Prime Minister's strong expression of opinion, I asked the attention of the Lord Chancellor to the matter. All this appeared in the newspapers, and I then allowed the matter to drop, feeling no doubt what would be the effect of this correspondence in reference to the Commission of the Peace for the county of Huntingdon. I was not mistaken. About two years afterwards, Mr. Bright, in a public speech, alluded to my complaint, and on the following day, the Lord-Lieutenant of Huntingdon rose in the House of Lords, and after a political attack upon myself, which has no importance, repudiated the charge of improper exercise of his powers, stated that there were Nonconformists on the Commission of the Peace for Huntingdon, and informed the House of Lords that when Mr. Gladstone's and Lord Selborne's letters to the writer were published, he had consulted the Duke of Richmond, and had followed the advice of his Grace, which was to take no notice whatever of the matter. I was well prepared for this disingenuous and misleading reply, and was in a position to point out the next day

in the newspapers that the Lord-Lieutenant had, in the
most significant manner, taken notice of the complaint,
and had qualified himself for speaking in this way in
his place in Parliament, because he had met my complaint by placing the names of the gentlemen I had
indicated—the mayor, whom I had mentioned by name—
upon the Commission of the Peace. The incident is not
without importance as bearing upon the matter of rural
government, because it is thoroughly characteristic.
The administration of the law by the rural magistracy
is tainted from the source of their authority. They
are for the most part well-meaning, kindly-hearted, and,
as to the affairs of their neighbours, well-informed men ;
but they are essentially representatives of property, and
their judgments are remarkable for tenderness to rights
of property and for comparative disregard towards the
far more important rights of persons. It is a matter of
daily experience that rural magistrates inflict heavy
sentences for larcenous crimes, and deal lightly with
murderous offences. Mr. Henry Crompton, in delivering
a lecture at Sheffield upon " the reform of the magistracy
and of the law relating to summary justice," said, " I
have for many years watched the administration of
criminal justice, and one of its worst features is the
extraordinary leniency with which crimes of violence
are treated, as compared with the severity with which
crimes against property are punished. I have collected
vast numbers of these cases. In one instance of a dreadful
assault, the magistrates fined the offender forty shillings.
But the victim of the outrage died, and the offender was
tried for manslaughter and sentenced by Mr. Justice

Denman to ten years' penal servitude. Instances like
this are of every-day occurrence. Men get a few months'
imprisonment for outrages upon their wives, when, if
the case was brought before the Judge of Assize, there
would be a sentence of twice as many years as the
magistrate gives months. I think that if the option of
trial by jury were given to the prosecutor in such cases,
the result would be a more vigorous administration of
justice." This, then, is the charge which is made concerning the administration of justice founded upon
acreage over the greater part of the kingdom—that the
judicial origin and qualification of the magistracy being
based on property, they reflect this characteristic in
their judgments with injurious consequences to the
morality and to the personal rights of the people. After
all, the most popular educational classes are those
assembled in a court of law, before the official seat of
justice. The education of the people is nearly concerned
with the administration of the law, and it cannot be
denied that the administration of justice in England is
sometimes grossly immoral in its teaching. From the
representative seat of the divine principle of justice,
the people of our counties have been taught again and
again that it is more wicked to strike a hare to death
in a public road than to bruise a wife and mother; that
it is worse to steal a plant from a garden or a stick
from a hedge than to neglect an aged parent or an infant
child. I say that this fault—a fault not doubtful, but
admitted and observed by all—must be charged to our
land system, and that with the establishment of free
land it would certainly tend to disappear.

But again, the costly and confusing complications of rural government are due to nothing so much as to blind idolatry of the English system of landed life-tenure. During this age of reform in local and sanitary government, the representative and the acreage principles were brought into contact, the former full of life and vigour, the latter strong in ancient privilege and real power of possession. Both have survived, and the dual existence has been the plea for that most absurd and extravagant system of local government, which is exhibited in the multiplicity of governing bodies. I will quote from Messrs. Rathbone and Whitbread's interesting and useful "Memorandum" an illustration of the result: "The inhabitant of a borough lives in a fourfold area for purposes of local government; namely, in the borough, in a parish, in a union, and in a county: none of these are conterminous (unless by accident) with any of the others; and different parts of the borough are, or may be, in different parishes and in different unions and in different counties. He is, or may be, governed by a sixfold authority—the council, the vestry, the burial board, the school board, the guardians, and the county quarter sessions: all these are different bodies: and inhabitants of different parts of the same borough are, or may be, under different vestries, burial boards, guardians, and county quarter sessions. He is, or may be, subject to a borough rate, a general district rate, a poor rate, a burial rate, and a county rate.

"The inhabitant of a local-board district also lives in four kinds of districts—the local-board district, the parish, the union, and the county. He also is, or may be, under six governments—the local board, the vestry, the union, the burial board, the quarter sessions, and the school board. And any of these districts or authorities, except the local board and its district, may be different for inhabitants of different parts of the same local-board district.

"The inhabitant of a rural parish lives in a parish, in a union, probably in a highway district, and in a county. He is, or may be, governed by a vestry, a school board, a burial board, a highway board, the guardians, and the justices." A case is mentioned of a farm of 200 acres in Gloucestershire, which, some years ago, was in 12 parishes, and subject to about 50 rates. Of course this complication of areas and authorities is very far from conducive to good government. Local government loses greatly in dignity and importance by such extreme subdivision. By making over local affairs to a number of petty governments, the persons of greatest influence, authority, and cultivation are not attracted to the labour. Full publicity cannot be given to the concerns of so many different bodies, and the consequence is that they work in gloom which is highly favourable to the development of noxious habits of jobbery and malversation. The result is wantonly wasteful, not only of the ratepayers' money, but also of the gratuitous labour of the members of these numerous boards.

One of the most needful reforms is the enactment of consolidated rating. That was, in fact, proposed by Mr. Gladstone's Administration in 1871. In the Rating and House Tax Bill, it was provided that only one tax should be levied; and that every authority now entitled to raise funds should obtain those funds by a requisition upon one single local authority. By that Bill, it was proposed that the boards of guardians, the highway boards, the county justices, the local boards, the town councils, and all the bodies who have a claim on a particular parish, should each, on a particular day in the year, send in an estimate of the particular amounts which they would require in the course of that year. These were to be added together by the parish officers in order to arrive at the total sum that would be needed for the whole of the year. Mr. Goschen, when he introduced the Bill, said that this one reform would be of considerable use and convenience, because not only would it effect a considerable saving in the cost of collection, but it would introduce such simplicity into the rating system that every ratepayer would know, what he never knows now—namely, the amount which he has to pay in the course of the year in the shape of rates. As showing how great is the saving to be effected by consolidation of rates, I will quote part of a letter addressed to myself by the town clerk of Manchester, in 1874. There are, together with the city of Manchester, four townships included in the municipal area, and Sir Joseph Heron, writing in 1874, said: "Township rates are, at the present time, levied in each township comprised within the city; but, under powers recently obtained, the amount of such rates is obtained by precepts issued to the overseers, in the same way as the borough rate is recovered under the Municipal Acts. In this way the expense and trouble of levying and collecting separate rates (amounting to about £3000 per annum) has been saved."

Mr. Gladstone's Government proposed to adopt the parish as the unit of their local system; Messrs. Rathbone and Whitbread prefer the union. A comparison of the arguments is very interesting. The president of the Poor Law Board said, in 1871: "We have chosen the parish. It has been said that the Poor Law Union might be utilized so as to be made the principal area for local government. An examination has proved that it is almost impossible to adopt that view, and for this reason—that, out of the total number of 650 unions, there are 250, at least, partly situate in one county and partly in another; and, what is still more serious, that, in the case of boroughs, a borough is very rarely coincident with a union. A borough is generally partly in a union and partly out of it. Again, unions do not coincide with highway districts; and the question, therefore, to determine is whether a union is an area which you can so touch, as by a rectification of its boundaries, to bring it into a more regular form. Examination shows that a union is precisely an area the most difficult to touch, and that because of the poor-rate. And again, unions have been so mapped out that the workhouses might be in the central part of the union; and if you were to do anything to rectify the boundaries of the union, it would be necessary for you to consider what distance the poor would have to travel in order to get to the workhouse. You would have to reconstruct the whole of the unions in the country in order to make them coincide with the boundaries of boroughs, with the boundaries of highway districts, with the boundaries of counties."

The contrary argument is that parishes are very unequal in size and population; that "the unions start with this not inconsiderable presumption in their favour, that they have been formed within the last 40 years, and formed deliberately for a purpose of local administration—and that a purpose which, of all the then purposes of local administration, the most demanded a strong and active administrative body, and a not unwieldy area,—and formed systematically by one central authority acting presumably on one principle, so far as it seemed applicable after local inquiry in the interested localities. Something is no doubt detracted from the weight of this consideration by the admitted circumstances—that there was, in 1834, a more pressing need for getting the principle of the poor-law union accepted in some form than for getting the best areas accepted; that local influences and the accidents of situation of workhouses, were necessarily permitted to make themselves felt; that, in many cases, the grouping, which was convenient 30 or 40 years ago, has become inconvenient, or not the most convenient, through changes of population and of the means of communication, and that in many more cases the carving out of urban districts from rural unions has left the remains of the latter in a disjected condition. The unions have the advantages of an existing representative constitution which can easily be modified so far as may be necessary : they have capable officers acquainted with much of the various business of administration; and they are accustomed to central control and audit. Lastly, Parliament has, to a certain extent, committed itself to their adoption, by adding to their original functions of

S

poor relief the important functions of the rural sanitary authority, and, in the absence of school boards, large powers with reference to elementary education. These considerations appear to warrant the acceptance of the union or rural sanitary district as the basis of rural local government."

This reasoning appears conclusive in favour of the unions, but it was disregarded by Mr. Sclater-Booth in his first County Government Bill. He selected, not the parish, nor the union, but the petty sessional area, in order—for there could be no other reason—to confirm the rule of the landed gentry in the counties. The provisions of Mr. Sclater-Booth's Bill, it was seen at once, were calculated to check the tendency of modern progress, as regards the reform of rural government. His attempts to remodel county government have been utter and complete failures. Where simplification and consolidation are the principal needs, his Bill, by setting up a new area, tended to make the existing confusion worse confounded. There can be no question that the county justices include some who would make the most valuable members of county boards. But the just complaint is that at present these gentlemen have not a valid title to control expenditure. Give them the title that direct representation alone can confer, and their administration will have a sanction it does not now possess. Let the tendency of legislation be that the highest elected authority in the county should as far as possible absorb the functions of other bodies, so as to render elections less numerous, to simplify local government as far as possible, and to increase the dignity of its operations.

All this is directly opposed to the Bills of Lord Beaconsfield's Government, which have silently perished, because
they displayed once more the selfish, uninstructed, unpro-
gressive policy of "the landed interest."

No one denies that in many counties the management
of affairs by the landed gentry is admirable, but no one
who is not blind to the inevitable tendencies of legislation and government can suppose that ratepayers will
be content with government by persons with whose
nomination they have no concern whatever. It is a
fiction which represents that the owners of property
need protection against the occupiers. It would be far
better for both to give both a fair field and no favour.
That is what it must come to in the end. But before
that time arrives, there will probably be many exhi-
bitions of selfishness and timidity on the side of the
possessors of power, and imputations against the honesty
and fair dealing of those who seek enfranchisement in
regard to rural government. That principle of Mr.
Goschen's Bill which provided that the payment of rates
should be divided between owners and occupiers was
a just principle, and its corollary is, of course, a just
representation of the owners of property. At present,
the owners of property secure, by contract with their
tenants, an exemption from any unlooked-for excess of
local taxation,—a contract which would be void if it
were made with regard to imperial taxation; and as to
the representation of property in local government, they
obtain it so far as it is obtained by nomination instead
of by election. In connection with the Rating and
House Tax Bill, introduced by Mr. Gladstone's Adminis-

tration, it was shown that the result of the present state of things has been that many great improvements in the metropolis, in Liverpool, in Manchester, and in other large towns, have been made within the last twenty years, exclusively at the cost of the occupiers, without the landlords contributing a single shilling towards the expense; and a provision was inserted in the Bill rendering void any engagements by which owners contract themselves out of the payment of a due share of local taxation. It would be a simple matter to make this operative, as far as yearly tenancies are concerned; the larger question to consider is whether the terms of any lease may be interfered with. In the Memorandum to which reference has been made in this chapter, it is suggested that "possibly a distinction may be supported between leases not originally exceeding twenty-one years and leases for a longer term; and it may be that, even if the enactment is thought not to be properly applicable to existing leases for the shorter term, it might, without injustice, become applicable after a certain period of grace to longer leases, especially perhaps those which commenced before the great modern increase in taxation." With that cautious suggestion we may close the subject.

CHAPTER XVI.

TAXATION OF LAND.

THE economic and equitable principles which demand that land shall be as free as possible from needless complexity of title, and from difficulty and cost of transfer, would be offended by the maintenance of the present inequitable taxation, due to the self-interested legislation of landowners. The landlord party in the State—always possessed of a substantial majority in Parliament, —including, probably, at the present day, together with cadets and collaterals, 800 or 900 out of the 1100 or 1200 members of the Legislature—have, in the matter of taxation, regarded with a single and undivided mind the interest of their class. We have all been accustomed to speak of "the landed interest," meaning only those persons who obtained rent from agricultural land; we have all been too unmindful of the fact that the "interest" of the people in the soil is far greater than theirs. In regard to taxation, they have been permitted to deal with the land as though the supreme interest of the country was that the deduction for taxation from rent made unnaturally low by our land system, should be as light as possible.

There is no tax the principle of which has been more widely accepted and adopted than a land-tax. " In most countries of Europe," said Mr. Mill, "the right to tax, as exigency might require, an indefinite portion of the rent of land, has never been allowed to slumber. In several parts of the Continent, the land tax forms a large proportion of the public revenues, and has always been confessedly liable to be raised or lowered without reference to other taxes. In England, land tax has not been varied since the early part of the last century." We shall see the reason for this, and at the same time obtain a pretty correct view as to what has been the ruling influence in the government of England, by a further reference to the history of the land tax. In 1660, the landed interest, liable in respect of their lands to many feudal dues and services, had restored monarchy in the person of Charles II., the worst sovereign that ever reigned in London. There have been monarchs as sensual, as wasteful, as frivolous, as the second Charles, but our history does not supply a parallel to his squandering the affections of a people. To him, more perhaps than to any other sovereign, much was given; it was required of him, who had not been without experience of adversity, that this wealth of opportunity should not be wasted. But by Charles II. all this was shamelessly, wantonly cast away; and for his misconduct no body of men were so responsible as those landed cavaliers who ruled in the Convention, and who taught him, by their dealings with this matter of taxation, and by other ways, that the people existed in order that their rulers might enjoy wealth, luxury, licence, and indulgence.

It was the Convention Parliament which resolved to commute these feudal dues into a fixed sum to be given as pecuniary Supply to the King. The first idea was that it should be paid as a land rate or tax, which was clearly equitable because the dues to be dealt with formed in fact the charge, in consideration of the payment of which, the landlords held their lands from the King, as the representative in chief of the State. But the majority eagerly seized upon a proposal to transfer the charge from themselves to the people, and especially upon the poor, who were then so helpless. On November 21st (six months after Charles had landed at Dover), the Convention Parliament resolved that, instead of a rent-charge on their lands, the people of England should pay a tax of fifteen pence per barrel upon all their beer and ale, and a proportionate sum upon all other liquors *sold* in the kingdom. Their object would have been less clear, their conduct somewhat less scandalous, had they not been careful to exempt themselves even from any share of this taxation, by relieving the home-brewed beer and the home-made spirits in their own cellars from the charge. The brief and partial annals of the time do contain some protests against this flagrant act. There were members of Parliament who contended that " the land ought to pay, it ought not to be charged upon the poor people by way of Excise." * Mr. Prynne protested against such a way of making " free the nobility." Mr. Bainton predicted that " there would be strange commotions among the common people about it," and Sir Thomas Clarges warned the Convention Parliament that

* 4 Parl. Hist. 146.

"the rebellion in Naples came from impositions and excises." In spite, however, of all protestation, the thing was done. Twenty-eight years afterwards there was another revolution, and the first Parliament of William and Mary overcame, with the aid of the King, the opposition of the landed interest, and imposed by statute a land tax. The 4 W. & M. c. 1, granted, by way of pecuniary Supply to his Majesty, a tax of 4s. in the pound, not upon any past valuation, nor upon any fixed assessment, but upon the true annual value of all real property. The words of the statute are clear upon this point. The tax was to be "according to the full true yearly value thereof, without any respect had to the present rents reserved for the same, if such rents have been reserved upon such leases or estates made for which any fine or income hath been paid or reserved, or have been lessened or abated upon consideration of money laid out, or to be laid out in improvements, and without any respect had to any former rates or taxes thereupon imposed, or making any abatement in respect to reparations, taxes, parish duties, or any other charges whatsoever." * The "most sufficient" inhabitants, who were to be parochial assessors, were directed to assess all real property "after the rate of four shillings for every twenty shillings of the full yearly value, as the same were let for, or worth to be let, at the time of assessing thereof." † It is quite clear that the land tax thus imposed was to be a tax rising in amount with the increasing value of land. To defeat this was the object

---

* Sec. 3 in Record Commissioners' edition of the Statutes.
† Sec. 5, Ibid.

of the landed interest, as their power waxed when the
ardour of 1688 had faded away. In 1697 their object
was fully attained. The Assessments Act of that year
put personal property forward to make the promised
supply of £1,484,015 1s. 11¾d. Personalty was to pay 3s.
in the pound, and then lands, etc., were to be "charged
with as much equality and indifferency as was possible,
by a pound rate for or towards the said several or respective sums of money by this Act set and imposed." *
From and after this period there was no more question
of assessment of land to the tax. It was merely liable
for so much of the residue which could not be obtained
by taxation of personalty. The matter was dealt with
again in 1702 by the statute of Anne, to which Mr. Mill
alluded in the passage I have quoted; but the triumph
of the landowners and their supremacy in Parliament
has remained unquestioned since 1697.

Now, supposing the policy of the 4 W. & M. c. 1
to have been a just and right policy, let us see what
would have been the amount of land tax in the United
Kingdom at the present time. I ought, however, first
to state that up to 1798 the land tax was continued by
annual acts, the rate falling at one time as low as 1s.
in the pound, but always upon the assessment made in
compliance with the 4 W. & M. c. 1, that of 1692. By an
Act passed in 1798, the 38 Geo. III. c. 5, the tax was fixed
as a perpetual charge of 4s. in the pound, and the tax
was apportioned—so much to each county of England,
Wales, and Scotland, provision being made for redemption. Mr. Pitt, in introducing this measure, said that

* Sec. 3, Ibid.

it would not preclude that or any other Parliament
from imposing another land tax, or from augmenting
or reassessing the existing tax; * but he comforted the
House of Commons with the assurance that Parliament
was not likely to adopt any one of these courses. The
produce of this stationary land tax in 1798 was
£2,037,629 ; in 1876 it was £1,109,289. The balance,
amounting to £928,340, we may suppose had been
redeemed. The result of an elaborate calculation, the
fairness and accuracy of which I have as far as
possible tested, is thus stated:† "It appears that on the
assessments of 1870-1, and on the produce of the land
tax in 1875-6, in no one instance did the quotas of
the several counties of Great Britain reach 6d. in the
pound. The highest was Rutland with 5¾d., the next
Suffolk with 5¼d.—all the rest were below 5d., several
below 1d., and some less than ¼d. in the pound.
The general average for Great Britain was only 1⅝d.
From a return dated, 'Inland Revenue Office, July 25,
1875,' we learn that the gross annual value of property,
including mines, quarries, etc., in Great Britain in 1873,
was £198,275,717, a real 4s. in the pound on which would
yield £39,655,143, instead of £1,078,362, the paltry
produce of its phantom namesake in 1875-6. Finally,
these two facts seem worthy of consideration ; in 14
years of the reign of William III., the whole public
income from all sources, including £51,946,621 2s. 8d.
raised by creation of debt, was £107,437,540, to which
the land tax contributed £20,776,865, i.e., more than
a fifth part of the total amount; whereas in 1875-6 the

* "Financial Reform Almanack."   † Ibid.

public income from taxes and ordinary receipts amounted to £78,636,043, towards which the land tax yielded £1,109,289 only, which was about £16,500 more than a seventieth part of the total ordinary income, exclusive of money raised by creation of debt."

Before we arrive at any conclusion upon this matter of the taxation of land, we must look at the Succession Duty—another scandal of class legislation. We need not look further back than 1780. In that year, Mr. Pitt introduced a Legacy Bill, providing for the payment of duty upon both real and personal property. By the influence of the landed interest, the Bill was divided into two. The House of Commons passed both, but in the House of Lords the Bill relating to personalty only was accepted, and the charge, which would have fallen upon their lordships, was rejected. In the present day such misuse of power in Parliament seems monstrous, almost incomprehensible, and altogether impossible; that the people should have been so tacit in their submission appears strange, and almost wonderful. For 70 years,— years of terrible expenditure—the landed interest enjoyed this audaciously self-made exemption. But I think it would be unjust to suppose that the nobility did this in the mere lust of power, by mere insolence of authority. It is more fair, and, to me, far more agreeable, to believe, as I do, that they looked upon the British institution of primogeniture and life-tenancy as a system to be encouraged at all costs, and upon the custom of settling estates as the very ark of the covenant, and the essential basis of the British State. Of course they exempted settled personalty from the tax. While I cannot exonerate

the peers of that day from the imputation of a selfish
and inconsiderate regard for their own interests in
rejecting Mr. Pitt's Bill, I admit they were to some
extent blinded by a belief in entail and settlement,
which I hope the further experience of 100 years
has driven from the minds of those to whom the
reality of power has at last been transferred in this
country.

In 1853, there arose a master of finance greater even
than Mr. Pitt, who essayed in his first Budget to march
out against the Goliath of privilege. Mr. Gladstone's
language was most wary. He proposed "that the exemption of real property should no longer exist," and
"that the exemption of settled personalty should no
longer exist." But he had no power to burst the bonds
of settlement, and he was therefore constrained to enact
that the exemption of land should continue in this
form,—namely, that the charge upon rateable property
should be upon the life interest of the legatee or inheritor, and not, as in the case of personalty, whether
settled or not settled, upon the value of the legacy or
inheritance. It was impossible for the House of Lords
in the latter half of the nineteenth century, to reject a
proposal thus attenuated in their favour. Mr. Gladstone
followed the line of his great predecessor in proposing, as
did Mr. Pitt, that this tax on land should be payable by
eight half-yearly instalments. His Bill, no less than Mr.
Pitt's, did homage to the great principle of life-tenure
which is now understood to be the bane of British agriculture and the denial of free land. The tax must not be
equitable, because, as Mr. Gladstone said in making his

proposal, "as a matter of fact, under the social arrangements of this country, our great estates are settled
estates." * And because "our great estates are settled
estatcs," Mr. Gladstone exempted from the duty on
capital value, those which were not settled estates.
Ostensibly the difference was permitted because of the
liability of rateable property to local charges. But on
the other hand, is there nothing to be admitted concerning the increase in the value of land by accumulation of personalty, and the tendency to decline in the
value of personalty, as a result of that accumulation? We
shall make further reference to this point. Let us conclude this unpleasant duty of exposition. Let us finish it
with a statement—authentic and official—of the amount
which land, exclusive of houses, paid towards imperial
taxation in 1870. Mr. Goschen stated as the result of
prolonged and laborious inquiry, that "with respect to
amount, land by itself pays only £3,000,000 out of the
£65,000,000 of taxation, and the percentage is 5¼ per
cent." † "In Holland land alone pays 9 per cent.; in
Austria 17½ per cent.; in France 18½ per cent.; in
Belgium 20½ per cent., and in Hungary 32½ per cent."‡
That is how the case stands as to imperial taxation.
We will look fully and fairly, without prejudice or
partiality, into the matter of local taxation before we
arrive at conclusions. But nothing that we shall find
in that department of inquiry can rectify this wrong
with regard to the succession to land, concerning which
we may quote the grave warning Mr. Cobden delivered

* Financial Statement, April 18, 1853.
† "Local Taxation," p. 184.   ‡ Ibid.

in the course of his struggle for Free Trade. He said,*—" I warn Ministers and I warn landowners and the aristocracy of this country, against forcing upon the attention of the middle and industrious classes the subject of taxation. For great as I consider the grievance of the protective system ; mighty as I consider the fraud and injustice of the Corn Laws, I verily believe if you were to bring forward the history of taxation. in this country for the last 150 years you will find as black a record against the landowners as even in the Corn-law itself. I warn them against ripping up the subject of taxation. If they want another League at the death of this one,—if they want another organization, and a motive—for you cannot have these organizations without a motive and principle,—then let them force the middle and industrious classes of England to understand how they have been cheated, robbed and bamboozled upon the subject of taxation; and the end will be—if they force a discussion of this question of taxation ; if they make it understood by the people of this country, how the landowners here, 150 years ago, deprived the sovereign of his feudal rights over them ; how the aristocracy retained their feudal rights over the minor copyholders ; how they made a bargain with the King to give him 4s. in the pound upon their landed rentals, as a quit charge for having dispensed with these rights of feudal service from them ; if the country understand, as well as I think I understand, how afterwards this landed aristocracy passed a law to make the valuation of their rental final—the bargain originally being that they should pay

* Speech in London, December, 17, 1845.

4s. in the pound of the yearly rateable value of their rental, as it was worth to be let for, and then stopped the progress of the rent by a law, making the valuation final,—that the land 'has gone on increasing ten-fold in many parts of Scotland, and five-fold in many parts of England, while the land tax has remained the same as it was 150 years ago ;—if they force us to understand how they have managed to exempt themselves from the probate and legacy duty on real property—how they have managed, sweet innocents that taxed themselves so heavily, to transmit their estates from sire to son without taxes or duties, while the tradesman who has accumulated with thrifty means his small modicum of fortune is subject at his death to taxes and stamps before his children can inherit his property;—if they force us to understand how they have exempted their tenants' houses from taxes, their tenants' horses from taxes, their dogs from taxes, their draining tiles from taxes,—if they force these things to be understood, they will be making as rueful a bargain as they have already made by resisting the abolition of the Corn-law. Again and again I warn the aristocracy of this country that they do not force us into a discussion of the peculiar burthens upon land."

Well, they have forced us into this discussion by raising a loud and continuous cry against the pressure of local taxation. The challenge to discussion has been accepted and must now be carried on to the end, which will not come until the people of the counties are enfranchised and the might of the English nation is arrayed to do justice and judgment in this great matter.

The local burthens upon land are heavy indeed. I do not deny their incidence, but I shall contend that they are in great part, especially in regard to pauperism, the vicious consequence of our land-system, and that they have been accepted by the landowners as the price of maintaining that ownerless condition of the soil, which is a primary cause of British and of Irish misery. It will be seen that pauperism, the peculiar curse of wealthy England, is hereditary in the counties where our system of landlordism has most extended and unmitigated sway. Mr. Goschen's laborious work * is admitted by all to be the highest authority upon the subject of local taxation. Mr. Goschen says (p. 185), " In many counties pauperism is actually hereditary, and throughout the whole of this century, such counties have been amongst the highest rated on account of the administration of the Poor Law. One of these counties is Sussex, in which the rate at one time was 8s. 7½d., in the pound. I do not wish to place before the House the list of peccant counties in this respect; but, singularly enough, they are, with only one exception, all situated in the south of England. If a line were drawn across the country from west to east, from Monmouth to the Wash, there would be found below it all the counties in which the rates are above the average, with one single exception." Mr. Goschen is probably too sagacious to have, in his own mind, any belief that this is "singular;" it is the sure and certain result of laws and customs which forbid free land. Why should the sparsely populated agricultural division of

* "Local Taxation," by the Right Honourable G. J. Goschen. Macmillan, 1872.

England be more pauperized than the northern and manufacturing division? Good agriculture does not breed paupers; of all industries it is that in which unskilled and feeble labour can most easily win the reward of an honest and independent livelihood. There are fewer paupers per square mile in Jersey than in any English county. It is reasonable to expect that if the soil of England were made free by such legislation as I have indicated, it would be redeemed from the greater portion of this incubus which is part, and only a part, of the terrible tribute we have been paying, and are still paying, for the stupid, ingrained superstition that our land must be held by life-tenure rather than by freehold tenure.

Many can repress pauperism more easily than few; when the ownership of land is widely diffused, the able-bodied applicant for relief will be much more shy of presenting himself. Our Poor Law does not differ in principle from what it was when Mr. Malthus wrote, "I feel persuaded that if the poor laws had never existed in this country, though there might have been a few more instances of very severe distress, the aggregate mass of happiness among the common people would have been much greater than it is at present. . . . A man who might not be deterred from going to the ale-house from the consideration that on his death or sickness he should leave his wife and family upon the parish, might yet hesitate in thus dissipating his earnings if he were assured that in either of these cases his family must starve or be left to the support of casual bounty. . . . The poor laws are strongly calculated to eradicate a spirit

T

of independence." * Professor Fawcett, in his work on
"Pauperism, its Causes and Remedies," has said that
"such warnings were as absolutely unheeded then as
they would be now. It was thought sufficient to say
that Malthusianism was hardhearted and degrading.
The words of warning have, however, lost none of their
significance. Assume that all the social and economic
reforms which are most popular were secured; suppose,
for instance, that the National Debt was paid off; that
standing armies were abolished; that primogeniture and
entail were things of the past, and that the land was
more equally divided. All this might take place, and in
a few years everything would be in as unsatisfactory a
condition as before unless these reforms were accompanied by a more general development of prudential
habits." This is true; but surely it is also true that
these prudential habits would follow upon the greater
diffusion of property in land. In regard to such habits,
we are undoubtedly the least prudent people of the
world. Must we then suppose that this imprudence is
peculiar and ineradicable? Is it not more rational to
ascribe it to the unique condition of the British people
in regard to that chiefest of all schools for thrift,
frugality, and prudence—the possession of land? Who
that journeys without thought in rural England would
suppose that he was traversing an island containing one
of the densest populations of Europe? Our people are
forced, in deference to the institution of a landed gentry,
into towns. "Great Britain and Ireland contain 55 towns
of which the population is 40,000 and upwards; France

* "On the Principle of Population," chap. vi.

has but 28 of such towns; Italy only 24; Russia no
more than 14, and Austria has 6."* In every one of those
55 towns, as in every town of less population, the
master evil of the British land system is distinctly felt.
Generally the larger part of the area covered by the
town is "settled land." A freehold cannot be obtained.
The people are overcrowded. Squalid habitations are
the result of fettered land—and from squalid habitations proceed drunkenness and pauperism.

Of direct local taxation, an amount not much less
than half is due to the relief of the poor. In Mr.
Goschen's Report, the total amount is £16,600,000, of
which £7,500,000 are charged for "Poor relief proper."
The "Poor Rate" represents a much larger sum. To the
£7,500,000 must be added £300,000 for expenses incurred
under Vaccination, Registration, and Assessment Acts
and in collectors' salaries; £600,000 contributed to the
Highway Rate; and £2,500,000 contributed to the
County, Hundred, Police and Borough Rates, making
a total of £10,900,000 under the head of Poor Rate.
With the exception of about £1,500,000 levied separately
for the Highway, County, and other Rates, the balance
of the whole sum of £16,600,000 appears to be raised
for purposes exclusively urban. But that which is most
striking when we look closely into his Report is that
the increase of local taxation which has taken place
within the last fifty years, and concerning which the
landed interest have made outcry, has been chiefly taken
from the pockets, not of the landlords, but from the
occupiers of houses in towns on account of works of

* *Journal of Statistical Society*, vol. xxxviii. p. 379.

public utility and sanitary improvement. The " general results " of the inquiry are thus stated :—

" 1. The increase in Local Taxation in England and Wales has been very great, less than in other countries, but nevertheless so considerable, as to justify the special attention which it has aroused.

" 2. Speaking broadly, the increase in Direct Local Taxes has been from £8,000,000 to £16,000,000.

" 3. The greater portion of this increase, at least £6,500,000 has fallen upon urban, not upon rural districts.

" 4. Of the total increase, £2,000,000 are due to the Poor Rate, £5,000,000 to Town Improvement Rates, and £1,000,000 to Police and Miscellaneous purposes.

" The statistics of separate counties, the division of the country between urban and rural unions, the analysis of the various kinds of rates, the comparison of the imposts on houses in England with corresponding burdens in other countries, the mode of valuation in England as compared with that followed elsewhere,—all point to the conclusion that house property in England is very heavily taxed.

" An historical retrospect seems to prove that as regards the burdens on lands they are not heavier than they have been at various periods of this century, nor so heavy as they are in most foreign countries, the increase in the special rates falling on lands, such as county and highway rates, having been insignificant as compared with urban rates. As regards the poor rate, the burden on lands in the country generally, whatever may be the case in special districts, has increased very slightly in

amount, and not at all as regards the rate in the pound.
The poor rate as regards towns has undoubtedly increased and caused new burdens in many places. In
those rural districts where the poor rate is now high, it
has, with few exceptions, always been high, and constitutes an hereditary burden which has at all times
been heavy, but which has gradually been lightened
by the transfer of a portion of it to other kinds of
property."

It appears certain that the burden of local taxation
upon agricultural land has not greatly increased in the
last fifty years, during which time so much has been
added to the wealth of towns, to their capacity for con-
suming produce, and to the improvement, at the expense
of urban populations, of the means of communication.
Agriculture has had to surrender the protection which
at times caused the price of the quarter of wheat to
rise above 100s. But what has been the improvement in
the value of agricultural land ? " The income-tax returns
are most instructive on this point, and as they show the
rental of land in England, Scotland, and Ireland separately, they afford the means of comparing the rate of
improvement in each country. From 1858, the rise has
been progressive and continuous, and with an average
increase of £470,000 a year. The capital value of the
total increase at the present selling price of land in this
country will be reckoned something prodigious, especially
by those of us who are old enough to recall the dismal
prophecies of the agricultural ruin which would surely
follow the free admission of foreign corn :—

GROSS ANNUAL VALUE OF LAND ASSESSED TO THE INCOME TAX IN
1857 AND 1875.

	1857.	1875.	Increase.	Increase per cent.	Capital value of increase at thirty years' purchase.
	£	£	£		£.
England	41,177,000	50,125,000	8,948,000	21	268,440,000
Scotland	5,932,000	7,493,000	1,561,000	26	46,830,000
Ireland from 1862	8,747,000	9,293,000	546,000	6	16,380,000
	55,856,000	66,911,000	11,055,000		331,650,000

" We here see that the capital wealth of the owners of
landed property has been increased by three hundred and
thirty-one millions sterling in these twenty years. This
increase has arisen chiefly from the great advance in the
consumption and value of meat and dairy produce, and
is thus only in part the result of land improvement." *

Although the burden of local taxation has not
materially increased, it is still heavy, and I should not
propose any addition to it. But I am firmly convinced
that a sum between £5,000,000 and £10,000,000 might
be added to local and imperial revenue, by way of charge
upon the land, when it is freed from the disabilities which
now oppress the soil, without making any addition whatever to its burdens. There can be no doubt that with
free land the character of pauperism will be wholly
changed. There would be quite a different administration of the Poor Law of England when free land was
established and an enfranchised people ruled in all
departments of local expenditure. The landowner's ability
to pay would further be immensely increased by the

* " The Landed Interest and the Supply of Food," by James Caird.

augmented value of his land—not merely owing to comparative freedom from pauperism, but by the positive increment of value contributed by security of title and simplicity of transfer. The English Law Reform Association estimated that this " would add four or five years' purchase to the marketable value of land." If it added but two years' purchase to the annual value of landed property, that would amount to nearly £150,000,000, which would allow a very adequate margin for taxation, and yet leave the landowner in a better position than he occupies at present. The Government that establishes free land may, without any increase of pressure upon the landed interest, impose a reasonable land tax, or succession duty, or both, and obtain, as I have said, an increase of between £5,000,000 and £10,000,000 of revenue. And if the sum so obtained, or a considerable part of it, were permanently devoted to the reduction of the National Debt, there would soon be a further reduction of the burdens on land, upon which that debt may be regarded as a charge.

CHAPTER XVII.

PEASANT PROPRIETORSHIP.

I BELIEVE there is no matter connected with agriculture and agricultural production which has been the subject of more thoughtless dogmatism and ill-considered judgment, than that of peasant proprietorship. If we recollect, however, that the idea which is raised by these words is so extremely opposed to the distribution of land in the United Kingdom, this ignorance will not perhaps appear surprising. No public man has, so far as I am aware, delivered in Parliament any utterance which has displayed mastery of the social and economic causes and results of such ownership, and the scattered allusions to the subject in our public journals have tended only to confirm the extraordinary indifference of the British public concerning this not unimportant matter. It is indeed probable, that if, even in parliamentary debate, a member of the legislature were to hazard an opinion favourable to the results of peasant proprietorship, some one, in a tone of authority and with the air of superior knowledge, would expect the topic to be quashed by reference to a few isolated cases of small proprietorship carried on in the midst of that which a noble lord, whose words I have quoted in a preceding chapter, condemned as a system for the centralization of land in huge estates. No one with the slightest claim to authority has ever supposed or suggested that a peasant proprietary can flourish where the land is not free; that the population can acquire the methods and habits indispensable to the success of small farming where the general condition of the soil is the opposite of freedom, and where, consequently, peasant proprietary can exist only in a few and isolated cases, always tending to decay and disappearance.

The Prime Minister, though he has certainly no taste for agricultural pursuits, has regarded it as his duty, in the county of Bucks, to exhibit some study of the economic laws which regulate the productiveness of agriculture. Yet is it not astonishing to find Lord Beaconsfield, on September 18, 1879, speaking at Aylesbury on peasant proprietorship, making no reference to the defects of English agriculture, owing to the practically exclusive system of large farms which prevails in this country, and actually devising an argument against the existence of peasant proprietary in this country, from the agriculture of Canada and the United States of America? It seems almost incomprehensible that a Statesman occupying the office of Prime Minister should, on the one hand, ignore the disadvantageous extent to which we, in this country, are dependent on the Continent of Europe for vegetable produce, and, on the other hand, should have been so unsuccessful in mastering the economics of agriculture, as to propound as a surprising discovery the

obvious fact that very small farms—such as those of
Jersey, for example—are not numerous in a new country.
Lately, in many parts of England, I have made careful
inquiry at ports and towns as to the supply of vegetables. In the summer and autumn of 1879, I found that
in the south a very large quantity, sometimes the greater
quantity, of the cabbages and other green vegetables
were imported into this country, than which there is no
part of the world better adapted for the production of
such commodities. In the winter of 1879, I find that in
London a great many of the potatoes sold are imported
from Germany. Why is this? There is no better
potato ground in Germany than in England. The fact
is that German farmers, like the Jersey growers, are
more successful than the British farmers in the production
of potatoes. We shall see presently what is the careful
method of Jersey husbandry in regard to potato growing, and we may learn how impossible it is for an
equivalent success to be achieved by farmers who, in the
British fashion, give nothing but superintendence to
agriculture upon a landlord's ground. In the production
of vegetables, the minute details of husbandry are all-
important, and there can be no equal competition
between the farmer who superintends the details upon
an area so large that he can rarely be upon the spot,
and one who has a personal interest in the proper
handling of every plant and of every potato. The
British people are paying millions sterling per annum
for foreign vegetables, of which a great part is in
reality a pecuniary and most unnecessary tribute to the
unique institutions of Great Britain and Ireland in

regard to the distribution of the soil. All practical
authorities upon British agriculture, such as Mr. Caird,
Mr. J. B. Lawes, and Mr. Mechi, observe this defect,
and are well aware that we have carried the large-farm
system to great excess. Mr. Lawes—to whom Mr. Caird
has stated that in his opinion "the agriculture of this
country is more indebted than to any other man"—in a
communication addressed to myself, says: "The production of milk, butter, and the highest qualities of
cheese; the production of fruit and vegetables, appear to
be the direction in which agriculture points at the
present moment." For the greatest success in that
direction, there must be an increase of small farms and
of peasant proprietorship, which, however, cannot be had
by natural processes without free land. It is in a
country where the direction of agriculture is such, that
what is known as a peasant proprietary—the proper
meaning of which I take to be a proprietary by whom
the greater part of the manual work of the farm is
carried on—is most needed, and will be most successful.
The conditions of agriculture are, as far as possible,
reversed in the United States and in Canada. There, the
simplest, the least laborious agriculture wins the most
reward; there, the least perishable crops must be produced at the least cost. This is so evident, that it is
with surprise we find a Statesman in the position of
Prime Minister expounding with the air of discovery,
and with the notion that he was refuting the ideas of
agricultural reformers in this country, the plain facts
of American agriculture. Said Lord Beaconsfield in the
speech referred to: "Now, it is a peculiar circumstance,

but to be noted, that the Dominion of Canada is not in
favour of peasant proprietorship;" and then his lordship
proceeded to exhibit the well-known fact that Cana-
dian farms are generally 160 acres or more in extent.
Virtually, the principle of peasant proprietary does
prevail, because, even upon those considerable farms,
the larger share of the labour is performed by the
proprietor and his family. But, of course, the agriculture which is most profitable in America is utterly
dissimilar from that which would obtain the greatest
profit in this country. We need the liberation of the
land in order that our soil may pass to the most
profitable occupation. What is the agriculture of the
United States and of North America generally ? In the
official report with regard to the tenure of land which
has already been quoted, we find, as we should expect
to find in any new country, " that the general mode of
cultivation, when judged by the standard of European
countries, may be characterized as extremely defective.
Owing to the marvellous fertility, abundance, and cheapness of land, proprietors make but little effort to prolong
the productiveness of their fields, either by rotation of
crops or the use of fertilizers. The cultivators of wheat
are accused of being less of farmers than of wheat-
growers, of neglecting suitable rotation of crops, and of
persisting in the cultivation of their wheat-fields until
the soil is exhausted, or utterly consumed by weeds.
It is said in defence of this system (or want of system)
of wheat culture, that wheat is raised in the manner
best adapted to the circumstances; that high farming
involves heavy expenses; and that the fertility and

cheapness of lands do not render a strict attention to careful husbandry as essential as in older countries, where the area of land is limited, and labour is easily procured." There is nothing which it is more needful to avoid in the discussion of agricultural reform, than a loose and unscientific comparison of the agriculture of two countries in which the circumstances of production are entirely different. We have now seen how patent is the error of such crude comparison between the agriculture of the Old World and that of the New World; we shall presently observe how error of the same character has become inveterate in regard to comparison of the agricultural production of England and France.

The direct establishment of peasant proprietary forms however no part of the plan of free land; it is contended that of the results of the freedom of the land, not the least beneficial to the community would be found in the growth of such a proprietary. There are some who say, and possibly a majority of Englishmen who believe, that this would not be the case. Their fixed idea is that high farming implies large farms,—an idea to which Lord Derby has given somewhat frequent expression. These views have found expression also by the pen of Mr. Froude. That gentleman has none of the caution of Lord Derby, who, so far as I understand, objects to the manufacture, as I do, of a peasant proprietary, but not to the establishment of such a proprietary by the free operation of economic laws. Mr. Froude has written an essay " On the Uses of a Landed Gentry." In that production, he made an announcement which is a flat contradiction of Adam Smith, of Ricardo,

of Mill, of Cairnes, of every distinguished writer, dead
as well as living, upon political economy.　One is almost
constrained to suppose that Mr. Froude did not know
what he was about when, in defiance of this vast weight
of opinion, he announced, with much approval of the
existing system, that " in a free country like ours, the
distribution of land depends on economic laws as absolute as the law of gravity."　No one appears to have
thought the economists all wrong and Mr. Froude right,
and the essay has been very appropriately placed by the
author in a volume of " Short Studies of Great Subjects."
This essay is, however, valuable, because nowhere do
we meet common errors expressed with equal plainness.
Shortly after the declaration I have just quoted, we find
the confession that " in England, the process [of buying
a piece of land] is so expensive as to put a few acres
beyond a poor man's reach."　But while Mr. Froude
concurs, as most Englishmen do who have made but
short study of this great subject, with the opinion that
improvement in agriculture and increase of production
are not possible fruits of peasant proprietary, he roundly
states an opinion which is even more widespread, and
which is received with all the force of an axiom in this
country, namely, that the possession of land is and must
be the luxury of the few, and those the rich, because
of its great price.　He declares—and his opinion is for us
important, because it is the common opinion—that it is
in consequence of the wealth and prosperity of this
country that the small proprietors have dwindled in
number and are not renewed.　" The soil will be again
divided among ambitious agricultural freeholders," when

"the grass will grow in the streets of Manchester."
"Abolish primogeniture,"—Mr. Froude does not say
anything about entail and settlement, but he may be
taken to mean, abolish those things also ; "you may
cheapen conveyancing, yet the poor man will not get his
acres. The more easy the transfer, the faster the land
will flow in the channels which it tends of itself to
follow." This is somewhat incoherent, but it undoubtedly expresses the view of most English gentlemen.

The business of those who seek the establishment of
free land is not the direct creation of peasant proprietary.
But they regard the fact that free land would have the
result of greatly increasing the number of proprietors as
of political, social, and economic importance among its
beneficial consequences. They know that the demand
for such legislative changes as are necessary to establish
free land will not be idly made ; that the people at
large must be convinced of the advantages—first, in
regard to increase of the home production of food ; and,
second, in regard to the closer association of a larger
body of the population with the soil. Foreign observers
frequently remark upon the political danger of England,
owing to the unnatural distribution of the soil consequent
upon the survival of feudal methods. M. de Laveleye, a
writer of great authority, says that " the distribution of
a number of small properties among the peasantry forms
a kind of rampart and safeguard for the holders of large
estates ; and peasant property may, without exaggeration, be called the lightning conductor that averts
from society dangers which might otherwise lead to
violent catastrophes. The concentration of land in large

estates, among a small number of families, is a sort of provocation of levelling legislative measures. The position of England, so enviable in many respects, seems to me to be in this matter full of danger for the future." *

Englishmen who foretell strange things concerning the future of Russia will, I fancy, find themselves mistaken. Perhaps to the absolute impossibility of general revolution in Russia, such as has occurred in other and westward countries, may be ascribed some part of the bloodthirsty violence of a few insane and immoderate fanatics, who find no sympathy among the great mass of the population. The hold of the peasantry upon the soil of Russia will, I believe, secure a general steadiness, though progress in so poor a country must be slow. It is well to note that which the military correspondent of the *Times* in Bulgaria, during the late war, wrote of the Russian soldier : " A popular fallacy in England is that the Russian soldier lives in an atmosphere of blows—that the knout and the stick are his only ruling motives. The fact is that nowhere, not even among the Germans, is the soldier managed more entirely by moral means. A word, or even a look, from his officer suffices. He seems to feel a reproof—and it is rarely deserved—as much as an Englishman would a blow. The bulk of the Russian privates are themselves small landowners, and have an interest and a stake in the country accordingly." † The Russians cherish the wide distribution of their land as a political security against " a proletariat and against pauperism," which, they see, is an English speciality. The prominence of pauperism in this country they, as I think,

---

* Cobden Club Essays, 1st Series. † *Times*, October 16, 1877.

rightly ascribe to laws and customs concerning the
tenure of land. Mr. Mackenzie Wallace, observing these
facts in his long intercourse with Russians, says: "Of
course, it is quite possible that their view of the subject
is truer than ours, and that we may some day, like the
people who live tranquilly on the slopes of a volcano, be
rudely awakened from our fancied security. But this
is an entirely different question. I am at present not
endeavouring to justify our habitual callousness with
regard to social changes, but simply wishing to explain
why the Russians, who have little or no practical acquaintance with pauperism, should have taken such
elaborate precautions against it." *

Englishmen are, and are entitled to be, without fear
in this matter, because they know there is no power in
this country capable of resisting, even for a moment, a
general impulse towards reform. Every extension of the
franchise is an assurance against revolution, and an assurance that beneficial changes cannot be withstood by supposed "interests" when the people are convinced of the
advantages to be attained. One of the major difficulties
in winning acceptance for such moderate proposals as
constitute the plan of free land, is contained in the obstinate adherence of most English people to the belief that
nothing less than conpulsory distribution of the soil would
stay, or could reverse, the process of aggregation in large
estates. We say that the consequence of free land would
be a large increase in the number of small proprietors
who would also be cultivators, and in support of this
opinion, we assert (1) that it is a fallacy which assumes

* "Russia," vol. i. p. 227.

that it is the high price of land in England which prevents the small capitalist from becoming a purchaser, and
(2) that it is another fallacy which assumes that the
produce of large farms is, and must be, greater than that
of small farms. We shall now proceed to consider these
assertions; and then, having maintained these two posi-
tions, we shall be enabled to contend that were free land
established, the result would be ownership by many
classes, and not as at present, practically by none but
the leisure, and luxurious, and most wealthy classes.

The first fallacy is that the aggregation of land in the
hands of the rich is the result of economic law, with
similar operation to that which brings diamonds exclusively to their possession—namely, that commodities of
which there is, in proportion to the demand of the
wealthiest classes, a very limited supply, and the possession of which is desired by all, must obtain so high
a price as to be inaccessible to any but the wealthy.
Sometimes the fallacy is put in this way: "Will men,
whose idea of life is to earn an industrial income of 10
per cent. from their capital, invest or retain an investment of a large part of that capital, in the purchase of
land, for a return certainly not exceeding 3 per cent. ?"
The supposition thus raised is regarded as preposterous.
The addition of small properties to great estates, which is
taking place every day, is referred to, and the subject is
dismissed as affording no basis for argument. Now, as a
matter of fact, the highest price is never obtained where
land is purchased by the rich and leisure classes for occupation or investment, but always where it is purchased in
suitable divisions by the industrial classes. This is as

true of the Poultry compared with Park Lane, as it is of
any rural district of England compared with the Channel
Islands, not to speak of Flanders, France, or Switzerland.
This part of the subject may be well illustrated by
reference to a portion of the United Kingdom—the
portion in which the land is most free, and in which the
transfer of land is effected by the act of registration.
Jersey and Guernsey ought, until free land is obtained by
the people of the United Kingdom, to be distinguished
as the Happier Isles. If free land is pernicious,—if to be
entailed and settled, and to be ownerless, is the proper
condition of the European dominions of the Queen,—then,
we may ask, why are these boons and blessings withheld from the Channel Islands? Virtually without inter-
ruption, those islands have been held with the English
Crown since the Norman Conquest. Entail has been
specially permitted in the case of several small estates,
but just as the larger part of Great Britain is no-man's
land, so that of those smaller islands is and has always
been as saleable as the corn and potatoes which it
produces. I would rather be Governor of Cyprus in
summer-time than Governor of Jersey with orders to
introduce the British land-system to that happier island.
In which island would it be supposed land is more valuable—in Great Britain, or in Jersey? In Great Britain
of course, will be the common reply. Land, it will be said,
in this island, is not merely land; it is the best security
in the securest place. Nor is that all. Land in England
has, close at hand, within reach by road, by rail, by canal,
the richest population in the world, together with the
largest and the most luxurious city, as purchasers of its

fruit. All other competitors must send their produce by sea; the British landowner has the dearest markets always at command. But even that is not all. The purchaser of British land may desire to have a vote for a county; he may increase his bidding with the hope of seeing his name on the commission of the peace; and if the area is large, he may be consciously buying a step, not only in county society, but towards a baronetcy, or even a peerage; for after all these things do the British purchasers of land seek. Who could doubt, it will be said, that the price of land is higher here than in Jersey, where no peer of the realm cares to live? Land must be dearer here than in Jersey, we might be told, because this is the market in which the produce of Jersey is sold. Land, we are given to understand, belongs to the rich because they are rich; and as the people of Jersey are a people of very moderate fortunes, as none of them use the land as a "luxury," which is the character it bears in Britain, of course the price is lower in the smaller island. Reasoning of this sort would be sound and true if such arguments as those used by Mr. Froude had anything of scientific accuracy in them. But it is not true, and indeed the very opposite is the truth. The price of agricultural land in Jersey, no better in quality or situation, is very much higher than in Great Britain.

I have lately spent some time in the Channel Islands, with the object of investigating the consequences of the approximation which may there be witnessed to the system of free land. I had heard much of the prosperity of those islands, but the reality exceeded my expectations. In sight of Jersey, no one could doubt the truth of Lord Derby's remark, confirmed by Lord Leicester, that the agricultural produce of England might be doubled. It would be doubled, and more than doubled, if the land of England were farmed as is the land of Jersey. The soil is not of uniformly good quality ; the winter is as mild as that of South Devon, and of the Isle of Wight, but less mild than that of parts of the west coast of Great Britain. There is one circumstance I have omitted which, in Jersey, should tend, according to English ideas, to depress the price of land : a purchaser cannot devise it to whom he will. He cannot, at death, deprive his wife of a reasonable share of his property, and, within certain limitations, each one of his children must have a portion. At the same time, extreme subdivision is prevented by a limited form of primogeniture. If an owner's real estate at death is not more than 1½ acres, he can make no division,—the whole goes to the eldest son, or, if no son, then to the eldest daughter. The average size of farms in Jersey is about eleven acres, and subdivision rarely takes place upon death of the proprietor. By the law of Jersey, the eldest son (or, if no son, the eldest daughter) inherits the house, together with 30 (Jersey) perches of garden, and (supposing the estate to be larger than 1½ acres) he has the power of choosing—after valuation by public officers elected in each parish—a tenth, before partition, over and above his distributive share in the division. The consequence may readily be imagined. The eldest purchases or pays an annuity to the younger. Sometimes a girl claims her share when she marries the owner of an adjoining property. But all this is not material to our inquiry; no such law of distribution' is proposed for England.

In order to test fairly the price of land in Jersey, I called upon a land agent and obtained particulars of all the farms he had for sale. There were four. The extent of farms in Jersey is reckoned not in acres, but in vergées, of which 2¼ are equal to our statute acre. The four farms, of which I obtained particulars, were separated by intervals of about two miles. The extent of the first was 22 vergées—not quite 10 acres. The land was unlevel—so unlevel that I could not see the entire area from the small cottage and homestead. Near the house there were vegetables on the land: of the outlying portions, one had lately produced a crop of wheat; the other was permanent pasture and orchard. One horse, two cows, two heifers, and four pigs were upon this little farm, which, I was told, was the usual number of stock. The farmer and proprietor had lately died, and his heirs desired to sell the property, in order to divide the proceeds. In England, in a similar position— that is, within two miles from a town of 40,000 population—the extreme value of the little farm would have been, in my opinion, about £3 an acre (including the house), and the saleable value certainly not more than £100 per acre. The price of this farm was £95 per vergée, or £214 per acre. The vendors would take £2,000 for the property. The second farm was larger; the extent was 38 vergées—about 17 acres. The house was well built, and contained six rooms; the stable, cowhouse, and piggery were all paved and drained into a liquid manure tank. The land was rather high in position, and had certainly not great natural fertility. An English farmer would think 30s. an acre quite sufficient rent for such land; but then, he would farm it very differently from the manner of the tenant with whom I inspected every plot of the little property. This man had a lease for nine years, and paid £4 10s. per vergée, which is equal to £10 2s. 6d. per acre. The price asked per vergée for the freehold was the same as that of the first farm—£95, or about £214 per acre. On the land there were two horses, six cows, seven calves, and six pigs. The tenant said he could manage that number of live stock without difficulty. His crop of potatoes had been dug about a month before I visited the farm. The produce, he said, was about three cabots a perch, which is equal to 130 lbs. English. There are 90 Jersey perches in a statute acre, and the crop would therefore be at the rate of more than $5\frac{1}{2}$ tons of "new" potatoes per acre. In preparing for that crop, he had laid on 10 tons of stable manure and 2 cwt. of guano, per vergée, at a cost of about £8 per vergée, or £18 per acre. His wheat stubbles contained no weeds, and a strong heavy crop had just been harvested. His average of wheat was, he said, a cabot (34 lbs.) a perch. Nine cabots are equal to five English bushels. This man's produce of ninety cabots per acre was therefore equal to fifty bushels, which is nearly double Mr. Caird's estimate of the average produce of English wheat lands. The tenant said he had the help of one man, and (he was a bachelor) a dairymaid. Between them they did all the work. "But," I remarked, "you have been threshing your wheat with a steam engine—how did you manage that?"

"Oh," he replied, "we never use anything but steam,
and we arrange that among ourselves, paying 36s. a day
for the machine, with an engineer and a stoker." Bearing
in mind what is commonly said in England as to the
utter impossibility of small farmers using machinery,
and knowing that a steam-threshing machine costs about
£300, I was curious to know "how they managed" in
Jersey. The farmer said there was no difficulty whatever; he had never known any unpleasant dispute.
When the machine was at work it required eighteen
men besides the engineer and stoker. He had never
known any trouble in finding men, and he said that
money very rarely passed on account of the work; "one
helped the other." "Me and my man are going down
yonder to do half a day's work with the machine at that
farm" (pointing to a house); "they came and helped us
half a day last week: and so it goes round." "But," I
asked, "do you never quarrel as to which is to have
the machine and the labour first?" "Oh no," he said;
"the rule is, that if two of us want the machine, it goes,
and we go, to the farm which is nearest the machine."
"It's just the same with ploughing," he added; "one
does a day's work for the other, and so on." I said,
"I suppose when some one gets a steam plough over
it will be just the same?" "Just the same," he said,
laughing. "Why not?"

The British farmer who reads these notes may, perhaps, be wondering what becomes of the cattle on these
peasant estates, where every foot of land is too highly
valued to encourage the growth of fences. He is aware
that the Jersey cows (known in England as Alderney

cows) are the best "milkers" in the world. Not long ago, a Jerseyman lost a bet that his cow would produce twenty-four quarts of milk in as many hours, only by a single quart. Let him understand, then, that in Jersey the cattle are as a rule tethered. A rope fastened round the horns, and secured by an iron spike driven into the ground, not only enables the Jersey farmer to do without fences, but the common belief is that a cow thus tethered will do as well upon one-fourth the quantity of grass which would be required if she roamed at large, and so destroyed a large part of the herbage. When the eight or ten feet radius has been closely fed, the peg is lifted and removed to "pastures new." The last question I put to this tenant—a fair sample of a Jersey farmer—was as to the wages he gave "his man;" to which he replied, "A shilling a day, and board him in the house."

The third farm on my list was, as to the larger part, permanent pasture. The cottage and premises were in a very ruinous state. The proprietor was also the occupier; but he and his family, from causes which occur everywhere, had none of them that look of independence and comfort which it is rare not to see in the farmers of Jersey. We talked in Jersey-French, which is queerly pronounced French mixed up with a few words of English. The price of the land, of which there were 16 vergées, was £85 a vergée, more than £190 an acre. There were a very few old, decaying apple-trees in the meadow of 10 vergées. The farm lay about three miles from the town of St. Heliers. But on this seven acres there were four cows. The fourth farm lay almost

as far as possible from the town and port of Jersey.
The farmer's potatoes must be carried more than five
miles before they could be shipped for England. The
extent of his property was about 15 vergées; the farming
proprietor was also the village schoolmaster, an intelligent middle-aged man, whom I found busily engaged
making a wheat stack. He wanted to sell the farm
because he desired to move nearer to St. Heliers. The
house was good, and the farmstead was sound and well
built. He asked £112 a vergée, or £252 per acre. The
farm was less than seven acres in extent; he mentioned
£1700 as the lowest price, of which perhaps £300 or
£350 might be allowed for the house and buildings. He
had three cows, two heifers, a horse, and six pigs on the
land, which he said he could let at the rate of £6 a vergée,
or £13 10s. per acre. There was a crop of parsnips on
part of the land, which the farmer said would average
5 cwt. a perch, or 22½ tons per acre.

If I were to go to any country town in England, and
obtain, in like manner, particulars of lands for sale, the
nearest to be at least two miles distant from a town or
from a railway station, the average price of four farms
lying in different directions would certainly not be much
more than £50 an acre. Places might be selected where
this average would be exceeded. But I made no selection
in Jersey. There is not a road or parish in the island
in which I did not made inquiry. From more than a
score of farmers, in different parts of Jersey, I obtained
an answer to the question, " What is your average crop
of wheat?" and I am understating the general level of
their response, when I say that the average of Jersey is

30 cabots to the vergée, which is equal to 37½ bushels per acre; while the highest estimate of the average produce of the large farms of England that I have ever met with, is only 28 bushels to the acre. But even with this large production, wheat is not regarded by the Jersey farmer as a highly profitable crop. Wheat is grown upon a considerable extent of land because the farmer must have straw; and although the soil is by no means very suitable, the largest area, second only to that under potatoes, is occupied by wheat. In 1876, there were no fewer than 6233 vergées under wheat. In the same year, there were in Jersey nearly 9000 vergées, equal to a tenth of the whole island, under potatoes, to the growth of which the wheat-straw of the previous year, in the shape of manure, had been devoted. It is a common saying in Jersey that the English go to the "workhouse," which in the happier island is called the "hospital," as they have no workhouse, in the English sense of the word. Jerseymen look upon the English as an unthrifty people (as indeed they are), as a people who in farming have never learnt to work early and late, and to eat the bread of carefulness. An Englishman, it is quite proverbial, rarely succeeds as a Jersey farmer ; he has been trained in a land where the example of frugality, such as pro- prietors only afford, has never been before his eyes. A Frenchman rarely fails : an Englishman not seldom goes to the "hospital." What little pauperism has to be dealt with is for the most part (I write after careful inquiry and observation) imported from the larger islands of the United Kingdom.

I asked one of the most prosperous men in Jersey

whether he should like to change his condition in life,
and for what ? His reply came without hesitation. " I
should like to be an English farmer," he said. " Why ? "
" Why ?—why, because they walk about all day with
their hands in their pockets." " But," I urged, " they
don't in any five years get much more than half as much
produce out of the land as you do ? " " That's true, I
believe," he said; " but I should like to drive a gig, like
an English farmer, and take it easy." " You could take
it easy," I replied, " if you liked; but you have trained
yourself differently. I know of no 20,000 acres in
England on which the farmers have as much money as
you Jerseymen. The British farmer has no hold on the
land, and he is not thrifty; but you—did you not tell me
that Jerseymen have lost lately, in foreign bonds and
unsound companies, not less than a million sterling ? "
" Ah yes," he said, " there's no lounging about here, and
looking at a ploughman instead of doing the work
yourself." Rain came on, and the farmer went indoors,
but not to " take it easy." The Jersey farmer is never
idle. There is not a potato sown in that area of more
than 4000 acres, which has not been " sprouted " in
boxes or trays, stored one upon another, either in the
farmer's house or in some outbuilding. During his
" leisure " hours in the autumn, the Jersey farmer selects
his seed—always good potatoes, and generally of large size.
He has prepared his trays, four or five inches deep, and
about fifty inches in length by eighteen wide. He takes
every seed potato separately in his hand, and sets it on
end with the " eyes " carefully placed uppermost. Sometimes this is done on the floor of spare rooms, where the

potatoes stand on end, each supported by others, in thousands, to be transferred, by another careful handling, to boxes when the sprouting has commenced. In the winter months the sprouting seeds are sometimes thinly covered with sawdust or cut straw. The farmer's object is to get them as forward as possible before the time of planting, and to secure them against being nipped by frost. It is usually in November that the seed potatoes are arranged in trays to sprout for early planting. When the new year comes, the Jersey farmer knows that his potatoes are growing faster in the boxes than they would in the ground; he is in good time if he plants his potatoes by the end of March. The greatest authority upon potato-growing in Jersey writes: "If the seed has been well sprouted in boxes in February, the produce [of those planted at the end of March] will be fit for digging within a week or ten days later than those planted in January, with the probability of double the crop."* There is nothing of the rude style of English farming; no sprout is allowed to remain above the surface until danger of frost is past; "covering at night must not be neglected [and it is not neglected], if the sky is clear and the wind ranging from N. to N.E." That is the direction for the end of March. In April, the Jersey farmer is still on the watch against frost; but, as a rule, he then puts about 500 lbs. of guano to the acre, and points it to its work with a fork. The result is an export of about 30,000 tons of potatoes at a high price, because they arrive early in the English markets.

We have seen that the average price of agricultural

* "The Gardener's Calendar," Jersey, 1877.

land is very much higher in Jersey than in England, that
the farms are, according to English ideas, very small, and
that the farmer is usually the proprietor. We have also
seen that the produce is much greater. Jersey is prosperous because the people have free land ; because, with
insignificant exceptions, the land is saleable ; because insolvency is followed by sale : and the price is high because
there are many buyers; the small capitalist who can
make ten per cent. on his purchase money is not driven
away by fear of delay and the cost of law, to make way
for the buyer who will give half as much and make only
three per cent. The customs of Jersey are not all that
could be desired, and the title to land is sometimes
needlessly complicated, but the process of transfer by
registration is simple and popular. I had the pleasure
of meeting one of the largest proprietors in the island ;
his immense property, for such it seems to most Jerseymen, is 300 vergées, more than 100 acres, in extent. He
told me that he thought his expenses for the purchase
of that land, which cost £8000, rather high—and he
added that the amount was under £5. He said, and his
statement was confirmed by others, that in the purchase
of property worth £500, all costs would not exceed £1.
He showed me his " deeds." A Jerseyman has no fear that
his parchments are the records of forgery, nor is his rest
troubled as to their custody. He does not, like the less
happy Englishman, leave his "deeds" with his solicitor,
with the knowledge that there will be costs attending
upon every application concerning those documents. A
Jerseyman's "deeds" are worth 3d. per 100 words, just so
much and no more. He would have no objection to your

throwing them on the fire, if you will take the trouble
to call at the registrar's office, and pay for new copies,
which, upon his application, will be given to you readily
and with much courtesy.   Is it wonderful that those are
" happier isles," where men can deal thus freely with the
foundation of all prosperity!   Yet they have nothing
but this.   The cost of the necessaries of life, take things
all round, is greater in Jersey than in England.   But
their soil is not, as ours is, blighted by entail and settlement.   It will be said that by their toil upon their
small farms they employ and feed the greater labour
which the land obtains, and that is all.   Let us see.
The total area of Jersey, in statute acres, is 28,717 acres.
The cultivated portion is 20,623 acres in extent—a
proportion, we may remark by the way, which obtains
nowhere without peasant proprietary.   The number of
occupiers of agricultural land, is 2309,* giving an
average of about nine acres for each holding.   If we
take each occupier to represent six persons, including
helpers, that will be a liberal allowance for the number
directly engaged in, and living by, the cultivation of the
soil.   That would account for 13,854 of the population.
The total population of Jersey, according to the census
of 1871, was 56,627, of whom more than 34,000 live in
the parish and suburbs of St. Heliers.   The estimate of
13,854 as that of the purely agricultural population
cannot be very incorrect.   In each of the other eleven
parishes there is a village in which there is some non-
agricultural population.   Now, my assertion is this :
that these 13,854 persons produce a very far greater

* Parish Returns for 1876, " British Press Almanack," Jersey, 1877.

quantity of food from 20,623 acres, than any other equal number of population, upon any equal area, in the United Kingdom. In regard to the chief articles of food, the large non-agricultural population of the island is supported by the surplus produce of the Jersey farms ; and during the months of summer, there is an average of 4000 visitors resident in the island, who are also, for the most part, sustained by the productions of Jersey agriculture. But in addition to this vast consumption of food within an island more densely populated than the larger islands of the United Kingdom, and in which the people enjoy a higher standard of comfort than the people of Great Britain or Ireland, the exports from Jersey for 1876, the last year I have at hand, were as follows :

Cattle	...	...	...	...	...	2,134 head.
Bricks	...	...	...	...	...	1,152,500
Butter	...	...	...	...	...	2,712 lbs.
Raw Fruit ...	...	...	...	...	63,889 cwt.
Potatoes	...	...	...	...	...	26,493 tons.
Vegetables	...	...	...	...	2,206 cwt.

Jersey, and the same may be said of Guernsey, is thus productive, and prosperous, and populous, because the people are not divorced from the soil. In England there are not a few societies for the encouragement of thrift, of frugal and saving habits. How is it that we need so grievously, and that the teeming population of Jersey have no need for, such institutions ? Is it not clearly because our people are debarred, by the continuance of obsolete laws and customs, from learning lessons of carefulness from the land, the mother of all thrift ? What is the first, and greatest, and most universal lesson of economy, which is taught to all people,

and to all countries, but least of all to the people of Great
Britain and Ireland ?   Is it not the periodical recurrence
of harvest ?   Is it not in the fact that there is a seed-
time and a harvest; that there is no continual harvest;
that store must be made for those seasons in which there
is no harvest ? The population who never learn economy
in that school, the greatest of all elementary schools,
have never displayed, and will never display, the cardinal
virtues of thrift and frugality.   In the subservience
of our Legislature to the maintenance of those perishing
laws and systems which are here denounced, which
favour the aggregation of the land in the possession of a
few families, there have been displayed from time to time
feeble and futile efforts to teach thrift to our population.
But it would be as easy for these well-meaning philan-
thropists to push this island from its solid foundation
in the earth to a junction with France, as to make the
British and Irish people thrifty while access is denied to
the natural instruction of the soil.

CHAPTER XVIII.

PEASANT PROPRIETORSHIP (*Continued*).

I HAVE now given some reasons for the belief that, with
a system of free land, not only would the peasant proprietor be a buyer of land even at higher prices than are
now common, but also, that when he acquired habits of
frugality and spontaneous industry which have been
banished from the United Kingdom by the divorce of
the people from the soil, he need not fear the competition
of the larger farmers, nor would he have any inducement
to part with the freehold of his land. What has led to
the belief, so general in the minds of Englishmen, that none
but a rich man will buy a security of which the stated
annual value to an average tenant will return but two
or at most three per cent. ? Do the working classes club
their savings together to buy a Turkish or Honduras bond ?
Are they not in all countries investors in the firmest class
of securities ? Here they cannot buy land, because they
know nothing of the custody of deeds, and are altogether
turned away by habit from the incalculable costs, the
intricacy, the delay, the difficulty of purchasing land.
But to the extent of sixty or seventy millions they

accept a security in the Savings Banks, much less remunerative than the estates of the landowner. In those countries where, most wisely and beneficially, every facility is afforded to them as well as to others, for investment in land, and equally in public funds, they avail themselves largely of such opportunities. It is not only due to the law of subdivision, but also to economic law, that in France there are 5,000,000 landowners who are also farmers. It is chiefly due to economic law that the debt of France is held by 4,000,000, while that of England is in the hands of only 250,000 persons. The beadles of the Bank of England, and of the Auction Mart, like true representatives of English systems, frown upon small men. A man who looks as if he gained his livelihood by the labour of his hands cannot be a buyer at the Auction Mart—it is quite contrary to the habits of the country. Why? Plainly because he cannot afford, and will not consent, to encounter a long delay and an incalculable cost in the business of purchase. The large buyer is encouraged, for upon his purchase the cost of conveyance can amount only to a small percentage. Say that a man has saved £500, and that the idea, so delightful to the minds of most men, of purchasing a small property upon which to spend his loving labour and the remainder of his life, presents itself to his imagination. In this country, and in this country only, the thought is chilled and checked, because he has no assurance that the cost of purchase may not amount to a fourth or even to a third of his store; and if the purchase money exceed his possessions, and he wishes to raise a further sum by way of mortgage, that process, to be repeated perhaps at the end of three years, may involve him in a life-long charge for legal costs equal to the amount of the mortgagee's interest.

How differently is his fellow-subject in the happier island of Jersey situated ! To begin with, he knows that the whole business can be settled in a day. The brief contract which declares that the land has passed from the vendor to himself is certified in their presence by a judicial officer, and transcribed upon the registration books, protected, in duplicate, and in separate buildings (in fire-proof chambers), by the Government of the island. After searching those books for some hours, I did not succeed in finding a deed containing more words than do three of these pages. The registration fees are well known. The tariff is public,—100 words, 1s. ; not exceeding 200 words, 2s. 3d. ; for every additional 100, or part of 100, 1s. Very many contracts are under 200 words, for which the charge would be 2s. 3d. About 6d. more ($\frac{1}{4}$th) is charged for the duplicate copy. Contracts are registered in duplicate for greater security and convenience. The solicitor's charge is three times the amount of the first registration, so that the total cost would be less than 10s., and the purchaser's mind is not weighted with custody of deeds. It may be asked, "How do the lawyers live under a system of this sort ?" I am inclined to believe that while there is no waste of labour, the amount received in fees by lawyers in Jersey is much larger per acre than in England. In Jersey, in 1876, there were 2,754 contracts relating to real property admitted by the Royal Court. Are there 2,000—are there 300—conveyances a year in regard to any 28,000 acres of rural England ?

With reference to production, the Isle of Wight is

barren compared with the Channel Islands. "The Isle of
Wight has not one peasant proprietor, and with 86,810
acres of land has a population of 55,362, and scarcely any
commerce or shipping." * Compare this with Jersey, an
island not more favoured in soil and climate, and with all
the disadvantage of lying remote from England. Jersey
has, on the same reckoning, 20,623 acres, and 56,627 population, including the owners of not less than 23,349 tons of
shipping,† by which trade is carried on with all quarters
of the world. To argue that the price of land is high in
England displays ignorance of facts; to argue that it is
high because its possession is a "luxury" could receive
no more signal contradiction than by comparison of the
value of agricultural land in Jersey and in the Isle
of Wight. In the former the price is nearly double that
which obtains in the latter. How indeed should it be
otherwise ? "To improve land with profit," says Adam
Smith, most truly, "like all other commercial projects,
requires an exact attention to small savings and small
gains, of which a man born to a great fortune, even
though naturally frugal, is very seldom capable. The
situation of such a person naturally disposes him to
attend rather to ornament which pleases his fancy, than
to profit for which he has so little occasion. He em-
bellishes perhaps four or five hundred acres in the
neighbourhood of his house, at ten times the expense
which the land is worth after all his improvements, and
finds that if he was to improve all his estate in the same
manner, and he has little taste for any other, he would be

---

* " Land Systems," by T. E. Cliffe Leslie, 1870.
† Jersey Shipping List, corrected to 31st Oct., 1876.

a bankrupt before he had finished the tenth part of it." *
In another page, Adam Smith has drawn a picture. "The
small proprietor—who knows every part of his little
territory, who views it with all the affection which
property, especially small property, naturally inspires,
and who, upon that account, naturally takes pleasure, in
not only cultivating, but in adorning it—is generally of
all improvers the most industrious, the most intelligent,
and the most successful."

Look at him in Belgium! That is a country, like
England, of great manufacturing industry. But it is a
country of very inferior soil. It is a country in which
I saw, in the summer of 1879, women scratching with
their fingers, fair crops of potatoes from nearly white
sand—a miracle of agricultural industry, of thrift, and
of perseverance, such as belong only to peasant proprietorship. It is a country from which we may learn,
as well as from the Channel Islands, the error of that
dogma in British agriculture—that large farms are
invariably more productive than small farms.

In these Chapters we maintain the following propositions : 1. That the large farms of England produce more
than the large farms of the Continent, because, as a rule,
the soil is superior and the farming capital is greater.
2. That the largest produce of grain of all sorts, as well
as of meat, is gathered from small farms, from the land
of peasant proprietors. 3. That rent and saleable value
are highest upon peasant properties. We do not propose
to "make" peasant proprietors ; we say that were free
land established the force of economic law would intro-

* "Wealth of Nations," book iii. c. ii.

duce such persons to the possession of land. In England there is no training for peasant farmers; the peasant is encouraged to be thriftless. Why should he be frugal when the workhouse is the almost certain bourne of his old age? The peasant farmer where he exists in England is one of a scattered, an unnatural, class, generally a "ne'er-do-weel," a "wastrel," attempting on a patch of land the routine of husbandry adopted by his neighbours who are farmers of hundreds of acres. He has no knowledge whatever of the frugal ways and means, of the incessant industry, of those who live in communities of peasant farmers. The business of turning sand or clay into gold is altogether foreign to his habits. He spends all or nearly all he can get. And so much is this the rule, that every Englishman regards the manner of life or the standard of comfort adopted by a peasant, as the exact measure of his means. The Englishman indeed carries this home-grown view abroad, and accordingly blunders in his estimate of the wealth of peasant proprietors. "So little are English travellers accustomed to consider it possible that a labourer should not spend all he earns, that they habitually mistake the signs of economy for those of poverty." * "The advocate of great estates and large farms," says Mr. Clife Leslie (referring to Ireland though the remark is of general application), "points to a squatter here and there, who has cleared a piece of land, and becomes the fee-simple proprietor, yet farms no better, and lives perhaps in more squalor than the neighbouring tenants at will. Small farming is a difficult art, which will not grow spontaneously from out the

* J. S. Mill, "Political Economy," book ii. c. 4.

ground as soon as a peasant is planted upon it as owner. Such a peasant proprietor will probably not thrive; he will do as his fathers did and as his neighbours do, with that which he regards as the privilege of doing it more lazily. Improvement—civilisation in every one of its forms—must be the work of many." Who desires to understand the spirit which animates peasant proprietorship, " let him," as the same writer advises from personal observation, "for instance, look round the roots of the lean firs, beside the station of Mille-Pommes, the next station to St. Nicholas, in the Pays de Waes. What would an English large farmer give for land like that— what could he make of it ? What the Fleming will give for it, and what small farming can make of it, may be stated in figures. By the side of a cultivated hectare which would sell for £120, a hectare in a state of nature, sells for £12." To a landlord, not intending to be an occupier, such land, which is much like many of the unenclosed lands of Surrey, would be worth £12; he could make three or four per cent. by letting it for sporting. But the peasant makes ten per cent., and the value— which he would never impart were he not the owner— doubles, and doubles, and doubles. "The £12 are given " continues Mr. Leslie, "for the natural hectare, only because it can afterwards be made worth £120. It is potential value only—or, in other words, room for the peasant to work in, for the bestowal of his time, his thrift, and his long labor of love—that the hectare brings of its own." Contrast this, which is characteristic of every country in which there is simplicity of transfer, and no wholesale withdrawal of land from markets by

entail and settlement,—contrast this with the late Sir
Robert Peel's description of English agriculture, in his
letter to Mr. Caird: "You will find immense tracts of
good land, in counties with good roads, good markets,
and a moist climate, that remain pretty nearly in a
state of nature. Nothing has hitherto been effectual
in awakening the proprietors to a sense of their own
interests." *

It is common, in making comparison between English
and Belgian agriculture, to dismiss the matter with a
decisive reference to the larger production of wheat per
acre in this country. As for green crops, it is one of
what Mrs. Norton called "dear boastful England's
proudest blind boasts," that she invented them all.
Yet it is to the land now known as Belgium that we
owe the hop and the carrot; and from one of the earliest
works on English agriculture, written in 1650, by a
Sir Richard Weston, upon "The Husbandry used in
Brabant and Flanders," and entitled "A Discourse
Showing Wonderful Improvement of Land There, and
Serving as a Pattern for our Practice in this Commonwealth,"—we learn that persons then living recollected
"the first gardener who came into Surrey to plant
cabbages, cauliflowers, and to sow turnips, carrots, parsnips, and pease, all which at that time were great
wonders, we having few or none but what came from
Holland and Flanders." Farming in Flanders has
always been "small farming," and it is from Flanders,
Weston states, that Englishmen learnt the value of
crops of clover. But to return to wheat—a crop for

* "English Agriculture," by James Caird.

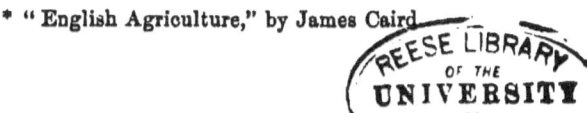

which the soil of Belgium is peculiarly unsuitable. Peasant proprietorship is denounced as a failure because the yield of wheat per acre is inferior to that of England and the case of large farms against small farms is tried upon this single issue. To prove that this is a false comparison, it will be sufficient to show that there are large farms in Belgium, and that those large Belgium farms produce much less wheat per acre than the small farms; and that, of the small farms, the least productive are those which do not belong to the cultivators, but which are farmed by rack-rented peasants upon short leases or yearly tenancies. The large farms of Belgium are in the south-east; in Hainault, Liège, Namur, and Luxembourg: West and East Flanders, in the opposite direction, are much subdivided. We learn from official statistics that the proportion of farms of 100 hectares and upwards in the two last provinces is respectively 0.02 and 0.01 per cent.; while in the former, the figures are 0.11, 0.26, 0.93, 0.77. * But the cultivation of Flanders is far superior to that of the eastern provinces. " The large farmers of Hainault and Namur do not buy manure, fancying they would ruin themselves by doing so. The Flemish small farmers invest from fifteen to twenty millions of francs in guano every year, and quite as much in other kinds of manure. Where does large farming make such advances?"† "On the ten-acre farms of Flanders, the crops are heavier by a fourth than on the hundred-acre farms of La Hesbaie [in the province of Liège], and as heavy again as on the farms of two hundred and fifty acres in Le Condroz."‡

---

* "Cobden Club Essays," 1870, p. 244.   † Ibid. p. 246.
‡ "Peasant Proprietors," by W. T. Thornton, C.B.

Of this latter district, M. de Laveleye writes: "The Condroz [provinces of Namur and Liège] is the region of Belgium which counts the greatest number of large farms; those which reach 250 acres, so rare in the Flemish provinces, being met here often enough. As soon as a farm is divided in Condroz, the land is better cultivated, and the number of cattle increases. The small proprietors who farm their own five or six acres know no fallow; their crops are more varied and better kept; the produce is much larger; they raise beetroot, colza, and turnips; their corn is taller and carries more grain. Thus, then, a too large size of the farms is one cause of the inferiority of the farming in Condroz."

The average production of wheat in Belgium is diminished by including the large farms; and of small farms, the most productive are only that minority belonging to peasant proprietors. We learn from an official statement of recent date and conclusive authority, that in East Flanders, of 88,300 * cultivators of less than three hectares (little more than 7¼ acres), only 32,201 are proprietors, and 37,283 are tenants under leases generally for nine years. But on an average of the farms in that district, the yield of wheat is six or eight bushels higher than that of England. Mr. Rham, a very careful writer on " Flemish Husbandry," † set the average of the Pays de Waes, in Flanders, at 32 to 36 bushels, and he wrote at a time when Mr. Caird set the average of England at 26 bushels. ‡ " Of barley, a more congenial cereal, the

---

* Enquête Agricole, Paris.
† "Outlines of Flemish Husbandry," by W. Rham.
‡ " English Agriculture," by James Caird.

average is in Flanders 41 bushels, and on good ground
60 bushels; while in England it is probably under 33,
and would certainly be overstated at 36 bushels." *

Perhaps the surest test of productive agriculture is
the number of cattle, and in this respect England is not
superior to Belgium. According to recent Agricultural
Returns, there were in Great Britain 9,730,000 cattle and
32,220,000 sheep. At the calculation of six sheep to one
head of cattle, this would give a total of about 15,000,000
cattle, which is at the rate of one to three acres of the
cultivated land. The Belgian does as much with smaller
capital, and upon terribly inferior land. Mr. Rham says,
" A beast for every three acres is a common Flemish proportion; and on very small occupations, where spade
husbandry is used, the proportion is still greater." In
1873, Mr. Thornton counted on a farm of 32 acres near
Ypres, besides horses, eight cows, six bullocks, a calf and
four pigs; and was told by the farmer that over and
above what his own cattle yielded, he purchased no less
than £200 worth of manure annually. But from what
soil do these averages come, to compare with the rich
lands of England, where sandy districts are so few and
far between? "It is the worst soil in all Europe; sterile
sand like that of La Campine and of Brandenburg. A
few miles from Antwerp, land sells for 20 francs (16s.)
an acre, and those who buy it for the purpose of cultivation get ruined. Having been fertilised by ten centuries
of laborious husbandry, it does not yield a single crop
without being manured—a fact unique in Europe. If in
a Flemish farm of 25 acres, there were but five or six

* " Peasant Proprietors," by W. T. Thornton, C.B.

acres of Irish soil, forming good natural pasture, it would
be worth one-third more. Not a blade of grass grows in
Flanders without manure. Irish soil might be bought
to fertilise the soil of the Fleming. The ideal, the dream
of the Flemish farmer—is a few acres of good grass. In
Ireland [as in England] nature supplies grass in
abundance." * M. de Laveleye, in the same essay, has
furnished a table showing that the small-farm provinces,
the Flanders, own more cattle, yield more produce, are
more carefully cultivated, and have more agricultural
capital, than those in which large estates are predominant.
In the table, East Flanders is compared with Namur,
and it is to be noticed that in the former province the
land is poorer than in the latter.

	Namur.	East Flanders.
Heads of cattle per 100 hectares	35	68
Working capital per hectare	250 francs	450 francs
Products per hectare	300 „	600 „
Rent per hectare	50 „	93 „
Average selling price of land per hectare ...	1804 „	3218 „
Number of inhabitants per 100 hectares ...	138	263

It is the same everywhere. In Lombardy, in the
province of Como, where small farming prevails, the
value of the cattle per hectare in cultivation is 161
francs; whilst in the province of Mantua, with its large
farms and fine pasture-land, it is but 94 francs.†

It is the same in France. Agricultural land fetches
a higher price than in England, and the average produce
of France is diminished by including the inferior yield

* "Land System of Belgium," by M. de Laveleye, 1870.
† "La Proprietà fondiaria in Lombardia," by Sig. Tacini.

of the large farms. "At the present day," says M. Hippolyte Passy, "on the same area and under equal circumstances, the largest clear produce is yielded by small farming, which besides, by increasing the population, opens a safe market to the products of manufacturing industry." [*] M. Léonce de Lavergne, writing to Mr. Cliffe Leslie under date November 6, 1869, said, "The best cultivation in France, on the whole, is that of the peasant proprietors." It is not merely that the land is divided by the compulsory law of succession, but "the French peasant is the great buyer of land." M. de Laveleye asks, "Which are the richest and most productive provinces of France? Precisely those in which the small landowners are in a majority;" [†] and this agrees with the official report of M. Monny de Mornay, quoted by Mr. Cliffe Leslie in the same volume. M. de Mornay says, "The fact which manifests itself most forcibly, is the profound and continuous alterations in the distribution of the soil among the different classes of the population. In the greater number of departments, the estates of 100 hectares might now be easily counted; and taken altogether, they form but an insignificant part of the national territory. The proportion cannot be stated in figures, because it varies from one department to another; one must confine one's self to saying that the west and south [where cultivation is inferior] have preserved more large estates than the north and east." The prosperity of France is wonderful, but it´ is not due to the law of subdivision; [‡] "it

[*] "Memoire de l'Académie de Sciences."
[†] "Cobden Club Essays," p. 255.
[‡] "A Second Visit to La Creuse," by T. E. Cliffe Leslie, 1870.

is observed throughout France that the subdivision
of peasant properties among children by succession
diminishes, instead of increasing, as the owners themselves increase in prosperity." I have myself gathered
evidence to the same effect, both in France and in the
Channel Islands. M. de Mornay, the writer of the
official report upon the Enquête Agricole, to whom I
have before referred, says, " The price of parcels of land
which are within reach of the industry and thrift of the
peasant, increases at a remarkable rate. The competition of buyers is active, and sales in small lots take place
on excellent terms for the seller, when the interval has
been sufficient to allow fresh savings to accumulate."
I know, however, of no more remarkable testimony to
this prosperity, than that of the *Times*, which I hope will
advocate free land in our own country. On the 8th
January, 1877, the *Times* said, " The prosperity of France
makes her the wonder of the world. A yearly revenue
of £109,000,000 is a marvellous proof of what France
can bear without any visible distress. We see how
eminently the national resources are agricultural in the
great contributions from the soil. The Land Tax yields
nearly £7,000,000, and the receipts of the Registration
and Mortgage Duties came to more than £18,600,000.
In great part, these duties are so fruitful because the
French Law of Succession makes the ownership of the
soil constantly move from one hand to another. Small
as well as large patches of land, are sold every day in
all the communes, and they form the favourite investment
of the peasantry. Thus, in 1869, the registration fees on
the sale of land yielded nearly £6,000,000, and they will

give M. Léon Say a considerably larger sum during the present year. The proceeds of the Succession Duties for 1869 were also large, amounting as they did to nearly £4,000,000." That was the largest revenue ever raised by any nation in time of peace, and it was mainly the fruit of peasant proprietorship.

CHAPTER XIX.

PEASANT PROPRIETORSHIP (*Continued*).

WE do not demand free land in order to create peasant proprietary. We join cordially with Mr. Caird in recommending the extension of the provisions of the " Bright " clauses of the Irish Land Act to England and Scotland, and agree with him in thinking that there would be here a much more rapid appropriation of the advantages than has occurred in Ireland. In both islands, however, the enactment of free land would make a vast difference in the disposition of the people towards such provisions. We do not advocate any interference with the power of a landowner to bequeath his land undivided. We say, that the consequence of free land would be (1) an active competition for small lots of agricultural land; (2) the increase of farming capital, by attracting investors, and by leading farmers to hold fewer acres with more capital ; (3) a very large increase in the number of owners of agricultural land, and a disposition to sell land in small lots in order to suit small purchasers, who would, with advantage to themselves, give prices much above those now obtained ; and (4) that the tendency—which is a political danger as well as a hindrance to production—towards a diminution

Y

in the number of landowners would be arrested and reversed. We have seen that the distribution of land in this country is not the result of economic law, by observing that where economic law prevails there is a tendency to increase in the number of small proprietors. The possession of land where the unrestricted action of economic law is permitted, must tend towards those who will give the highest price for it; and, as a broad rule, it may be said, those are they in whose possession it can be made most productive.

We have seen that the large farms of England are more productive, because they are better supplied with capital, than the large farms of the Continent; but, that they are much less productive than the small farms of our own islands in the Channel, and than many of the less fertile farms of Flanders,—and the same might be said of not a few of the small farms of France and Switzerland. The reason why those small farms are more productive than our large farms is probably the same as that which makes our large farms produce more than those of the Continent. It may be that in money, or saleable stock, some of our farmers have a capital per acre larger than that of the peasants of Jersey and Flanders. But the calculators who make much of this, have for the most part forgotten to assess the extraordinary value of the peasant and his family, who, as they toil from morning till night, in a manner which belongs only to proprietorship, are good for a considerable sum of tenant's capital.

It is a very common error to suppose that there is invariably great economy in extensive agricultural opera-

tions, and that therefore much higher income per acre
will be earned in wages of superintendence by large
farmers, than by labouring farmers upon small areas.
Lord Derby delivered in 1871 a speech, to which further
reference will be made in connection with Ireland, in
which he appears to have made a mistake of this sort.
He assumed that the peasant cultivator, "honest, industrious, and frugal," was a man who in the nature of
things must always be in antagonism to the "combination of capital and science," just as is the hand-loom
weaver in these days of steam power. But that, we
have seen, is a fallacy. We have seen the peasant cultivator in Jersey and Flanders employing the combination
of science and capital in steam-threshing machines, the
use of which is far more universal in Jersey than in the
Isle of Wight. And the error will be still more patent
when steam-ploughing becomes more extended. The
large farmers of England do not face the combination of
capital and science. Each one of them does not purchase
for himself a steam plough at £800, and a steam threshing-
machine at £300. If ten peasant farmers join together
to work a steam-threshing machine, as we have seen them
doing in Jersey, they may unite in laying their lands
open to a steam plough. And the future of agriculture,
so far as the delving of the soil is concerned, will tend to
be divided between hand labour and steam power—the
spade and the steam plough.

The British farmer finds himself in difficulties because
his capital is spread over too much land. Superintendence is not so profitable in agriculture as in manufacture.
The agricultural labourer for wages can never be made to

work with the zeal of the peasant proprietor. If free land were fully established in England, the intelligent among the large farmers would prosper with security of tenure, with ample capital, and a superintendence sufficiently but not too widespread. I have no belief in a universal system of small farms. It is probable that the largest farms in Western Europe are not to be found in England. The farm of M. Cail at La Briche, near Tours, is nearly 4000 acres in extent. His barns and beet-root sugar factory are almost perfect in arrangement. But M. Cail's crops would appear small beside the crops of a Jersey farmer. It is not possible for M. Cail or for any one else to distribute over 4000 acres the personal care and energy, in the way of superintendence, that is given by the smaller farmers. When machinery was first largely introduced into agriculture, it was the opinion of many that there would be such an increase in the average size of farms as would admit of the possession and constant employment of the best machinery by each farmer. But that idea is now entirely exploded. If a farmer of 200 or 300 acres were to possess himself of all the best steam and horse machinery, he must devote a considerable part of his time to the business of letting it out for hire among his neighbours, and neglect the proper affairs of his farm. The size of farms is, and must ever remain, an open question. The machinery test has not proved valid. Indeed, even in a business admitting so easily of supervision as the cotton manufacture, machinery is engaged with several capitals. It is common in some parts of Lancashire for the steam power to belong to one man, and the manufacturing machinery

which is set in motion by that power to belong to several
persons, each having a separate floor in the same mill.
With free land, the size of farms would depend upon
the character of soil, the circumstances of the neighbourhood, and especially upon the capital and capacity of
individuals. It should be in farming as in other business ;—the man with extraordinary faculty of organization and control would have a wide area; the man of
opposite characteristics would have greater success upon
twenty acres, and he would obtain them in England as
he does on the mainland of the Continent, when, by the
establishment of a free land system, he had forgotten that
terror of legal proceedings which ages of bitter experience have engrained in the national character, and when
the taste for a thrifty and more independent life had, by
means of such reform, become established. The small
farmer would outbid all other purchasers in certain
places, as he does in all countries where the land is not
settled, and where there is simplicity and certainty in
the transfer and the title. If he did not farm well and
profitably, with the hire, when necessary, of the best
machinery, his property would quickly pass from him ;
and it would probably not be added, as it now is, to the
next large estate, because another small capitalist, the
farm being suitable, would probably give more than the
squire could afford to give for the land. Why should he
not ? There are thousands of persons of that class who
are now giving 40 years' purchase for the income they
derive from the Post Office Savings Banks ; and if the
vague fear of law were removed, and equal certainty and
simplicity given in obtaining possession of land, the small

capitalist would often prove to be the highest bidder. Rents are falling, farmers are in difficulty now in England, because the land is for the most part held by tenants who have neither the capital nor the energy to obtain, as they otherwise might, a greater and more profitable produce from the soil. Instead of making large investments in manure, and feeding stuffs, and labour, and manufacturing £5 worth of fat meat for every acre of land they hold—which Mr. Mechi and others have proved to be possible,—they obtain permission from their landlords to lay down more and more land in permanent pasture, for which they can, if need be, pay more rent, because upon such land they require little capital or labour. That is the sort of farming which free land would drive from the soil, because it would introduce to the business of agriculture active and intelligent men of the industrial classes. There are large farmers who achieve great results. Let us look at the case of one—a Norfolk farmer, Mr. John Hudson of Castle Acre. Mr. Hudson told Mr. Mechi * that during his long tenure (25 to 30 years) of a farm of 1200 acres, he had expended £70,000 in cake, and £50,000 in artificial manures; and Mr. Mechi saw for himself that, in a favourable year, Mr. Hudson had produced upon a 40-acre field of wheat, the amazing crop of 8½ quarters = 68 bushels per acre. But Mr. Mechi says something more than this of Mr. Hudson;—" He jocularly said to his landlord, 'The top or ploughed soil is mine; I made it; the subsoil belongs to your lordship.'" With regard to security therefore, this enterprising man was farming over a volcano, and few men would do that

* "How to Farm Profitably," p. 491.

after the manner of Mr. Hudson. He was dependent for the security of his capital upon the honour and upon the uncertain life of his landlord. There are small farmers in Jersey, in Belgium, in France, and in Switzerland, who make quite as great an outlay per acre as did Mr. Hudson, but they never do this unless they have the security of ownership; and to obtain that, which is the only sufficient security, they give enormous prices for the freehold of their land. Instead of farms becoming larger, a very great number must be diminished in England, in order to become more profitable. The capital and labour must be more concentrated, and must penetrate deeper into the soil. "We all farm too much land," says Mr. Mechi, "and so complain of want of capital.* Experience teaches me that our cultivation is too shallow, our manure too little, and our produce too small. No man ever ruined his root and green crops by filling the land to the depth of 2 feet with good manure. When I told my farming friends that Mr. Bagley of Fulham grew 70 tons of mangel per acre, and sold them, at 20s. per ton, to Mr. Rhodes the cow-keeper, there was a shout of laughter, and something said about a 'crammer;' but market gardeners, who cultivate four times as deeply, and manure four times as heavily as ordinary farmers, look upon such a crop as nothing extraordinary. Our tillage is miserably shallow . . . I see before me," adds Mr. Mechi, "a man who lost most of his money on 50 acres, but now, keeping the same amount of stock upon 10 acres, he is recovering himself and paying his way." † There are other method of doubling our produce. Thou-

* "How to Farm Profitably," p. 493.　　† Ibid. p. 501.

sands of acres of grass land in England might be made
to keep more than double the number of cattle and
sheep, by irrigation with river water, or, better still, with
the sewage of towns.

It is likely that in future the cultivation of the soil
will, for the most part, be by steam power and by manual
labour.   Deep cultivation by horse power is very costly.
On average land, a farm horse, to be kept in good condition, requires the produce of four to five acres.   The
animal is liable to sickness and to death ; and is continually approaching a useless condition of old age.
Moreover, cultivation by horse power has this inalienable
defect on clay land, that the horses, by treading the subsoil, diminish the fertility of the ground.   It is essential
for the best cultivation that the surface soil should be
rich, and that the subsoil should freely admit both air
and water to the artificial or natural drainage ; and on
clay soils, however deep the cultivation, the pressure of
horses dragging a plough, which cause a great addition
to their own weight, tends to place an impermeable
stratum between the plant and the drain pipes, to the
serious injury of the crop.   Deep cultivation and a porous
subsoil are especially essential for root crops.   Mr. Dixon,
on a farm near Witham, produced a parsnip the root
of which broke off at a length of thirteen feet six inches.
Mr. Mechi saw that extraordinary growth, and asked
himself, " Why did that parsnip go so deep ? Because the
earth had all been moved to the depth of fourteen feet.
It had been a brick-earth pit, filled up with soil from the
adjoining land, when it was necessary to open a new pit ;
air and water had circulated freely to the depth of four-

teen feet." In cultivation by steam or with spade, the subsoil is not trodden and kneaded into watertight puddle. Manure is wasted if the roots of plants cannot penetrate the subsoil. There can be no doubt whatever that spade cultivation with abundant manure would treble the produce of many lands in England. Nor can there be any question that a continually increasing area will be thus cultivated by manual labour. The area of separate properties cultivated in this way will be small, but there is no reason whatever why both small and large growers of wheat should not make use of the steam plough. When I next visit Jersey, I expect to see reaping machines and probably steam ploughs passing over the lands of three or four farmers in one operation. They themselves tell me there would be no difficulty in the matter; that they could co-operate in the use of a reaping machine or steam plough as easily as they do with regard to the steam threshing machine. It is not likely that in future the produce of agriculture will be drawn to market towns and to railway stations, to any great extent, by horse power. The traction engine must win its way, and it will not be the property of the farmer. Corn might be carried to mill or railway station by steam power, at less than one-third the cost at present expended. In these times, country gentlemen are all-powerful in counties, and they dislike, for obvious reasons, to meet with traction engines on rural roads. The regulations under which the use of such locomotive power is permitted are vexatious and harassing. But such opposition will tend to disappear, and the extravagant costly team of horses will in time become a rare sight on a country road.

There is a wide difference between the labour and the cost of eight horses, and the work and cost of an engine of eight-horse power.   It is expensive to attempt and impossible to succeed in making eight horses pull all together and with continuously equal strain.   The effort to do this, which must involve expenditure and failure, is accomplished with perfect success by one hand upon a steam engine.   A horse which costs at least 2s. for care and keep during five hours, cannot work longer than that time.   Continuous labour during five hours is a day's work for horses at plough.   A single-horse power in a steam engine is, in other words, the evaporation of six gallons, or sixty pounds, of water per hour ; and with an engine of good construction, twelve pounds of coal, worth five farthings, will give a power equivalent to that of a horse costing two shillings. Where hand labour is not more suitable, the general application of steam power to the cultivation of the soil may be deferred, but it must in the end be accomplished ; and perhaps the time is not very distant when it will appear as strange, that a farmer of clay land should allow his subsoil to be trodden into a watertight stratum by four horses, as that a Lancashire weaver should fill his sheds with hand looms.

A comparison of the results of Continental agriculture with that of England is not really important to the question in hand.   The capital employed in every country is insufficient for the best cultivation.   The fact that the largest produce is obtained from small farms merely proves this—that under a system of free land small farms would find and would maintain a place in the national agriculture. I suppose there are no farms in England which produce a larger rent and profit than the dairy farms of Cheshire, the greater number of which range from 30 to 60 acres in extent. Probably the small farms of England under a system of free land would be occupied chiefly with the production of vegetables, meat, milk, cheese and butter.

Before we leave this subject of peasant proprietorship, it would be well to .glance at the views of Mr. James Howard, M.P., an eminent manufacturer of agricultural machinery, and a careful, though somewhat prejudiced, inquirer into matters relating to "Continental Farming and Peasantry," which is the title of a work published by Mr. Howard in 1870. It deserves notice, not only for its intrinsic merits, but because it was received with something like enthusiasm by those who are opposed to the views of the present writer.

Subdivision in France is most notable in the north-west. But even in the department of the North, about Valenciennes, Mr. Howard tells us there are farms of 400 to 600 acres, though we have the report of M. Hamoir, the best known agriculturist of the province, to the effect that 25 acres are considered a large extent, and that 10 acres may be taken as the average. M. Hamoir has known agricultural land in that region sell as high (to peasant proprietors) as £192 per acre. As usual with large farmers, or large proprietors, he deprecates such an outlay; he thinks it "better that the small farmer should not be a proprietor or landowner at the price he pays." Then M. Hamoir, repeating the argument which is so often employed in England to prove that the small capitalist would not buy land, says, "The interest of his money invested in ordinary securities would permit him to hire, even at a high rate, double the quantity of land that he could hold as an owner, but he does not enter upon this path." Now here is a phenomenon! This French peasant, taxed all over the world with morbid thrift, with unnatural frugality, is told that he is reckless in the outlay of his painful savings, and the large landowners and farmers in France, and in foreign countries, look upon him as a stubborn, contumacious animal, with a wonderful faculty for existing on hard fare and for raising the price of land to unheard-of figures. Is this likely to be true? Is it reasonable to suppose that the people who, generation after generation, have put sou to sou, and franc to franc, till a purse was made for purchase, would be thus duped in their expenditure? M. Hamoir, to do him justice, is not so ignorant as to believe this, though he professes to trace such conduct in part to the "ignorance" of the Continental peasantry. M. Hamoir gives, in Mr. Howard's pages, a subordinate place to that which is the real and the abundantly sufficient motive with the peasantry. Their purchase is, in truth, the result of prudence, not of ignorance. They know that their unremitting labour will turn sand to gold, and they know that there is but one way to security—that of ownership. As M. Hamoir puts it, the peasant fears "the short duration of leases, at the end of which he dreads to be ousted for some competitor." There it is; that is the whole story; the full and complete justification of the peasant's prudence and judgment. To be secure he must be proprietor. Mr. Howard makes the common error, the great mistake to which we have already alluded, of confusing that most wretched agriculturist, the cottier tenant, with the peasant proprietor. Referring to the farming of Belgium, in the neighbourhood of Brussels, he heard from M. Verheyden, the principal farmer of the place, occupying 140 acres, at a rental of £240, " that farmers were no politicians, and voted as their landlords wished," and he heard a good deal more to the disadvantage of the small farmers. But that which is most interesting is that M. Verheyden said of the small proprietor class, that they " could never live and pay their way by mere farming; that their mainstay was fruit, vegetables, and poultry." It is strange that this, which is just what their friends would advance as the security of their position, should be said by way of depreciation—that they abandon the common rotation of farming for the production of more valuable crops. Mr. Howard well knows that the secret of successful agriculture is security of tenure, and that wherever land is free from settlement, and transfer is secure and simple, the industrial classes show their sense of these advantages by acquiring the only real security—that of proprietorship. Mr. Howard bears indirect testimony to this fact in regard to that province of Holland—Groningen —which he says possesses " the greatest agricultural wealth of any part of Europe. Here the tenancy is hereditary; and," continues Mr. Howard, " I mention this, not by way of advocating the principle of fixity or perpetuity of tenure, but as a proof that the tendency of length of tenure is to increase production."

The most valuable part of Mr. Howard's work consists of replies to a series of questions relative to the tenure and cultivation of land, which he obtained from persons practically conversant with Continental agriculture. It is a testimony to the straightforwardness of Mr. Howard's work, that I am able to use these replies to destroy his own prejudices. With regard to Belgium, Mr. Howard inquired of the highest official authority— M. Leclerc, Inspector-General of Agriculture,—first, What was the average extent of the farms in the nine provinces of the kingdom? secondly, What was the average rent? thirdly, What was the average selling-price of land in the various provinces? The following is a tabular statement of M. Leclerc's replies:—

	Average Extent of Farms.	Average Rent of Farms.	Average Selling Price per Acre.
	Acres.	£ s. d.	£ s. d.
East Flanders	6¾	1 14 0	69 11 8
Hainault	8	1 15 2	70 14 8
Brabant	8¾	1 12 0	68 17 8
West Flanders	9½	1 6 8	50 19 2
Liège	11¼	1 12 4	57 10 2
Antwerp	12	1 4 0	47 17 6
Limburg	17	0 19 10	34 18 6
Namur	18¾	1 0 4	39 8 6
Luxembourg	28	0 14 0	16 13 10

The testimony of these figures is interesting. They show conclusively that the rent and price, and, we may be sure, the produce of land, are highest where land is most divided; and the reply of Baron Peers, President of the Agricultural Society of West Flanders, is also remarkable. He says, "For third-class land, in large farms, farmers pay 21s.; for medium quality, 29s.; and for the best land, 38*s*. 6*d*. per acre. Small farms let for 29*s*., 40*s*., and 45*s*. per acre, for land of similar quality to the above." The replies Mr. Howard received from France have a similar tendency. M. Hamoir, in the north, says that land sells in large lots at £96, and in small at £144 an acre; and that when there has been a succession of good crops for several years, and the farmer has saved money, the price of small lots is considerably augmented. All those who report to Mr. Howard are what may be called large holders or large proprietors, and they deprecate, as persons in their position always do, the keen competition of smaller capitalists for land. One says that "the peasants are possessed by the demon of property," and another refers to "the land mania so characteristic of the Flemish," while a third declares of the small farmers of France, that "they do not and will not appreciate any other investment than land." I remember that one of the largest proprietors in Jersey, a man possessing about 100 acres, made exactly the same complaint. I thought it fell very naturally from his lips; but, after all, these poorer men are not mad; they have neither demon nor mania; they seek security and they obtain it, at a heavy price, but in the only way in which it can be obtained in their respective countries. Without absolute security they would not, they could not, labour from morning till night for the improvement of their land. Where they have sufficient capital they can double and quadruple the rental value in a few years. But they will not do that on another man's land. No man will do that; no man ever did or ever could do that. Sometimes they are miserably destitute of working capital, and then it is only by a long and painful process that peasant proprietorship produces good crops. But their capital is, as a rule, always much greater per acre than that of the large farmers in their neighbourhood; and that is one of the reasons why in France and Belgium, in Switzerland, and in the Channel Islands, the largest produce is obtained from small farms. Baron Peers, of Flanders, no great admirer of small proprietorship, says of the class of larger farmers, "They often enter upon a farm of from 100 to 125 acres, with a capital of £40, whilst they ought to have £80 to £100. It is only by dint of economy, and privations that they get round, and this at the end of 30 or 40 years." I have never yet heard of a peasant proprietor who entered upon a farm of 10 acres with a working capital of less than 8s. an acre.

I believe I have now established in the minds of all who will give fair consideration to these statements, a conviction that if we had free land in this country, there would be farming proprietors, not established by force of any law of subdivision, but rather establishing themselves, by natural selection of the fittest for such occupation, in which the right men could afford to give very much higher prices than are now obtained for agricultural land. I have myself no fear whatever that the dwindling in the number of agricultural landowners, which is now a dangerous feature of our social system, would not be arrested if the country were made free from settlement, and the transfer were secure and simple; and, as Mr. J. S. Mill has truly said, "Whatever facilitates land passing into new hands tends to increase its productiveness, and thereby its usefulness to the nation at large; since those among the owners who are least provided with skill, enterprise, and capital, are those who are under the strongest inducement to sell their land."

CHAPTER XX.

IRELAND.

IF there were debate in Parliament upon the subject of peasant proprietorship, it is by no means improbable that some of those who spoke in favour of the distribution resulting from entail and settlement, would refer with decisive emphasis to the past and present condition of Ireland; and although it cannot be supposed that Lord Derby himself, when he delivered in 1871 so emphatic an opinion upon the peasant cultivator, was at the time confounding tenancy with ownership, there can be no doubt that of the hundreds of thousands who studied his lordship's remarks, there were not many who supposed that the following observations had no proper relation whatever to the matter of peasant proprietorship. Lord Derby said, " Of course a man may go on, after the fashion of the Irish cottiers, scratching the earth for a bare subsistence—but that is not farming; and I am only repeating an opinion which I have expressed before, and which I hold very strongly, when I say that the cottier, the peasant cultivator, honest and industrious and frugal as he may be, has just as much chance of holding his own against the combination of capital and science as bows and arrows have of superseding breech-loading rifles, or hand-loom weaving of driving the power-loom out of the field."

That is a very favourable example of the remarks by which the idea of peasant proprietorship has been dismissed from the minds of multitudes in this country. Lord Derby is certainly aware, but the great majority of his readers are certainly not aware, that peasant proprietorship has never existed in Ireland. There is much in this quotation which might lead to the supposition that the fact was not in Lord Derby's mind. If a people engage—though it be with a spade—in agriculture, and are "honest, industrious, and frugal," how should they come to desolation ? The Irish cottier did not deserve this encomium. He lived under a system which is not distinguished by "honesty," and he certainly was not "industrious," nor was he "frugal." If he lived on potatoes, and died miserably when potatoes failed, it was because he could not help himself. He was a rack-rented farmer, living in constant remembrance that he had no encouragement to be either industrious or frugal; that the improvement which every day's labour effected was not his own, but was absolutely the property of another, and might be made use of as a plea for increasing the burden of his rent. "Ireland," says Mr. W. T. Thornton, "is one of the few countries in which there neither are, nor ever were, peasant properties. From the earliest appropriation of the soil down to the present day, estates have always been of considerable size, and though these estates are now cut up into many small holdings, the actual occupiers of the soil, far from being landowners, are not even leaseholders, but are rack-rented tenants at will. In this single phrase may be found a complete explanation of all the evils of their condition, and all the defects of their character. They are indolent, because they have no inducement to work after they have obtained from their labour wherewithal to pay their rent and to save themselves from starvation. Whatever additional produce they might raise would only subject them to additional exactions. They are careless of the future, because they cannot, by taking thought, improve the gloomy prospects of the morrow; they are reduced to the verge of destitution, because they are permitted to retain no more of the fruits of their labour than will barely suffice for their subsistence; and they set at nought all other laws, divine or human, partly in obedience to the first law of nature—that of self-preservation, and partly because familiarity with misery has rendered them desperate." * Wherever we find peasant holders as a numerous body, we shall meet with this want of "honesty" on the part of their land-lords, this want of "industry" and of true "frugality" on the part of the tenants. We shall find this nowhere so strongly marked as in Ireland, because there a large population has been driven, by the absence of other occupation, to beggar itself in competition for the soil. Look where we will, we shall find little that is admirable or useful resulting from peasant tenancy; and equally, look where we will, we shall find the peasant proprietor, where he has free land, and where the system of peasant farming is well understood and established, not only

* " Peasant Proprietorship," by W. T. Thornton, C.B.

holding his own, not only displaying a high degree of honesty, industry, and frugality, but also making a larger produce than the farmers of any other class.

At the present moment, Ireland occupies much of the thoughts, but rarely the lips, of English statesmen. I will not hesitate to express my conviction that there is a lack of courage in this silence which is to be regretted. The only positive statement concerning Ireland from the mouth of a responsible statesman has been made by Mr. Bright at Manchester (October 25, 1879), to the effect that further legislation is needed with reference to agricultural land. I shall here deal only with the land question, and in reference to that great question, I shall show that the state of Ireland calls for serious attention; that to leave Ireland alone to seethe in discontent and disaffection is unjust and impolitic. Nothing would tend more surely to forward the separatist movement than that English politicians should proclaim that the question of Home Rule is the only question between England and Ireland. Before putting the matter in the most disadvantageous and irritating form, they would do well to have regard to some of the grievances of Ireland, especially to those which, it is complained, are due to neglect, indifference, or injustice at Westminster. Surely the most evident dictates of prudence demand that we should first see what can be fairly alleged against the Imperial Parliament as regards its work for Ireland, before we enter upon the question of separate Legislatures.

Much has appeared lately with reference to the political action of the Irish in Great Britain; and when we consider what is their numerical strength in this island, I fancy that not only those who are just but those who are prudent will listen to their complaints. I have obtained from Dr. Neilson Hancock, of Dublin, trustworthy statistics, which show that in the census of 1871, the persons of Irish birth in Scotland were 207,770 in number, those in England and Wales 566,540; making together a total of 774,310. This large factor in our population was, however, very peculiar as to age. Of the whole number of persons of Irish birth in England and Wales, only 67,616 were under 20 years of age; 498,733 were of 20 years of age and upwards. If the 207,770 of Irish birth in Scotland were in a similar position in regard to age, which it is reasonable to suppose was the case, there would be more than 184,000 of 20 years and upwards—making in Great Britain a total of more than 682,000 of Irish birth of 20 years and upwards. At the same time, there were of that age in Ireland only 2,900,000 persons of Irish birth. The result, therefore, of Dr. Hancock's calculations is that of Irish in the United Kingdom, of the age of 20 years and upwards, considerably more than one-fifth reside in Great Britain. That is a fact which I think does not receive sufficient attention at the hands of English and Scotch politicians.

To the circumstances of the present time in Ireland, arising in great part from the prevalent agricultural distress, I must make some allusion before passing on to deal with the general relations of landlord and tenant in Ireland. The agricultural distress is enlarging, but indications of distress have been observed during the last three years. From the latest statistics relative to

savings and poor-law relief in Ireland, we learn that the
deposits and cash balances in joint-stock banks show
a falling off of £1,554,000 : from £31,745,000 at Midsummer, 1878, to £30,191,000 at Midsummer, 1879. The
last preceding year when there was a falling off in bank
deposits at all comparable to this, was the very unfavourable year of 1863. The falling off then was £1,422,000.
The Trustee Savings Banks show a decrease in deposits
for the first six months of 1879, of £92,000 : from
£2,208,000 in 1878, to £2,116,000 in 1879; indicating
that the pressure which had affected bank deposits had
reached the artisan and servant class in the 36 chief
towns where these banks are situate. At Midsummer,
1879, the number in receipt of poor relief, in workhouses
and outdoor, was 6156 above the number in the preceding year. The statistics of crime in Ireland continue
to exhibit the well-known features. Serious crimes committed against property are much fewer in Ireland than
in England, and very much fewer than in Scotland. The
Scotch offences against morals are double the number
of the Irish—281 as compared with 142. " In the most
serious punishments," says Dr. Hancock, " the comparison
of Irish with French, English, and Scotch proportional
figures is as follows:—

" (a) Those sentenced to imprisonment for one year and upwards were,
for the same population in Ireland, 87 ; in France, 220; in Scotland,
241 ; in England, 266.

" (b) The Irish figure of sentences to penal servitude was 170; the
Scotch, 198 ; the French, 4 ; and the English, 364.

" (c) In sentences of death, the Scotch figure was 0, the Irish 2, the
French 3, and the English "

With regard to the agitating question of reduction of

rent, that cannot be treated as invariable, because agricultural rents are very unequal, and in no part of the
United Kingdom so much so as in Ireland. The rent in
Ireland is, unquestionably, in many cases largely composed of the value of tenants' improvements. I know
of no part of Europe in which landlords have obtained
so large a share of the fruits of the soil, and have done
so little to promote and to increase the best cultivation
and the produce, as in Ireland. In this respect, Irish
agriculture differs widely from that of England and Scotland. I do not wish to see the small farmers disturbed
in their holdings; I would rather see their number increased. Ireland, with reformed and rational land laws,
would be all the better for another million of agricultural
population. I should like to see some of her sons and
daughters returning to retake possession of their fatherland; and I will presently quote evidence of the very
highest authority, showing how and why this increase of
population is desirable and would be advantageous from
an economic point of view. But before going into that
matter, which is connected with the general relations of
landlord and tenant, it is desirable that there should be
a clear understanding as to what it is together with the
immediate pressure of cruelly hard tunes, which almost
disturbs the reason of the Irish farmer, and I will state
it very briefly. In Ulster, if a tenant cannot pay his
rent, he does not lose that which is equivalent to compensation upon ejectment. But over all the rest of
Ireland, if a tenant cannot in the severe times pay
his rent, he may be ejected, with loss of the compensation
which Mr. Gladstone's Land Act awards for disturbance.

Now, it is a fact, which may be read upon the face of that Act, that Irish landlords have a patent and plain interest in clearing their lands of the smaller tenants, while there can be no doubt that to these tenants eviction may imply a sentence to pauperism; and if they are evicted without compensation, the proceeding probably involves the confiscation of much of the work of their lives. The scale of compensation for disturbance to be given by landlords to tenants under the provisions of the Land Act decreases as the rent becomes larger; and while a landlord must give seven years' rent upon ejectment, except for non-payment of rent, to a tenant paying £10 and under, he gives only one year's rent to a tenant paying £100.

This condition of security in one province, and of insecurity in the other three provinces of Ireland, may be well illustrated by the case of Lord Headfort, who, I believe, is a good landlord, and who in 1879, together with his agent, received threatening letters. That nobleman has two estates, separated only by the imaginary line which divides the counties of Meath and Cavan. A tenant upon his lordship's Cavan estate can sell the tenant-right of his farm; he cannot be ejected for non-payment of rent without such an amount of compensation as would enable him to emigrate, or, in any case, would secure him from destitution. But upon Lord Headfort's Meath estate, in case of inability to pay rent, the tenants may be ejected with loss of that compensation which the Land Act is supposed by some people in this country to have secured to them under any circumstances of disturbance. It will appear strange, no doubt, to many English readers, that the word "compensation" should be used in connection with the ejectment of a tenant who cannot pay rent. But the peculiar circumstances of Irish agriculture, to which I shall presently make fuller reference, will more clearly explain the extraordinary position of landlord and tenant in Ireland. It may be supposed that small tenants in the circumstances of those upon Lord Headfort's Meath property feel that they are in some jeopardy. There can, however, be no reason to fear that so upright a landlord as Lord Headfort would take any advantage of their necessities; and in relation to my argument, it is no small assistance that I am able to quote evidence recently given before the Select Committee appointed to inquire into the operation of the "Bright" clauses of the Land Act, by Lord Headfort's former agent, of whom he wrote as "my valued and lamented kinsman, Major Dalton." Speaking of these two estates, Major Dalton said that "on the Cavan estate, where tenant-right exists, the tenantry are in a more thriving condition than on the Meath property; and he thought the interest thus conceded to the tenants had been an incentive to industry and thrift, and had given a *status* to the occupiers, who feel invested with a *quasi* property in the land." It should be observed that there has been no disquiet upon Lord Headfort's Cavan estate, and this fact alone must lead Englishmen to wish to know more of the Ulster custom. At its best, the Ulster custom implies continuous occupancy, a fair rent, and a power of sale. The tenant holds the land as long as he pays the rent. A fair rent is a rent which does not on the one side confiscate the tenant's improvements, nor deprive the landlord of the progressive value of his estate, due to material progress of the country. The power of selling tenant-right is the right to sell by public auction or private contract the occupancy of the farm, subject, of course, to the discharge of all arrears of rent, and to the purchaser being a solvent and acceptable person. Lord Headfort's former agent, continuing his evidence, said he was strongly in favour of creating a peasant proprietary in Ireland. This is what he said: "I think it would be a most conservative measure—not using the word in a political sense—but as giving the occupiers of land that which they have not got now, namely, an attachment to the Constitution under which they live." Considering that Sir Stafford Northcote appears to have gone over to Ireland in 1879 mainly for the purpose of sneering at this most conservative measure, which may be established by a thorough reform of the land laws of the United Kingdom, and by the more effective operation of those clauses of the Land Act which bear the honoured name of Mr. Bright, it is well not to use the word in a political sense.

I will again refer to Major Dalton's evidence with respect, first, to the class of persons whom it is most desirable " to fix upon the soil; " and second, in regard to the alleged danger of subdivision. On the first point, Major Dalton said, " There are a good many tenants on Lord Headfort's estate holding from one to five acres. They are rather labouring men than farmers. They live chiefly by labour. Now, these are men whom I should like to fix upon the soil; I think it is one way of dealing with the most perplexing question of all, perhaps—namely,

the labourers' question, and how to house them. It costs
the farmers much to build cottages, and, moreover, thatch
is getting more expensive every year; they do not like
to waste it on the roofs of their cabins. Then, on the
other hand, landlords cannot do it on a very large scale,
except upon the land which they have in their hands;
they are not rich enough; but if you give the labourer a
property in his small allotment or holding, I think he
would be very likely to do it himself, and I know instances where they have done it." Any attempt to
exclude such a class from any facilities offered by the
State would, in his opinion, be impolitic and most in-
vidious. "I think that it would be fatal to the measure,
from a conservative point of view, at all events, because
it would create so much disaffection that I would rather
do nothing." And with regard to subdivision, he said,
"Of course, it would take place in some cases, but I have
found from my own experience, which is a tolerably long
one now, that the wish for subdivision is dying out
altogether on the Headfort estates; the tendency is
rather the other way, towards the consolidation of farms,
which is generally brought about by emigration. Before
the famine, the tendency to subdivision existed to a very
great extent, but since then the opening afforded in the
Colonies and the United States has exercised what I may
call a centrifugal force upon the home population, and
instead of subdividing the holding among the family,
one of the sons retains the farm, and the others emigrate
or adopt other employments. Of course, subdivision
would take place in some cases, but then the neighbouring tenant would buy the property of the man who was

going away, and in that way it would tend rather to increase the size of the holding than otherwise." On this subject, the evidence of Mr. Murrough O'Brien is very interesting. Mr. O'Brien said, "I think the subdivision which took place formerly, of which I have no knowledge except from reading, arose from this: that the tenants subdivided and misused land which was not their own; they had little or no interest in it, and they did not care how they misused it. Now when tenants invest in land, and more especially when they have a permanent interest in it, I think they are much more likely (contrasting my experience with what I have read of in the past) to use it judiciously and wisely, and to make their possessions of the greatest advantage to themselves and the country. I think that farmers in Ireland are just as unlikely as anywhere else to subdivide their farms in a manner which would be injurious to their property; they are quite aware of the disadvantages of a farm being left among a whole family of children; they generally make wills, even where they have nothing to leave but a yearly tenancy, and they would be much more likely to make wills when they have freeholds to leave. There is also a much higher standard of living than there was formerly; moreover, the younger men of the families go to other countries; it is a thing which has been said to me over and over again when I have visited farms in Ireland, that the whole family cannot expect to live upon the land; the sons and daughters go to America or to England. There are, therefore, three distinct causes to render subdivision less likely than it was formerly: first, that the tenant will be the owner of the land, and have a permanent interest in it; second, the higher standard of living; and third, that the young people are more in the habit of going to America and elsewhere."

There is one class of landlords to whom I wish to make particular allusion—I mean the absentee landlords, the men who drain an agricultural island of rent, and return little or nothing in the shape of expenditure. I think many, if not all, would do well to follow the policy of Lord Derby, and arrange for the sale, in partition, of their properties; yet, if all made the outlay which the late Lord Derby, I believe, annually expended upon his Irish estates, there would be less cause for complaint. There must be during this winter deep distress in Ireland, and very heavy burdens will be cast upon the resident ratepayers. I should like to know what, in these circumstances, will be the contribution of the absentee landlords—the gentlemen who are drawing, say, from £1000 to £20,000 a year from the soil of Ireland? If Parliament were sitting, I would suggest that inquiry be made of Lord Beaconsfield as to what is his opinion of the following proposition, which I will quote from a well-known work:—" I cannot help expressing a wish that some arrangement may be made connected with the levying of the poor-rate in Ireland by which absentee landlords may be made to contribute in something like a fair proportion to the wants of the poor in the districts in which they ought to reside. I think if there were two poor-rates introduced into Ireland, the one applying to all occupiers of land, and the other to all those who did not spend a certain portion of the year upon some portion of their estates in Ireland, it would prove useful. I think that by thus appealing to their interests it might induce absentee landlords to reside much more in Ireland than is now unfortunately the case." That is not my proposition. Perhaps, if a Liberal politician were to make such a proposal, it would be called "communistic." Those are words spoken in the House of Commons by a former leader of the Conservative party, and published, with great eulogy of their author, by Lord Beaconsfield, in his biography of his friend and leader, Lord George Bentinck. I have no doubt whatever that if those words had issued lately from the lips of an Irish member of Parliament, many ugly things would have been said of them which will not be said because they belong to a Conservative nobleman and statesman. I will venture, however, to say this of the suggestion, that never have I heard from any Irishman a proposal which would more surely tend to abolish that which,—whether Lord George Bentinck's short way with absentee landlords be sound or unsound, —is, as every one admits, a sore disadvantage for Ireland.

In the Irish Land Act, Mr. Gladstone did the best he could in a Parliament which, for 200 years, has been composed, as to the majority, of very determined representatives of what is called the landed interest. But he did not do enough. He left the Irish farmer—and, I may add, he left Irish agriculture, which concerns every man in England—a prey to that tenure of which Lord Dufferin, a great Ulster proprietor, and a thorough Irishman, exclaimed in the House of Lords: "What is the spectacle presented to us by Ireland! It is that of millions of persons, whose only dependence and whose chief occupation is agriculture—for the most part cultivating their lands—that is, sinking their past, their present, and their future upon yearly tenancies. But what is a yearly tenancy? Why, it is an impossible tenure—a tenure which, if its terms were to be literally interpreted, no Christian man would offer, and none but a madman would accept." From the figures of the leading official statistician of Ireland, it appears that at present no fewer than 75 per cent., or 440,000, of the tenant farmers of Ireland, hold their lands upon this "insane and unchristian" tenure, of which Adam Smith wrote: "It is against all reason and probability to suppose that yearly tenants will improve the soil."

Of the 592,000 tenant farmers in Ireland, 423,000 hold less than thirty acres of land. The great bulk of the purchasers of the Church property were tenants of this class; the average holdings in Ulster are also of this class. In the opinion of Mr. Murrough O'Brien, it is even more important that ownership should be encouraged among the smaller tenants than among the larger. Speaking of small farmers, averaging about ten acres each, he said, "I think that lots of this sort are just as suitable for sale, and that the small farmers are most desirable members of society to encourage. It makes them orderly, and it gives men labouring in England or America a home to come back to." Speaking of holdings of about five acres, he said, "For one thing, it is the best mode of housing the labouring population; it does not pay the landlord to build houses for them, and it is a matter of experience that, when they have the opportunity, they, not all at once, but from time to time, invest their little savings of money and labour in building themselves houses, and improving their little plots of land. The holders of these small plots do not also require so much capital in proportion as those with larger holdings. The labour of the man and his family is his capital, and is sufficient for the cultivation of a small farm." He adds, " I think the fact of the tenants having only a yearly tenure is the reason why the Irish are the worst-housed nation in civilized Europe."

Englishmen generally have but slight knowledge of the dearth of other industry in Ireland, and of the fearful obligations by which Irishmen are bound to cling to the occupation of the soil. I dare say but few Englishmen know much about conacre, by which a man hires a part of the lands of some landlord or of some large farmer during the growth of, and for the purpose of harvesting, the crop, whether of corn, hay, or potatoes. Not long ago, when I was a visitor in the house of an Irish landlord, who is a member of the House of Peers, his lordship pointed from his window towards some meadows, and said to me, "Would you believe it, such is the hunger of these people for land, that I could let those meadows in conacre for more than I could get for the crop, after I have paid the cost of making the hay and of sending it to market?" Through the operation of what Mr. Cobden called free trade in land, or of what I call free land, that hunger, which it is so distressing to witness, would be satisfied by the transfer, through processes beneficial alike both to landlord and tenant, of the greater part of the soil of Ireland into the hands of the people.

I am thankful beyond my powers of expression to see that our land laws have become an intolerable burden to Englishmen as well as to Irishmen, and that both are beginning to comprehend that we cannot possibly prosper in competitive trade while four-fifths of the land of the United Kingdom are bound in the unfertile bonds of strict settlement. I long for the emancipation of the soil of this country, and not less for the freedom of the land of Ireland from those fetters which so cruelly gall the agriculture of both islands.

We ought now to consider—What is the condition, and what are the peculiar features, apart from the unusual circumstances of the moment, of Irish husbandry? With reference to that question, I propose to cite two witnesses, one of the highest authority in Ireland, the other of not less eminence in Great Britain. As a cure for the complaints of farmers, the Government have administered a Royal Commission—a most cruel form of treatment, because it will take at least two years to operate. But when it was sought to dignify that Commission by entrusting the practical inquiry in Ireland to a gentleman whose name would command respect, the Government fixed upon Professor Baldwin, of Glasnevin Agricultural College. We are, however, already in possession of Mr. Baldwin's opinions upon Irish farming. Mr. Baldwin has reported to the Irish Executive that " wide areas of land in Ireland are not yielding a fourth of the produce which could be obtained from them. The dwellings of a vast number of small farmers in Ireland are wretched. In this age of progress it is unsatisfactory to find that there are in Ireland very many

small farmers with large families whose dwellings consist
of a single apartment, in which cattle and pigs are also
housed. There are 4,000,000 acres of medium land, now
growing poor herbage, which would pay far better in
tillage. At present the gross return of these 4,000,000
acres does not amount to twice the rent; if put under
a proper system, the yield would amount to five times
the rent, and the wealth of the country would be increased to the extent of several millions. The want of
drainage is a crying defect in Irish agriculture. In Ireland, at least 6,000,000 acres are in need of drainage.
This work could be effected at a cost of £5 an acre.
The annual letting value would be thereby increased by
£3,000,000."* We shall do well to consider what this
means. We have here, at least two years in advance
of the report of the Government Commission, their distinguished assistant's views concerning the agriculture
of Ireland, and he condemns as wasteful the reckless
system of converting tillage into pasture, which has
driven hundreds of thousands of Irish people from their
country, and which threatens to make of Ireland a green
desert. How is it possible to exaggerate the benefit
which would result from enlarging the income from Irish
agriculture "to the extent of several millions"? With
regard to the labour requisite to obtain this result, Mr.
Baldwin continues: "Many persons will ask, Where is
all the capital to execute this work to come from? I
answer, that the greater part of it is in the labour of
the people. The working farmers of Ireland have a

* "The Working of the 'Bright' Clauses of the Irish Land Act, 1870,"
by G. Shaw Lefevre, M.P.

great deal of labour in their families, which could be most usefully employed in draining their lands." Mr. Baldwin's conclusions are of the greatest importance. He says, "Every experienced agriculturist will agree that the smaller farmers of Ireland could, by adopting modes of management which are within their reach, double their income." And why, then, do they not double their income? Mr. Baldwin tells us in the fewest words. He says the small farmers fear that any improvement in their agriculture would be taken hold of by their landlords "as a cloak for raising rents." There it is; that is the matter with which we must deal, not more for the sake of the Irish farmer than for the interest of the whole community. The cause of the backward and unproductive condition of Irish agriculture is declared, upon the authority of the man selected by their Graces and their Lordships of the Government Commission, to be the fear that landlords will confiscate improvements.

It now and then happens that partisans of abuses in the land laws, finding a few cases in which even Irish freeholders are unthrifty bad farmers, where such persons show a tendency to injurious subdivision of small properties, parade these cases in the *Times* as if they were in some way or other conclusive against the arguments of reformers. We must repeat that the proper management of small farms is a habit of slow growth, and one which cannot co-exist with the land system of the United Kingdom. The destruction of their argument is the invariable tendency to increase of production and to avoidance of minute subdivision which small farmers display in all countries where they have been long and widely established. There are gentlemen, even in Ireland, who have a vague idea that at the time of the famine of 1846 Ireland was a land of peasant proprietors. They have a notion that peasant proprietary has been tried in Ireland, and has proved a failure. But, as I have shown in the words of Mr. Thornton, Ireland is one of the few countries in which there neither are, nor ever were, peasant proprietors. With regard to Ireland, the study of the political economy of the Channel Islands is very useful, because that is the only part of the United Kingdom where the proprietorship of land is widely distributed among the people. Those people differ somewhat in race from the English, but in that respect they are more nearly allied to the Irish, and in the Channel Islands there is agricultural prosperity and produce unequalled in any other part of her Majesty's dominions. There are some people who are ready at any moment, and without any consideration, to say that Ireland, with 5,500,000 people, has still too many. I do not undertake to say that Ireland should be half as thickly populated as Jersey, but Ireland would certainly not appear to be over-populated if she could obtain reform of the desolating land laws of the United Kingdom, and it is evident that if unhappy Ireland were populated in the same proportion to area as is happy Jersey, she would have nearly 30,000,000 of people within her borders.

I believe that with regard to Irish agriculture the problem to be considered is this: How can the Irish farmer best obtain security of tenure at a fair rent? And it is in dealing with that question that I propose to cite my second witness, who is the highest authority upon agriculture in Great Britain—I mean Mr. Caird. Last year, Mr. Caird was asked by the Council of the Royal Agricultural Society, a body including the Prince of Wales and leading representatives of the great nobility and landed gentry of England, to report upon the agriculture of the United Kingdom for the information of the world, then assumed to be assembled somewhere about the Champ de Mars, in Paris. This is what he reported concerning Ireland: "In Ireland the relation between landlord and tenant is altogether different from that of England and Scotland. Previous to the famine of 1846, the great landowners were non-resident, and the land was still in a great measure in the hands of middlemen on leases for lives, with leave to subdivide and sublet for the same time. These men had no permanent interest in the property; their business was to make an income out of it at the least cost, and their intermediate position severed the otherwise natural connection between landlord and tenant. The famine of 1846 prostrated the class of middlemen entirely, and brought the landowners and the real tenants face to face. But the hold which the latter had been permitted to obtain led them to consider the landowners very much as only the holders of the first charge upon the land, and they were in the habit of selling and buying their farms among themselves, subject to this charge—a course which, as a matter of practice, was tacitly accepted by the landowner. He had security for his rent in the money paid by the incoming tenant, who, for his own safety, required the landowner's consent to the change of tenancy; and

the landowner's agent thus received the 'price' of the
farm—for that was the term used—and handed it over
to the outgoing tenant, after deducting all arrears of
rent. This suited the convenience of landowners, the
most of whom had no money to spend in improvements,
many of them non-resident and taking little interest in
the country, and dealing with a numerous body of small
tenants with whom they seldom came into personal
contact. In the north of Ireland, this custom of sale
became legally recognized as tenant-right. The want of
it in other pars of Ireland produced an agitation which
ultimately led to the Irish Land Act, under which legislative protection is given to customs capable of proof.
The customs of 'selling' the farm, subject to the approval
of the landowner, by a tenant on yearly tenure, is rapidly
gaining ground in Ireland; and so firmly are the people
imbued with this idea of their rights, that the clauses
of the Irish Land At which enabled the tenant by the
aid of a loan of Government money on very easy terms
to purchase the prope ownership of his farm, are rarely
acted upon, from the relief that the farm is already his
under the burden of a moderate rent-charge to his
nominal landlord. Circumstances have thus brought
about a situation in which the landowner cannot deal
with the same freedom with his property as in England or Scotland, either in the selection of his tenants
or in the fair readjustment of rent; and this has in a
great measure arisen naturally from the neglect by the
landlord of his proper dutes in not himself executing
those indispensable permannt improvements which the
tenant was thus obliged to undertake, and who, in this

way, established for himself the claim to co-partnership in the soil itself."

This report was accepted by the Council of the Royal Agricultural Society; and in sight of that fact and of Mr. Caird's admirable and conclusive statement, I cannot understand how men like the Duke of Richmond, who are leading members of that Council, can refuse to take into consideration, or to undertake without delay, a measure for giving security of tenure to Irish farmers. I should have supposed that if any one had not been ready to give an earnest and hopeful consideration to a reasonable proposal for carrying out that which is miscalled fixity of tenure, the statement of Mr. Caird would have convinced him that it was his duty to take that course. The land question is the question of questions for Ireland and for Irishmen. If Englishmen will not have regard to it, can we wonder that Irishmen say, "Let us have a Parliament in Dublin, and we will do it for ourselves?" Cottier tenancy has meant in Ireland that the peasantry were to accomplish all the improvement of the land, to do the drainage and building, which in England and Scotland fall upon the landlord; and they have had to do this without security of tenure, and to be subject to the competition of a half-starving population. If ever there was in the world a school, framed and fenced by law, for the encouragement of idleness, of dishonesty, and of improvidence that has existed in the land system of Ireland.

The evidence of Mr. Baldwin, which I have quoted shows that the conversion of arable land into pasture and the consequent depopulation of the country, have been injurious to the interests of production. I read not very long since in the *Times* a statement that, in the county of Wexford, more than 350,000 acres had gone out of cultivation—that is, I suppose, had been converted into pasture—within 30 years; that, within the same period, the population of that county had decreased by 70,000, and that more than 9000 houses had been levelled to the ground. It can hardly be doubted that such a statement is calculated to excite very bitter feelings in the minds of Irishmen, especially when they realize, as all intelligent people must realize, that this change is not due to the natural operation of economic law, but is rather the consequence of laws and customs with reference to the tenure and transfer of property in land, which prevail in no other part of the world.

British Secretaries of Legation find so much to admire in the tenure and transfer of land in foreign countries, that, after even a short residence abroad, they grow quite disrespectful to the institutions of the United Kingdom. Mr. Ford, writing from Washington, in 1869, exclaimed, in concluding his report to the Foreign Office : " May not some of the discontent that has been ripening in the minds of Irishmen (since their great Exodus in 1848) towards British institutions and the system of land tenure in Ireland, be partially traced to the easy acquisition of real estate in the United States ? " Mr. Sackville West, of the British Embassy in Paris, was very strongly moved from another quarter in a similar direction. He was aware that small farms are common in Ireland as in France. But, he says, that which " has caused, in the one case, discontent and agrarian outrage,

has, in the other, been productive of social order and
general contentment. It must be borne in mind that
75 per cent. of the agricultural population in France are
proprietors, and that the number of proprietors is still
increasing. In this fact consists the difference—a difference depending upon the ownership of land by the
masses, as opposed to the ownership of land by the
minority. Tenant-right and fixity of tenure arising
from land occupation are phrases scarcely heard in
France in connection with landed property, for the
simple reason that there can be no such right or fixity
of tenure which does not result from free and undisputed
possession; and as such possession appertains in the
majority of cases more or less to the tenant and labourer
as well as to the landlord, the disputed questions which
occupy attention as regards the Irish land question can
scarcely ever arise in France. Proprietary rights can
never be called in question. Whether a property consists of one acre or one hundred acres, the owner is
absolute in all matters relating to possession. The small
proprietor is seen under more advantageous circumstances
in France than in any other country in Europe, for he
has been in fact the creation of a system, which, whatever may be urged against it, has reconstituted the rural
economy of the nation, and more than doubled the produce of the soil. His mode of life presents a striking
and instructive illustration of the system, for it is based
upon the proceeds of the land in which he has a direct
personal interest, and he lives, therefore, as an independent
member of society, rising according to his means in the
social scale. The amount of capital expended by the

small proprietor upon his land is proportionately small. The condition, however, of the small proprietors varies very much in different departments, as also does the mode of cultivation; but they will generally be found in easy circumstances, and living always in the hope of bettering them; and it is this hope which absolute possession engenders that stimulates them to fresh exertions, beneficial not only to themselves, but to the community in general."

Owing to well-known circumstances, there has been an approach to the conditions of "free land," in the offer of the lands of the disestablished Church of Ireland to the tenants. There was certainty of title, and a rare simplicity of transfer. These are among the attractions which free land would offer. The habits of a people with regard to investment, are not quickly formed nor abandoned, and it would take time, after the establishment of free land, to change the method of our people in this respect. But it is surprising to note with what alacrity the invitation was accepted in Ireland. I will describe what happened in the words of the illustrious author of the Irish Church Act. "I learn," said Mr. Gladstone, in Dublin, on November 9, 1877, "that a body of 5000 purchases of all possible varieties has been created under the Church Act, which, although we contemplated such results, we never thought or supposed it to be capable of producing them on such a very large scale. . . . The sales and purchases are spread all over Ireland; they are not merely in the north; they have spread all over Ireland, and they go down to the smallest proprietors; and in all these cases, Captain Godley (Secretary to the Church Commissioners) has been bold to assert before a Committee of the House of Commons, with the experience and information he possessed, through the officers of the court, that in all these classes of moderate purchases—small purchases, and even very small purchases—the result of the acquisition of landed property by small holders has been most satisfactory, and has tended to the development of industry and enterprise in a remarkable degree." This successful operation appearing in remarkable contrast to the redistribution of ownership of land through operation of the "Bright" clauses of the Irish Land Act, naturally attracted the attention of Parliament; and Mr. Shaw Lefevre, with assiduity and success, undertook the suggestion and direction of inquiry. In order to qualify himself for this task, Mr. Shaw Lefevre sought the advice of Mr. Murrough O'Brien, the valuator employed by the Irish Church Temporalities Commission; and visited, as samples of these transactions, two landed estates, distant about six and twelve miles from Newry, one of which was sold in 1873 to the tenants, and the other in 1877. The object of his visit was that he might personally judge of the motives which the tenants had or have in view in effecting purchase, and of the results, so far as they could be ascertained by ocular proof and by conversation with the new owners.

I intend to quote in this place a few of Mr. Shaw Lefevre's notes of conversation, because these notes afford striking evidence of the desire for the acquisition of land, of the sense of security obtained by possession as owner, and of the stimulus, so far more powerful than any other that can be suggested, which is by such ownership imparted to improvement in cultivation, to thrift, to sobriety, to industry, and to general good conduct. I regard these notes of conversation as affording very strong evidence in support of the arguments advanced in this volume.

The following are notes of Mr. Shaw Lefevre's conversation with the new owners:—

1. A. B. farms twenty acres, for which he paid the Church Commissioners £516, the whole of which he paid down. He spent some years of his life as an engineer in the merchant service; later at Liverpool as a marine store dealer. A few years ago he inherited the tenant's interest of a small farm of eight acres, and subsequently bought the tenant's interest of an adjoining farm of twelve acres, for which he paid £350, or thirty times the rent. Since his purchase of the fee from the Commissioners, he has built a range of superior farm buildings, at a cost of £500, tiled the floor of his house, put in an excellent kitchen-range, and has drained and reclaimed a part of his land. He would not have done this, he said, but for the security of ownership. There was general satisfaction, he told me, among his neighbours at having become owners. Those, however, who had to borrow the balance of the purchase money, beyond the amount left on loan by the Commissioners, had a hard struggle. A neighbouring lawyer lent them money at five per cent., which they were paying off by degrees, and they could not lay out money on improvements until these debts were discharged. Those who had not borrowed were making improvements. He himself works harder now than ever before; likes the life.

2. Farm of two and a half acres, rented at £2 15s., bought for £77, of which the tenant paid down £39. This he borrowed in small sums from different persons—giving £1 for the use of £10 for ten months; 10s. to a sister for £11 for a year, and so on. Has repaid most of it, and will soon be free. Is a labouring man, working at wages for the clergyman, to whom he has let a part of his land for grazing; his wife does washing, and uses the remainder of the land for drying clothes. They are well pleased to have the land for their own; expect to have it free before they die. Wife said, "It all seems like winning (saving) now; we never could save before."

3. Tenant bought his little farm of five and a half acres for £164. Is ninety-two years of age; has nine sons and two daughters. Seven sons at sea; one of them, sailing out of Newry, gave the money for purchase, and last year gave more to build an additional farm building; has a neat

slated cottage; gate piers, and iron gates to fields. A son, aged forty, who was for some time in hospital at New York and Dublin, far gone in consumption, told me he had every comfort and all the care he needed at home.

4. Farm of seventeen acres, rented at £27, bought by tenant for £648, of which he paid down £226; saved this at sea—"many a salt wave went over his head for it." Since his purchase he paid £87 for building materials, has converted his thatched cottage into a two-storied slated house; would have rebuilt the house in any case, but would have had no security unless he bought, and is well pleased to be the owner; has seven little girls, too young to help him, and lives wholly by his labour on the farm.

5. Tenant bought ten acres for £273, of which he paid down £75, but borrowed this from friends. Wife says her husband is an able seaman in a vessel trading between Liverpool and Rotterdam; borrowed the money lest they should be turned out of the farm. Four months ago her eldest son, "a fine, quiet boy of twenty-five," died; he used to work on the farm. She now finds it hard to struggle on, her second son being only thirteen. No improvements effected; but they hope to pay off the debt.

6. Tenant, a widow, bought nine and a half acres for £314, of which she paid down £79. Family consists of mother, two daughters, and a boy of fifteen. The eldest daughter, a fine, able young woman, full of spirits, says they borrowed £75 at six per cent. All but £15 has now been repaid. She works on the farm, and the family have no means of living except from it. A brother in Liverpool sent a few pounds towards the price. "How do they manage?" I asked. "Well, just cooling and supping." "Last year they had a good bit of flax, and paid off £10." "Why did they buy?" "Every one said, 'If ye don't, yez 'ill be thrown out, and may go lie behind a hedge.'" House is thatched, clean, neat, and comfortable.

7. Farm, fifty-one acres, bought by tenant for £1583, which he paid in full. Is now farmed by the son; the father lives on an adjoining property.

8. Tenant bought the farm of fifteen acres for £421, of which he paid down £106; leaves the remainder on mortgage. Purchaser died, leaving farm to his son, but in charge of his widow. Son, aged fifteen, is at sea; will soon be able to help his mother out of his earnings. Father, a Scotchman, was tenant of a farm of ninety-five acres in Fermanagh; sold the tenant-right of it for £600, and bought this farm. Widow says he preferred being the owner of a small farm to being tenant of a larger farm. Since they came they have greatly improved the house.

9. Farm of eighteen acres, bought for £508, of which £128 paid down. Purchaser died three years ago, leaving farm to his widow for life, and then to his youngest son. Other house property was to be sold; £300 to

go to his eldest son, and remainder to second son. Property sold for less than was expected, and only sufficed for eldest son's portion. Widow is laying by for second son. " Please God, when she has done this, she will pay off the debt to the Commissioners." She is well pleased with the purchase of the farm. It enables them to be independent, and to save. She added that those who had to borrow from other quarters have had a hard struggle.

Inquiry by a Select Committee of the House of Commons into the operation of the " Bright " clauses was made in two sessions—those of 1877 and 1878. Mr. Shaw Lefevre, the Chairman of the Committee, has described its operations: " The first witness examined was Dr. Hancock. He gave to the Committee a general review of the measures which had been taken by successive Governments in the direction aimed at, and he pointed out at length the legal difficulties in the way of the creation and maintenance of small proprietors in Ireland, in the present state of the law of real property. The other witnesses examined in the session of 1877 were chiefly officers of the Landed Estates Court and of the Board of Works, who have had charge of the machinery for working the clauses of the Irish Land Act, which were the subject of inquiry. Captain Godley, the Secretary to the Church Temporalities Commission, gave a very full description of the sale to the tenants of the Church property, and the results thereof so far as they had gone under the observation of the Commission ; and two or three witnesses were examined who had special complaints to make of the mode in which proceedings were carried out by the Landed Estates Court. On the reappointment of the Committee in 1878, Mr. Vernon gave evidence which produced a most favourable impression. He showed that the causes of failure of the Act

had been deeper than had been supposed; that the duties
of the Landed Estates Court, as vendors of property in
the interest of the owners, were inconsistent with duties
which the Irish Land Act endeavoured to cast upon them,
of giving perferential opportunities to the tenants of
purchasing their holdings, and that no result could ever
be expected so long as these two duties were combined.
He was of opinion that if the Legislature desired to create
a peasant proprietary, or a body of small proprietors,
whoever should sell to the tenants must be in the position
that the Church Temporalities Commissioners were put
into—that is to say, they must be absolute owners. He
proposed, therefore, that a Special Commission should be
appointed by the Government, who should be charged
with this duty."

"In the draft report presented by Mr. David Plunket
(which was accepted by the Committee), the existing
machinery of the Landed Estates Court and the Board of
Works was proposed to be retained, but certain amend-
ments were suggested which would or might facilitate
their working. He proposed that the advance to be made
to the purchasing tenant by the Board of Works should
be increased from two-thirds to three-fourths of the value
of holding; that the Landed Estates Court should have
the power of sanctioning fee-farm grants by owners to
tenant purchasers; that the clauses against alienation
and assignment during the continuance of the loan should
be repealed; and that where an estate should be offered
for sale in the Landed Estates Court, an officer acting
under the authority of that court, or of the Board of
Works, should visit the lands, and personally explain

to the tenants the advantages offered to them . . . Mr. Plunket's report studiously abstained from expressing any opinion in favour of the creation of small proprietors. The first amendment made in it was one proposed by Mr. Law, to the effect ' that the Committee, having considered the evidence, are of opinion that it is very desirable that further facilities should be given for the purchase by tenants of the fee-simple of their holdings.' "

The next amendment proposed by Mr. Law was to add the words, " Your Committee find that there is a general desire on the part of the tenantry of Ireland to become absolute owners of their farms." This was amended by a majority of one, on the motion of Mr. Heygate, by inserting the words, " when estates are offered for sale ; " thus limiting very much the scope of the amendment of Mr. Law, which was then added to the report. A subsequent amendment, moved by Mr. Shaw Lefevre, to the effect that, " The Committee believe that a substantial increase in the number of small proprietors would give stability to the social system, and would tend to spread contentment and promote industry and thrift, among the Irish peasantry," was then added to the report by a majority of one. The most important amendment, however, was one moved by Mr. Law, which struck at the whole root of the question, and which practically imported into Mr. Plunket's report conclusions at variance with his draft report. Mr. Plunket had proposed a paragraph to the effect " that a suggestion had been made to the Committee that funds should be entrusted to some existing public functionary, or to a Commission appointed for

2 B

the purpose, for the purchase and re-sale of estates to occupying tenants and others, but that the Committee saw serious objections to such a proposal, and were not prepared to recommend its adoption." This paragraph was struck out, and on the motion of Mr. Law, an amendment was carried, " That, for the purpose of promoting the purchase of land by occupying tenants, the Committee are of opinion that some provision must be made to meet what the evidence showed to be the fundamental difficulty of the present system—that is to say, the difficulty, if not impossibility (save in rare cases), of forming the lands into lots to suit the tenant purchasers, and at the same time having due regard to the interests of those whose property is being sold in the Court. That so long as these practically inconsistent duties continued to be imposed on one and the same functionary, the Committee believe that no substantial results can reasonably be expected. They, therefore, think that, whilst leaving to one body the function of selling to the best advantage such estates as may be offered for sale, another distinct and independent body should be constituted specially charged with the duty of superintending and facilitating the purchase of their several farms by the occupying tenants. The Committee, therefore, recommend that some properly constituted body should be entrusted with sufficient funds to enable them to purchase suitable estates, or parts of estates when offered for sale, with the view of afterwards selling to as many of the tenants as, with the aid of advances through the Board of Works, may be able and willing to buy ; and disposing of the residues (if any) at such times and in such manner as they may think would be most productive."

The report of the Committee was laid before Parliament in June, 1879, and no project of legislation has been based upon its recommendations.

THE END.

PRINTED AT THE CAXTON PRESS, BECCLES.

A LIST OF

C. KEGAN PAUL AND CO.'S

PUBLICATIONS.

10.79.

A LIST OF
C. KEGAN PAUL AND CO.'S
PUBLICATIONS.

ABDULLA (Hakayit).

Autobiography of a Malay Munshi. Translated by J. T. Thomson, F. R. G. S. With Photolithograph Page of Abdulla's MS. Post 8vo. Cloth, price 12s.

ADAMS (F. O.), F.R.G.S.

The History of Japan. From the Earliest Period to the Present Time. New Edition, revised. 2 volumes. With Maps and Plans. Demy 8vo. Cloth, price 21s. each.

ADAMS (W. D.).

Lyrics of Love, from Shakespeare to Tennyson. Selected and arranged by. Fcap. 8vo. Cloth extra, gilt edges, price 3s. 6d.
Also, a Cheap Edition. Fcap. 8vo. Cloth, price 2s. 6d.

ADAMS (John), M.A.

St. Malo's Quest, and other Poems. Fcap. 8vo. Cloth, 5s.

ADAMSON (H. T.), B.D.

The Truth as it is in Jesus. Crown 8vo. Cloth, price 8s. 6d.

ADON.

Through Storm & Sunshine. Illustrated by M. E. Edwards, A. T. H. Paterson, and the Author. Crown 8vo. Cloth, price 7s. 6d.

A. J. R.

Told at Twilight; Stories in Verse, Songs, &c. Fcap. 8vo. Cloth, price 3s. 6d.

A. K. H. B.

A Scotch Communion Sunday, to which are added Certain Discourses from a University City. By the Author of "The Recreations of a Country Parson." Second Edition. Crown 8vo. Cloth, price 5s.

From a Quiet Place. A New Volume of Sermons. Crown 8vo. Cloth, price 5s.

ALBERT (Mary).

Holland and her Heroes to the year 1585. An Adaptation from Motley's "Rise of the Dutch Republic." Small crown 8vo. Cloth, price, 4s. 6d.

ALLEN (Rev. R.), M.A.

Abraham; his Life, Times, and Travels, 3,800 years ago. Second Edition. With Map. Post 8vo. Cloth, price 6s.

ALLEN (Grant), B.A.

Physiological Æsthetics. Large post 8vo. 9s.

ALLIES (T. W.), M.A.

Per Crucem ad Lucem. The Result of a Life. 2 vols. Demy 8vo. Cloth, price 25s.

AMOS (Prof. Sheldon).

Science of Law. Third Edition. Crown 8vo. Cloth, price 5s. Volume X. of The International Scientific Series.

ANDERSON (Rev. C.), M.A.

New Readings of Old Parables. Demy 8vo. Cloth, price 4s. 6d.

Church Thought and Church Work. Edited by. Second Edition. Demy 8vo. Cloth, price 7s. 6d.

The Curate of Shyre. Second Edition. 8vo. Cloth, price 7s. 6d.

ANDERSON (Col. R. P.).

Victories and Defeats. An Attempt to explain the Causes which have led to them. An Officer's Manual. Demy 8vo. Cloth, price 14s.

ANDERSON (R. C.), C.E.

Tables for Facilitating the Calculation of every Detail in connection with Earthen and Masonry Dams. Royal 8vo. Cloth, price £2 2s.

ARCHER (Thomas).

About my Father's Business. Work amidst the Sick, the Sad, and the Sorrowing. Crown 8vo. Cloth, price 5*s.*

Army of the North German Confederation.

A Brief Description of its Organization, of the Different Branches of the Service and their *rôle* in War, of its Mode of Fighting, &c. &c. Translated from the Corrected Edition, by permission of the Author, by Colonel Edward Newdigate. Demy 8vo. Cloth, price 5*s.*

ARNOLD (Arthur).

Social Politics. Demy 8vo. Cloth, price 14*s.*

AUBERTIN (J. J.).

Camoens' Lusiads. Portuguese Text, with Translation by. With Map and Portraits. 2 vols. Demy 8vo. Price 30*s.*

Aunt Mary's Bran Pie.

By the author of " St. Olave's." Illustrated. Cloth, price 3*s.* 6*d.*

Aurora.

A Volume of Verse. Fcap. 8vo. Cloth, price 5*s.*

BAGEHOT (Walter).

Physics and Politics; or, Thoughts on the Application of the Principles of "Natural Selection" and "Inheritance" to Political Society. Fourth Edition. Crown 8vo. Cloth, price 4*s.*

Volume II. of The International Scientific Series.

Some Articles on the De-preciation of Silver, and Topics connected with it. Demy 8vo. Price 5*s.*

The English Constitution. A New Edition, Revised and Corrected, with an Introductory Dissertation on Recent Changes and Events. Crown 8vo. Cloth, price 7*s.* 6*d.*

Lombard Street. A Description of the Money Market. Seventh Edition. Crown 8vo. Cloth, price 7*s.* 6*d.*

BAGOT (Alan).

Accidents in Mines: their Causes and Prevention. Crown 8vo. Cloth, price 6*s.*

BAIN (Alexander), LL.D.

Mind and Body: the Theories of their relation. Sixth Edition. Crown 8vo. Cloth, price 4*s.*

Volume IV. of The International Scientific Series.

Education as a Science. Crown 8vo. Second Edition. Cloth, price 5*s.*

Volume XXV. of The International Scientific Series.

BAKER (Sir Sherston, Bart.).

Halleck's International Law; or Rules Regulating the Intercourse of States in Peace and War. A New Edition, Revised, with Notes and Cases. 2 vols. Demy 8vo. Cloth, price 38*s.*

The Laws relating to Qua-rantine. Crown 8vo. Cloth, price 12*s.* 6*d.*

BALDWIN (Capt. J. H.), F.Z.S.

The Large and Small Game of Bengal and the North-Western Provinces of India. 4to. With numerous Illustrations. Second Edition. Cloth, price 21*s.*

BANKS (Mrs. G. L.).

God's Providence House. New Edition. Crown 8vo. Cloth, price 3*s.* 6*d.*

Ripples and Breakers. Poems. Square 8vo. Cloth, price 5*s.*

BARING (T. C.), M.A., M.P.

Pindar in English Rhyme. Being an Attempt to render the Epinikian Odes with the principal remaining Fragments of Pindar into English Rhymed Verse. Small Quarto. Cloth, price 7*s.*

BARLEE (Ellen).

Locked Out: a Tale of the Strike. With a Frontispiece. Royal 16mo. Cloth, price 1*s.* 6*d.*

BARNES (William).

An Outline of English Speechcraft. Crown 8vo. Cloth, price 4*s.*

Poems of Rural Life, in the Dorset Dialect. New Edition, complete in 1 vol. Crown 8vo. Cloth, price 8*s.* 6*d.*

BARTLEY (George C. T.).
Domestic Economy ; Thrift
in Every Day Life. Taught in
Dialogues suitable for Children of
all ages. Small crown 8vo. Cloth,
limp, 2s.

BAUR (Ferdinand), Dr. Ph.
A Philological Introduction
to Greek and Latin for Students.
Translated and adapted from the
German of. By C. KEGAN PAUL,
M.A. Oxon., and the Rev. E. D.
STONE, M.A., late Fellow of King's
College, Cambridge, and Assistant
Master at Eton. Second and re-
vised edition. Crown 8vo. Cloth,
price 6s.

BAYNES (Rev. Canon R. H.)
At the Communion Time.
A Manual for Holy Communion.
With a preface by the Right Rev.
the Lord Bishop of Derry and
Raphoe. Cloth, price 1s. 6d.
. Can also be had bound in
French morocco, price 2s. 6d.; Per-
sian morocco, price 3s.; Calf, or
Turkey morocco, price 3s. 6d.
Home Songs for Quiet
Hours. Fourth and cheaper Edi-
tion. Fcap. 8vo. Cloth, price 2s. 6d.
*This may also be had handsomely
bound in morocco with gilt edges.*

BECKER (Bernard H.).
The Scientific Societies of
London. Crown 8vo. Cloth,
price 5s.

BELLINGHAM (Henry), Barris-
ter-at-Law.
Social Aspects of Catholi-
cism and Protestantism in their
. Civil Bearing upon Nations.
Translated and adapted from the
French of M. le Baron de Haulle-
ville. With a Preface by His Emi-
nence Cardinal Manning. Crown 8vo.
Cloth, price 6s.

BENNETT (Dr. W. C.).
Narrative Poems & Ballads.
Fcap. 8vo. Sewed in Coloured Wrap-
per, price 1s.
Songs for Sailors. Dedicated
by Special Request to H. R. H. the
Duke of Edinburgh. With Steel
Portrait and Illustrations. Crown
8vo. , Cloth, price 3s. 6d.
An Edition in Illustrated Paper
Covers, price 1s.

BENNETT (Dr.W.C.)—*continued*.
Songs of a Song Writer.
Crown 8vo. Cloth, price 6s.

BENNIE (Rev. J. N.), M.A.
The Eternal Life. Sermons
preached during the last twelve years.
Crown 8vo. Cloth, price 6s.

BERNARD (Bayle).
Samuel Lover, the Life and
Unpublished Works of. In 2
vols. With a Steel Portrait. Post
8vo. Cloth, price 21s.

BERNSTEIN (Prof.).
The Five Senses of Man.
With 91 Illustrations. Second
Edition. Crown 8vo. Cloth,
price 5s.
Volume XXI. of The International
Scientific Series.

BETHAM - EDWARDS (Miss
M.).
Kitty. With a Frontispiece.
Crown 8vo. Cloth, price 6s.

BEVINGTON (L. S.).
Key Notes. Small crown
8vo. Cloth, price 5s.

BISSET (A.)
History of the Struggle for
Parliamentary Government in
England. 2 vols. Demy 8vo.
Cloth, price 24s.

BLASERNA (Prof. Pietro).
The Theory of Sound in its
Relation to Music. With nume-
rous Illustrations. Second Edition.
Crown 8vo. Cloth, price 5s.
Volume XXII. of The International
Scientific Series.

Blue Roses ; or, Helen Mali-
nofska's Marriage. By the Author
of " Véra." 2 vols. Fifth Edition.
Cloth, gilt tops, 12s.
. Also a Cheaper Edition in 1
vol. With Frontispiece. Crown 8vo.
Cloth, price 6s.

BLUME (Major W.).
The Operations of the German Armies in France, from Sedan to the end of the war of 1870-71. With Map. From the Journals of the Head-quarters Staff. Translated by the late E. M. Jones, Maj. 20th Foot, Prof. of Mil. Hist., Sandhurst. Demy 8vo. Cloth, price 9s.

BOGUSLAWSKI (Capt. A. von).
Tactical Deductions from the War of 1870-71. Translated by Colonel Sir Lumley Graham, Bart., late 18th (Royal Irish) Regiment. Third Edition, Revised and Corrected. Demy 8vo. Cloth, price 7s.

BONWICK (J.), F.R.G.S.
Egyptian Belief and Modern Thought. Large post 8vo. Cloth, price 10s. 6d.

Pyramid Facts and Fancies. Crown 8vo. Cloth, price 5s.

The Tasmanian Lily. With Frontispiece. Crown 8vo. Cloth, price 5s.

Mike Howe, the Bushranger of Van Diemen's Land. With Frontispiece. Crown 8vo. Cloth, price 5s.

BOSWELL (R. B.), M.A., Oxon.
Metrical Translations from the Greek and Latin Poets, and other Poems. Crown 8vo. Cloth, price 5s.

BOWEN (H. C.), M.A.
English Grammar for Beginners. Fcap. 8vo. Cloth, price 1s.

Studies in English, for the use of Modern Schools. Small crown 8vo. Cloth, price 1s. 6d.

Simple English Poems. English Literature for Junior Classes. In Four Parts. Parts I. and II., price 6d. each, now ready.

BOWRING (L.), C.S.I.
Eastern Experiences. Illustrated with Maps and Diagrams. Demy 8vo. Cloth, price 16s.

BOWRING (Sir John).
Autobiographical Recollections. With Memoir by Lewin B. Bowring. Demy 8vo. Price 14s.

BRADLEY (F. H.).
Ethical Studies. Critical Essays in Moral Philosophy. Large post 8vo. Cloth, price 9s.

Brave Men's Footsteps. By the Editor of "Men who have Risen." A Book of Example and Anecdote for Young People. With Four Illustrations by C. Doyle. Fifth Edition. Crown 8vo. Cloth, price 3s. 6d.

BRIALMONT (Col. A.).
Hasty Intrenchments. Translated by Lieut. Charles A. Empson, R. A. With Nine Plates. Demy 8vo. Cloth, price 6s.

BROOKE (Rev. S. A.), M. A.
The Late Rev. F. W. Robertson, M.A., Life and Letters of. Edited by.
I. Uniform with the Sermons. 2 vols. With Steel Portrait. Price 7s. 6d.
II. Library Edition. 8vo. With Two Steel Portraits. Price 12s.
III. A Popular Edition, in 1 vol. 8vo. Price 6s.

Theology in the English Poets. — COWPER, COLERIDGE, WORDSWORTH, and BURNS. Third Edition. Post 8vo. Cloth, price 9s.

Christ in Modern Life. Thirteenth Edition. Crown 8vo. Cloth, price 7s. 6d.

Sermons. First Series. Eleventh Edition. Crown 8vo. Cloth, price 6s.

Sermons. Second Series. Third Edition. Crown 8vo. Cloth, price 7s.

The Fight of Faith. Sermons preached on various occasions. Third Edition. Crown 8vo. Cloth, price 7s. 6d.

Frederick Denison Maurice: The Life and Work of. A Memorial Sermon. Crown 8vo. Sewed, price 1s.

BROOKE (W. G.), M.A.
The Public Worship Regulation Act. With a Classified Statement of its Provisions, Notes, and Index. Third Edition, Revised and Corrected. Crown 8vo. Cloth, price 3s. 6d.

BROOKE (W. G.)—*continued.*

Six Privy Council Judg-
ments—1850-1872. Annotated by.
Third Edition. Crown 8vo. Cloth,
price 9s.

BROUN (J. A.).

Magnetic Observations at
Trevandrum and Augustia
Malley. Vol. I. 4to. Cloth,
price 63s.
The Report from above, separately
sewed, price 21s.

BROWN (Rev. J. Baldwin), B.A.

The Higher Life. Its Reality,
Experience, and Destiny. Fifth and
Cheaper Edition. Crown 8vo. Cloth,
price 5s.

Doctrine of Annihilation
in the Light of the Gospel
of Love. Five Discourses. Third
Edition. Crown 8vo. Cloth, price
2s. 6d.

BROWN (J. Croumbie), LL.D.

Reboisement in France; or,
Records of the Replanting of the
Alps, the Cevennes, and the Pyre-
nees with Trees, Herbage, and Bush.
Demy 8vo. Cloth, price 12s. 6d.

The Hydrology of Southern
Africa. Demy 8vo. Cloth, price
10s. 6d.

BRYANT (W. C.)

Poems. Red-line Edition.
With 24 Illustrations and Portrait of
the Author. Crown 8vo. Cloth extra,
price 7s. 6d.
A Cheaper Edition, with Frontispiece. Small crown 8vo. Cloth, price
3s. 6d.

BUCHANAN (Robert).

Poetical Works. Collected
Edition, in 3 vols., with Portrait.
'Crown 8vo. Cloth, price 6s. each.

Master-Spirits. Post 8vo.
Cloth, price 10s. 6d.

BULKELEY (Rev. H. J.).

Walled in, and other Poems.
Crown 8vo. Cloth, price 5s.

BURCKHARDT (Jacob).

The Civilization of the Pe-
riod of the Renaissance in Italy.
Authorized translation, by S. G. C.
Middlemore. 2 vols. Demy 8vo.
Cloth, price 24s.

BURTON (Mrs. Richard).

The Inner Life of Syria,
Palestine, and the Holy Land.
With Maps, Photographs, and
Coloured Plates. 2 vols. Second
Edition. Demy 8vo. Cloth, price 24s.
⁎⁎ Also a Cheaper Edition in
one volume. Large post 8vo. Cloth,
price 10s. 6d.

BURTON (Capt. Richard F.).

The Gold Mines of Midian
and the Ruined Midianite
Cities. A Fortnight's Tour in
North Western Arabia. With numerous Illustrations. Second Edition. Demy 8vo. Cloth, price 18s.

The Land of Midian Re-
visited. With numerous illustrations on wood and by Chromo-
lithography. 2 vols. Demy 8vo.
Cloth, price 32s.

CALDERON.

Calderon's Dramas: The
Wonder-Working Magician—Life is
a Dream—The Purgatory of St.
Patrick. Translated by Denis
Florence MacCarthy. Post 8vo.
Cloth, price 10s.

CANDLER (H.).

The Groundwork of Belief.
Crown 8vo. Cloth, price 7s.

CARLISLE (A. D.), B. A.

Round the World in 1870.
A Volume of Travels, with Maps.
New and Cheaper Edition. Demy
8vo. Cloth, price 6s.

CARNE (Miss E. T.).

The Realm of Truth. Crown
8vo. Cloth, price 5s. 6d.

CARPENTER (E.).

Narcissus and other
Poems. Fcap. 8vo. Cloth, price 5s.

CARPENTER (W. B.), M.D.

The Principles of Mental
Physiology. With their Applica-
tions to the Training and Discipline
of the Mind, and the Study of its
Morbid Conditions. Illustrated.
Fifth Edition. 8vo. Cloth, price 12s.

CAVALRY OFFICER.

Notes on Cavalry Tactics,
Organization, &c. With Diagrams. Demy 8vo. Cloth, price 12s.

CHAPMAN (Hon. Mrs. E. W.).
A Constant Heart. A Story.
2 vols. Cloth, gilt tops, price 12s.
Children's' Toys, and some
Elementary Lessons in General
Knowledge which they teach. Illus-
trated. Crown 8vo. Cloth, price 5s.
CHRISTOPHERSON (The late
Rev. Henry), M.A.
Sermons. With an Intro-
duction by John Rae, LL.D., F.S.A.
Second Series. Crown 8vo. Cloth,
price 6s.
CLERK (Mrs. Godfrey).
'Ilâm en Nâs. Historical
Tales and Anecdotes of the Times
of the Early Khalifahs. Translated
from the Arabic Originals. Illus-
trated with Historical and Explana-
tory Notes. Crown 8vo. Cloth, price 7s.
CLERY (C.), Major.
Minor Tactics. With 26
Maps and Plans. Fourth and Revised
Edition. Demy 8vo. Cloth, price 16s.
CLODD (Edward), F.R.A.S.
**The Childhood of the
World :** a Simple Account of Man
in Early Times. Sixth Edition.
Crown 8vo. Cloth, price 3s.
A Special Edition for Schools.
Price 1s.
**The Childhood of Reli-
gions.** Including a Simple Account
of the Birth and Growth of Myths
and Legends. Third Thousand.
Crown 8vo. Cloth, price 5s.
A Special Edition for Schools.
Price 1s. 6d.
COLERIDGE (Sara).
Pretty Lessons in Verse
for Good Children, with some
Lessons in Latin, in Easy Rhyme.
A New Edition. Illustrated. Fcap.
8vo. Cloth, price 3s. 6d.
Phantasmion. A Fairy Tale.
With an Introductory Preface by the
Right Hon. Lord Coleridge, of
Ottery St. Mary. A New Edition.
Illustrated. Crown 8vo. Cloth,
price 7s. 6d.
Memoir and Letters of Sara
Coleridge. Edited by her Daughter.
With Index. 2 vols. With Two
Portraits. Third Edition, Revised
and Corrected. Crown 8vo. Cloth,
price 24s.
Cheap Edition. With one Portrait.
Cloth, price 7s. 6d.

COLLINS (Mortimer).
The Secret of Long Life.
Small crown 8vo. Cloth, price 3s. 6d.
Inn of Strange Meetings,
and other Poems. Crown 8vo.
Cloth, price 5s.
COLLINS (Rev. R.), M.A.
Missionary Enterprise in
the East. With special reference
to the Syrian Christians of Malabar,
and the results of modern Missions.
With Four Illustrations. Crown
8vo. Cloth, price 6s.
COOKE (M. C.), M.A., LL.D.
Fungi ; their Nature, Influ-
ences, Uses, &c. Edited by the Rev.
M. J. Berkeley, M.A., F.L.S.
With Illustrations. Second Edition.
Crown 8vo. Cloth, price 5s.
Volume XIV. of The International
Scientific Series.
COOKE (Prof. J. P.)
The New Chemistry. With
31 Illustrations. Fourth Edition.
Crown 8vo. Cloth, price 5s.
Volume IX. of The International
Scientific Series.
Scientific Culture. Crown
8vo. Cloth, price 1s.
COOPER (T. T.), F.R.G.S.
The Mishmee Hills : an
Account of a Journey made in an
Attempt to Penetrate Thibet from
Assam, to open New Routes for
Commerce. Second Edition. With
Four Illustrations and Map. Post
8vo. Cloth, price 10s. 6d.
COOPER (H. J.).
The Art of Furnishing on
Rational and Æsthetic Prin-
ciples. New and Cheaper Edition.
Fcap. 8vo. Cloth, price 1s. 6d.
COPPÉE (François).
L'Exilée. Done into English
Verse with the sanction of the Author
by I. O. L. Crown 8vo. Cloth,
price 5s.
Cornhill Library of Fiction
(The). Crown 8vo. Cloth, price
3s. 6d. per volume.
Half-a-Dozen Daughters. By
J. Masterman.
The House of Raby. By Mrs. G.
Hooper.

Cornhill Library of Fiction—
continued.

A Fight for Life. By Moy Thomas.
Robin Gray. By Charles Gibbon.
One of Two; or, A Left-Handed Bride. By J. Hain Friswell.
God's Providence House. By Mrs. G. L. Banks.
For Lack of Gold. By Charles Gibbon.
Abel Drake's Wife. By John Saunders.
Hirell. By John Saunders.

CORY (Lieut. Col. Arthur).
The Eastern Menace; or, Shadows of Coming Events. Crown 8vo. Cloth, price 5s.
Ione. A Poem in Four Parts. Fcap. 8vo. Cloth, price 5s.
Cosmos. A Poem. Fcap. 8vo. Cloth, price 3s. 6d.

COURTNEY (W. L.).
The Metaphysics of John Stuart Mill. Crown 8vo. Cloth, price 5s. 6d.

COWAN (Rev. William).
Poems : Chiefly Sacred, including Translations from some Ancient Latin Hymns. Fcap. 8vo. Cloth, price 5s.

COX (Rev. Sir G. W.), Bart.
A History of Greece from the Earliest Period to the end of the Persian War. New Edition. 2 vols. Demy 8vo. Cloth, price 36s.
The Mythology of the Aryan Nations. New Edition. 2 vols. Demy 8vo. Cloth, price 28s.
A General History of Greece from the Earliest Period to the Death of Alexander the Great, with a sketch of the subsequent History to the present time. New Edition. Crown 8vo. Cloth, price 7s. 6d.
Tales of Ancient Greece. New Edition. Small crown 8vo. Cloth, price 6s.
School History of Greece. With Maps. New Edition. Fcap. 8vo. Cloth, price 3s. 6d.
The Great Persian War from the Histories of Herodotus. New Edition. Fcap. 8vo. Cloth, price 3s. 6d.

COX (Rev. Sir G. W.), Bart.—
continued.
A Manual of Mythology in the form of Question and Answer. New Edition. Fcap. 8vo. Cloth, price 3s.

COX (Rev. Samuel).
Salvator Mundi; or, Is Christ the Saviour of all Men? Sixth Edition. Crown 8vo. Cloth, price 5s.

CRAUFURD (A. H.).
Seeking for Light : Sermons. Crown 8vo. Cloth, price 5s.

CRESSWELL (Mrs. G.).
The King's Banner. Drama in Four Acts. Five Illustrations. 4to. Cloth, price 10s. 6d.

CROMPTON (Henry).
Industrial Conciliation. Fcap. 8vo. Cloth, price 2s. 6d.

D'ANVERS (N. R.).
The Suez Canal : Letters and Documents descriptive of its Rise and Progress in 1854-56. By Ferdinand de Lesseps. Translated by. Demy 8vo. Cloth, price 10s. 6d.
Parted. A Tale of Clouds and Sunshine. With 4 Illustrations. Extra Fcap 8vo. Cloth, price 3s. 6d.
Little Minnie's Troubles. An Every-day Chronicle. With Four Illustrations by W. H. Hughes. Fcap. Cloth, price 3s. 6d.
Pixie's Adventures; or, the Tale of a Terrier. With 21 Illustrations. 16mo. Cloth, price 4s. 6d.
Nanny's Adventures; or, the Tale of a Goat. With 12 Illustrations. 16mo. Cloth, price 4s. 6d.

DAVIDSON (Rev. Samuel), D.D., LL.D.
The New Testament, translated from the Latest Greek Text of Tischendorf. A New and thoroughly Revised Edition. Post 8vo. Cloth, price 10s. 6d.
Canon of the Bible : Its Formation, History, and Fluctuations. Second Edition. Small crown 8vo. Cloth, price 5s.

DAVIES (G. Christopher).
Mountain, Meadow, and Mere : a Series of Outdoor Sketches of Sport, Scenery, Adventures, and Natural History. With Sixteen Illustrations by Bosworth W. Harcourt. Crown 8vo. Cloth, price 6s.

DAVIES (G. Chris.)—*continued.*
Rambles and Adventures
of Our School Field Club. With
Four Illustrations. Crown 8vo.
Cloth, price 5*s.*

DAVIES (Rev. J. L.), M.A.
Theology and Morality.
Essays on Questions of Belief and
Practice. Crown 8vo. Cloth, price
7*s.* 6*d.*

DAVIES (T. Hart.).
Catullus. Translated into
English Verse. Crown 8vo. Cloth,
price 6*s.*

DAWSON (George), M.A.
Prayers, with a Discourse
on Prayer. Edited by his Wife.
Fifth Edition. Crown 8vo. Price 6*s.*
Sermons on Disputed
Points and Special Occasions.
Edited by his Wife. Third Edition.
Crown 8vo. Cloth, price 6*s.*
Sermons on Daily Life and
Duty. Edited by his Wife. Second
Edition. Crown 8vo. Cloth, price 6*s.*

DE L'HOSTE (Col. E. P.).
The Desert Pastor, Jean
Jarousseau. Translated from the
French of Eugène Pelletan. With a
Frontispiece. New Edition. Fcap.
8vo. Cloth, price 3*s.* 6*d.*

DENNIS (J.).
English Sonnets. Collected
and Arranged. Elegantly bound.
Fcap. 8vo. Cloth, price 3*s.* 6*d.*

DE REDCLIFFE (Viscount
Stratford), P.C., K.G., G.C.B.
Why am I a Christian?
Fifth Edition. Crown 8vo. Cloth,
price 3*s.*

DESPREZ (Philip S.).
Daniel and John; or, the
Apocalypse of the Old and that of
the New Testament. Demy 8vo.
Cloth, price 12*s.*

DE TOCQUEVILLE (A.).
Correspondence and Con-
versations of, with Nassau William Senior, from 1834 to 1859.
Edited by M. C. M. Simpson. 2
vols. Post 8vo. Cloth, price 21*s.*

DE VERE (Aubrey).
Legends of the Saxon
Saints. Small crown 8vo. Cloth,
price 6*s.*

A 2

DE VERE (Aubrey) - *continued.*
Alexander the Great. A
Dramatic Poem. Small crown 8vo.
Cloth, price 5*s.*
The Infant Bridal, and
Other Poems. A New and En-
larged Edition. Fcap. 8vo. Cloth,
price 7*s.* 6*d.*
The Legends of St. Patrick,
and other Poems. Small crown
8vo. Cloth, price 5*s.*
St. Thomas of Canterbury.
A Dramatic Poem. Large fcap. 8vo.
Cloth, price 5*s.*
Antar and Zara: an Eastern
Romance. INISFAIL, and other
Poems, Meditative and Lyrical.
Fcap. 8vo. Price 6*s.*
The Fall of Rora, the
Search after Proserpine, and
other Poems, Meditative and Lyrical.
Fcap. 8vo. Price 6*s.*

DOBSON (Austin).
Vignettes in Rhyme and
Vers de Société. Third Edition.
Fcap. 8vo. Cloth, price 5*s.*
Proverbs in Porcelain. By
the Author of "Vignettes in Rhyme."
Second Edition. Crown 8vo. 6*s.*

DOWDEN (Edward), LL.D.
Shakspere: a Critical Study
of his Mind and Art. Fourth Edition.
Large post 8vo. Cloth, price 12*s.*
Studies in Literature, 1789-
1877. Large post 8vo. Cloth, price
12*s.*
Poems. Second Edition.
Fcap. 8vo. Cloth, price 5*s.*

DOWNTON (Rev. H.), M.A.
Hymns and Verses. Original and Translated. Small crown
8vo. Cloth, price 3*s.* 6*d.*

DRAPER (J. W.), M.D., LL.D.
History of the Conflict be-
tween Religion and Science.
Eleventh Edition. Crown 8vo. Cloth,
price 5*s.*
Volume XIII. of The International
Scientific Series.

DREW (Rev. G. S.), M.A.
Scripture Lands in con-
nection with their History.
Second Edition. 8vo. Cloth, price
10*s.* 6*d.*

DREW (Rev. G. S.), M.A. *continued*.

Nazareth: Its Life and Lessons. Third Edition. Crown 8vo. Cloth, price 5*s*.

The Divine Kingdom on Earth as it is in Heaven. 8vo. Cloth, price 10*s*. 6*d*.

The Son of Man: His Life and Ministry. Crown 8vo. Cloth, price 7*s*. 6*d*.

DREWRY (G. O.), M.D.

The Common-Sense Management of the Stomach. Fifth Edition. Fcap. 8vo. Cloth, price 2*s*. 6*d*.

DREWRY (G. O.), M.D., and BARTLETT (H. C.), Ph.D., F.C.S.

Cup and Platter: or, Notes on Food and its Effects. New and cheaper Edition. Small 8vo. Cloth, price 1*s*. 6*d*.

DRUMMOND (Miss).

Tripps Buildings. A Study from Life, with Frontispiece. Small crown 8vo. Cloth, price 3*s*. 6*d*.

DU MONCEL (Count).

The Telephone, the Microphone, and the Phonograph. With 74 Illustrations. Small crown 8vo. Cloth, price 5*s*.

DURAND (Lady).

Imitations from the German of Spitta and Terstegen. Fcap. 8vo. Cloth, price 4*s*.

DU VERNOIS (Col. von Verdy).

Studies in leading Troops. An authorized and accurate Translation by Lieutenant H. J. T. Hildyard, 71st Foot. Parts I. and II. Demy 8vo. Cloth, price 7*s*.

EDEN (Frederick).

The Nile without a Dragoman. Second Edition. Crown 8vo. Cloth, price 7*s*. 6*d*.

EDMONDS (Herbert).

Well Spent Lives: a Series of Modern Biographies. Crown 8vo. Price 5*s*.

The Educational Code of the Prussian Nation, in its Present Form. In accordance with the Decisions of the Common Provincial Law, and with those of Recent Legislation. Crown 8vo. Cloth, price 2*s*. 6*d*.

EDWARDS (Rev. Basil).

Minor Chords; or, Songs for the Suffering: a Volume of Verse. Fcap. 8vo. Cloth, price 3*s*. 6*d*.; paper, price 2*s*. 6*d*.

ELLIOT (Lady Charlotte).

Medusa and other Poems. Crown 8vo. Cloth, price 6*s*.

ELLIOTT (Ebenezer), The Corn Law Rhymer.

Poems. Edited by his Son, the Rev. Edwin Elliott, of St. John's, Antigua. 2 vols. Crown 8vo. Cloth, price 18*s*.

ELSDALE (Henry).

Studies in Tennyson's Idylls. Crown 8vo. Cloth, price 5*s*.

Epic of Hades (The). By the author of "Songs of Two Worlds." Seventh and finally revised Edition. Fcap. 8vo. Cloth, price 7*s*. 6*d*.

*** Also an Illustrated Edition with seventeen full-page designs in photomezzotint by GEORGE R. CHAPMAN. 4to. Cloth, extra gilt leaves, price 25*s*.

Eros Agonistes. Poems. By E. B. D. Fcap. 8vo. Cloth, price 3*s*. 6*d*.

Essays on the Endowment of Research. By Various Writers. Square crown 8vo. Cloth, price 10*s*. 6*d*.

EVANS (Mark).

The Gospel of Home Life. Crown 8vo. Cloth, price 4*s*. 6*d*.

The Story of our Father's Love, told to Children. Fourth and Cheaper Edition. With Four Illustrations. Fcap. 8vo. Cloth, price 1*s*. 6*d*.

A Book of Common Prayer and Worship for Household Use, compiled exclusively from the Holy Scriptures. Fcap. 8vo. Cloth, price 2*s*. 6*d*.

EX-CIVILIAN.

Life in the Mofussil; or, Civilian Life in Lower Bengal. 2 vols. Large post 8vo. Price 14*s*.

EYRE (Maj.-Gen. Sir V.), C.B., K.C.S.I., &c.

Lays of a Knight-Errant in many Lands. Square crown 8vo. With Six Illustrations. Cloth, price 7*s*. 6*d*.

FARQUHARSON (M.).
I. **Elsie Dinsmore.** Crown 8vo. Cloth, price 3s. 6d.

II. **Elsie's Girlhood.** Crown 8vo. Cloth, price 3s. 6d.

III. **Elsie's Holidays at Roselands.** Crown 8vo. Cloth, price 3s. 6d.

FERRIS (Henry Weybridge).
Poems. Fcap. 8vo. Cloth, price 5s.

FIELD (Horace), B.A., Lond:
The Ultimate Triumph of Christianity. Small crown 8vo. Cloth, price 3s. 6d.

FINN (the late James), M.R.A.S.
Stirring Times; or, Records from Jerusalem Consular Chronicles of 1853 to 1856. Edited and Compiled by his Widow. With a Preface by the Viscountess STRANGFORD. 2 vols. Demy 8vo. Price 30s.

FLEMING (James), D.D.
Early Christian Witnesses; or, Testimonies of the First Centuries to the Truth of Christianity. Small crown 8vo. Cloth, price 3s. 6d.

Folkestone Ritual Case (The). The Argument, Proceedings, Judgment, and Report, revised by the several Counsel engaged. Demy 8vo. Cloth, price 25s.

FOOTMAN (Rev. H.), M.A.
From Home and Back; or, Some Aspects of Sin as seen in the Light of the Parable of the Prodigal. Crown 8vo. Cloth, price 5s.

FOWLE (Rev. Edmund).
Latin Primer Rules made Easy. Crown 8vo. Cloth, price 3s.

FOWLE (Rev. T. W.), M.A.
The Reconciliation of Re-ligion and Science. Being Essays on Immortality, Inspiration, Miracles, and the Being of Christ. Demy 8vo. Cloth, price 10s. 6d.

The Divine Legation of Christ. Crown 8vo. Cloth, price 7s.

FOX-BOURNE (H. R.).
The Life of John Locke, 1632—1704. 2 vols. Demy 8vo. Cloth, price 28s.

FRASER (Donald).
Exchange Tables of Ster-ling and Indian Rupee Currency, upon a new and extended system, embracing Values from One Farthing to One Hundred Thousand Pounds, and at Rates progressing, in Sixteenths of a Penny, from 1s. 9d. to 2s. 3d. per Rupee. Royal 8vo. Cloth, price 10s. 6d.

FRISWELL (J. Hain).
The Better Self. Essays for Home Life. Crown 8vo. Cloth, price 6s.

One of Two; or, A Left-Handed Bride. With a Frontispiece. Crown 8vo. Cloth, price 3s. 6d.

FYTCHE (Lieut.-Gen. Albert), C.S.I., late Chief Commissioner of British Burma.
Burma Past and Present, with Personal Reminiscences of the Country. With Steel Portraits, Chromolithographs, Engravings on Wood, and Map. 2 vols. Demy 8vo. Cloth, price 30s.

GAMBIER (Capt. J. W.), R.N.
Servia. Crown 8vo. Cloth, price 5s.

GARDNER (H.).
Sunflowers. A Book of Verses. Fcap. 8vo. Cloth, price 5s.

GARDNER (J.), M.D.
Longevity: The Means of Prolonging Life after Middle Age. Fourth Edition, Revised and Enlarged. Small crown 8vo. Cloth, price 4s.

GARRETT (E.).
By Still Waters. A Story for Quiet Hours. With Seven Illustrations. Crown 8vo. Cloth, price 6s.

GEBLER (Karl Von).
Galileo Galilei and the Roman Curia, from Authentic Sources. Translated with the sanction of the Author, by Mrs. GEORGE STURGE. Demy 8vo. Cloth, price 12s.

G. H. T.
Verses, mostly written in India. Crown 8vo. Cloth, price 6s.

GILBERT (Mrs.).
Autobiography and other Memorials. Edited by Josiah Gilbert. Third Edition. With Portrait and several Wood Engravings. Crown 8vo. Cloth, price 7s. 6d.

GILL (Rev. W. W.), B.A.
Myths and Songs from the
South Pacific. With a Preface by
F. Max Müller, M.A., Professor of
Comparative Philology at Oxford.
Post 8vo. Cloth, price 9s.

GLOVER (F.), M.A.
Exempla Latina. A First
Construing Book with Short Notes,
Lexicon, and an Introduction to the
Analysis of Sentences. Fcap. 8vo.
Cloth, price 2s.

GODKIN (James).
The Religious History of
Ireland: Primitive, Papal, and
Protestant. Including the Evange-
lical Missions, Catholic Agitations,
and Church Progress of the last half
Century. 8vo. Cloth, price 12s.

GODWIN (William).
William Godwin: His
Friends and Contemporaries.
With Portraits and Facsimiles of the
handwriting of Godwin and his Wife.
By C. Kegan Paul. 2 vols. Demy
8vo. Cloth, price 28s.
The Genius of Christianity
Unveiled. Being Essays never
before published. Edited, with a
Preface, by C. Kegan Paul. Crown
8vo. Cloth, price 7s. 6d.

GOETZE (Capt. A. von).
Operations of the German
Engineers during the War of
1870-1871. Published by Authority,
and in accordance with Official Documents. Translated from the German
by Colonel G. Graham, V.C., C.B.,
R.E. With 6 large Maps. Demy
8vo. Cloth, price 21s.

GOLDIE (Lieut. M. H. G.)
Hebe: a Tale. Fcap. 8vo.
Cloth, price 5s.

GOLDSMID (Sir Francis Henry).
Memoir of. With Portrait.
Crown 8vo. Cloth, price 5s.

GOODENOUGH (Commodore J.
G.), R.N., C.B., C.M.G.
Memoir of, with Extracts from
his Letters and Journals. Edited by
his Widow. With Steel Engraved
Portrait. Square 8vo. Cloth, 5s.
*** Also a Library Edition with
Maps, Woodcuts, and Steel En-
graved Portrait. Square post 8vo.
Cloth, price 14s.

GOSSE (Edmund W.).
Studies in the Literature of
Northern Europe. With a Frontis-
piece designed and etched by Alma
Tadema. Large post 8vo. Cloth,
price 12s.
New Poems. Crown 8vo.
Cloth, price 7s. 6d.

GOULD (Rev. S. Baring), M.A.
Germany, Present and Past.
2 Vols. Demy 8vo. Cloth, price 21s.
The Vicar of Morwenstow:
a Memoir of the Rev. R. S. Hawker.
With Portrait. Third Edition, revised. Square post 8vo. Cloth, 10s. 6d.

GRANVILLE (A. B.), M.D.,
F.R.S., &c.
Autobiography of A. B.
Granville, F.R.S., &c. Edited,
with a brief Account of the concluding
Years of his Life, by his youngest
Daughter, Paulina B. Granville. 2
vols. With a Portrait. Second Edi-
tion. Demy 8vo. Cloth, price 32s.

GREY (John), of Dilston.
John Grey (of Dilston):
Memoirs. By Josephine E. Butler.
New and Revised Edition. Crown
8vo. Cloth, price 3s. 6d.

GRIFFITH (Rev. T.), A.M.
Studies of the Divine Mas-
ter. Demy 8vo. Cloth, price 12s.

GRIFFITHS (Capt. Arthur).
Memorials of Millbank, and
Chapters in Prison History.
With Illustrations by R. Goff and
the Author. 2 vols. Post 8vo. Cloth,
price 21s.

GRIMLEY (Rev. H. N.), M.A.
Tremadoc Sermons, chiefly
on the SPIRITUAL BODY, the UNSEEN
WORLD, and the DIVINE HUMANITY.
Second Edition. Crown 8vo. Cloth,
price 6s.

GRÜNER (M. L.).
Studies of Blast Furnace
Phenomena. Translated by L. D.
B. Gordon, F.R.S.E., F.G.S. Demy
8vo. Cloth, price 7s. 6d.

GURNEY (Rev. Archer).
Words of Faith and Cheer.
A Mission of Instruction and Sugges-
tion. Crown 8vo. Cloth, price 6s.

Gwen: A Drama in Monologue. By the Author of the "Epic of Hades." Second Edition. Fcap. 8vo. Cloth, price 5*s.*

HAECKEL (Prof. Ernst).
The History of Creation. Translation revised by Professor E. Ray Lankester, M.A., F.R.S. With Coloured Plates and Genealogical Trees of the various groups of both plants and animals. 2 vols. Second Edition. Post 8vo. Cloth, price 32*s.*

The History of the Evolution of Man. With numerous Illustrations. 2 vols. Large post 8vo. Cloth, price 32*s.*

Freedom in Science and Teaching. From the German of Ernst Haeckel, with a Prefatory Note by T. H. Huxley, F.R.S. Crown 8vo. Cloth, price 5*s.*

HAKE (A. Egmont).
Paris Originals, with twenty etchings, by Léon Richeton. Large post 8vo. Cloth, price 14*s.*

Halleck's International Law; or, Rules Regulating the Intercourse of States in Peace and War. A New Edition, revised, with Notes and Cases. By Sir Sherston Baker, Bart. 2 vols. Demy 8vo. Cloth, price 38*s.*

HARCOURT (Capt. A. F. P.).
The Shakespeare Argosy. Containing much of the wealth of Shakespeare's Wisdom and Wit, alphabetically arranged and classified. Crown 8vo. Cloth, price 6*s.*

HARDY (Thomas).
A Pair of Blue Eyes. New Edition. With Frontispiece. Crown 8vo. Cloth, price 6*s.*

The Return of the Native. New Edition. With Frontispiece. Crown 8vo. Cloth, price 6*s.*

HARRISON (Lieut.-Col. R.).
The Officer's Memorandum Book for Peace and War. Second Edition. Oblong 32mo. roan, elastic band and pencil, price 3*s.* 6*d.*; russia, 5*s.*

HAWEIS (Rev. H. R.), M.A.
Arrows in the Air. Crown 8vo. Second Edition. Cloth, price 6*s.*

HAWEIS (Rev. H. R.)—continued.
Current Coin. Materialism— The Devil—Crime—Drunkenness— Pauperism—Emotion—Recreation— The Sabbath. Third Edition. Crown 8vo. Cloth, price 6*s.*

Speech in Season. Fourth Edition. Crown 8vo. Cloth, price 9*s.*

Thoughts for the Times. Eleventh Edition. Crown 8vo. Cloth, price 7*s.* 6*d.*

Unsectarian Family Prayers, for Morning and Evening for a Week, with short selected passages from the Bible. Second Edition. Square crown 8vo. Cloth, price 3*s.* 6*d.*

HAWKER (Robert Stephen).
The Poetical Works of. Now first collected and arranged, with a prefatory notice by J. G. Godwin. With Portrait. Crown 8vo. Cloth, price 12*s.*

HELLWALD (Baron F. von).
The Russians in Central Asia. A Critical Examination, down to the present time, of the Geography and History of Central Asia. Translated by Lieut.-Col. Theodore Wirgman, LL.B. Large post 8vo. With Map. Cloth, price 12*s.*

HELVIG (Major H.).
The Operations of the Bavarian Army Corps. Translated by Captain G. S. Schwabe. With Five large Maps. In 2 vols. Demy 8vo. Cloth, price 24*s.*

Tactical Examples: Vol. I. The Battalion, price 15*s.* Vol. II. The Regiment and Brigade, price 10*s.* 6*d.* Translated from the German by Col. Sir Lumley Graham. With numerou s Diagrams. Demy 8vo. Cloth.

HERFORD (Brooke).
The Story of Religion in England. A Book for Young Folk. Crown 8vo. Cloth, price 5*s.*

HEWLETT (Henry G.).
A Sheaf of Verse. Fcap. 8vo. Cloth, price 3*s.* 6*d.*

HINTON (James).
Life and Letters of. Edited by Ellice Hopkins, with an Introduction by Sir W. W. Gull, Bart., and Portrait engraved on Steel by C. H. Jeens. Second Edition. Crown 8vo. Cloth, 8*s.* 6*d.*

HINTON (James)—*continued*.

Chapters on the Art of Thinking, and other Essays. With an Introduction by Shadworth Hodgson. Edited by C. H. Hinton. Crown 8vo. Cloth, price 8s. 6d.

The Place of the Physician. To which is added ESSAYS ON THE LAW OF HUMAN LIFE, AND ON THE RELATION BETWEEN ORGANIC AND INORGANIC WORLDS. Second Edition. Crown 8vo. Cloth, price 3s. 6d.

Physiology for Practical Use. By various Writers. With 50 Illustrations. 2 vols. Second Edition. Crown 8vo. Cloth, price 12s. 6d.

An Atlas of Diseases of the Membrana Tympani. With Descriptive Text. Post 8vo. Price £6 6s.

The Questions of Aural Surgery. With Illustrations. 2 vols. Post 8vo. Cloth, price 12s. 6d.

The Mystery of Pain. New Edition. Fcap. 8vo. Cloth limp, 1s.

HOCKLEY (W. B.).

Tales of the Zenana; or, A Nuwab's Leisure Hours. By the Author of "Pandurang Hari." With a Preface by Lord Stanley of Alderley. 2 vols. Crown 8vo. Cloth, price 21s.

Pandurang Hari; or, Memoirs of a Hindoo. A Tale of Mahratta Life sixty years ago. With a Preface by Sir H. Bartle E. Frere, G. C. S. I., &c. New and Cheaper Edition. Crown 8vo. Cloth, price 6s.

HOFFBAUER (Capt.).

The German Artillery in the Battles near Metz. Based on the official reports of the German Artillery. Translated by Capt. E. O. Hollist. With Map and Plans. Demy 8vo. Cloth, price 21s.

HOLMES (E. G. A.).

Poems. First and Second Series. Fcap. 8vo. Cloth, price 5s. each.

HOLROYD (Major W. R. M.).

Tas-hil ul Kālām; or, Hindustani made Easy. Crown 8vo. Cloth, price 5s.

HOOPER (Mary).

Little Dinners: How to Serve them with Elegance and Economy. Thirteenth Edition. Crown 8vo. Cloth, price 5s.

Cookery for Invalids, Persons of Delicate Digestion, and Children. Crown 8vo. Cloth, price 3s. 6d.

Every-Day Meals. Being Economical and Wholesome Recipes for Breakfast, Luncheon, and Supper. Second Edition. Crown 8vo. Cloth, price 5s.

HOOPER (Mrs. G.).

The House of Raby. With a Frontispiece. Crown 8vo. Cloth, price 3s. 6d.

HOPKINS (Ellice).

Life and Letters of James Hinton, with an Introduction by Sir W. W. Gull, Bart., and Portrait engraved on Steel by C. H. Jeens. Second Edition. Crown 8vo. Cloth, price 8s. 6d.

HOPKINS (M.).

The Port of Refuge; or, Counsel and Aid to Shipmasters in Difficulty, Doubt, or Distress. Crown 8vo. Second and Revised Edition. Cloth, price 6s.

HORNE (William), M.A.

Reason and Revelation: an Examination into the Nature and Contents of Scripture Revelation, as compared with other Forms of Truth. Demy 8vo. Cloth, price 12s.

HORNER (The Misses).

Walks in Florence. A New and thoroughly Revised Edition. 2 vols. Crown 8vo. Cloth limp. With Illustrations.
Vol. I.—Churches, Streets, and Palaces. 10s. 6d. Vol. II.—Public Galleries and Museums. 5s.

HOWARD (Mary M.).

Beatrice Aylmer, and other Tales. Crown 8vo. Cloth, price 6s.

HOWELL (James).

A Tale of the Sea, Sonnets, and other Poems. Fcap. 8vo. Cloth, price 5s.

HUGHES (Allison).

Penelope and other Poems. Fcap. 8vo. Cloth, price 4s. 6d.

HULL (Edmund C. P.).
The European in India.
With a MEDICAL GUIDE FOR ANGLO-INDIANS. By R. R. S. Mair, M.D., F.R.C.S.E. Third Edition, Revised and Corrected. Post 8vo. Cloth, price 6s.

HUTCHISON (Lieut. Col. F. J.), and Capt. G. H. MACGREGOR.
Military Sketching and Reconnaissance. With Fifteen Plates. Small 8vo. Cloth, price 6s.
The first Volume of Military Handbooks for Regimental Officers. Edited by Lieut.-Col. C. B. BRACKENBURY, R.A., A.A.G.

INCHBOLD (J. W.).
Annus Amoris. Sonnets.
Fcap. 8vo. Cloth, price 4s. 6d.

INGELOW (Jean).
Off the Skelligs. A Novel.
With Frontispiece. Second Edition. Crown 8vo. Cloth, price 6s.
The Little Wonder-horn.
A Second Series of "Stories Told to a Child." With Fifteen Illustrations. Small 8vo. Cloth, price 2s. 6d.

Indian Bishoprics. By an Indian Churchman. Demy 8vo. 6d.

International Scientific Series (The).
I. **Forms of Water:** A Familiar Exposition of the Origin and Phenomena of Glaciers. By J. Tyndall, LL.D., F.R.S. With 25 Illustrations. Seventh Edition. Crown 8vo. Cloth, price 5s.
II. **Physics and Politics;** or, Thoughts on the Application of the Principles of "Natural Selection" and "Inheritance" to Political Society. By Walter Bagehot. Fourth Edition. Crown 8vo. Cloth, price 4s.
III. **Foods.** By Edward Smith, M.D., &c. With numerous Illustrations. Fifth Edition. Crown 8vo. Cloth, price 5s.
IV. **Mind and Body:** The Theories of their Relation. By Alexander Bain, LL.D. With Four Illustrations. Sixth Edition. Crown 8vo. Cloth, price 4s.
V. **The Study of Sociology.** By Herbert Spencer. Seventh Edition. Crown 8vo. Cloth, price 5s.

International Scientific Series (The)—*continued.*
VI. **On the Conservation of Energy.** By Balfour Stewart, LL.D., &c. With 14 Illustrations. Fifth Edition. Crown 8vo. Cloth, price 5s.
VII. **Animal Locomotion;** or, Walking, Swimming, and Flying. By J. B. Pettigrew, M.D., &c. With 130 Illustrations. Second Edition. Crown 8vo. Cloth, price 5s.
VIII. **Responsibility in Mental Disease.** By Henry Maudsley, M.D. Third Edition. Crown 8vo. Cloth, price 5s.
IX. **The New Chemistry.** By Professor J. P. Cooke. With 31 Illustrations. Fourth Edition. Crown 8vo. Cloth, price 5s.
X. **The Science of Law.** By Prof. Sheldon Amos. Third Edition. Crown 8vo. Cloth, price 5s.
XI. **Animal Mechanism.** A Treatise on Terrestrial and Aerial Locomotion. By Prof. E. J. Marey. With 117 Illustrations. Second Edition. Crown 8vo. Cloth, price 5s.
XII. **The Doctrine of Descent and Darwinism.** By Prof. Oscar Schmidt. With 26 Illustrations. Third Edition. Crown 8vo. Cloth, price 5s.
XIII. **The History of the Conflict between Religion and Science.** By J. W. Draper, M.D., LL.D. Eleventh Edition. Crown 8vo. Cloth, price 5s.
XIV. **Fungi;** their Nature, Influences, Uses, &c. By M. C. Cooke, LL.D. Edited by the Rev. M. J. Berkeley, F.L.S. With numerous Illustrations. Second Edition. Crown 8vo. Cloth, price 5s.
XV. **The Chemical Effects of Light and Photography.** By Dr. Hermann Vogel. With 100 Illustrations. Third and Revised Edition. Crown 8vo. Cloth, price 5s.
XVI. **The Life and Growth of Language.** By Prof. William Dwight Whitney. Second Edition. Crown 8vo. Cloth, price 5s.
XVII. **Money and the Mechanism of Exchange.** By W. Stanley Jevons, F.R.S. Fourth Edition. Crown 8vo. Cloth, price 5s.

International Scientific Series (The)—*continued.*

XVIII. The Nature of Light: With a General Account of Physical Optics. By Dr. Eugene Lommel. With 188 Illustrations and a table of Spectra in Chromo-lithography. Second Edition. Crown 8vo. Cloth, price 5*s.*

XIX. Animal Parasites and Messmates. By M. Van Beneden. With 83 Illustrations. Second Edition. Crown 8vo. Cloth, price 5*s.*

XX. Fermentation. By Prof. Schützenberger. With 28 Illustrations. Second Edition. Crown 8vo. Cloth, price 5*s.*

XXI. The Five Senses of Man. By Prof. Bernstein. With 91 Illustrations. Second Edition. Crown 8vo. Cloth, price 5*s.*

XXII. The Theory of Sound in its Relation to Music. By Prof. Pietro Blaserna. With numerous Illustrations. Second Edition. Crown 8vo. Cloth, price 5*s.*

XXIII. Studies in Spectrum Analysis. By J. Norman Lockyer. F.R.S. With six photographic Illustrations of Spectra, and numerous engravings on wood. Crown 8vo. Second Edition. Cloth, price 6*s. 6d.*

XXIV. A History of the Growth of the Steam Engine. By Prof. R. H. Thurston. With numerous Illustrations. Second Edition. Crown 8vo. Cloth, price 6*s. 6d.*

XXV. Education as a Science. By Alexander Bain, LL.D. Second Edition. Crown 8vo. Cloth, price 5*s.*

XXVI. The Human Species. By Prof. A. de Quatrefages. Second Edition. Crown 8vo. Cloth, price 5*s.*

XXVII. Modern Chromatics. With Applications to Art and Industry, by Ogden N. Rood. With 130 original Illustrations. Crown 8vo. Cloth, price 5*s.*

Forthcoming Volumes.

Prof. W. Kingdon Clifford, M.A. The First Principles of the Exact Sciences explained to the Non-mathematical.

W. B. Carpenter, LL.D., F.R.S. The Physical Geography of the Sea.

Sir John Lubbock, Bart. F.R.S On Ants and Bees.

International Scientific Series (The)—*continued.*

Forthcoming Volumes— continued.

Prof. W. T. Thiselton Dyer, B.A., B.Sc. Form and Habit in Flowering Plants.

Prof. Michael Foster, M.D. Protoplasm and the Cell Theory.

H. Charlton Bastian, M.D., F.R.S. The Brain as an Organ of Mind.

Prof. A. C. Ramsay, LL.D., F.R.S. Earth Sculpture: Hills, Valleys, Mountains, Plains, Rivers, Lakes; how they were Produced, and how they have been Destroyed.

P. Bert (Professor of Physiology, Paris). Forms of Life and other Cosmical Conditions.

Prof. T. H. Huxley. The Crayfish: an Introduction to the Study of Zoology.

The Rev. A Secchi, D.J., late Director of the Observatory at Rome. The Stars.

Prof. J. Rosenthal, of the University of Erlangen. General Physiology of Muscles and Nerves.

Francis Galton, F.R.S. Psychometry.

J. W. Judd, F.R.S. The Laws of Volcanic Action.

Prof. F. N. Balfour. The Embryonic Phases of Animal Life.

J. Luys, Physician to the Hospice de la Salpétrière. The Brain and its Functions. With Illustrations.

Dr. Carl Semper. Animals and their Conditions of Existence.

Prof. Wurtz. Atoms and the Atomic Theory.

George J. Romanes, F.L.S. Animal Intelligence.

Alfred W. Bennett. A Handbook of Cryptogamic Botany.

JACKSON (T. G.). Modern Gothic Architecture. Crown 8vo. Cloth, price 5*s.*

JACOB (Maj.-Gen. Sir G. Le Grand), K.C.S.I., C.B. Western India before and during the Mutinies. Pictures drawn from life. Second Edition. Crown 8vo. Cloth, price 7*s. 6d.*

JENKINS (E.) and RAYMOND (J.), Esqs.
A Legal Handbook for Architects, Builders, and Building Owners. Second Edition Revised. Crown 8vo. Cloth, price 6s.

JENKINS (Rev. R. C.), M.A.
The Privilege of Peter and the Claims of the Roman Church confronted with the Scriptures, the Councils, and the Testimony of the Popes themselves. Fcap. 8vo. Cloth, price 3s. 6d.

JENNINGS (Mrs. Vaughan).
Rahel: Her Life and Letters. With a Portrait from the Painting by Daffinger. Square post 8vo. Cloth, price 7s. 6d.

Jeroveam's Wife and other Poems. Fcap. 8vo. Cloth, price 3s. 6d.

JEVONS (W. Stanley), M.A., F.R.S.
Money and the Mechanism of Exchange. Fourth Edition. Crown 8vo. Cloth, price 5s.
Volume XVII. of The International Scientific Series.

JONES (Lucy).
Puddings and Sweets. Being Three Hundred and Sixty-Five Receipts approved by Experience. Crown 8vo., price 2s. 6d.

KAUFMANN (Rev. M.), B.A.
Utopias; or, Schemes of Social Improvement, from Sir Thomas More to Karl Marx. Crown 8vo. Cloth, price 5s.

Socialism: Its Nature, its Dangers, and its Remedies considered. Crown 8vo. Cloth, price 7s. 6d.

KAY (Joseph), M.A., Q.C.
Free Trade in Land. Edited by his Widow. With Preface by the Right Hon. John Bright, M. P. Third Edition. Crown 8vo. Cloth, price 5s.

KER (David).
The Boy Slave in Bokhara. A Tale of Central Asia. With Illustrations. Crown 8vo. Cloth, price 5s.

The Wild Horseman of the Pampas. Illustrated. Crown 8vo. Cloth, price 5s.

KERNER (Dr. A.), Professor of Botany in the University of Innsbruck.
Flowers and their Unbidden Guests. Translation edited by W. OGLE, M.A., M.D., and a prefatory letter by C. Darwin, F.R.S. With Illustrations. Sq. 8vo. Cloth, price 9s.

KIDD (Joseph), M.D.
The Laws of Therapeutics, or, the Science and Art of Medicine. Crown 8vo. Cloth, price 6s.

KINAHAN (G. Henry), M.R.I.A., &c., of her Majesty's Geological Survey.
Manual of the Geology of Ireland. With 8 Plates, 26 Woodcuts, and a Map of Ireland, geologically coloured. Square 8vo. Cloth, price 15s.

KING (Alice).
A Cluster of Lives. Crown 8vo. Cloth, price 7s. 6d.

KING (Mrs. Hamilton).
The Disciples. A Poem. Third Edition, with some Notes. Crown 8vo. Cloth, price 7s. 6d.

Aspromonte, and other Poems. Second Edition. Fcap. 8vo. Cloth, price 4s. 6d.

KINGSLEY (Charles), M.A.
Letters and Memories of his Life. Edited by his WIFE. With 2 Steel engraved Portraits and numerous Illustrations on Wood, and a Facsimile of his Handwriting. Thirteenth Edition. 2 vols. Demy 8vo. Cloth, price 36s.
*** Also a Cabinet Edition in 2 vols. Crown 8vo. Cloth, price 12s.

All Saints' Day and other Sermons. Second Edition. Crown 8vo. Cloth, price 7s. 6d.

True Words for Brave Men: a Book for Soldiers' and Sailors' Libraries. Fifth Edition. Crown 8vo. Cloth, price 2s. 6d.

KNIGHT (A. F. C.).
Poems. Fcap. 8vo. Cloth, price 5s.

KNIGHT (Professor W.).
Studies in Philosophy and Literature. Large post 8vo. Cloth, price 7s. 6d.

LACORDAIRE (Rev. Père).
Life: Conferences delivered at Toulouse. A New and Cheaper Edition. Crown 8vo. Cloth, price 3s. 6d.

8	*A List of*

Lady of Lipari (The).
A Poem in Three Cantos. Fcap.
8vo. Cloth, price 5*s.*

LAIRD-CLOWES (W.).
Love's Rebellion: a Poem.
Fcap. 8vo. Cloth, price 3*s.* 6*d.*

LAMBERT (Cowley), F.R.G.S.
A Trip to Cashmere and
Ladâk. With numerous Illustrations. Crown 8vo. Cloth, 7*s.* 6*d.*

LAMONT (Martha MacDonald).
The Gladiator: A Life under
the Roman Empire in the beginning
of the Third Century. With four
Illustrations by H. M. Paget. Extra
fcap. 8vo. Cloth, price 3*s.* 6*d.*

LAYMANN (Capt.).
The Frontal Attack of
Infantry. Translated by Colonel
Edward Newdigate. Crown 8vo.
Cloth, price 2*s.* 6*d.*

LEANDER (Richard).
Fantastic Stories. Translated from the German by Paulina
B. Granville. With Eight full-page
Illustrations by M. E. Fraser-Tytler.
Crown 8vo. Cloth, price 5*s.*

LEE (Rev. F. G.), D.C.L.
The Other World; or,
Glimpses of the Supernatural. 2 vols.
A New Edition. Crown 8vo. Cloth,
price 15*s.*

LEE (Holme).
Her Title of Honour. A
Book for Girls. New Edition. With
a Frontispiece. Crown 8vo. Cloth,
price 5*s.*

LENOIR (J.).
Fayoum; or, Artists in Egypt.
A Tour with M. Gérome and others.
With 13 Illustrations. A New and
Cheaper Edition. Crown 8vo. Cloth,
price 3*s.* 6*d.*

LEWIS (Edward Dillon).
A Draft Code of Criminal
Law and Procedure. Demy 8vo.
Cloth, price 21*s.*

LEWIS (Mary A.).
A Rat with Three Tales.
With Four Illustrations by Catherine
F. Frere. Crown 8vo. Cloth, price 5*s.*

LINDSAY(W. Lauder), M.D.,&c.
Mind in the Lower Animals
in Health and Disease. 2 vols.
Demy 8vo. Cloth, price 32*s.*

LOCKER (F.).
London Lyrics. A New and
Revised Edition, with Additions and
a Portrait of the Author. Crown 8vo.
Cloth, elegant, price 6*s.*
Also, a Cheaper Edition. Fcap.
8vo. Cloth, price 2*s.* 6*d.*

LOCKYER (J. Norman), F.R.S.
Studies in Spectrum Analysis; with six photographic illustrations of Spectra, and numerous
engravings on wood. Second Edition. Crown 8vo. Cloth, price 6*s.* 6*d.*
Vol. XXIII. of The International
Scientific Series.

LOMMEL (Dr. E.).
The Nature of Light: With
a General Account of Physical Optics.
Second Edition. With 188 Illustrations and a Table of Spectra in
Chromo-lithography. Second Edition. Crown 8vo. Cloth, price 5*s.*
Volume XVIII. of The International Scientific Series.

LORIMER (Peter), D.D.
John Knox and the Church
of England: His Work in her Pulpit,
and his Influence upon her Liturgy,
Articles, and Parties. Demy 8vo.
Cloth, price 12*s.*

John Wiclif and his
English Precursors, by Gerhard
Victor Lechler. Translated from
the German, with additional Notes.
2 vols. Demy 8vo. Cloth, price 21*s.*

LOTHIAN (Roxburghe).
Dante and Beatrice from
1282 to 1290. A Romance. 2 vols.
Post 8vo. Cloth, price 24*s.*

LUCAS (Alice).
Translations from the
Works of German Poets of the
18th and 19th Centuries. Fcap.
8vo. Cloth, price 5*s.*

MACAULAY (J.), M.A., M.D.,
Edin.
The Truth about Ireland:
Tours of Observation in 1872 and
1875. With Remarks on Irish Public
Questions. Being a Second Edition
of "Ireland in 1872," with a New
and Supplementary Preface. Crown
8vo. Cloth, price 3*s.* 6*d.*

MAC CLINTOCK (L.).
Sir Spangle and the Dingy
Hen. Illustrated. Square crown
8vo., price 2s. 6d.

MAC DONALD (G.).
Malcolm. With Portrait of
the Author engraved on Steel. Fourth
Edition. Crown 8vo. Price 6s.

The Marquis of Lossie.
Second Edition. Crown 8vo. Cloth,
price 6s.

St. George and St. Michael.
Second Edition. Crown 8vo. Cloth, 6s.

MAC KENNA (S. J.).
Plucky Fellows. A Book
for Boys. With Six Illustrations.
Second Edition. Crown 8vo. Cloth,
price 3s. 6d.

At School with an Old
Dragoon. With Six Illustrations.
Second Edition. Crown 8vo. Cloth,
price 5s.

MACLACHLAN (A. N. C.), M.A.
William Augustus, Duke
of Cumberland : being a Sketch of
his Military Life and Character,
chiefly as exhibited in the General
Orders of His Royal Highness,
1745—1747. With Illustrations. Post
8vo. Cloth, price 15s.

MACLACHLAN (Mrs.).
Notes and Extracts on
Everlasting Punishment and
Eternal Life, according to
Literal Interpretation. Small
crown 8vo. Cloth, price 3s. 6d.

MACNAUGHT (Rev. John).
Cœna Domini: An Essay
on the Lord's Supper, its Primitive Institution, Apostolic Uses,
and Subsequent History. Demy
8vo. Cloth, price 14s.

**MAGNUSSON (Eirikr), M.A.,
and PALMER (E.H.), M.A.**
Johan Ludvig Runeberg's
Lyrical Songs, Idylls and Epi-
grams. Fcap. 8vo. Cloth, price 5s.

MAIR (R. S.), M.D., F.R.C.S.E.
The Medical Guide for
Anglo-Indians. Being a Compen-
dium of Advice to Europeans in
India, relating to the Preservation
and Regulation of Health. With a
Supplement on the Management of
Children in India. Second Edition.
Crown 8vo. Limp cloth, price 3s. 6d.

MALDEN (H. E. and E. E.)
Princes and Princesses.
Illustrated. Small crown 8vo. Cloth,
price 2s. 6d.

**MANNING (His Eminence Car-
dinal).**
Essays on Religion and
Literature. By various Writers.
Third Series. Demy 8vo. Cloth,
price 10s. 6d.

The Independence of the
Holy See, with an Appendix containing the Papal Allocution and a
translation. Cr. 8vo. Cloth, price 5s.

The True Story of the
Vatican Council. Crown 8vo.
Cloth, price 5s.

MAREY (E. J.).
Animal Mechanics. A
Treatise on Terrestrial and Aerial
Locomotion. With 117 Illustrations.
Second Edition. Crown 8vo. Cloth,
price 5s.
Volume XI. of The International
Scientific Series.

**MARRIOTT (Maj.-Gen. W. F.),
C.S.I.**
A Grammar of Political
Economy. Crown 8vo. Cloth,
price 6s.

Master Bobby : a Tale. By
the Author of "Christina North."
With Illustrations by E. H. Bell.
Extra fcap. 8vo. Cloth, price 3s. 6d.

MASTERMAN (J.).
Worth Waiting for. A New
Novel. 3 vols. Crown 8vo. Cloth.

Half-a-dozen Daughters.
With a Frontispiece. Crown 8vo.
Cloth, price 3s. 6d.

MAUDSLEY (Dr. H.).
Responsibility in Mental
Disease. Third Edition. Crown
8vo. Cloth, price 5s.
Volume VIII. of The International
Scientific Series.

MAUGHAN (W. C.).
The Alps of Arabia; or,
Travels through Egypt, Sinai, Ara-
bia, and the Holy Land. With Map.
Second Edition. Demy 8vo. Cloth,
price 5s.

MAURICE (C. E.).
Lives of English Popular Leaders. No. 1.—STEPHEN LANGTON. Crown 8vo. Cloth, price 7s.6d. No. 2.—TYLER, BALL, and OLDCASTLE. Crown 8vo. Cloth, price 7s. 6d.

MEDLEY(Lieut.-Col.J. G.),R.E.
An Autumn Tour in the United States and Canada. Crown 8vo. Cloth, price 5s.

MEREDITH (George).
The Egoist. A Comedy in Narrative. 3 vols. Crown 8vo. Cloth.

The Ordeal of Richard Feverel. A History of Father and Son. In one vol. with Frontispiece. Crown 8vo. Cloth, price 6s.

MERRITT (Henry).
Art - Criticism and Romance. With Recollections, and Twenty-three Illustrations in eau-forte, by Anna Lea Merritt. Two vols. Large post 8vo. Cloth, 25s.

MICKLETHWAITE (J. T.), F.S.A.
Modern Parish Churches: Their Plan, Design, and Furniture. Crown 8vo. Cloth, price 7s. 6d.

MIDDLETON (The Lady).
Ballads. Square 16mo. Cloth, price 3s.6d.

MILLER (Edward).
The History and Doctrines of Irvingism; or, the so-called Catholic and Apostolic Church. 2 vols. Large post 8vo. Cloth, price 25s.

MILLER (Robert).
The Romance of Love. Fcap. 8vo. Cloth, price 5s.

MILNE (James).
Tables of Exchange for the Conversion of Sterling Money into Indian and Ceylon Currency, at Rates from 1s. 8d. to 2s. 3d. per Rupee. Second Edition. Demy 8vo. Cloth, price £2 2s.

MIVART (St. George), F.R.S.
Contemporary Evolution: An Essay on some recent Social Changes. Post 8vo. Cloth, price 7s. 6d.

MOCKLER (E.).
A Grammar of the Baloochee Language, as it is spoken in Makran (Ancient Gedrosia), in the Persia-Arabic and Roman characters. Fcap. 8vo. Cloth, price 5s.

MOFFAT (Robert Scott).
The Economy of Consumption; an Omitted Chapter in Political Economy, with special reference to the Questions of Commercial Crises and the Policy of Trades Unions; and with Reviews of the Theories of Adam Smith, Ricardo, J. S. Mill, Fawcett, &c. Demy 8vo. Cloth, price 18s.

The Principles of a Time Policy: being an Exposition of a Method of Settling Disputes between Employers and Employed in regard to Time and Wages, by a simple Process of Mercantile Barter, without recourse to Strikes or Locks-out. Reprinted from "The Economy of Consumption," with a Preface and Appendix containing Observations on some Reviews of that book, and a Re-criticism of the Theories of Ricardo and J. S. Mill on Rent, Value, and Cost of Production. Demy 8vo. Cloth, price 3s. 6d.

MOLTKE (Field-Marshal Von).
Letters from Russia. Translated by Robina Napier. Crown 8vo. Cloth, price 6s.

MOORE (Rev. D.), M.A.
Christ and His Church. By the Author of "The Age and the Gospel," &c. Crown 8vo. Cloth, price 3s. 6d.

MORE (R. Jasper).
Under the Balkans. Notes of a Visit to the District of Philippopolis in 1876. With a Map and Illustrations from Photographs. Crown 8vo. Cloth, price 6s.

MORELL (J. R.).
Euclid Simplified in Method and Language. Being a Manual of Geometry. Compiled from the most important French Works, approved by the University of Paris and the Minister of Public Instruction. Fcap. 8vo. Cloth, price 2s. 6d.

MORICE (Rev. F. D.), M.A.
The Olympian and Pythian Odes of Pindar. A New Translation in English Verse. Crown 8vo. Cloth, price 7s. 6d.

MORLEY (Susan).
Margaret Chetwynd. A Novel. 3 vols. Crown 8vo. Cloth.

MORSE (E. S.), Ph.D.
First Book of Zoology.
With numerous Illustrations. Crown
8vo. Cloth, price 5*s.*

MORSHEAD (E. D. A.)
The Agamemnon of Æs-
chylus. Translated into English
verse. With an Introductory Essay.
Crown 8vo. Cloth, price 5*s.*

MUSGRAVE (Anthony).
Studies in Political Eco-
nomy. Crown 8vo. Cloth, price 6*s.*

Mystery of Miracles, The.
By the Author of "The Supernatural
in Nature." Crown 8vo. Cloth,
price 6*s.*

NAAKÉ (J. T.).
Slavonic Fairy Tales.
From Russian, Servian, Polish, and
Bohemian Sources. With Four Illus-
trations. Crown 8vo. Cloth, price 5*s.*

NEWMAN (J. H.), D.D.
Characteristics from the
Writings of. Being Selections
from his various Works. Arranged
with the Author's personal approval.
Third Edition. With Portrait.
Crown 8vo. Cloth, price 6*s.*
** A Portrait of the Rev. Dr. J. H.
Newman, mounted for framing, can
be had, price 2*s. 6d.*

NEW WRITER (A).
Songs of Two Worlds.
Fourth Edition. Complete in one
volume with Portrait. Fcap. 8vo.
Cloth, price 7*s. 6d.*
The Epic of Hades. Seventh
and finally revised Edition. Fcap.
8vo. Cloth, price 7*s. 6d.*

NICHOLAS (Thomas), Ph.D.,
F.G.S.
The Pedigree of the English
People: an Argument, Historical
and Scientific, on the Formation and
Growth of the Nation, tracing Race-
admixture in Britain from the earliest
times, with especial reference to the
incorporation of the Celtic Abori-
gines. Fifth Edition. Demy 8vo.
Cloth, price 16*s.*

NICHOLSON (Edward B.).
The Christ Child, and other
Poems. Crown 8vo. Cloth, price
4*s. 6d.*
The Rights of an Animal.
Crown 8vo. Cloth, price 3*s. 6d.*

NICHOLSON (Edward B.)—con-
tinued.
The Gospel according to
the Hebrews. Its Fragments trans-
lated and annotated with a critical
Analysis of the External and Internal
Evidence relating to it. Demy 8vo.
Cloth, price 9*s. 6d.*

NOAKE (Major R. Compton).
The Bivouac ; or, Martial
Lyrist, with an Appendix—Advice to
the Soldier. Fcap. 8vo. Price 5*s. 6d.*

NORMAN PEOPLE (The).
The Norman People, and
their Existing Descendants in the
British Dominions and the United
States of America. Demy 8vo.
Cloth, price 21*s.*

NORRIS (Rev. Alfred).
The Inner and Outer Life
Poems. Fcap. 8vo. Cloth, price 6*s.*

Notes on Cavalry Tactics,
Organization, &c. By a Cavalry
Officer. With Diagrams. Demy 8vo.
Cloth, price 12*s.*

Nuces : Exercises on the
Syntax of the Public School
Latin Primer. New Edition in
Three Parts. Crown 8vo. Each 1*s.*
** The Three Parts can also be
had bound together in cloth, price 3*s.*

O'BRIEN (Charlotte G.).
Light and Shade. 2 vols.
Crown 8vo. Cloth, gilt tops, price
12*s.*

O'MEARA (Kathleen).
Frederic Ozanam, Professor
of the Sorbonne ; His Life and
Works. Second Edition. Crown
8vo. Cloth, price 7*s. 6d.*

Oriental Sporting Magazine
(The).
A Reprint of the first 5 Volumes,
in 2 Volumes. Demy 8vo. Cloth,
price 28*s.*

PALGRAVE (W. Gifford).
Hermann Agha ; An Eastern
Narrative. Third and Cheaper Edi-
tion. Crown 8vo. Cloth, price 6*s.*

PANDURANG HARI;
Or, Memoirs of a Hindoo.
With an Introductory Preface by Sir
H. Bartle E. Frere, G.C.S.I., C.B.
Crown 8vo. Price 6*s.*

PARKER (Joseph), D.D.
The Paraclete : An Essay
on the Personality and Ministry of
the Holy Ghost, with some reference
to current discussions. Second Edition. Demy 8vo. Cloth, price 12s.

PARR (Harriet).
Echoes of a Famous Year.
Crown 8vo. Cloth, price 8s. 6d.

PARSLOE (Joseph).
Our Railways : Sketches,
Historical and Descriptive. With
Practical Information as to Fares,
Rates, &c., and a Chapter on Rail-
way Reform. Crown 8vo. Cloth,
price 6s.

PATTISON (Mrs. Mark).
The Renaissance of Art in
France. With Nineteen Steel
Engravings. 2 vols. Demy 8vo.
Cloth, price 32s.

PAUL (C. Kegan).
Mary Wollstonecraft.
Letters to Imlay. With Prefatory
Memoir by, and Two Portraits in
eau forte, by Anna Lea Merritt.
Crown 8vo. Cloth, price 6s.

Goethe's Faust. A New
Translation in Rime. Crown 8vo.
Cloth, price 6s.

William Godwin : His
Friends and Contemporaries.
With Portraits and Facsimiles of the
Handwriting of Godwin and his
Wife. 2 vols. Square post 8vo.
Cloth, price 28s.

The Genius of Christianity
Unveiled. Being Essays by William
Godwin never before published.
Edited, with a Preface, by C.
Kegan Paul. Crown 8vo. Cloth,
price 7s. 6d.

PAUL (Margaret Agnes).
Gentle and Simple : A Story.
2 vols. Crown 8vo. Cloth, gilt tops,
price 12s.
⁂ Also a Cheaper Edition in one
vol. with Frontispiece. Crown 8vo.
Cloth, price 6s.

PAYNE (John).
Songs of Life and Death.
Crown 8vo. Cloth, price 5s.

PAYNE (Prof. J. F.).
Lectures on Education.
Price 6d.
II. Fröbel and the Kindergarten
system. Second Edition.

PAYNE (Prof. J. F.)—*continued.*
A Visit to German Schools :
Elementary Schools in Germany. Notes of a Professional Tour
to inspect some of the Kindergartens,
Primary Schools, Public Girls'
Schools, and Schools for Technical
Instruction in Hamburgh, Berlin,
Dresden, Weimar, Gotha, Eisenach,
in the autumn of 1874. With Critical
Discussions of the General Principles
and Practice of Kindergartens and
other Schemes of Elementary Education. Crown 8vo. Cloth, price
4s. 6d.

PEACOCKE (Georgiana).
Rays from the Southern
Cross : Poems. Crown 8vo. With
Sixteen Full-page Illustrations
by the Rev. P. Walsh. Cloth elegant,
price 10s. 6d.

PELLETAN (E.).
The Desert Pastor, Jean
Jarousseau. Translated from the
French. By Colonel E. P. De
L'Hoste. With a Frontispiece. New
Edition. Fcap. 8vo. Cloth, price
3s. 6d.

PENNELL (H. Cholmondeley).
Pegasus Resaddled. By
the Author of " Puck on Pegasus,"
&c. &c. With Ten Full-page Illustrations by George Du Maurier.
Second Edition. Fcap. 4to. Cloth
elegant, price 12s. 6d.

PENRICE (Maj. J.), B.A.
A Dictionary and Glossary
of the Ko-ran. With copious Gram-
matical References and Explanations
of the Text. 4to. Cloth, price 21s.

PERCIVAL (Rev. P.).
Tamil Proverbs, with their
English Translation. Containing
upwards of Six Thousand Proverbs.
Third Edition. Demy 8vo. Sewed,
price 9s.

PESCHEL (Dr. Oscar).
The Races of Man and
their Geographical Distribution.
Large crown 8vo. Cloth, price 9s.

PETTIGREW (J. Bell), M.D.,
F.R.S.
Animal Locomotion ; or,
Walking, Swimming, and Flying.
With 130 Illustrations. Second Edi-
tion. Crown 8vo. Cloth, price 5s.
Volume VII. of The International
Scientific Series.

PFEIFFER (Emily).

Quarterman's Grace, and other Poems. Crown 8vo. Cloth, price 5*s.*

Glan Alarch: His Silence and Song. A Poem. Second Edition. Crown 8vo. price 6*s.*

Gerard's Monument, and other Poems. Second Edition. Crown 8vo. Cloth, price 6*s.*

Poems. Second Edition. Crown 8vo. Cloth, price 6*s.*

PIGGOT (J.), F.S.A., F.R.G.S.

Persia—Ancient and Modern. Post 8vo. Cloth, price 10*s.* 6*d.*

PINCHES (Thomas), M.A.

Samuel Wilberforce: Faith—Service—Recompense. Three Sermons. With a Portrait of Bishop Wilberforce (after a Photograph by Charles Watkins). Crown 8vo. Cloth, price 4*s.* 6*d.*

PLAYFAIR (Lieut.-Col.), Her Britannic Majesty's Consul-General in Algiers.

Travels in the Footsteps of Bruce in Algeria and Tunis. Illustrated by facsimiles of Bruce's original Drawings, Photographs, Maps, &c. Royal 4to. Cloth, bevelled boards, gilt leaves, price £3 3*s.*

POLLOCK (W. H.).

Lectures on French Poets. Delivered at the Royal Institution. Small crown 8vo. Cloth, price 5*s.*

POOR (Henry V.).

Money and its Laws, embracing a History of Monetary Theories and a History of the Currencies of the United States. Demy 8vo. Cloth, price 21*s.*

POUSHKIN (A. S.).

Russian Romance. Translated from the Tales of Belkin, &c. By Mrs. J. Buchan Telfer (*née* Mouravieff). Crown 8vo. Cloth, price 7*s.* 6*d.*

POWER (H.).

Our Invalids : How shall we Employ and Amuse Them ? Fcap. 8vo. Cloth, price 2*s.* 6*d.*

POWLETT (Lieut. N.), R.A.

Eastern Legends and Stories in English Verse. Crown 8vo. Cloth, price 5*s.*

PRESBYTER.

Unfoldings of Christian Hope. An Essay showing that the Doctrine contained in the Damnatory Clauses of the Creed commonly called Athanasian is unscriptural. Small crown 8vo. Cloth, price 4*s.* 6*d.*

PRICE (Prof. Bonamy).

Currency and Banking. Crown 8vo. Cloth, price 6*s.*

Chapters on Practical Political Economy. Being the Substance of Lectures delivered before the University of Oxford. Large post 8vo. Cloth, price 12*s.*

PROCTOR (Richard A.), B.A.

Our Place among Infinities. A Series of Essays contrasting our little abode in space and time with the Infinities around us. To which are added Essays on "Astrology," and "The Jewish Sabbath." Third Edition. Crown 8vo. Cloth, price 6*s.*

The Expanse of Heaven. A Series of Essays on the Wonders of the Firmament. With a Frontispiece. Fourth Edition. Crown 8vo. Cloth, price 6*s.*

Proteus and Amadeus. A Correspondence. Edited by Aubrey De Vere. Crown 8vo. Cloth, price 5*s.*

PUBLIC SCHOOLBOY.

The Volunteer, the Militiaman, and the Regular Soldier. Crown 8vo. Cloth, price 5*s.*

Punjaub (The) and North Western Frontier of India. By an old Punjaubee. Crown 8vo. Cloth, price 5*s.*

QUATREFAGES (Prof. A. de).

The Human Species. Second Edition. Crown 8vo. Cloth, price 5*s.*

Vol. XXVI. of The International Scientific Series.

RAM (James).

The Philosophy of War. Small crown 8vo. Cloth, price 3*s.* 6*d.*

RAVENSHAW (John Henry), B.C.S.

Gaur: Its Ruins and In-scriptions. Edited with considerable additions and alterations by his Widow. With forty-four photographic illustrations and twenty-five fac-similes of Inscriptions. Super royal 4to. Cloth, 3*l.* 13*s.* 6*d.*

READ (Carveth).

On the Theory of Logic : An Essay. Crown 8vo. Cloth, price 6*s.*

REANEY (Mrs. G. S.).

Blessing and Blessed ; a Sketch of Girl Life. With a frontispiece. Crown 8vo. Cloth, price 5*s.*

Waking and Working ; or, from Girlhood to Womanhood. With a Frontispiece. Crown 8vo. Cloth, price 5*s.*

English Girls : their Place and Power. With a Preface by R. W. Dale, M.A., of Birmingham. Second Edition. Fcap. 8vo. Cloth, price 2*s.* 6*d.*

Just Anyone, and other Stories. Three Illustrations. Royal 16mo. Cloth, price 1*s.* 6*d.*

Sunshine Jenny and other Stories. Three Illustrations. Royal 16mo. Cloth, price 1*s.* 6*d.*

Sunbeam Willie, and other Stories. Three Illustrations. Royal 16mo. Cloth, price 1*s.* 6*d.*

RHOADES (James).

Timoleon. A Dramatic Poem. Fcap. 8vo. Cloth, price 5*s.*

RIBOT (Prof. Th.).

English Psychology. Second Edition. A Revised and Corrected Translation from the latest French Edition. Large post 8vo. Cloth, price 9*s*

Heredity : A Psychological Study on its Phenomena, its Laws, its Causes, and its Consequences. Large crown 8vo. Cloth, price 9*s.*

RINK (Chevalier Dr. Henry).

Greenland : Its People and its Products. By the Chevalier Dr. HENRY RINK, President of the Greenland Board of Trade. With sixteen Illustrations, drawn by the Eskimo, and a Map. Edited by Dr. ROBERT BROWN. Crown 8vo. Price 10*s.* 6*d.*

ROBERTSON (The Late Rev. F. W.), M.A., of Brighton.

Notes on Genesis. New and cheaper Edition. Crown 8vo., price 3*s.* 6*d.*

Sermons. Four Series. Small crown 8vo. Cloth, price 3*s.* 6*d.* each.

Expository Lectures on St. Paul's Epistles to the Corinthians. A New Edition. Small crown 8vo. Cloth, price 5*s.*

Lectures and Addresses, with other literary remains. A New Edition. Crown 8vo. Cloth, price 5*s.*

An Analysis of Mr. Tenny-son's " In Memoriam." (Dedicated by Permission to the Poet-Laureate.) Fcap. 8vo. Cloth, price 2*s.*

The Education of the Human Race. Translated from the German of Gotthold Ephraim Lessing. Fcap. 8vo. Cloth, price 2*s.* 6*d.*

Life and Letters. Edited by the Rev. Stopford Brooke, M.A., Chaplain in Ordinary to the Queen.

I. 2 vols., uniform with the Sermons. With Steel Portrait. Crown 8vo. Cloth, price 7*s.* 6*d.*

II. Library Edition, in Demy 8vo., with Two Steel Portraits. Cloth, price 12*s.*

III. A Popular Edition, in one vol. Crown 8vo. Cloth, price 6*s.*

The above Works can also be had half-bound in morocco.

*** A Portrait of the late Rev. F. W. Robertson, mounted for framing, can be had, price 2*s.* 6*d.*

ROBINSON (A. Mary F.).

A Handful of Honey-suckle. Fcap. 8vo. Cloth, price 3*s.* 6*d.*

RODWELL (G. F.), F.R.A.S., F.C.S.
Etna : a History of the Mountain and its Eruptions. With Maps and Illustrations. Square 8vo. Cloth, price 9s.

ROOD (Ogden N.).
Modern Chromatics, with Applications to Art and Industry. With 130 Original Illustrations. Crown 8vo. Cloth, price 5s. Vol. XXVII. of The International Scientific Series.

ROSS (Mrs. E.), ("Nelsie Brook").
Daddy's Pet. A Sketch from Humble Life. With Six Illustrations. Royal 16mo. Cloth, price 1s.

ROSS (Alexander), D.D.
Memoir of Alexander Ewing, Bishop of Argyll and the Isles. Second and Cheaper Edition. Demy 8vo. Cloth, price 10s. 6d.

RUSSELL (Major Frank S.).
Russian Wars with Turkey, Past and Present. With Two Maps. Second Edition. Crown 8vo., price 6s.

RUTHERFORD (John).
The Secret History of the Fenian Conspiracy; its Origin, Objects, and Ramifications. 2 vols. Post 8vo. Cloth, price 18s.

SADLER (S. W.), R.N.
The African Cruiser. A Midshipman's Adventures on the West Coast. With Three Illustrations. Second Edition. Crown 8vo. Cloth, price 3s. 6d.

SAMAROW (G.).
For Sceptre and Crown. A Romance of the Present Time. Translated by Fanny Wormald. 2 vols. Crown 8vo. Cloth, price 15s.

SAUNDERS (Katherine).
Gideon's Rock, and other Stories. Crown 8vo. Cloth, price 6s.
Joan Merryweather, and other Stories. Crown 8vo. Cloth, price 6s.
Margaret and Elizabeth. A Story of the Sea. Crown 8vo. Cloth, price 6s.

SAUNDERS (John).
Israel Mort, Overman : A Story of the Mine. Cr. 8vo. Price 6s.
Hirell. With Frontispiece. Crown 8vo. Cloth, price 3s. 6d.
Abel Drake's Wife. With Frontispiece. Crown 8vo. Cloth, price 3s. 6d.

SCHELL (Maj. von).
The Operations of the First Army under Gen. von Goeben. Translated by Col. C. H. von Wright. Four Maps. Demy 8vo. Cloth, price 9s.
The Operations of the First Army under Gen. von Steinmetz. Translated by Captain E. O. Hollist. Demy 8vo. Cloth, price 10s. 6d.

SCHELLENDORF (Maj.-Gen. B. von).
The Duties of the General Staff. Translated from the German by Lieutenant Hare. Vol. I. Demy 8vo. Cloth, price 10s. 6d.

SCHERFF (Maj. W. von).
Studies in the New Infantry Tactics. Parts I. and II. Translated from the German by Colonel Lumley Graham. Demy 8vo. Cloth, price 7s. 6d.

SCHMIDT (Prof. Oscar).
The Doctrine of Descent and Darwinism. With 26 Illustrations. Third Edition. Crown 8vo. Cloth, price 5s. Volume XII. of The International Scientific Series.

SCHÜTZENBERGER (Prof. F.).
Fermentation. With Numerous Illustrations. Second Edition. Crown 8vo. Cloth, price 5s. Volume XX. of The International Scientific Series.

SCOTT (Leader).
A Nook in the Apennines: A Summer beneath the Chestnuts. With Frontispiece, and 27 Illustrations in the Text, chiefly from Original Sketches. Crown 8vo. Cloth, price 7s. 6d.

SCOTT (Patrick).
The Dream and the Deed, and other Poems. Fcap. 8vo. Cloth, price 5s.

SCOTT (W. T.).
Antiquities of an Essex Parish ; or, Pages from the History of Great Dunmow. Crown 8vo. Cloth, price 5s. Sewed, 4s.

SCOTT (Robert H.).
Weather Charts and Storm Warnings. Illustrated. Second Edition. Crown 8vo. Cloth, price 3s. 6d.
Seeking his Fortune, and other Stories. With Four Illustrations. Crown 8vo. Cloth, price 3s. 6d.

SENIOR (N. W.).

Alexis De Tocqueville.
Correspondence and Conversations with Nassau W. Senior, from 1833 to 1859. Edited by M. C. M. Simpson. 2 vols. Large post 8vo. Cloth, price 21s.

Journals Kept in France and Italy.
From 1848 to 1852. With a Sketch of the Revolution of 1848. Edited by his Daughter, M. C. M. Simpson. 2 vols. Post 8vo. Cloth, price 24s.

Seven Autumn Leaves from Fairyland.
Illustrated with Nine Etchings. Square crown 8vo. Cloth, price 3s. 6d.

SHADWELL (Maj.-Gen.), C.B.

Mountain Warfare.
Illustrated by the Campaign of 1799 in Switzerland. Being a Translation of the Swiss Narrative compiled from the Works of the Archduke Charles, Jomini, and others. Also of Notes by General H. Dufour on the Campaign of the Valtelline in 1635. With Appendix, Maps, and Introductory Remarks. Demy 8vo. Cloth, price 16s.

SHAKSPEARE (Charles).

Saint Paul at Athens:
Spiritual Christianity in Relation to some Aspects of Modern Thought. Nine Sermons preached at St. Stephen's Church, Westbourne Park. With Preface by the Rev. Canon FARRAR. Crown 8vo. Cloth, price 5s.

SHAW (Major Wilkinson).

The Elements of Modern Tactics.
Practically applied to English Formations. With Twenty-five Plates and Maps. Small crown 8vo. Cloth, price 12s.
*** The Second Volume of "Military Handbooks for Officers and Non-commissioned Officers." Edited by Lieut.-Col. C. B. Brackenbury, R.A., A.A.G.

SHAW (Flora L.).

Castle Blair: a Story of
Youthful Lives. 2 vols. Crown 8vo. Cloth, gilt tops, price 12s. Also, an edition in one vol. Crown 8vo. 6s.

SHELLEY (Lady).

Shelley Memorials from
Authentic Sources. With (now first printed) an Essay on Christianity by Percy Bysshe Shelley. With Portrait. Third Edition. Crown 8vo. Cloth, price 5s.

SHERMAN (Gen. W. T.).

Memoirs of General W. T. Sherman,
Commander of the Federal Forces in the American Civil War. By Himself. 2 vols. With Map. Demy 8vo. Cloth, price 24s. *Copyright English Edition.*

SHILLITO (Rev. Joseph).

Womanhood: its Duties,
Temptations, and Privileges. A Book for Young Women. Second Edition. Crown 8vo. Price 3s. 6d.

SHIPLEY (Rev. Orby), M.A.

Principles of the Faith in
Relation to Sin. Topics for Thought in Times of Retreat. Eleven Addresses. With an Introduction on the neglect of Dogmatic Theology in the Church of England, and a Postscript on his leaving the Church of England. Demy 8vo. Cloth, price 12s.

Church Tracts, or Studies
in Modern Problems. By various Writers. 2 vols. Crown 8vo. Cloth, price 5s. each.

SHUTE (Richard), M.A.

A Discourse on Truth.
Large Post 8vo. Cloth, price 9s.

SMEDLEY (M. B.).

Boarding-out and Pauper
Schools for Girls. Crown 8vo. Cloth, price 3s. 6d.

SMITH (Edward), M.D., LL.B., F.R.S.

Health and Disease, as In-
fluenced by the Daily, Seasonal, and other Cyclical Changes in the Human System. A New Edition. Post 8vo. Cloth, price 7s. 6d.

Foods.
Profusely Illustrated. Fifth Edition. Crown 8vo. Cloth, price 5s.
Volume III. of The International Scientific Series.

Practical Dietary for
Families, Schools, and the Labouring Classes. A New Edition. Post 8vo. Cloth, price 3s. 6d.

Tubercular Consumption
in its Early and Remediable Stages. Second Edition. Crown 8vo. Cloth, price 6s.

SMITH (Hubert).

Tent Life with English Gipsies in Norway. With Five full-page Engravings and Thirty-one smaller Illustrations by Whymper and others, and Map of the Country showing Routes. Third Edition. Revised and Corrected. Post 8vo. Cloth, price 21s.

Songs of Two Worlds. By the Author of "The Epic of Hades." Fourth Edition. Complete in one Volume, with Portrait. Fcap. 8vo. Cloth, price 7s. 6d.

Songs for Music. By Four Friends. Square crown 8vo. Cloth, price 5s. Containing songs by Reginald A. Gatty, Stephen H. Gatty, Greville J. Chester, and Juliana Ewing.

SPEDDING (James).

Reviews and Discussions, Literary, Political, and Historical not relating to Bacon. Demy 8vo. Cloth, price 12s. 6d.

SPENCER (Herbert).

The Study of Sociology. Seventh Edition. Crown 8vo. Cloth, price 5s. Volume V. of The International Scientific Series.

SPICER (H.).

Otho's Death Wager. A Dark Page of History Illustrated. In Five Acts. Fcap. 8vo. Cloth, price 5s.

STAPLETON (John).

The Thames: A Poem. Crown 8vo. Cloth, price 6s.

STEPHENS (Archibald John), LL.D.

The Folkestone Ritual Case. The Substance of the Argument delivered before the Judicial Committee of the Privy Council. On behalf of the Respondents. Demy 8vo. Cloth, price 6s.

STEVENSON (Robert Louis).

An Inland Voyage. With Frontispiece by Walter Crane. Crown 8vo. Cloth, price 7s. 6d.

Travels with a Donkey in the Cevennes. With Frontispiece by Walter Crane. Crown 8vo. Cloth, price 7s. 6d.

STEVENSON (Rev. W. F.).

Hymns for the Church and Home. Selected and Edited by the Rev. W. Fleming Stevenson. The most complete Hymn Book published.
  The Hymn Book consists of Three Parts:—I. For Public Worship.—II. For Family and Private Worship. —III. For Children.
  ** Published in various forms and prices, the latter ranging from 8d. to 6s. Lists and full particulars will be furnished on application to the Publishers.

STEWART (Prof. Balfour), M.A., LL.D., F.R.S.

On the Conservation of Energy. Fifth Edition. With Fourteen Engravings. Crown 8vo. Cloth, price 5s. Volume VI. of The International Scientific Series.

STONEHEWER (Agnes).

Monacella: A Legend of North Wales. A Poem. Fcap. 8vo. Cloth, price 3s. 6d.

STORR (Francis), and TURNER (Hawes).

Canterbury Chimes; or, Chaucer Tales retold to Children. With Illustrations from the Ellesmere MS. Extra Fcap. 8vo. Cloth, price 3s. 6d.

STRETTON (Hesba). Author of "Jessica's First Prayer."

Michel Lorio's Cross, and other Stories. With Two Illustrations. Royal 16mo. Cloth, price 1s. 6d.

The Storm of Life. With Ten Illustrations. Twenty-first Thousand. Royal 16mo. Cloth, price 1s. 6d.

The Crew of the Dolphin. Illustrated. Fourteenth Thousand. Royal 16mo. Cloth, price 1s. 6d.

Cassy. Thirty-eighth Thousand. With Six Illustrations. Royal 16mo. Cloth, price 1s. 6d.

The King's Servants. Forty-third Thousand. With Eight Illustrations. Royal 16mo. Cloth, price 1s. 6d.

Lost Gip. Fifty-ninth Thousand. With Six Illustrations. Royal 16mo. Cloth, price 1s. 6d.
  ** Also a handsomely bound Edition, with Twelve Illustrations, price 2s. 6d.

STRETTON (Hesba)—*continued.*

David Lloyd's Last Will.
With Four Illustrations. Royal 16mo., price 2*s.* 6*d.*

The Wonderful Life.
Thirteenth Thousand. Fcap. 8vo. Cloth, price 2*s.* 6*d.*

A Man of His Word.
With Frontispiece. Royal 16mo. Limp cloth, price 6*d.*

A Night and a Day. With
Frontispiece. Twelfth Thousand. Royal 16mo. Limp cloth, price 6*d.*

Friends till Death. With
Illustrations and Frontispiece. Twenty-fourth Thousand. Royal 16mo. Cloth, price 1*s.* 6*d.*; limp cloth, price 6*d.*

Two Christmas Stories.
With Frontispiece. Twenty-first Thousand. Royal 16mo. Limp cloth, price 6*d.*

Michel Lorio's Cross, and
Left Alone. With Frontispiece. Fifteenth Thousand. Royal 16mo. Limp cloth, price 6*d.*

Old Transome. With
Frontispiece. Sixteenth Thousand. Royal 16mo. Limp cloth, price 6*d.*

*** Taken from "The King's Servants."

The Worth of a Baby, and
how Apple-Tree Court was won. With Frontispiece. Nineteenth Thousand. Royal 16mo. Limp cloth, price 6*d.*

Through a Needle's Eye :
a Story. 2 vols. Crown 8vo. Cloth, gilt top, price 12*s.*

STUBBS (Lieut.-Colonel F. W.)

The Regiment of Bengal
Artillery. The History of its Organization, Equipment, and War Services. Compiled from Published Works, Official Records, and various Private Sources. With numerous Maps and Illustrations. 2 vols. Demy 8vo. Cloth, price 32*s.*

STUMM (Lieut. Hugo), German Military Attaché to the Khivan Expedition.

Russia's advance Eastward. Based on the Official Reports of. Translated by Capt. C. E. H. VINCENT. With Map. Crown 8vo. Cloth, price 6*s.*

SULLY (James), M.A.

Sensation and Intuition.
Demy 8vo. Cloth, price 10*s.* 6*d.*

Pessimism : a History and
a Criticism. Demy 8vo. Price 14*s.*

Sunnyland Stories.
By the Author of "Aunt Mary's Bran Pie." Illustrated. Small 8vo. Cloth, price 3*s.* 6*d.*

Supernatural in Nature, The.
A Verification by Free Use of Science. Demy 8vo. Cloth, price 14*s.*

Sweet Silvery Sayings of
Shakespeare. Crown 8vo. Cloth gilt, price 7*s.* 6*d.*

SYME (David).

Outlines of an Industrial
Science. Second Edition. Crown 8vo. Cloth, price 6*s.*

Tales of the Zenana.
By the Author of "Pandurang Hari." 2 vols. Crown 8vo. Cloth, price 21*s.*

TAYLOR (Algernon).

Guienne. Notes of an Autumn
Tour. Crown 8vo. Cloth, price 4*s.* 6*d.*

TAYLOR (Rev. J. W. A.), M.A.

Poems. Fcap. 8vo. Cloth,
price 5*s.*

TAYLOR (Sir H.).

Works Complete. Author's
Edition, in 5 vols. Crown 8vo. Cloth, price 6*s.* each.

Vols. I. to III. containing the Poetical Works, Vols. IV. and V. the Prose Works.

TAYLOR (Col. Meadows), C.S.I., M.R.I.A.

A Noble Queen : a Romance
of Indian History. 3 vols. Crown 8vo. Cloth.

Seeta. 3 vols. Crown 8vo.
Cloth.

Tippoo Sultaun : a Tale of
the Mysore War. New Edition with Frontispiece. Crown 8vo. Cloth price 6*s.*

Ralph Darnell. New and
Cheaper Edition. With Frontispiece. Crown 8vo. Cloth, price 6*s.*

The Confessions of a Thug.
New Edition. Crown 8vo. Cloth, price 6*s.*

Tara : a Mahratta Tale.
New Edition. Crown 8vo. Cloth, price 6*s.*

TELFER (J. Buchan), F.R.G.S., Commander, R.N.
The Crimea and Trans-Caucasia. With numerous Illustrations and Maps. 2 vols. Medium 8vo. Second Edition. Cloth, price 36s.

TENNYSON (Alfred).
The Imperial Library Edition. Complete in 7 vols. Demy 8vo. Cloth, price £3 13s. 6d.; in Roxburgh binding, £4 7s. 6d.
Author's Edition. Complete in 6 Volumes. Post 8vo. Cloth gilt; or half-morocco, Roxburgh style :—
VOL. I. Early Poems, and English Idylls. Price 6s.; Roxburgh, 7s. 6d.
VOL. II. Locksley Hall, Lucretius, and other Poems. Price 6s.; Roxburgh, 7s. 6d.
VOL. III. The Idylls of the King (*Complete*). Price 7s. 6d.; Roxburgh, 9s.
VOL. IV. The Princess, and Maud. Price 6s.; Roxburgh, 7s. 6d.
VOL. V. Enoch Arden, and In Memoriam. Price 6s.; Roxburgh, 7s. 6d.
VOL. VI. Dramas. Price 7s.; Roxburgh, 8s. 6d.
Cabinet Edition. 12 vols. Each with Frontispiece. Fcap. 8vo. Cloth, price 2s. 6d. each.
CABINET EDITION. 12 vols. Complete in handsome Ornamental Case. 32s.
Pocket Volume Edition. 13 vols. In neat case, 36s. Ditto, ditto. Extra cloth gilt, in case, 42s.
The Royal Edition. Complete in one vol. Cloth, 16s. Cloth extra, 18s. Roxburgh, half morocco, price 20s.
The Guinea Edition. Complete in 12 vols., neatly bound and enclosed in box. Cloth, price 21s. French morocco, price 31s. 6d.
The Shilling Edition of the Poetical and Dramatic Works, in 12 vols., pocket size. Price 1s. each.
The Crown Edition. Complete in one vol., strongly bound in cloth, price 6s. Cloth, extra gilt leaves, price 7s. 6d. Roxburgh, half morocco, price 8s. 6d.
*** Can also be had in a variety of other bindings.

TENNYSON (Alfred)—*continued.*
Original Editions :
The Lover's Tale. (Now for the first time published.) Fcap. 8vo. Cloth, 3s. 6d.
Poems. Small 8vo. Cloth, price 6s.
Maud, and other Poems. Small 8vo. Cloth, price 3s. 6d.
The Princess. Small 8vo. Cloth, price 3s. 6d.
Idylls of the King. Small 8vo. Cloth, price 5s.
Idylls of the King. Complete. Small 8vo. Cloth, price 6s.
The Holy Grail, and other Poems. Small 8vo. Cloth, price 4s. 6d.
Gareth and Lynette. Small 8vo. Cloth, price 3s.
Enoch Arden, &c. Small 8vo. Cloth, price 3s. 6d.
In Memoriam. Small 8vo. Cloth, price 4s.
Queen Mary. A Drama. New Edition. Crown 8vo. Cloth, price 6s.
Harold. A Drama. Crown 8vo. Cloth, price 6s.
Selections from Tennyson's Works. Super royal 16mo. Cloth, price 3s. 6d. Cloth gilt extra, price 4s.
Songs from Tennyson's Works. Super royal 16mo. Cloth extra, price 3s. 6d. Also a cheap edition. 16mo. Cloth, price 2s. 6d.
Idylls of the King, and other Poems. Illustrated by Julia Margaret Cameron. 2 vols. Folio. Half-bound morocco, cloth sides, price £6 6s. each.
Tennyson for the Young and for Recitation. Specially arranged. Fcap. 8vo. Price 1s. 6d.
Tennyson Birthday Book. Edited by Emily Shakespear. 32mo. Cloth limp, 2s.; cloth extra, 3s.
*** A superior edition, printed in red and black, on antique paper, specially prepared. Small crown 8vo. Cloth, extra gilt leaves, price 5s.; and in various calf and morocco bindings.

THOMAS (Moy).
A Fight for Life. With
Frontispiece. Crown 8vo. Cloth,
price 3s. 6d.

THOMPSON (Alice C.).
Preludes. A Volume of
Poems. Illustrated by Elizabeth
Thompson (Painter of "The Roll
Call"). 8vo. Cloth, price 7s. 6d.

THOMPSON (Rev. A. S.).
Home Words for Wan-
derers. A Volume of Sermons.
Crown 8vo. Cloth, price 6s.

THOMSON (J. Turnbull).
Social Problems; or, an Inquiry into the Law of Influences.
With Diagrams. Demy 8vo. Cloth,
price 10s. 6d.

Thoughts in Verse.
Small Crown 8vo. Cloth, price 1s. 6d.

THRING (Rev. Godfrey), B.A.
Hymns and Sacred Lyrics.
Fcap. 8vo. Cloth, price 5s.

THURSTON (Prof. R. H.).
A History of the Growth
of the Steam Engine. With
numerous Illustrations. Second
Edition. Crown 8vo. Cloth, price
6s. 6d.

TODHUNTER (Dr. J.)
Alcestis : A Dramatic Poem.
Extra fcap. 8vo. Cloth, price 5s.

Laurella; and other Poems.
Crown 8vo. Cloth, price 6s. 6d.

TOLINGSBY (Frere).
Elnora. An Indian Mytho-
logical Poem. Fcap. 8vo. Cloth,
price 6s.

TRAHERNE (Mrs. A.).
The Romantic Annals of
a Naval Family. A New and
Cheaper Edition. Crown 8vo.
Cloth, price 5s.

Translations from Dante,
Petrarch, Michael Angelo, and
Vittoria Colonna. Fcap. 8vo.
Cloth, price 7s. 6d.

TURNER (Rev. C. Tennyson).
Sonnets, Lyrics, and Trans-
lations. Crown 8vo. Cloth, price
4s. 6d.

TYNDALL (John), LL.D., F.R.S.
Forms of Water. A Fami-
liar Exposition of the Origin and
Phenomena of Glaciers. With
Twenty-five Illustrations. Seventh
Edition. Crown 8vo. Cloth, price 5s.
Volume I. of The International
Scientific Series.

VAN BENEDEN (Mons.).
Animal Parasites and
Messmates. With 83 Illustrations.
Second Edition. Cloth, price 5s.
Volume XIX. of The International
Scientific Series.

VAUGHAN (H. Halford), some-
time Regius Professor of Modern
History in Oxford University.
New Readings and Ren-
derings of Shakespeare's Tra-
gedies. Vol. I. Demy 8vo. Cloth,
price 15s.

VILLARI (Prof.).
Niccolo Machiavelli and
His Times. Translated by Linda
Villari. 2 vols. Large post 8vo.
Cloth, price 24s.

VINCENT (Capt. C. E. H.).
Elementary Military
Geography, Reconnoitring, and
Sketching. Compiled for Non-
Commissioned Officers and Soldiers
of all Arms. Square crown 8vo.
Cloth, price 2s. 6d.

VOGEL (Dr. Hermann).
The Chemical effects of
Light and Photography, in their
application to Art, Science, and
Industry. The translation thoroughly
revised. With 100 Illustrations, in-
cluding some beautiful specimens of
Photography. Third Edition. Crown
8vo. Cloth, price 5s.
Volume XV. of The Internationa
Scientific Series.

VYNER (Lady Mary).
Every day a Portion.
Adapted from the Bible and the
Prayer Book, for the Private Devo-
tions of those living in Widowhood.
Collected and edited by Lady Mary
Vyner. Square crown 8vo. Cloth
extra, price 5s.

WALDSTEIN (Charles), Ph. D.
The Balance of Emotion
and Intellect: An Essay Introductory to the Study of Philosophy.
Crown 8vo. Cloth, price 6s.

WALLER (Rev. C. B.)
The Apocalypse, Reviewed under the Light of the Doctrine of the Unfolding Ages and the Restitution of all Things. Demy 8vo. Cloth, price 12s.

WALTERS (Sophia Lydia).
The Brook: A Poem. Small crown 8vo. Cloth, price 3s. 6d.
A Dreamer's Sketch Book.
With Twenty-one Illustrations by Percival Skelton, R. P. Leitch, W. H. J. Boot, and T. R. Pritchett. Engraved by J. D. Cooper. Fcap. 4to. Cloth, price 12s. 6d.

WARTENSLEBEN (Count H. von).
The Operations of the South Army in January and February, 1871. Compiled from the Official War Documents of the Head-quarters of the Southern Army. Translated by Colonel C. H. von Wright. With Maps. Demy 8vo. Cloth, price 6s.
The Operations of the First Army under Gen. von Manteuffel. Translated by Colonel C. H. von Wright. Uniform with the above. Demy 8vo. Cloth, price 9s.

WATERFIELD, W.
Hymns for Holy Days and Seasons. 32mo. Cloth, price 1s. 6d.

WATSON (Sir Thomas), Bart., M.D.
The Abolition of Zymotic Diseases, and of other similar enemies of Mankind. Small crown 8vo. Cloth, price 3s. 6d.

WAY (A.), M.A.
The Odes of Horace Literally Translated in Metre. Fcap. 8vo. Cloth, price 2s.

WELLS (Capt. John C.), R.N.
Spitzbergen—The Gateway to the Polynia; or, A Voyage to Spitzbergen. With numerous Illustrations by Whymper and others, and Map. New and Cheaper Edition. Demy 8vo. Cloth, price 6s.
Wet Days, by a Farmer. Small crown 8vo. Cloth, price 6s.

WETMORE (W. S.).
Commercial Telegraphic Code. Second Edition. Post 4to. Boards, price 42s.

WHITAKER (Florence).
Christy's Inheritance. A London Story. Illustrated. Royal 16mo. Cloth, price 1s. 6d.

WHITE (A. D.), LL.D.
Warfare of Science. With Prefatory Note by Professor Tyndall. Second Edition. Crown 8vo. Cloth, price 3s. 6d.

WHITNEY (Prof. W. D.)
The Life and Growth of Language. Second Edition. Crown 8vo. Cloth, price 5s. *Copyright Edition.*
Volume XVI. of The International Scientific Series.
Essentials of English Grammar for the Use of Schools. Crown 8vo. Cloth, price 3s. 6a.

WICKHAM (Capt. E. H., R.A.)
Influence of Firearms upon Tactics: Historical and Critical Investigations. By an OFFICER OF SUPERIOR RANK (in the German Army). Translated by Captain E. H. Wickham, R.A. Demy 8vo. Cloth, price 7s. 6d.

WICKSTEED (P. H.).
Dante: Six Sermons. Crown 8vo. Cloth, price 5s.

WILLIAMS (A. Lukyn).
Famines in India; their Causes and Possible Prevention. The Essay for the Le Bas Prize, 1875. Demy 8vo. Cloth, price 5s.

WILLIAMS (Charles), one of the Special Correspondents attached to the Staff of Ghazi Ahmed Mouktar Pasha.
The Armenian Campaign: Diary of the Campaign of 1877 in Armenia and Koordistan. With Two Special Maps. Large post 8vo. Cloth, price 10s. 6d.

WILLIAMS (Rowland), D.D.
Life and Letters of, with Extracts from his Note-Books. Edited by Mrs. Rowland Williams. With a Photographic Portrait. 2 vols. Large post 8vo. Cloth, price 24s.
Stray Thoughts from the Note-Books of the Late Rowland Williams, D.D. Edited by his Widow. Crown 8vo. Cloth, price 3s. 6d.

WILLIAMS (Rowland), D.D.—
continued.
Psalms, Litanies, Counsels and Collects for Devout Persons. Edited by his Widow. New and Popular Edition. Crown 8vo. Cloth, price 3*s. 6d.*

WILLIS (R.), M.D.
Servetus and Calvin : a Study of an Important Epoch in the Early History of the Reformation. 8vo. Cloth, price 16*s.*

William Harvey. A History of the Discovery of the Circulation of the Blood. With a Portrait of Harvey, after Faithorne. Demy 8vo. Cloth, price 14*s.*

WILLOUGHBY (The Hon· Mrs.).
On the North Wind — **Thistledown.** A Volume of Poems. Elegantly bound. Small crown 8vo. Cloth, price 7*s. 6d.*

WILSON (H. Schütz).
Studies and Romances. Crown 8vo. Cloth, price 7*s. 6d.*
The Tower and Scaffold. A Miniature Monograph. Large fcap. 8vo. Price 1*s.*

WILSON (Lieut.-Col. C. T.).
James the Second and the Duke of Berwick. Demy 8vo. Cloth, price 12*s. 6d.*

WINTERBOTHAM (Rev. R.), M.A., B.Sc.
Sermons and Expositions. Crown 8vo. Cloth, price 7*s. 6d.*

WINTERFELD (A. Von).
·A Distinguished Man. A Humorous Romance. Translated by W. Laird-Clowes. 3 vols. Crown 8vo. Cloth.

Within Sound of the Sea. By the Author of "Blue Roses," "Vera," &c. Third Edition. 2 vols. Crown 8vo. Cloth, gilt tops, price 12*s.*
*** Also a cheaper edition in one Vol. with frontispiece. Crown 8vo. Cloth, price 6*s.*

WOINOVITS (Capt. I.).
Austrian Cavalry Exercise. Translated by Captain W. S. Cooke. Crown 8vo. Cloth, price 7*s.*

WOLLSTONECRAFT (Mary).
Letters to Imlay. With a Preparatory Memoir by C. Kegan Paul, and two Portraits in *eau forte* by Anna Lea Merritt. Crown 8vo. Cloth, price 6*s.*

WOOD (C. F.).
A Yachting Cruise in the South Seas. With Six Photographic Illustrations. Demy 8vo. Cloth, price 7*s. 6d.*

WOODS (James Chapman).
A Child of the People, and other poems. Small crown 8vo. Cloth, price 5*s.*

WRIGHT (Rev. David), M.A.
Waiting for the Light, and other Sermons. Crown 8vo. Cloth, price 6*s.*

WYLD (R. S.), F.R.S.E.
The Physics and the Philosophy of the Senses ; or, The Mental and the Physical in their Mutual Relation. Illustrated by several Plates. Demy 8vo. Cloth, price 16*s.*

YOUMANS (Eliza A.).
An Essay on the Culture of the Observing Powers of Children, especially in connection with the Study of Botany. Edited, with Notes and a Supplement, by Joseph Payne, F. C. P., Author of "Lectures on the Science and Art of Education," &c. Crown 8vo. Cloth, price 2*s. 6d.*

First ˏ Book of Botany. Designed to Cultivate the Observing Powers of Children. With 300 Engravings. New and Cheaper Edition. Crown 8vo. Cloth, price 2*s. 6d.*

YOUMANS (Edward L.), M.D.
A Class Book of Chemistry, on the Basis of the New System. With 200 Illustrations. Crown 8vo. Cloth, price 5*s.*

YOUNG (William).
Gottlob, etcetera. Small crown 8vo. Cloth, price 3*s. 6d.*

ZIMMERN (H.).
Stories in Precious Stones. With Six Illustrations. Third Edition. Crown 8vo. Cloth, price 5*s.*